Banished Into The Interior

To order additional copies, please contact us.
BookSurge, LLC
www.booksurge.com
1-866-308-6235
orders@booksurge.com

Banished Into The Interior

The Making of Peter Dorn - Fur Trader

To Diana with gratitude as a so special member of the writers group

Love

Shirley Keran

S.T. Keran

2006

Banished Into The Interior

Dedicated to all of us who share a love for the diverse fruits of wilderness and of civilizations.

Chapter 1.

The Promise

And I listened. The long forehead and scraggly white brows half-hid the sunken eyes glinting like coals in flesh, spare and of a waxen hue. The whisk of chin beard and pale thin lips scarcely moved, yet his words erupted as from some deep rising well. And I listened. Listened to him tell of my half-brothers Pieter Willem III, Gregor, and Dirck. Each brother was old enough to be my father, while my father, old enough to be my grandfather, still burned with a single, inexhaustible passion.

I, sitting on a low stool leaned into my student table, his words caressing my brain like holy oil so sacred to him were the workings of The Trade. From time to time I would whisper, "Yes, Papa" and "No, Papa," all the while staring at the glass buttons on his embroidered waistcoat heave in and out, the frayed velvet stretching the length of his upraised arm. His hand, cuffed in yellowed-lace, dangled a gold chain before my eyes, bearing a three-tiered oval of carved ivory.

"*Der Vogel de Nederlands*, Pieter."

"Yes, Papa."

"And who owned the ship, Pieter?"

"Meneer Van Rensselaer, Papa."

"And who sailed this ship, Pieter?"

"Your father—my grandfather, Meneer Pieter Willem Van Doorn the First, Papa."

"And who is his last namesake and who bears his trust?"

"I, Pieter Van Doorn the Fourth, Papa."

How often I'd sat with him thus, my father. Within his shriveled body dwelt a mind alert to every erroneous calculation of his last son to be instructed in the pathways of heavenly bodies, and the sciences and instruments of astronomy and navigation. The far wall framed the continents, hung so that North America, lying between the Atlantic and Pacific Oceans, was at the level of my father's eyes.

Along the inner wall amid dusty volumes of the philosophers were the works of Kepler and Newton. Merchant account books mingled with logs of ship captains and narratives of explorers. Among them were Hudson's failed expedition in the Hopewell to find a passage by way of the North Pole to Japan and China. Three volumes of Champlain's voyages took up a corner (which, because they were in French, I was obliged to read). Under a faded chart of Bode's astronomical observations, a small table harbored an astrolabe.

Coarse damask draperies aside the hearthstone stayed the dampness permeating the lone casement or, when the sun was favorable, were hitched to the corners of the room with silken cords. Small rectangular windowpanes exposed a row of ill-kept hedges and beyond, tired fruit trees huddled like old men. Seated in the waning light, my daily lesson always ended with my father's self-same incantation, no less earnest than the churchman's prayer for all its mercantile nature.

"The English harvest furs where the Dutch have sown."

"Yes, Papa."

The same lament had tendered into service his three eldest sons, and I, coaxed from his loins to carry on where they might fail, knew no other lullaby. And what of my mother? I remember her best, head bent, dark auburn hair parted down the middle pulling tight her fair skin. Did I think her pretty? I hardly know now. Younger by thirty-odd years than my father, she adopted his fevered mission and with wifely vows gave him his fourth son. I, then, was the second son to be named for our paternal grandfather, and the fourth he would send to redeem the ancestral wealth, wealth that could be bought in the New World with hard courage and baubles. My mother's dark eyes always shone with a peculiar glow when, rocking me close as a small child, she first began to recount the family history.—Nor did they lose their brightness upon her retellings as I grew beyond boyhood.

"Your father's father, Pieter, captained a merchant ship with the Dutch East Indies trade and, in 1636 came back, built this house and filled it with fine furniture, paintings, porcelains from China. And, when guests came the table was extended the length of the room and overflowed with food. It was said that music rang in these rooms then, Pieter!"

I was about seven or eight, then, and Ma-ma stopped long enough to search through our family cupboard, and hand me a faded song book. Her intent was for the music; but only the engraving of

Admiral Piet Heyn caught my interest. In school we had sung songs about this Dutch hero, who in the 1620's, captured fifteen Spanish galleons loaded with silver and filled our nation's coffers. How well he'd earned the title, pirata!

Ma-ma's voice would turn melancholy when talking on about my father. "Your father sailed but once with your grandfather, Pieter. His first wife, Matilde, took to her bed in 1654, giving birth to a third son, Dirck. And, it was while she lay dying that news of your grandfather's near-certain shipwreck reached this house. Your father, the poor man, was cast into a double mourning. Yet, he made a solemn vow, Pieter, before God the Almighty that he would recompense both his own and his father's losses; he would restore all and more than had been lost!

"Now, Matilde's death had certainty, but not his father's. Day after day,—for two long years your father awaited some word of a rescue. None came. And so it was, in 1656, he undertook a second and his last voyage, this with the East India Company's trade in spices off the Cape of Good Hope. Your father was well suited to arguing the laws of trade and plying contracts, and took to the sea, too, until this strange, unknown sickness struck him. The Company returned him to Amsterdam in the next year's sailing.... And, here he remains," she'd end on a sigh.

The deathbed promise to restore the family fortune that took hold in my father's mind only grew in strength as his crippling lameness worsened, and forestalled forever his own ambition to sail for The Trade. In the ensuing years he apprenticed his sons to Amsterdam merchants: Pieter Willem III in 1660, Gregor in 1662, and Dirck in 1671, sending them to the New World, each by their seventeenth birthday.

I think it not unlikely that he married one so young and impressionable as my mother, Johanna, that he might mold her mind to his own necessity. Why else would she slavishly prosper his wishes, knowing that three sons by his first wife had sailed for New Amsterdam; yet none had returned. Why would she zealously bless my departure, unless it were to fuel the flame that consumed my father. One communication only we received and that from Dirck, nineteen years my senior. "The land," Dirck wrote, "is as fair as can be imagined along this great, wide river called the Hudson. But only the land. I look up and down both of its banks upon vast landholdings of a few families. Small patches are rented to poor farmers for prices far in excess of their worth. The savages they use or dismiss as no account. I can find no trace of Gregor, and of Willem only a rumor at best."

As the time of my leaving grew close, she smiled less and less, my mother. At the age of seventeen, primed with my ill-begotten destiny, I would be the last son to sail out of Amsterdam. I was to sail, not on *Der Vogel de Nederlands*, but on *De Engelenburg*, in the year Sixteen Hundred and Ninety, knowing the world only as well—or as ill—as my father had instructed me.

"So, Pieter Van Doorn! You come to say goodbye and your head hangs before you like the bowed head of a goat! Why should your leaving bother my maidenhood? You're but a clumsy bookish fellow with no future to make you the more welcome."

"Kristina, don't talk so." I felt caught between shame and anger that my betrothed should speak so; her blue eyes bright with mocking, her head raised at a haughty angle and tendrils of fair hair escaping the starched white cap tied beneath her chin. She stood, clutching close her blue cape. Her full skirts trailed in the early morning dampness as a tiny foot, encased in red leather boot, tapped peevishly on the wet stones of the pathway leading to the Planck household.

"Kristina, don't talk so," she spat back at me. "And why not, Pieter Van Doorn! Do you think because our parents locked our cradles, scarcely before we could talk, that such a promise ought bind us when you sail off on a fool's errand? Ah, when we were small and ran hand-in-hand across the fields, Pieter, that was a lovely time for us to remember, but as your legs grew, you became strange. Oh, you are fair enough a man to look upon, but there is inside you only maps and tattered books and the longings of your mad father. Pieter," she said, stepping close to me, "There are no words in you to please a woman?"

This last she spoke more softly, for her almost gently, but my mind overrode the stirrings in my heart and fixed on the stinging insult to my aged parent. What did this fledgling of a woman know of familial loyalty bred of suffering? She had only to part her sweet young lips to receive whatever foolish whimsy of adornment she desired from that pig-snout of a father who used riches to worship wife and daughter. An unseeing swineherder was Meneer Planck!

I trusted myself not to speak, wrath making my back tall and my lip curl as I looked down on that upturned face. Yet, as she paled before me, my arms closed around her with an iron possessiveness from I knew not where. Our lips met but once, and in haste.

I remember her last as she leaned against the sidegate. I caught up my valise. Mist was rising off the lowlands; the ship's bell beckoned!

Chapter 2.

The Departure

De Engelenberg was a shallow-draught vessel with two gun decks. The beakhead curved upwards more than was usual on ships in northern waters. Atop the forecastle, carved lions painted a gaudy red, faced out to sea on either side of the ship's middle-most lantern. No feature of land along these coastal waters lent its name to the ship, nor at Hoorn where *De Engelenberg* was first launched; but in happy expectation of clear sky over an open sea, some mind's eye must have looked aloft at sails full and by, and named the ship *Angel Mountain*.

I stood gawking up at the rigging, forgetful of the stern warning laid on me before departing from my father, his voice a low murmur to keep my mother from overhearing. "Act the highborn gentleman-scholar. Avoid attention to yourself and do not let the breadth of your shoulders tempt the eyes of the mate. Do nothing for yourself that your servant can properly do. Keep your conversation modest and walk not alone on the deck."

Filial obedience stayed the laughter I felt; yet, had he been observing my face instead of measuring the progress of the sandglass for the hour of my leaving, my father would have noted how my cheeks quivered when he called Jan Carpentier my 'servant'. It was a ruse Jan and I arranged to prevent the only domestic left in my parents household from accompanying me on my voyage. My mother would not hear of a Van Doorn setting off alone and unattended; I was equally determined that they should not be deprived of their last servant. Besides, of what use could Kootermann be to me in this young man's venture, Kootermann, whose lumbago and cross disposition had plagued my youth for as long as I could remember.

"Jan," I'd said but days ago, announcing a decision sprung full-born of the moment, "You will go with me to the New World!"

My closest friend, though we saw one another but rarely over a stolen game of draughts, kept his eyes fastened on the board and captured two of my men before looking up. Swarthy, like a lean-faced Spaniard with cropped, curly hair, Jan fixed my gaze with a fierce expression and thus we sat, game forgotten, like head-locked rams.

When finally he spoke, he rose up, overturned the board, and clenched my hand in his calloused fist. "I will go with you, Pieter! It is sure you'd be meal for sharks, were you to go alone."

My passage being agreed upon to include myself and one male servant, and Jan being of questionable birth and no means, we set between ourselves the terms of our partnership. For the course of the voyage he would serve me in all outward manner. Upon reaching the New World he would be free to stay or to make off on his own. My parents took the plan with grace, and some relief. So habitual were we in our family intercourse, the slightest gesture or intake of breath held meaning. The stiff, ribboned bands fronting Mama's bodice relaxed and she looked on me with a gentle fondness I scarce remembered. My father's need presumed the greater, I had accustomed myself to thinking her more his wife than my mother.

From Amsterdam's fine harbour to reach the open waters of the Zuider Zee, a most ingenious scheme got underway this very year, whereby heavily-weighted ships such as East Indiaman were raised above harm's way by means of barges. Some hundred years of sand had silted in the shallow waters of the Pampas gulf and my gaze pinned on the two barges, water up to their gunwales, as they came alongside us. Once our hull was positioned to ride upon the heavy beams lashed tight to each barge, creaking and groaning. the barges were pumped dry. Yells rose up from all the company as De Engelenberg lifted just enough to cross the barrier.

Along the banks, all manner of maritime activity convenienced sea traffic from treadmill rope works and carpenter shops to smithies forging anchors. My Dutch heart swelled with pride on passing the Admiralty and arsenal. Warehouses of trading companies flanked the East Indies House high up on its stone foundation, and higher still, whirled the sweeping sails of the windmill in the naval dockyard that powered saws for cutting even the heaviest of timbers into planking. I stopped counting at forty, the warships at-ready in the docks as we left the bustling industry of the port.

A brisk wind stirred the sheets and a thin bead of rain freshened the air as our Captain gave orders to make ready to sail. He was a fair bearded, hard-faced man in his mid-fifties, Captain Von Streppe, squared like the broad-beamed East Indiaman; and like his half-warship, half-cargo vessel, he would prove himself to be of two-sided character and intention. Seamen sped to man the capstan. Coils of Manila rope screeched and furled, round and round, as a man on each side of the drumhead, turned the capstan's bars that heaved up the anchor. Sails set, the ship began moving out. But neither business above on the quarterdeck, nor the furious motions of the crew at the handspikes, nor the hands atop the triple masts kept my gaze from straying back around the carved rails securing the halyards.

I stared until only dim traces of the Groote Kerk remained. Its stone steeple, looming over houses and warehouses of Bickers and Fils and other prominent merchant families of Amsterdam, faded fast as a fair wind took us out to sea.

I stared on until water swelled high above the horizon and no shorebirds flew. How small then this wooden vessel seemed, breasted on four sides by churning gray seas. How it lifted and lowered, lifted, lowered, roved up, strove down.

"Go below, Piet!" Jan's voice echoed as he came toward me. My legs on that lurching ship were dead stumps refusing to move. Salt spray leapt around me and I became prey to the most foul, most unspeakable sensations. No! to the rocking ocean! No! to the rolling ship! I would not be primal actor on those tossing waters!

"Ah! I understand the truth now. The men of your family disappeared one by one into the sea from retching!" Slapping his hand full on my back, Jan pushed me close against the taffrail. I clung, rigid, my mind spinning out advice: *Let your movements be one with the motion of the ship.* The maxim sallied my brain, but can a limp sack tossed in a storm control its moves? Nor could I, grandson of a sea captain, son of a sea merchant keep from stupidly flinging out bread bits for scavenging seagulls.

"Give into it, my friend," Jan urged. "You are like a mad dog who foams the more for trying not to."

When at last my shoulders drooped and my head wobbled like a disgraced clout in the stocks, my breathing slowed and my stomach settled. Bleary-eyed and nose wet, I steadied my feet past the cursed winking, smirking deckhands. "And, you, Jan—" I muttered, he trailing behind me to my quarters, "I suppose a turbulent sea is of no more nub to you than your papist baptismal water is to me!"

Jan took my jibe with a laugh and said, "You forget, Pieter. My father was a Flemish sailor. To my mother he left only his name, but to me, his sea legs." His mirthful dark eyes then turned strangely thoughtful. "It may be, they prove enough...," he said, leaving his thought to wander unfinished in my brain as I sent him below, and entered my cabin.

I was alone. And grateful to be so, for this Dutchman was installed with English. To my astonished, but polite query as to why Captain Von Streppe countenanced aboard his ship subjects of the British Crown when their Navigation Acts interfered so ruinously with our Dutch carriers of trade and commerce, he all but snarled: "Either they suffer you in their quarters, Van Doorn, or you lodge below!" I met his steely-eyed glare full on, yet knew better than to push an argument with a ship's captain.

I'd had only a glimpse of the two English when they boarded, and supposed them to be at supper, a repast I wisely forsook. Here in the cabin, I looked upon two generously sized leather and gilded coffins. On each rested a pointed beaver hat with rolled brim like those a parading cleric or fashionable burgemeester wore. Hooked to a narrow wardrobe, silk-threaded frock coats spoke the quality of these gentlemen with whom I was to be so closely quartered for the length of our passage. I slipped off my pantaloons and shirt and sought a spot to stow my belongings. However fair my Dutchman's baggage seemed at the outset, it was as orphan's duds beside the raiment of these English walking so freely upon a Dutch ship.

I stretched on the topmost hammock with the roll of the North Sea trying my every limb. From a port hole, its gun being removed and readied elsewhere, light settled like a shaft on the brass fittings securing the carpentry. I might have slept had not my nose begun to twitch from the cunning scent of musk-sweet cologne vying with the reek of lamp oil, sea-damp wood, and my own foul breath.

Vanity greater than the weakness of my legs, I eased down from my hammock and, opening my bag—a close-stitched bundle of carpet—escorting the sea chests of the English, I removed the gold chained ivory entrusted me by my father.

"You, Pieter—," he had said, "were not even a snit in my farthest eye when your brothers sailed out of Amsterdam. They do not know you exist! But when you find them—and find them you must!—they will know this ivory. Its image is carved into their brains as much as in your own. Ah, the demise of our hard-won trade at the hands of kings, politicians, and fools shall not forever fatten the pockets of the almighty British!"

Well-schooled as I was to hate our foremost rival on the high seas—the Dutch being reduced from commanders of great fleets that scoured the three oceans to captains, shipbuilders, and sailors—in days to come, I would find myself beset in this tiny cabin by an intense curiosity about the two English, and would grow even somewhat careless in the regard of our two navies.

I hung my family talisman on an overhead peg, then lay in my berth. Through half-closed eyes I watched, transfixed by the uneven swing of that small piece of ivory stolen from some Asian elephant to be tooled into the semblance of a ship. A particular ship. It replicated the ship of my grandfather who procured it from an artisan-sailor, perhaps ordered it made. But where? On the Gulf of Siam, the China Sea, the Cape of Good Hope? It mattered not. I fell off to sleep leaving, bone white on its glittering chain *Der Vogel de Nederlands* to announce my ancestral claim to the English.

Chapter 3.

The English

Awakened by the iron bolt sliding across the door, I pretended sleep as they entered, my eyelids lowered to the merest squint. In the darkness, one struck a candle. They'd get no greeting from this Hollander abed in the topmost hammock.

The English began to disrobe. I stifled my laughter as, rump-to-rump, the full-bellied one worked himself out of his ruffled shirt and, the other, to disengage his satin breeches, crouched to keep his head from hitting the crossbeam. My muffled noises drew attention to my person and I kept my breathing steady. The fat one reached for the brass drip tray weighting the candle. My eyes shut as the light neared, still I felt their scrutiny.

"A well-chiseled nose for the scruffy son of a burgher."

"The devil, Sir James, look!" I knew the tall one spoke this last; his voice cackled close to my ear bringing with it a spittle of sour-smelling sherry. I kept my breathing measured. In the flickering candle light, the tall one had remarked my ivory pendant dangling on its gold chain.

"A sailor's trinket, Andrew. I'm to bed." The fat one yawned, and the ropes creaked as he sank into the lower hammock.

"I tell you, Sir James, I've seen it before."

"Poppycock, Andrew. For all his length, he's yet a lad. You saw him puke over the rail and gangly-foot it up the deck. It is sure he never navigated more than a Dutch puddle."

"Nonetheless. It is the same I saw in Portsmouth, though not, I grant you, around that neck."

It was the last they spoke before snuffing the candle and settling into sleep. With relief, I heard the whistled breathing of the tall one called Andrew with the cruel droop about his left eye. Soon after, the honking snore of Sir James began. He, I judged to be the least disagreeable of the two.

Sleep, I could not a second time. My eyes were wide open to that black darkness that covers the dead of night. As night wore on, I grew grateful that the small size of our quarters did not admit those shrouded phantoms that come and go as night turns gray. How was it, I wondered, that pork-stuffed cod of an English called me the son of a burgher, a scruffy burgher!—He knew not of me. Of more moment, why seemed Sir Andrew so certain of spying my ivory in Portsmouth? It had strayed from my father's brass box directly to me. Like enough, in some drunken stupor, one of his ilk would ogle a display of soaps and bones—or ivories—in a dockside pawnshop, and know not one from the other!

The fat Sir James, was surely the higher born gentlemen from the deference shown in addressing him, but the sot was none the better for it, deeming my ivory a sailor's 'trinket'. Me, he'd called gangly-footed; I would see he never had cause to again! Only the hold and oaken planks broke the roll of the sea beneath as I eased my limbs and learned to trust the tilt of that bed of rope!

To the pounding strike and fall of the ocean and the raucous snorting of the English, in the early hours before daylight a pleasantness stole over me in the visage of Kristina, blue-eyed and tremulous at the boldness of my leave taking. I smiled in remembrance. Yet, perhaps my smile was not only of Kristina, for during this interminably long night, I mastered my weakness. Hereafter, I would walk strong the decks of *De Engelenberg*. And why should I not, when our William III rules as Stadholder of Holland and King of England!

Captain Von Streppe had the gone-looking eyes of the lifelong sailor. The fringe of beard siding his weathered cheeks was met by thin, straggling gray hair anchored on top by a peaked and braided cap of command. He wore it even at supper. He sat at the end of our stout table, backed against a cot stowed to his cabin's innermost wall. The outside end was given the fat English, while Markham sat aft. I, being the only other gentleman aboard, was wedged in port side. Truth was, accepting my curiousness about the English, I would rather have supped with Jan and the company of ruffians that worked the ship. The stories Jan told! For in days gone by, I had devised means to have him near me while the English, the weather being fine, walked above.

"With your permission, Sirs," I'd preened before Sir James and Markham, "my servant will keep clean our quarters while you gentlemen take your airings. He needs some business, else his mind strays."

In the privacy of my cabin, not just wild tales of his shipmates Jan told me, but only this morning, a strange circumstance he'd had from the servant of Sir James concerning dealings to come at Fort Orange, a region above New Amsterdam our Dutch West Indies Company established as a trading post. The lad, Sarkey, told Jan his master carried secret papers from the King. With his own eyes he'd seen them.

"Sarkey is schooled in letters?" I asked.

"No, no, but he, himself, saw the Royal Seal and heard his master talk of the orders he had concerning himself and Andrew Markham. Be patient, Piet, I dare not question too closely or, it may be Sarkey's lips that bear a seal."

I promised Jan I would be patient. And, with patience, I waited my turn to be served supper. First, Captain Von Streppe was helped to a slab of cold brisket dripping in pickled brine, lard biscuit, and a tankard of claret. Sir James was served next. With a contented scowl he sucked his ration of lemon provisioned every other day to all on board. Andrew Markham was then served. No one spoke as was the Captain's wishes. But this habit of silence, I determined I would break even though they would think me an ill-mannered, ignorant Dutchman. If I could engage the Captain in talk with the English, I was certain to gain information useful to myself upon arrival in the Colony.

"Have ever you sailed from Portsmouth, Captain Von Streppe, to Fort Orange?"

As if by signal, the three raised their heads and each turned and stared at me. I felt a hot flush prickle my skin, but pursued my opening.

"I've heard it called a place of bustling commerce, Portsmouth."

The Captain, without a word, looked back at his plate. He began to eat again as though I'd not spoken. But, a sneer sat on Sir James's fleshy jowls at odds with what also seemed a smile.

"And so, Meneer Van Doorn," he said just above a whisper, "what can a lad of Amsterdam know of 'Portsmouth', being so uninformed about Fort Orange. That small outpost, now Albany, is secure and thriving under British rule since the Treaty of Westminster in 1674."

"You insult me, Sir!"—I knew of the treaty that put three of our

Dutch colonies into British hands, but that unfortunate piece of our history did not suit my purpose.

"How so, what insult do you claim?"

"Why, my knowledge of Portsmouth, of course! It is well known as a place of vast activity in the building of ships—as likewise is—Chatham." This unintended sting dropped off my lips unbidden, so often had my father recounted the burning of English ships by the Dutch Navy. And gratified I was to see those two British heads raise up and take notice! For, it was at Chatham, our raiders towed away England's pride ship—the *Royall Charles* from under the very noses of the British Admiralty. My tongue this night having no stopper, I locked my knees together, filled my lungs, and continued to bait these old men who bantered my youth about like the hard leather ball men toyed with to play kolf on frozen canals.

"My question to the Captain about sailing from Portsmouth to Fort Orange—or 'Albany', as you prefer it called—was to ask if, perhaps my country's salvaging of the Royall Charles was witnessed by you, Sir James. Or, you, Mister Markham," I added, innocently, to my partner across the table, "If not, to you, yourself, Captain Von Streppe?"

My last challenge was flung and met with cold silence, I kept to my plate, and unconcerned as I could manage, slid a wedge of brisket from my knife to my mouth. I chewed at the stringy beef as though it were a fine Christmas bloedworst. I tapped my biscuit to dislodge weevils, then dipped it in the sour, filmy liquid on my plate. Smacking my lips, I concentrated on the glowing pewter of my tankard then, suddenly, shot out my arm, and raised it in a toast to the Captain. The English were forced to oblige.

I met the eyes of Captain Von Streppe. He was, after all, my countryman. A rumble started at his gut and, reaching his mouth, laughter hit out like hailstones in the confines of his small cabin.

"Another toast, gentlemen!" he boomed. "More wine here, Steward, and there!" Our tankards filled, we all raised with him.

"We drink," said Captain Von Streppe, his watery eyes angling on me, "to all brave fools who die young!"

"Ay, and I'll raise to that!" said Sir James.

"Ay, and be it soon!" Markham added, his voice high and full of scorn.

I pretended dumb to any offense and reached out to clink my

tankard against Markham's with gusto. "Ay! and to such brave fools, let's drink!"

Whether it was wine to my head or suffusion of pride at being Prime Mover among these old men, I all but forgot my purpose for foisting fellowship on the Captain and the dirty English. The table was long cleared and still we sat on. More wine was swilled than ever I'd seen at a single sitting. Markham was chirping some silly English rhyme: "Dead Queen Bess, Be She Ever Blest," when most unexpectedly, Sir James, leaned close by me. He held up his knife as though to show me its inlay of pearl. He bade me stroke the handle. I did so and his free hand gripped my wrist with uncommon strength. He smiled unevenly as he forced the blade near, so near, surely my eyes crossed at its silvered point.

"I see it well enough!" I gaped. I alone heard his words as, ever so slowly, he let go my wrist.

"A warning, my young friend. No more Portsmouth-Chatham games—nor any other. I might press a stalwart hothead such as yourself into service for, say a half-pound.—Others would bundle you off for a pence or a geldstuck."

Wine numbed any quarrel over the stingy price he put on my head.

Chapter 4.

The Quarrel

"Fool, you are Piet! Must I cut out your tongue to keep the rest of you whole!" Jan's eyes flashed anger, nostrils flaring. I stiffened at his ridicule and hardened my fist to smash his insolent face. Was it dread of how alone we two would be in the New World that checked the swing of my arm and somewhat softened his look of contempt as he said, "Pieter, you're such a dolt! What good that you can spout Erasmus and scribble letters—you've no more sense among wolves than a wet babe."

His taunt stung. Never, had I jibed at him for his lack of studious ways. Who was Jan Carpentier to question the method of my education, or—for this was the crux of his argument—my disdain of the English. "You dare call my schooling to task?—you bastard son of a Flemish rake!"

"Better not knowing the father than be sired by that senile ancient who lumped your head with his rusty formulas and old hatreds! A viper can bite, Pieter, while you step on its tail!"

I lunged and would surely have cracked his scull on the mizzenmast, but for his cowardly duck. Instead, I felt a searing pain and clutched my hand, the knuckles raw and bloodied.

"Come," he said, tearing a strip from the tail of my shirt, "I goaded you too far." He dipped the rag in the tar bucket by the half deck and, with a rough gentleness, bandaged my hand. I let him. Our hot words, after all, had matched insult for insult.—Further, the morning watch coming on looked ready, eager for a row.

Shadowy outlines moved in iridescent orange as the sun crept up the watery horizon. Jan and I had arranged our rendezvous for just before daybreak when privacy was most assured. The English, it seemed, had taken to sleeping late rather than stare off at the endless reach of the Atlantic, the only diversion being a rare sighting of whale or porpoises. For some weeks, now, I'd not been alone in our cabin. When Jan came to empty pots and see to the hammocks, one of them always stayed behind. And, always, one of them delayed until I left. Worse, shortly after our third week out, our cabin door was fitted with a padlock to which only Sir James retained a key. The door was unlocked while we three slept should some disaster befalling the ship demand a hasty exit. Thus, I could go and come freely of early mornings, but could contrive no time to search if royal orders be among Sir James's possessions. It was these circumstances, along with a slip of the lip from Sarkey that stirred Jan to such a pitch. Sarkey had overheard Markham tell Sir James that he'd find cause to 'put a knife to the young pup.' Sir James replied that he 'had a better plan than the knife for Van Doorn, that Markham was to "Leave off." When Jan questioned him about the 'plan,' Sarkey, turning wary, veered away.

"No worry then, Jan, about Markham's knife in my back!" And, because I was certain that weasel of an English foppen would never strike from the front, I held Jan's suspicions of no account. Sir James, himself, was quite cordial since that first warning he'd laid on me against what he called "games" and, I must say, I had no wish to provoke another quarrel. This was our thirty-eighth day at sea—an excellent crossing, thus far, with but few storms. Captain Von Streppe conjectured our arrival to be within a fortnight if the winds held.

A light morning wind held the promise of rain as Jan left me to go below. In parting, he leaned forward so I looked down the sharp incline of his swarthy cheeks. He pointed to my neck. "What you wear like an amulet, may become a noose. Watch your step." I made no answer knowing that Jan, though misguided, spoke out of fear for me. I returned to my hammock for a few hours sleep before the English and I took breakfast.

My 'amulet' as Jan had called it was not the pastime incised on a whale's tooth by some voyage-weary sailor. This was Ceylon ivory near the size of a goose egg. Intricately carved in that white rock, was each detail from main royal down to spritsail. Minuscule figures raised along the grating were scarce visible without the aid of a glass, as was the speck of lion atop the beakhead. I do not know from just where the ivory came. Father thought it likely from Grandfather's voyage of 1640, when he sailed for the Dutch East India Company's venture to Malacca, wresting The Trade in spices from the Portuguese. I had thought Sir James merely ignorant to call my ivory a sailor's trinket; but later, this and other instances convinced me Sir James had, at least in uncertain light, weak eyesight. At times he walked like a man balancing from his forearms, and not from the roll of the ship. I even felt pity once to see such a proud man stumble close at the capstan. Yet, he nor anyone spoke of his affliction.

As silently as that creaking hunk of solid wood allowed, I opened the cabin door. Always, after fresh air on deck, the stench of sweating humans and unemptied filth pots bended the nostrils. Moldy, sour odors of rotting timber, which even on the brightest of days saw little light, hid all manner of slime. Our cabin was fit habitation for such as spiders and ship rats.

Easing up into my hammock, careful lest I rouse Markham in the berth below mine, I heard corpulent Sir James turn over. "Were it doable aboard this ship," he said, his groggy voice low and even, "I would think you had yourself a wench, young Master Van Doorn. Whom might you visit in early dawn when honest men sleep?"

"I like to rise with the sun!" Then quick to remember mornings I lay abed to catch some loose shred of gossip between thin-lipped Markham and Sir James, I hastened to add, "It was my habit before boarding this ship—to be up with the first light; my father bade me be at my studies."

"You rose before your servants lit the fires?" Slippery as silk sounded his sinister voice, but I made ready answer.

"Ha! Old Kootermann did little else than stoke the one fire my father permitted."

"Admirable, no? A careful man your father?"

All at once, I was oddly taken by the interest Sir James accorded me. He seemed to welcome a chat, and I, thinking at first only to allay his suspicions of my whereabouts, began to describe how I was introduced to the microscopy of Leeuwenhoek and the workings of a barometer for measuring pressure. His silence I took for disinterest, and rushed to tell him how my father admired one of his own countrymen, Isaac Newton, for his reflecting telescope. He made a thin smile, and thus encouraged, I ran on about having read my mother's copy of the Englishman Behn's The Dutch Lover and was roundly scolded, not because I'd filched it, but because Father thought novels and plays frivolous. Sir James yawned.

"So this was the sum total of your father's instruction?"

"Not at all!" In some detail I explained how Father began

instructing me in workings of The Trade at an early age, a subject perhaps more to Sir James's liking.

"Usually, we began by Father pointing to a stack of imagined pelts across the room, and his asking,'Combien de castores?' and I might answer, 'Deux!'

"Father would say, 'Ce n'est pas bon!' which was my clue to add more. Trois? Quatre!'

"If Father shouted, 'Non! Non!' I'd stand as tall and rigid as I could at age four or five and, in my eagerness to please him, shout out my numbers up through nine, and finish with 'Ten prime beaver!'"

Strange, that I should discover in talking to my enemy, an understanding of my father's method of instruction. The winds, steadily rising, beat the sails into a high whistle, yet between the lift and thump of the bow our talk went on. As for Markham, lost in the nightmares of early morning, he groaned with each lurch of the ship. "So, as well as workings of the The Trade, your father tutored you in languages, Van Doorn."

"He did. As I grew older, he quit my studies in Latin and Greek and, instead of Dutch, used the vernacular of our trade and industry and, spouting out in French or English, 'Three-quarter pound coloured beads?' I grew quick to answer. 'One made-beaver.'"

"Two pound Brazil tobacco?" And I, "One made-beaver."

"One gun; twenty flints?"

"Twelve made-beaver." And so I learned to trade goods for peltries, mastering your English ciphers and letters as I did the French.

"This Brazil tobacco—it is a recent commodity in the trade. I wonder that you know of it." I thought to answer, but at that moment the wind struck up. My head hit the side wall with such force my neck all but snapped. The wind wailed like ten million shrieking dervishes, and our wooden boat seemed a-whirl in the devil's own maelstrom with Lucifer himself our co-pilot. Markham jolted awake in a roll from his hammock and crashed to the boards.

"Damn the Dutch Captain!" he cursed, "he'll drive us to hell!" As though in answer, the ship leaned. I, on my back, clenched a weft of hammock in each fist, clinging-to and swinging about and envying the bulk of Sir James. The violent pitch of the ship buffeted Markham to and fro like a straw man. His eyes held the crazed look of fear that's turned far better men into piteous babblers.

The mounting seas howled and the mad morning wore on.

Ensnared in my rope cradle, I could barely see, only feel and hear each monstrous wave thunder down the deck, then retreat before the next wash strove against the creaking bulwarks. During one such lull, I heard Sir James muttering Pater Nosters. I lifted my head an instant to discern Markham wedged into the corner, shoulder tight against the doorjamb and cringing in his water-sodden nightclothes.

We rocked and heaved our way toward noon, each momentary break teasing up a more deadly rampage. Worse than the wrenching ship was the sound of sea when nothing but sea drums inside the head. How, I wondered, fared Jan and Sarkey. I imagined them drowned in the bilge or flung overboard. And could this stinking, tossing ship still have a helmsman? On and on screamed the eerie wind churning up all the souls of wasted sailors. These and other dark thoughts, exhaustion, and what must have been a gradual easing of the tempest, threw me into a fitful sleep of reptilian waves raising and wrapping, raising and wrapping.

When I awoke, all was quiet. I was alone. My head hurt and I felt a streak of dried blood on my forehead. Lulled by the spent ocean, I wished to sleep on. Yet, here—Now! This was the occasion I needed! I would ransack Sir James's leather cask, and should I discover secret papers of the enemy English, who knew of what use Jan and I might put such pilfered knowledge to in the New World.

Chapter 5.

The Leather Chest

Caution said to seek out Jan in the lower deck, be assured the storm left him his wits, and to warn me should the English approach our cabin door. Instead, I set a candle. Take your chance or lose it! I told myself, drawing the soggy leather chest out from under Sir James's berth. Grasping it around with all possible force, I smashed it, end-down, against the floorboards, soundly denting one of its brass corners. With my case knife, I tore a slit in the leather the length of my forearm. Reaching in, I felt among Sir James's woolen garments, sundry linen, the silk seam of a shirt, and felt a soft, plush cloth that wrapped around a box. Scarce thicker than my wrist, the box was wider and longer than a tobacco tin. I'd thought to feel out a rolled-up parchment, but how much better a sturdy box!

From the muddle of clothing, I eased it through the gap in the leather. In the dim light, the dun-colored metal glowed plain enough for a box such as a tradesman would carry. My heart pounded and water lapped my ankles as I squatted with the box on my knees. I worked open its small silver clasp and was lifting the lid when the cabin door creaked. Someone was about to enter. Was I to be caught naked in my own trap? I slid the metal box under my legs and postured up against Sir James's leather chest. The door swung wide. Daylight struck up a torch. I shielded my eyes.

"I came to see if you...Piet!—you look like a grain sack left in the rain. Are you stuck to the floor?"

"Markham—Sir James—their whereabouts?"

"By the roundhouse with the Captain, Sir James asking about lost days. The storm's taken us off course."

Saved from immediate danger, again I took up the metal box.

"They said you struck your head in the storm and did no great damage. God's blood, they lie! That must be your brains spread across your lap! And that beaten cask—swear it is not Sir James's!"

He gaffed on, while I swept aside a wood comb, a small brass thimble, pairs of gold buttons. A small looking glass reflected my swollen eye. Ugly and purple fleshed it was, and might serve me well in the hours ahead. Of the box, a better Christian would say God guided my hand. Underneath Sir James's bits and dabs of toiletry lay a folio. I spread it open and emblazoned thereon saw the royal seal of the Stuarts. "Jan!" I cried, "Listen!" for read it himself, he could not.

"CHARLES THE SECOND By the grace of God King of England Scotland France and Ireland defender of the Faith. To ALL to whom these presentes shall come greeting..."

Only a moment did I gape at the seal of a king dead these five years. "Here! Keep this!" I said, as restoring the triple fold, I thrust the orders at Jan to hide inside the blouse beneath his jerkin. "Now, go!" I said. "Tell Sir James I am in pain and raving. Make a compress for my head. Go quick! Before they return!"

He left, wearing his face like a clamp. No better friend than Jan. Nothing I had said, and nothing he had seen would quit his womanish fears for me, but Jan knows when to act. He can fly at me later. And so, restoring the box to its plush cloth, I coaxed it back inside the chest. There was more to do. Knife in hand, I bellied under Sir James berth and half-severed a shaft of ribbing along the wall planking. I wedged the torn, leather end of the chest over the jagged wood as though the storm had driven it. I didn't quibble over my handiwork, but crept out, flicked slime from my clothes, snuffed the candle, and, straightaway swung myself up into my hammock—to wait.

Like a heathen I lay, praising the dumb elements and thanking the wild storm that brought a young man of Amsterdam the wherewithal to cheat the dirty English.

Chapter 6.

Friends and Enemies

The ship's boy Sarkey came out of a London dockside knowing no parent or next of kin. A foundling, surely he must have suckled on rainwater or found pity at some engorged breast. Perhaps a barmaid flung him table scraps before he reached an age to steal his way in and out of back doors and alleys. But Sarkey had no past, no memory to guide him. He had no notion of his age and was of such slight build that were he thirty, he would seem but a boy of twelve. Sallow and taut skinned, his ferret eyes darted to and around searching for prey.

Instinct, honed no doubt by a scavenger's skill to make of every moment an eternal present, Sarkey moved by no feeling other than self-interest. Self-interest directed him to espy the folio lodged inside Jan's blouse, when Jan took pains in arranging his linen to face the wall, a caution one of Sarkey's stealthy habits did not fail to recognize. Unerring instinct, not design, steered Sarkey to whisper what he'd seen to Markham, not the substance mind you, but just the suspicion that 'certain papers' might turn up on the person of one Jan Carpentier. A word from Markham to the Captain, and Jan was seized and brought topside to be interrogated before the ship's company.

An evil leer on his flaccid features, Markham placed himself in front of Jan whose hands were roped behind his back. With his long white fingers Markham made as though to fondle Jan's chin and trace the line of his shoulders, all to the laughter of the crew who thought it better sport than mopping up after the storm. Markham placed his hands seductively on Jan's hips, when Sir James was heard to say he should leave off gesturing and get to the point of what himself and the Captain were brought to witness.

But Markham, enjoying the fullest attention, was not so easily put off. His hand slid to the neck of Jan's blouse and lightly stroked the throat of one who would have spit in his face, had he not been gagged and bound. He made a pretense of poking about Jan's chest, and then sensing his audience at their peak, sneered triumphantly and whipped out the paper hidden in Jan's shirt. A gasp went up from the men near enough to spot the royal seal. Sir James put out his hand and Markham relinquished the papers. The Captain ordered Jan's gag be removed, then Sir James, not the Captain, began the interrogation.

"How do you come by these?" Jan refused at first to speak.

"Fetch young Van Doorn. He is full of words. Let us see how he speaks on your behalf."

"No," Jan said. "My master knows nothing. He still lies on his back, aching and sore from ramming his head during the storm. It was while I was in seeing to his needs, and while he lay raving like a madman, that I broke open the baggage beneath your berth and stole the papers that you, Sir James, now hold."

"Hang him from the mast," someone murmured; then others joining in, "Ay, hang him!" sounded up from the deck. It was as though clamoring for punishment of a crime with such solid evidence would secure the crew's own desperate futures; hangings were dispensed for far lesser transgressions.

"Too easy a death for the thieving wretch from Amsterdam! Flog him first, nine times nine, for each day he's spent at sea." This, Markham called out, then faced about and dared Sir James to spoil the crew's entertainment. "What say you, Sir James? The parchment sealed by our former sovereign was in your custody."

"I say," Sir James began, speaking slowly, "I say there is more to be learned from a man in irons on a crust of bread and water, than from a flogged man dangling from the mast. Nothing will be lost. Jan Carpentier can stretch from the gallows on land as well as at sea."

"And, you, Captain Von Streppe," Markham challenged, "does the leniency of Sir James suit the law aboard your ship?" To his credit, the Captain was not a man to be cowed by the swaggering of an Andrew Markham. He sent the crew flying and gave Markham to understand that since the stolen property was restored to Sir James's possession, he was satisfied to leave justice to Sir James to dispense. That he gave not a sot for papers from a dead or living King of England!—or of France or from the Emperor of China; that he, a Dutch sea captain, served the merchants of any country who paid him in good Dutch guilders.

Jan was then lowered into the dark hole above the bilge, the only light a small iron grating above his head, which should his fingers slip around, anyone walking above had leave to trample.

The way of my learning Jan's black misfortune came much too late to affect his sentence. In the hours since giving Jan the English King Charles's orders for safekeeping, as we'd agreed I had kept inside the cabin. And, while not so grievous an injury in fact, the lump to my head was enough to feign my disablement for twenty-odd hours. And so, sometime later, when Sir James entered I made a low moan, one which were he my mother instead of my enemy would have brought him running to my bed. As it was, he began to question me.

"Jan Carpentier, your friend, no?"

"Friend? He is my servant." I spoke haltingly like a man with a pounding head should.

"Do you judge him trustworthy?"

"I'd trust him with my life!"

"A vicious thing for a a friend to betray a friend or, as you prefer, a servant to betray his master. Do you not think so?"

"I think so, of course!" My peevish response was less to feign sickness than at the game he was having with me.

"He brings me most interesting news, your friend, ah, servant. He says he found you breaking into my baggage." I shifted to see him more clearly. He was squatting down and puffing as he tried to dislodge the case beneath his berth. "Rather than see you hanged, he returned to me the papers you stole. A true friend, no?"

"You lie!" I cried, "Jan would never betray me!"

"Good. Then I have no need to worry that you would betray him." I stared at his fat reddened face for a sign of which way his riddle was intended, but could find none. In that moment of anguish I felt the lubber who would go by way of the hole to climb up the mast, not knowing the seaman's way around the outside.

"Tell me, of what use to you would be papers from our dead King Charles?" He brandished before my nose the same as I had stolen that very afternoon. "I could have you torn limb-from-limb with as little mercy as your countrymen showed in severing the parts of your Prime Minister, and restoring the House of Orange. —I am grateful, however, to have your William share the throne of England and rid us of the Stuarts. But, you," he said, dropping his satiric tone for one of disgust as, arms locked, he stood backed against Markham's bunk. "Rabid young Dutchman! you scarcely open your mouth but some foolhardy rashness slips out. Why do you vex me so, Van Doorn? You're like a thorn in my foot. No real threat, just a nuisance to one's walking. Yet," he continued and turned to face me, "it could go poorly for the lad you call your servant."

"Where is he? Why goes it poorly for Jan?"

"He's still alive, and out of harm's way."

"Still alive! What's happened? What trouble is he in?" All thought of protecting myself under the guise of injury vanished. My worry was for Jan. My agitation grew as the seconds ticked, and Sir James kept silent as a graven Buddha. He moved in, his elbow against the upright by my hammock, and leered at me, one hand supporting his chins. He had the pale, colorless eyes that change with the light and, in the gloom of our cabin, they fastened on me, grayly.

"Let me put it to you directly, Meneer Van Doorn—in any case, before Andrew returns. You may think us close. It is not so. I tolerate him because he is consigned to me, but he has only cunning and no silk in his brains, nor, more important for the business of The Trade, can he gain and hold the trust of men.

"In short," he said, one pudgy grayed eye half shut and the other full open, "though I believe the truth is, you stole the papers—and a botched copy of a Charter, they are, though few apart from an able scrivener would know it,—Carpentier will remain a prisoner until we reach the Colony. But before we speak of him, tell me why you would take such a risk to steal my papers. What did you hope to gain?"

"It was an act of rashness, I admit it—They were described as "secret papers." I wanted to know more—I..."

"In short, you put your life on the line—or that of your so-called "servant," to gratify, I think, your Dutch mistrust of anyone or thing British, in whatsoever way you could. Is it not so?" He spoke these last words with such irritating evenness, he could have been asking if I wanted a clot of cream on my pudding. I scowled, ready to reply when he held up a hand.

"No need to debase yourself, further, Van Doorn. Only listen.

"The papers I carry define territory claimed for the purpose of furthering British trade, territory already being mined. On my wanderings the far side of the Atlantic, I find it of interest to see how well words on parchment signed and sealed by a dead king, are matched to hard-held terra firma—land so greatly removed in size and distance—it's the beyond envisioning of those who seal the document. Having such a document, copy though it is, satisfies a whim of mine and, if I choose, persons who may value clarification. That is all.—Besides, I was quite fond of our Charles. He was a man of parts or, one might say, 'passions'. "

"What of Jan Carpentier! Since you know the truth, why must he remain a prisoner?"

"Ah, yes, young Carpentier. You must give me your word not to try to speak to him or get word to him of any kind. Markham is treacherous. If he but suspects you are to be his replacement, he has means as well as purpose to put you out of his way. His main virtue is his quickness with the knife.

"Replacement, Markham's—I? " But for his blocking my exit by the post near my head, I might have vaulted to the floor. As it was, I laughed outright and maneuvered my body past him. No longer prone, but standing upright, my height forced his head up to meet my gaze. "I, Pieter Willem Van Doorn the IV, loyal citizen of Amsterdam and the United Netherlands, am blooded by Dutch Sea Captains and merchants. I, in the employ of the stinking English? NEVER!

"I admire your spirit." His maddeningly quiet, sane-sounding voice only bespoke his insanity. "Sense," he continued, "will come your way within a very short time of your knocking about in the wilderness. Ploughing this world's oceans by-the-book means little to a river, to an overland portage. You'll find it to be so.

"Your main value to me is your proclivity for languages—or so I judge it to be from hearing your thick Dutch tongue spit out English and French. Your utter inexperience has value also; you can be trained. And, you come from a stock adept, so it would seem, in the workings of The Trade. Moreover, I have use for a quick pair of eyes—my own fail me from time to time." He paused like a Domine allowing his wisdom to seep into his dull-headed congregation.

"And, when you ripen and think more on history than hatred, you'll know that our British ascendancy is but the turn of the wheel. Yes, we defeated Phillip II of Spain. Still, you Dutch had a season. A short one, no?" His raised hand halted the torrent of stammerings I sought to unleash. He had me seething! Only his age and corpulence stayed my arm.

"Ah, but for some time, now," he went on in slow, honeyed tones, "while we British command the seas, your Dutch mercantiles do still maintain sole access to ports of Japan, no? As well, you conquered and rule your 'Batavias'. So learn from your colonials that seek to keep that which they have earned." He lumbered to the door, slid the door latch, and made a half turn in my direction. "And, you? You will do as I bid, Van Doorn. Mind, you hold your tongue. Remember whose life is in forfeit should you blabber about ship in your customary way."

I set the padlock, cursing like a stuttering idiot and clutching at my stupid skull that, not only was I found out, but Jan was made the scapegoat! When my rage cooled enough for me to think, I wondered how it was that Jan should still remain a prisoner. Sir James rightfully accused me of the theft, and I had not denied it nor given him any reason to doubt it.

Then it struck me. When Jan took the blame on himself, only Sir James had wit enough to guess the truth and, quick to seek his own advantage, kept silent, thereby boxing the two of us into a corner. Jan's valiant dissembling had entrapped us both! He would stink in that black hole not knowing that to save him, I must desert him; that should I speak the truth, he hangs! Oh, how I loathed my youth and inexperience among crafty men! How I despised my lack of wit and discernment! I, with advantages of birth and education was, it seemed, ill-suited to this New World of lying guttersnipes....Unless... I pondered, the thought slowly ensnaring my brain, unless after all I were to become a willing student of Master Guttersnipe!

I sat sometime, hunched on my berth, head down, arms crossed on my chest. And, even as I descried the forereach of De Engelenberg in coming about to turn and run before the wind, just so I felt a stirring in the sheets of my being to reconsider my own direction. Just how it would come about was unclear. All I knew was this: From none better could I learn the art of skullduggery than from that hornswoggler, Sir James. Use the English to turn the Dutch knife! Yet, at the height of my resolve, a shiver ran down my spine as, for a moment, I glimpsed the dark phantom of my soul bearing a likeness not my own, but like unto Sarkey's. Sarkey, who knowingly or not, had planted the mischief. And hadn't I, just as wantonly as he, rushed at the word 'orders'? King's orders indeed! A charter, twenty years under seal! A charter licensing a band of adventurers to claim half a continent. And it rankled like the sliver of wood in my thumb to learn that this was a mere copy, a "botched" copy.

Chapter 7.

Voyage Ends

We lay at anchor off the rocky coast of New Netherland, though to his shame, even our Dutch Captain called it by name of New York. "New York Town," he said, "has grown to some two hundred houses."

I bristled on seeing the Dutch standard De Engelenberg lowered, and the merchant flag of Britain, raised. My cooler mind was forced to acknowledge such subterfuge to be common practice among pirates, and even of merchant ships seeking harbour in foreign ports. But, if I were a Dutch sea captain off New Netherland Coasts, I would raise my country's standard!

So shrouded in fog we lay, for all I knew, beyond that thick gray wall lay the Patagonian Coast or the Isle of Texel. Gloom settled on all the company. For myself, fog only mirrored the melancholy that soured each new day that we were lodged, Jan and I, in our separate prisons. He caged in the hold and myself stifled always by the shadow of Sir James or Andrew Markham eying my whereabouts. Only later, would their hanging about take on purpose.

This voyage was now into its fifty-ninth day, slowed by storm-laden gale winds, rarer days with no wind, and now fog. My eager chatter when new aboard, had long since settled into a disagreeable silence when at meals with Captain Von Streppe and the English. Strain must have sat easy on me, or else our captain chose not to notice. A man of his pecuniary bent, was not likely to take up with a nearly impoverished countryman against the well-pocketed English. He was a man whose nose bent toward the fullest purse, nor did he deny it.

Of the strange bargain made with me in exchange for Jan's life, Sir James gave no sign. Not the slightest hint by word or glance. I began to think that bump to my head might truly be as grave as Jan described it. Had I imagined Sir James's plotting to replace Markham with myself? The prospect sickened me. — And, here was Jan, languishing, now, twenty-one days in that black pit!

Each day I felt more the sheer boredom of being trapped. The zeal I had upon beginning this voyage caught in my throat, and I struggled against dark despair. Was I to be the Sarkey of this New World?—I, born of sea captains, merchants, and traders who trafficked in cargoes on the world's great oceans East and West? My thoughts plunged to their lowest while at anchor, the ship holding fast as a steady thrash of waves lapped her hull, and the cable creaking back and forth ticked away the mindless hours.

By mid morning of the third day the bank of fog began to lift. Dark green forest hovered ghostlike above the horizon. With sails reefed and cargo readied for unloading. most of the hands idled out the long wait on the foredeck, gazing shoreward. So, too, did we on the quarterdeck. Markham lounged at my elbow, in a purple satin waistcoat and matching breeches, his thin British nose aloft. Sir James in plain dull frock coat stood at a short distance closer to the stern.

When the last of the fog rolled out to sea, the reefy shoreline of New Netherland lay suffused in yellow light, and with the calm waters, proffered a fair omen. Like the rising anticipation in every sea-worthy's breast, I felt the ivory ship at mine, quicken. This journey, was it truly ending? I prayed as the believer prays, that also ended was my feeble heartedness, that before we put to shore in the coble boats, Jan would be back at my side. Together we would walk that distant bank!—alongside which, I began to make out through my glass,—figures in strange attire and others in no attire as is customary among some savage races. Resolve swelled my lungs anew. Markham visibly stiffened as though discerning my intent though he made no move. I looked past him toward Sir James. He, leaning back from the taffrail, made a darting motion of his head to let me know I was to stay put. Then, just as clearly, Markham, when turning his way, was sent some signal the two must have prearranged for, immediately, Markham strode over below the poop deck and, calling up for the Captain's attention, raised a tight fist. Captain Von Streppe leaning over, hand-to-ear, nodded, then barked an order to the First Mate.

Meanwhile, Sir James in his sidewise gait was approaching. His demeanor, casual as always, gave no hint that more was afoot than the rising sun. When he spoke, it was from the side of his mouth so only I could hear. "Keep close and follow me into the boat."

"What of Jan?" I, too, scarcely moved my lips.

"Learn when to trust your friends, Van Doorn." Then, looking me full in the face, added, "and when to trust your enemies."

I followed, all the while determining what I should do next, and vowing I'd not leave the ship until Jan, unfettered, went with me.

The first boat was lowered for putting to shore. The boatswain helped steer Sir James over the side, saw him safely seated, then turned to me.

"Ye'll not need a hand, laddie?"

"No!" My mind whirled. No time was left, and where was Jan? Sir James's bidding me to trust had netted no result I could detect.

"Well, move then. Move afore me men see ye scared lookin' red face. Shame t'see one a such brawny makin's as yerself, Sir, so afeared o' a lit'le boat. T's safe enough. —Ye'll go nicely now, else I throw ye down and give ye a mate for the bad-lookin' eye ye wearin'." At odds with his gentle words, he clenched my arm with an iron grip and made ready to heave me over.

"Captain Von Streppe!" At my bellowing the hold on my arm slackened just enough. I jabbed him solidly, and, breaking loose, rushed forward, shouting up at the poop, "Captain! I paid my servant's passage. His unequal punishment, you exacted without trial and for a crime he did not do. Hand him over to me! Now! Before I quit your ship!"

"Look behind you, Van Doorn."

Turning from Von Streppe to look past the burly sailors rushing up to pin back my arms, I understood the signal that had passed from Sir James to Markham.

"Jan!"

At my shout, Jan, coming up the hatchway hands shackled, squinted into the flood of blinding light following his days of darkness. They brought him to stand by Markham. "Bastard Dutch Sea Dog!" I shot up at the captain and, kicking roundly at my captors trying to rough me over the side, I managed to bloody more than one mangy jack of them before, hoisting me up and over the side, they threw me down into the coble boat. An oarsman scuttled me into the stern.

Sir James, seated near the bow, faced the ship and called, "Loose his ropes!" And as I looked up, I saw Jan much weakened being unbound. He staggered hand-over-hand down the ladder, and clambered into the second coble boat.

My breath came lighter than in many a day, even as Andrew Markham, seated himself in relation to Jan as Sir James's was to me. Close to content I sat in spite of my forced entry. Jan and I were off the stinking ship!

"Heave to!" shouted the oarsmen. And thus began a furious rowing for shore.

"Pull! Sons of scum!" came a yell from the rival boat flashing past us.

"Lead in your groin!" sang out from one of our oarsmen.

We were racing ahead of them closely pursued when, suddenly, a movement so ominous or fortuitous or so coincidental—I know not which—I swear before God and all His angels, Sir James upraised his arm straight and high as any Oriental plying a scimitar, then let it fall. Another signal? Our companion boat was spinning so, I was sure it would founder. Then an oarsman rove up on his feet, and slammed his oar down over the bow as would split a man's head wide open. His weight and the force of his blow being all to the front, made the little boat swerve from side-to-side. So swiftly did all this occur that not until I sighted purple breeches floating above the surface, did I comprehend Sir James had orchestrated Markham's demise.

In one motion I was up and diving over the side. I swam madly off towards that speck of purple with no thought of whether Markham deserved such fate. The water was calm, my stroke strong, and the distance not great. To this day, I do not doubt that I would have succeeded, but for the coble boats closing in on either side of me.

Numb with cold, I was drawn from the water to huddle alone with what I had witnessed. No man spoke. Sir James in the bow held his back as straight as ever I'd seen it as he faced shoreward. My heart kept time with the tug and pull of the oars and, within the hour, we reached the banks of New Netherland.

Chapter 8.

The Invitation

"Fool!" Jan muttered in my ear, "When your purse is empty, there'll not be a stiver between us."

"You'd have me begin life in New Albany in their debt?" I whispered, too, although had we shouted, our two tablemates would have been scarce the wiser.

Dieter and Rolf seemed sober enough when first we came upon the Handelaar Tavern. Standing up as we entered, they'd welcomed us, heartily, we being the tavern's only other patrons. The first called himself son of Farmer Leek. The second, who described himself as 'Rolf Rutgarsz, son and partner to the Rutgar grain business.' We were to call him 'Rolf.'

"And so, the more talkative one inquired, "what news of het vaderland can you give us?"

"Ah, more than baskets of cheeses, herring and mackerel, mussels and eels! You'll be surprised to learn about the market held in Leiden. Leiden this year past encourages the business of The Trade with a far grander marktplein. I was not there to see it..." I left off as Dieter Leek rattled the table board, calling for an oyster bowl and a round of ale.

"Sit with us," Rolf offered, pointing to the empty chairs.

Jan, still stuck in his surly manner, stowed my piece of baggage between us at the table, one of such size, eight could sit at their ease.

We cracked and ate, merrily enough, and I ordered another. When Cook came, he set not one bowl, but a bowl before each of us. I paid before our companions could reach. I thought it a small matter and oysters not so costly. — Such cost was nothing if pumping these jovial citizens led me to my brothers. Dieter and Rolf joked back and forth, their garble a mix of Dutch and English, and neither easily understood. An unsmiling, suspicious-looking Jan nodded on occasion. For myself, I was for choosing the moment to break in with the question uppermost on my mind.

Before long, little oysters slipping around my empty stomach, I craved a dish of mutton stew, and called for a dish to share among us.

Cook came and, again, set a sturdy bowl before us each. "They'll need more ale with their pots!" he bellowed.

Through the dutch-doored kitchen, bungled an aproned old crone bearing a tray and a curse as the door's upper half smacked the back of her head. She shuffled over to us, filled our cups, and winked a gap-toothed smile, singling me out from the four at our table. "Y've th' look a one who'll pay me."

As fast as I set a coin down, her knobby fist closed in.

My moment had come and, Dieter, being the more dull of speech and countenance, I sought out Rolf. "Do you know the name 'Van Doorn?'"

"Well, and don't you call yourself 'Van Doorn?'

"I do. But, is the name 'Van Doorn' known here in the colonie?"

Dieter was about to speak, when Rolf's arms swinging out in a wide yawning stretch, the back of his hand caught Dieter straight on the mouth.

"Whaaaat...y' friggin-"

"Sorry, Diet! I'm clumsy as a wet bridegroom. I'll let y' yawn me in the face, Dieter, for sure I will." Rolf then turned my way, and in great earnest, asked, "Van Doorn. Now, what be the goin' name?"

"Gregor." Why of my three brothers, Gregor came most often to my mind, I do not know but, Rolf's face showing no recognition, I named the eldest. "Or, Willem Van Doorn?"

"Hmmm...Gre-gor, hmmm...Will-em." His chin and lips puckered to one side, weighing those precious names like schepels of grain, one bushel if even, the next will be less. Still, I leaned in to listen, ready to snatch the merest shred of understanding. Millers like brewers know their villagers and strangers.

"Perhaps, Dirck Van Doorn?"

"Dirck! hmmm.—Now as to 'Gregor,' No. Not likely. With 'Willem,' may be there's a bit of chance, all things bein' right a-tween us.—But 'Dirck?' Now, we've heard of a Dirck Van Doorn, eh, Dieter?" He got no answer and directed a solid kick at Dieter's foot, but with less effect than his hand to Dieter's mouth for Dieter was draining the last of his ale, making a great show of his empty cup with a satisfied belch.

He belched, again. "Oh, so may be we'ave heard a Dirck, al'right. 'E come from Amssssterdam, too, I reco'lect?"

"More ale!" I called to the crone. "Yes, yes," I assured him, "from Amsterdam. Do you know of him, Dieter?" So anxious I was for news, I told the crone to leave the ale pitcher in hopes that some worthwhile bit might drop from those two guzzlers of ale from my free-flowing fountain.

"Well, then, you've heard of Dirck. What do you know of him?"

Dieter's eyes rolled up toward the overhead crossbeam. Rolf sank his elbows on the table, swilled his ale, and gave me a slanty-eyed look. "Y' hear 'em say, 'may be we'ave'. An me sayin' if things be right a-tween us." He shifted back in his chair.

Jan leaned forward, his gaze cold and contemptuous. I felt a sermon coming on. "What addles you, Jan? Wouldn't I buy ale by the vat to learn anything at all of my brothers!"

"They're goading you! It's plain you're new to the low life of taverns, Piet. Pay for the ale, but make it the last. You'll see." His voice low, he plumped his arms across his chest with a lordly look at odds with his breeding. "You'll see, those two know nothing."

His tankard refilled, Dieter tottered to his feet, and raised it up. Ale slopped down his blotchy chin and dirty leather vest as he sang out, his words clearer than when he was sober.

From Amsterdam across th' sea
'E came one early mornin'
Now, Dirck's m' name 'e sez t' me
Where'z som place t' go a-whorin'?

Dieter sank under my fist. Whether the ale fogged my mind, I can't say. I have no memory of leaving my chair, so eager was I to smash his stinking face to the floor of the Handelaar Tavern. Then Rolf pulled himself up and, not as drunk, came at me.

I stood ready until Jan, breaking in between us, gripped my arm and, at the same time, clamped a hand around Rolf's throat. "SIT YOURSELF!" he spat, "before my hammer-handed friend, here, has a go at you. To the door, Piet!"

"Yer ale!" screamed the old crone, scrawny arms flailing. "Y' owe me a stiver'n two!"

"He's paid more this hour than you'll see all week!" Jan shouted from the door, his hand closing over the purse I was prepared to untie. Just then, Cook rushed in from the kitchen wielding a fire poker as could split open a man's skull. He stumbled on Dieter's sprawling bulk and, while still bent over, Jan and I departed.

We'd taken a room in a house to the rear of the Handelaar Tavern of stout timbers and Dutch bricks,—ballast, no doubt recovered from a ship's hold. The house raised memories for transplanted Hollanders. Though not nearly so fine as a tall-storied Amsterdam lodging, it loomed over the dreary huts to either side of it, and was amiable enough to serve itinerant traders. We climbed the creaky, wooden steps that zigzagged up its exterior. Our room, tucked high up between gables, faced a quadrangle of mud streets. Wilderness lay west of a clearing, and to the East, running North and South, flowed the River Hudson, the same we'd sailed up by sloop.

Scarce had Jan shut the door behind us, when he began to rattle at me. "I'll be plain about it. You're a trouble to me, Piet. On your account, I crossed the mad Atlantic amid ship rats in the bilge and shackles in the hole! I forgave you, thinking you'd learn caution at my expense. Now, here we are in Albany, but ten days! Already you've spent more than a month's keep.

"You've learned nothing of your brothers. Rich burghers look on us with loathing and poor ones with suspicion. You've made us enemies in a place where we have no friends—You've-"

"Have done!" I interjected, "you'd still be rotting in that foul hole were it not for my besting Sir James!"

"That may be, although it was to protect you I won that stinking hole in the first place!—I'd never call you coward, Piet, but you run off full sail! Your single-purposed courage lacks skill. Your mouth, alone, is enough to have us in chains or hanging from trees next to the scalps of those dead savages strung up outside the Fort.

"As for besting Sir James—there's something afoot with that English. I saw as you did, how his raised arm in the boat sent a signal. And next I knew, you were trying to save his drowning henchman! Why suppose you, did Sir James not let you drown?"

For words, I reached inside my shirt. A strange ripple coursed from my neck on down my arm and into my hand as I showed him my ivory talisman. His eyes flashed as he followed the swing of that white ship on its gold chain, fascinated as myself when I first studied it.

His study was short lived. "You'll not evil-eye me with that trinket like your father did you, Pieter Van Doorn. Leave all that behind! We're in a fresh land. Cut your family's cursed past out from your heart. Start by selling that bit of jewelry and get us passage to New Canada. There, Piet, I'm told footloose men like us have a future! Furs are abundant. And the French? They could hardly treat us worse than our own countrymen do, here."

I'd let him run on, admitting to myself some truth in what he'd said about my lack of caution. And, Jan, being my friend, I sought to teach myself to tolerate him when I was angered.—Good practice, too, I thought for holding my own with the fools and jackals I was certain to encounter here in the Colonie and elsewhere.

A loud thumping struck our door. Jan and I exchanged a knowing look. I swept the ivory back inside my shirt and stole aside the door to keep it shut. Had the irate tavern keeper mustered up the constable? Was he on my heels as the one having held the purse? Pay I would, even bribe; but be trailed off to the goal, I would not!

"Who knocks?" Jan called, his hand on the bolt.

In answer, we heard a scratchy, oddly familiar voice. "Ye's the same as lately's from Amsterdam, no? I 'ave a message for ye'."

"Tell it!"

"Not bein' a readin' man, ye' kin open th' door, o' nay. I've 'ad m' payment. Be no matter t' me."

Jan undid the latch. Through the crack, I saw first the gray smock, then the yellowish face of Sarkey. His scrawny fingers held out a paper. Jan reached for it, and we waited for him to slink down the length of the stairs before shutting the door. Jan gave me the folded paper creased with sealing wax. At least in letters Jan acknowledged me his superior.

He, as anxious as myself to know the matter of the message, I read aloud:

This day, 9 August, 1690
Greetings. I request your presence at a small supper to meet persons of importance in the Colonie. Pleased I am to provide my former shipmates with most suitable dress for the occasion. Such, arriving at your lodging late the afternoon of 10 August,

kindly present yourselves, in a timely manner, at the Widow Spence's Lodging, 'tis down from Rum Street.
Sir Richard Blackman James

"What gall!" I cried. "Does he think us London street beggars that he needs to robe us?"

"Beggars we are! And worse beggars we'll be by month's end. Don't question the giver, Piet, until we've had the gift!"

"So gloomy you were. And, now, you beam.—An invitation from the English shifts your spirits so easily?"

"And so ought yours! Take opportunity as it's handed.—It's perhaps not mine at all, Pieter. I may be but a foil for your opportunity, my friend."

I argued no more. But how irritatingly certain Sir James was of us! His messenger had not even been instructed to bring him a reply.

It came back to me then, his harangue aboard ship about the British 'star' being in ascendancy in regard to Europe's navies. Here in this British outpost wrested by treaty from the Dutch, Sir James must be the broker of that power he so readily flaunts; and, who better would know how to suck the blood from aspiring young men, only lately arrived in this New World.

Jan was right. And I would learn 'caution'.

Chapter 9.

The Gossips

Albany sits like a pebble on the edge of a region so vast and wild few venture beyond. The town's citizens number some four hundred persons, including women. Besides Dutch, I see on streets and sideways a Swede, a Scot, an Iberian, Irishman or renegade Frenchman; and on English farms, I've seen black slaves from Africa. Slaves of our Dutch patroons have likely been brought in at high cost from the West Indies.—Now, in Nederlands, our laws forbid the practice of slavery and a black domestic in the household of a wealthy burgher is a freed slave.

Yet, it is no secret that the Dutch, like the English, at high risk for higher profits, traffick in human cargo out of the dark continent. My knowledge of this is particular: Now, my father was not one to divulge a family 'secret' without cause.

And I believe he did so, not to enumerate the sins, but the exploits of his Great Uncle Andriesz. His words, I thought, were spoken with a modicum of pride. "Great Uncle Andriesz Vrooman, Pieter, sailed on a Dutch West Indies Company Slaver out of the Gold Coast all the way to the Spanish Brazil." His profits built a fine house upon his return to Nederlands. In Brazil, and other of Spain's colonies, a slave purchased in Angola for thirty guilders, would be worth ten to sixteen times more. Multiply that, Pieter, for each head that survived the voyage. Sugar plantations have need for many slaves."

"And my grandfather? Did he, too, captain a slave ship?"

Father stiffened. "A foolish question, Pieter. Why think you I talk always of furs? Besides, Great Uncle Andriesz Vrooman was not of blood lineage. We Van Doorns—you should already know this—sailed for the Dutch East Indies Company for porcelains and silks, and most fragrant of spices. Later on, our purpose with the Dutch West Indies Company was for the furs of North America." I had not known of this Vrooman uncle, nor am I now so certain these years later, that my father's telling held censure and not envy. At the time, convinced it was the former, my boy's heart swelled, thinking this slave trade an unholy business. And so it is.

Of those who labor as slaves on farms here in Albany, not all are from Africa or the West Indies. Natives of this land, I am told,—that is the males, do not take well to working a farmer's fields. But their females, some brought in as captives from more distant tribes, I myself see working a landholder's pease or bean crops. This very morning, embarked on my new, self-imposed errand, I delayed on passing a grain field to observe these females. And how strange! As they were bent over sheaves at the field's near side, wild birds and turkeys were left to feast at the far side! In my country, land is too scarce for such beneficence. Our household gardens are small. Our fields are verdant pasture for the famous produce of our dairy cows—Ah! to set my knife into a good solid Dutch cheese,—a firm ball of red-rind Edam. But here there is no cheese fair as in Alkmaar; and, I was fast upon the doorstep of my "errand."

My morning "errand" was eavesdropping. I am not ashamed to own it a new habit. Asking with directness after strangers—myself being a stranger—had yielded nothing useful to my search. While in the Old World one's servant can be relied upon for gossip, commerce properly takes place in shops and houses of trade. Here, both gossip and commerce might well be conducted along the streets and in the taverns. Especially the taverns. There, given time enough, conversations once thought private can escape a wagging tongue as news.

Establishments to discretely practice eavesdropping being few, I thought it wise to make amends at this early hour to the Proprietor of the Handelaar Tavern for last night's disturbance—most certain to have been reported to him by Cook and Crone.

Our exchange was brief. I made a slight bow, pulled out my purse, and ignored the outrage popping from his heavy-lidded eyes. "Henceforth, my friend and I will take more care in choosing those with whom we drink" I said, pressing a silver Rijksdaelder—nearly my last—into his upturned hand. His protruding lips spread quickly into a smile, and so, seating myself near two citizens, I prepared to listen.

According to one,—the one I took for a barrister fresh from London from the way he presented his facts,—told of his being present, some days earlier, at a meeting. The principals being none other than Sir James! and one whom he referred to by name as 'Sir William Graves,' and by title as the 'British Factor of Albany'.

"Sir William Graves," the lawyer said, "was bemoaning low receipts due to the steadily worsening trade in furs, and asked Sir James whether the London Company would see fit to extend trade beyond present boundaries and on into the 'Indian Country'.

Sir James was reported to have told him "not to hold his breath, that the Company was not ready to push for War with France."

Here, the lawyer's companion, a big rough-looking sort called 'Joost' interrupted. "If any Frenchman—or Pennsylvanian—or Dutchman. even though he be my countryman—pokes his nose around my Indians, there'll be war, and no mistake about it.'

Were I a Spaniel, my ears would have cocked!—Joost, dressed in skins and leather, I took for one of those boslopers who goes off unlicensed into the wilds for furs, and trades and cavorts with savages. But talk ceased just then as a savory dish of smoked kippers was set before them. Both began eating. I ordered a second ale and waited for their conversation to resume.

Before long, the lawyer sat back in his chair sipping kirsch, a grin on his face. "Sir William confided that he may be forced to send his daughter back to London or, if she remain, send for a bachelor.—It seems our Factor thinks the Colonie has no 'suitable husbands.'"

Joost set down his ale with a bawdy gesture, winked, and said, "Tell Graves, I'll husband her. There's only my wife to share our bed."

"As for husbanding," returned the lawyer, "Sir James invited Sir William to bring his daughter to sup with him at the Widow Spence's lodging."

"By Yivs! Sir William won't settle his daughter on that used-up old man! The poor, sweet maid needs more than a title."

I thought my fit of coughing discreet, until the lawyer looked up from his brandy and, turning my way, lowered his voice. I was preparing to leave just as Joost, not as cautious as his companion, said of the Widow Spence, "She has an easy way to support her establishment."

Mention of the widow and our summons to her lodging, hurried my departure. Jan, on waking, would suppose me up to no good, and rather than distress him further, I was eager to tell him all I'd learned about the troublesome trade and the British reluctance to provoke a war with France, by venturing into the hinterland,—land the man Joost called Indian Country.

Chapter 10.

Dinner at the Widow Spence's Lodgings

"Grootmoeder Vermulst!"

A stockily built man with a beet-red face and straw hair stormed out of his gate, all but knocking us aside on the narrow dirt path. "Grootmoeder Vermulst!" he bellowed, again, shaking a threatening finger at an old woman braced against the doorway of a sorry little hovel nearby. "Again your hogs stray into my house! My wife and children will feast on roast pig if you fail to box-in your swine!"

"Idioot!" she swore, "one of my hogs is missing! Fondle my piglets, Meneer Boek—you'll hang slender on my meat hook!"

Jan nudged my elbow, turning my attention away from the Vermulst woman's pigs grunting in the roadway. I followed his glance up to the second storey of a sturdy brick house. A young girl with a halo of yellow braids, leaning out the window, looked down upon her neighbors with amusement. Seconds later, a voice from within called, "Close the shutters, Mary, their squabbling will fill the streets another hour!" At once, the girl Mary backed out of sight, and the wooden shutters snapped tight.

"Did you see her face, Piet? Like the Madonna in the chapel at Bruges! Ah! If I could wear 'her' on this pleated-velvet sleeve." Jan crooked his elbow as though to encase the lady's hand.

"I saw her plain enough." Jan had never seen my Kristina's sunlit face and I had no miniature of her likeness to remind him of our fair Amsterdam women. He mooed on while we, done up in our borrowed clothes, walked to the Widow Spence's lodgings. A humiliation! I was certain the owner of our finery had been Andrew Markham whose sea-battered corpse fed bellies of fish in the mid-Atlantic.

We found the Widow Spence's place down Jonkheer Straat, the same Sir James called Rum Street. It lay just past the hipped-roof Dutch church that also serves the town as an arsenal. "This church would never have staved off the invading Spaniards," I muttered, half to myself.

"What nonsense you talk," Jan said, having no comprehension of my train of thought.

"You've not been to Spaarndam, then? A church stands on a mound, built there in the eleventh century of brick, and as round and high as a fortress. Villagers used it to defend themselves, not only from the soldiers when Spain invaded our shores but from flooding when the dikes overflowed, as they still do. I think it fine that churches are double-purposed. I..."

"Yes, I see." Jan's interruption held no trace of interest.

The widow's house sat half-hid and well shaded behind a huge linden tree, its heart-shaped leaves drooping in the August sun. Upon my flapping the brass knocker, a servant came, and led us to a small parlor, spare and plain, with whitewashed walls. We were still standing when Sir James came booming through the archway.

"Hah, my young shipmates!" He beamed upon us, but took no notice of the apparel he'd put at our disposal. Gaudy birds we were, too. The tailor who'd arrived at our door scarcely an hour past with an armful of garments, adjusted them to us with a snip and a stitch. Markham, though fuller, had been only half a head taller than me, though Jan required a few lops off a pair of bottoms. Sir James clasped my hand with the earnestness of friend rather than benefactor, but still I felt a beggar. My desire to explain that only Jan's insistence got me into a murdered man's clothes was cut off as he chortled on so cheerfully, and in a manner so pleasant for his being English, I held my tongue.

"Here," he said, holding out a silver tobacco box. Inside were rolled up tobaccos in thin paper-like substances. "Try one," he said. "See if these do not match a twist of Brazil for flavor." To smoke was not our custom. Jan drew deeply and choked and coughed lustily. Seeing his mistake, I drew lightly, sat back, and crossed my legs, stiff as birches in white silk-stockings met at the knees by blue satin breeches.

"I've made inquiries for you."

Sir James had my entire attention. I waited, impatient to hear more as his hand reached to the sideboard and lifted a heavy earthenware decanter, one with the look of Dutch majolica with a rich blue glaze. He proceeded, leisurely, and poured us each a cup of brandy. Then, one sharp grayed-eye raised, he looked from Jan to me, paused, and made a toast. "To your 'continued' good health, young gentlemen." I saved for later, wondering if I imagined a slight pressure on the word 'continued'.

"It seems that, indeed there was a Van Doorn here, when Albany was Fort Orange. The name is written in the Patroon's records as one 'Gregor Van Doorn sent to bargain with the Five Nations over a tract of land.' No date is entered, but the book naming Van Doorn mentions 1662 — the very year the Colonie first became subject to the English crown."

Could Sir James but fathom my joy at that moment! The business of the English Crown for me held no significance. But that the date was the same year as Gregor's departure. At the very least, I now knew my unmet brother arrived, safely, in New Netherland, and moreover, in New Albany.

Sir James sat, head back puffing tobacco, his triple chins disappearing as his smoke roved up to the ceiling; and I sat, valiantly hiding my need for him to get on with it!

"No one here, presently, can tell me anything of this brother," he said, with nonchalance. "Nor of any other by name of Van Doorn.

"My contacts are reliable. It's certain, your brothers will not be found in these parts, my young friend." Giving me this unwelcome assurance, his bulbous lips next hugged his glass, sloshing brandy inside his mouth from pockmarked cheeks to jowl, before he swallowed.

"Don't look so glum, Van Doorn. We sit on a tiny pinprick of land. You are young! There are many ways to take up your search, and I know most of them."   This last he said with a hard, direct look. My hand strayed to the talisman chilling my breast. I saw Jan watching me and dropped my hand in confusion. I am a Dutchman, I told myself at the questions besetting my mind. Why does this enemy English seek to help me find my brothers? And, why, when he as good as killed his own countryman, did he spare my life? Jan's life. Why, now, does he want us to meet important persons. And, why, unlike my father, can a man of his years be so moored to the present? What does he want of us — of me? These, and a rush of uncharted thoughts obscured whatever conversation he and Jan were going on about. At that moment, talk did not concern me if not about my brothers.

We were six at supper. The dark paneled room was lit by flaring rays of tall candles set in silver wall holders. An expansive round table covered in a white silken cloth shone like a full moon. The only other furnishing was a tall sideboard with pearl inlay, doubtless from the Orient. Sir James acted host. Across from him sat our hostess, the Widow Spence, a handsome looking woman about forty. Her glossy black hair was piled high. She had thin, arched eyebrows and bright dark eyes, the white skin of her face softened by an almost girlish chin and small red mouth. Her sharp voice and shrill laughter as her banter echoed around the room, was not to my liking. Nor, was I accustomed to seeing the rise and fall of fulsome breasts rounding like cream over the rim of a gray, shadowy-silk gown.

Jan, to the widow's left and across from me, took no notice. That steady rock, who was forever warning me of my lack of caution—in a single moment lost all his own. From the moment Sir William Graves and his daughter had been announced, Jan looked transformed. I'd never known him to stutter. He leaned forward, glory-struck as a pious pilgrim. Mary Graves—the very same that drew his notice on our walk—was as comely, I expect, as many a blue-eyed, fair-haired English female. Jan lingered over his soup and dallied over a plate of roast pork, drawing out each savory morsel. And she, seated to my left, had to be aware of his eyes fawning upon her across the table for, too often, Mistress Grave's right hand smoothed the skirt of her modest rose-color gown, and the other toyed with a spoon or rearranged her napkin; her appetite seeming to wane as Jan's waxed.

Her father, seated to Jan's right, was a tense-looking man with patrician features and silver hair. I could well imagine him, wigless and frowning, leaning over account books. A faint, not unpleasant smile grazed his pallid cheeks. No small matter, I learned, that glimmer of a smile. His usual solemnity led the town to wager whether it was Sir Graves' exalted position that caused his mournful countenance, or if his chiseled face was molded by his surname. As the only British trader of consequence among mainly Dutch merchants, he probably cared little for Albany gossip. Yet, he was not a man without humor. When Sir James asked the Widow Spence from whom she'd procured her succulent pig, and the widow answered, "Meneer Boek," Sir William came alive.

"Could Meneer Boek have sold your cook my neighbor Vermulst's missing sow?" he asked. His demeanor innocent, Sir William bent close to his plate, his long thin nostrils sniffing. "Ah, delicious! I must remind myself I am only the Factor of Albany, not its Constable."

None met his revelation with heartier laughter than the Widow Spence. I felt anxious. Caught in the midst of their gaiety, I was getting no answers to thoughts needling my brain. I had become the target of Widow Spence and Mistress Graves for conversation:

Did I know about the citizen drills at the stockade? The fire guardians?

What were my thoughts upon first seeing savages?

Was I to return to Amsterdam in spring?

Had we visited Albany's brick courthouse? Its blockhouse church?

Did I not think Albany more pleasant than Manhattan?

Another time, I might have responded with alacrity to well-meant questions raining on me, generously and unsolicited. Jan lent no support, incapable it seemed of uttering more than Ahs and Oh's as he gazed dumbly across at Mistress Mary. But my reasons for any lack of civility surely differed from his! With Sir William in conversation with Sir James, I, striving to hear every word passing between them, was obliged to mumble polite replies to the ladies.

These long weeks past, I'd had it in mind that Sir James's business must be for the English Crown and was anxious to learn more. From the little I overheard at the Widow Spence's table, it began to appear that he avoided politics, and was based in solid business as, indeed, were our own Dutch merchants. I grew eager to discover if his employer could be that ravisher-company to the North, only lately got underway at a Bay called Hudson, named after the English Captain Henry Hudson, who in the year 1609, sailed our ship, de Halve Maen, and explored this river, but footsteps away.

Supper ending before twilight, Widow Spence suggested a stroll to the South Gate before night settled in. Sir James and Sir William were disinclined. This was my cue to plead a festered toe, and not quite a lie, saddled as I was in these insufferable breeches, leggings, and brass buckled shoes.

Jan, of course, was ecstatic to be favored as sole escort to Mistress Mary, and on leaving made a polite bow and offered his other arm to the Widow, or 'Amelia', as Sir James was wont to call her. My hopes surged as the trio departed, Jan looking quite the gentleman in light satin breeches and dark velvet coat with a lady on each side, their skirts billowing out the door.

We three having moved to the parlor, Sir James supplied us with a rolled tobacco, and for the other hand a fine-tasting brandy. Sir William looked taken aback when, to initiate a conversation, I asked if it was the trade brandy of the British. Sir James sent me a knowing look and chortled, "Fur-rench."

I took a seat somewhat apart, feigning uncommon interest in a small book lying on a carved Spanish lowtable. The two English, I thought, and rightly so, might drift into intimate business if I appeared preoccupied. I squinted admiringly at the name in gold leaf on the book's leather binding—one John Dryden, and slid a finger down the ribbon marker. The book opened to a page with this verse:

Friend, once 'twas Fame that led thee forth,
To brave the tropic heat; the frozen North.
Later 'twas gold. Then beauty was the spur,
But now our gallants venture but for fur.

My lips mouthed verses as though in deep contemplation. As, indeed, they might; the poet's words echoed dreams of exploration.

Sir William was speaking low, but whether to accommodate their privacy or mine, I was no judge. "May I dare to hope, Sir James, that their Lordships in London will consider causes of dwindling profits as well as rising expenditures in the Colonie? Away in their Noble Street offices, they catch at figures with little mind to my dispatches."

Sir James made no answer. Perhaps, none was expected. I, unwilling to risk coughing, was content to inhale the sweetly pungent puffs of smoke he so expertly sent ceiling-ward.

"You know, Sir, the beaver can no longer be counted on from these parts. Our Mohawk and Seneca bring in peltries from ever increasing distances. Costs go higher, yet quantities steadily lower. And twice in my dispatches," the Factor said with considerable passion, "I've rendered stern warnings to the Lords of the threat to our trade from the French. They seem to care only for profits. They understand little of this land—less than the French. Nor, do they know how easy it may be to lose it!"

"As for that,..." Sir James began, then paused. He tilted back his balding head and thrust out his chins, drawing on the black roll balanced between his thumb and forefinger, swirls of dark smoke fleeing his nostrils..."our former abject King James when Duke of York only visited his women. He never laid eyes on his holdings on the upper Hudson—nor for that matter, did the Dutch owners, nor do our own! No, the Crown's only answer to the French threat lies in appeasement—except on the Bay—thanks to The Company aided now and again by our 'French conspirator'. It was our great good fortune that France refused to reward Radisson for his services. None knows the country and its natives so well, unless it be his brother-in-law, Groseilliers."

"But damnation, Sir!—to carry on the trade—to keep the peace—we need troops!" I stole a look at Sir William's flushed face. After a time, he quieted. "Perhaps, I could be of more service elsewhere." At that, Sir James turned adamant that Sir William must remain in Albany, there being no one ready to replace him.

"There is yet another matter," Sir William said, shortly. His lowered voice was enough to set me turning a page, and to peer at it as though all that interested me in the entire world was printed on vellum. I felt their glances.

"Speak, man," said Sir James. "You may speak as freely as were we alone." Ah, does wily Sir James perceive my game? I wondered.

"My daughter—I do not know that you have provided me a solution."

"Ha! You are too impatient. A little time, Sir William. Were you in such a hurry at her age?"

"She is fifteen and has little to occupy her attention here apart from myself and the few entertainments devised by the Dutch and by, our even fewer, English citizens. There are no persons here of her station of either sex.—Ah, Sir James, we must talk more of this another time. It seems our strollers are returning." I, too, could hear their voices nearing.

The two getting up, I closed the book with feigned reluctance, and rejoined them. "Sir James," Sir William said, "My daughter will think us remiss in courtesy, but I will take our leave before they enter. The evening grows late. Van Doorn,"—I took his outstretched, long English hand. "I do trust you will call on us."

"We will, Sir," I said, fully intending that Jan be half of such a visit.

The Factor of Albany bowed, and bid Sir James, then me, a good night.

The instant he left to rejoin his daughter, Sir James swung around, forestalling my own leave taking.

"Van Doorn, there is a matter I would discuss with you. Alone."

His bulky frame grew in stature as, shadowed in the purple hues of darkness, he stood facing the room's one small leaded windowpane. "For all that wild forest," he intoned, sweeping an arm out as though to penetrate the thick-built walls, "you'll discover how rare a thing is a private talk among men." His arm fell to his side, and he reached for a folded paper almost hidden by the ink pot on the writing desk. I restrained from telling him that, already in the Handelaar Tavern, I was privy to one of his own 'private' conversations.

"I've put the matter to paper, Van Doorn. I trust you'll keep it to yourself. Discuss it with no one. Not even Jan Carpentier—until, first, you've talked with me.

"Do I have your word on it?" He pressed the fold of paper in my hand, gripping with a strength that, despite his advancing years, locked on like an anvil.

"You have it." He released my hand, slowly. I met the iron look in his eye, undid the top buttons under the ruffed collar of dead Markham's jacket, and slid the paper inside. "Unless, Sir James, its contents force me to do otherwise."

"Just the honest, stubborn answer I expected, Van Doorn!" And to my surprise, he threw back his great, shaggy-rimmed bald pate, and laughed, giving me cause to wonder if in crossing an ocean, I had not exchanged my father's single-purposed nature, for a nature the more dangerous for being better humored—a nature skilled in bending wills to purposes known only to himself!

"I accept your first word, Van Doorn. But you must act soon. Come tomorrow. Before noon. I will expect you."

Chapter 11.

The Offer

He aims to hoodwink me! Make me think the very earth will chart a path for my feet if I but untangle his muddled message. So ran my thoughts as dawn swept over the darkly forested hills and bluffs above the river and lit the town; and I, opening Sir James's communication unraveled a botch of blobs and scribbles. I could do without the wind roses and rhumb lines of a cartographer, but the map—if this were a map—displayed no meridians, no marked seas, no landforms. Jan still slept. To have opened it upon our return last night, risked arousing his curiosity, and so I waited. I read by the slip of light our narrow windowpane admitted, a luxury my bedfellow assured me entitled our landlord to charge an extra sou.

A garble of languages! Fourrure-Pels-Fur fell on the page in broad cursive strokes, yet apportioned space by more than the size of their letters. Our Dutch pels was the merest speck on the Eastern edge, even smaller than the mite ascribed to Russia on the far Western margin of the map.—I had to wonder why Russia had a place at all, if furs were the missive's object. Fourrures, crossing the top of the Northeast quadrant, extended westward in dots and dashes. But the English 'fur' transgressed half and more of the total if, as I supposed, the map represented the continent of North America. While, surely, territory and acquisition was its meaning, this puzzle boded more. A series of crudely sketched vessels, canoes such as the savages use, ran from the east to the center and radiated outwards. And faintly discernible, a set of symbols marched from left to right across the paper's topmost edge. I turned the paper upside down to be sure the symbols were as I thought: the English crown, a fleur-de-lis, and a ship—Ah, there was no mistaking the Dutch East Indiaman. All three stood on their heads, but why?

I dressed, quietly, to avoid Jan's questions should he wake. He stirred as the door hinges creaked, and I whispered, "Sugar buns. I will buy us sugar buns for our breakfast."

"Before noon" Sir James had said, and the hour was far earlier. The town dogs growled sleepily. A light drizzle fell. I knew not what to make of Sir James nor the sport he had of me, only hoped his wits would be duller with the day being so young.

I took the wagon road that led past the mill and the brew house. Sturdy klompen such as I'd left behind in Amsterdam would serve better in the marshland around Fuyck Kill. The only stream inside the stockade, the Fuyck Kill flowed into the river with the town garbage, but my route was, as yesterday, up along Jonkheer Straat and past the blockhouse church.—How Jan's interest in its three gun slots and the cannons housed under it's hipped roof, had soared between the hours of afternoon and late evening!

"We should go to church come Sunday and examine its defenses," he'd said, nonchalantly, as we'd strolled from the Widow Spence's back to our quarters.

"I'm certain you'll hear a rousing sermon, Jan!" The night hour had hid my merriment, knowing as I did that the subject of Jan's 'examination' was one bonneted Mistress Mary Graves who, seated on a church bench with her father, might turn in profile from time to time for his benefit.

The uphill path to Widow Spence's lodging was not an incline to tax one's morning legs. Hers was a public lodging, yes? Well then, her door should stand ready to take one in. I rapped soundly, expecting the shutter to fly open in the cock loft and the servant maid to stick out her head. Though daylight, wary citizens of Albany chanced little with a stranger. Instead, I heard footsteps descending an inside stairway and, when the front door swung open, Sir James stood before me, fully clothed.

"Good! Just in time, just in time." He showed no surprise at the early hour of my visit; rather, he seemed to expect it. Widow Spence in night dress and cap came along behind, holding up a dark velvet frock coat for him to work his bulk into. She, too, was all cheerfulness as though nothing was amiss in my appearing on her doorstep before even a bake shop opened.

"Good morning to you, Widow Spence." I looked past her disorderly shift, thinking to spare her feelings, but of modesty, she cared not. She handed Sir James his wide-brimmed beaver, squashed his cheeks, and put her lips full and round on his own. When she made toward me as though to do the same, I must have reddened like a sheep boy, for the autumn lovers laughed like contra bass and twittering flute and, certain it is, I looked the dolt I felt.

"No doubt, we will meet with the Factor doubled over his books," Sir James said, stepping wide of a puddle on Rum Street in spite of his nearsightedness.

"I came to settle what concern you have with me over your missive, and a most strange, provocative one it is. Russia? on the western sea of North America?"

"Ah, then you question what you don't understand. Good," he said, amiably. "Once, on a trading mission to Moskva, I myself saw the young Peter's eyes flame and glow as he listened to men talk of the untold wealth in furs to be had for the taking. He would speak with any, from commanders of merchant fleets to traders and returning seamen—any whose knowledge could fatten his empire when his time came to take the throne. Should that burgeoning giant grasp at furs on this continent, who is to stop him! Hardly the Dutch. England? France? No, their royal highnesses William and Louis fill their coffers to battle each other at home and, only when urgently petitioned, send a pittance to wage war against each other on this side of the Atlantic."

"But Russia wars against the Turks," I ventured to argue. Sir James's head came up and his words came out softer than his critical stare.

"Perhaps word of the Treaty of Radzin was slow to reach you in the lowlands. Still, Van Doorn, your point though misaimed is solid. Other wars may indeed keep Russia occupied. Moreover, their eastern territory is a frozen wasteland and access to the sea, in any case, a formidable obstacle. Yet, should his desire be strong enough, I don't doubt that Tzar Peter's iron will would prevail. In time, Russia will have her turn.

"But, this night, our talk will be over matters closer at hand. Of that much, you can be certain."

"And, you seem certain of my presence. For what reason?"

"Come, come, lad. You are bright or I would not settle on you for my assistant. This is not the first we've spoken of it."

Assistant. I had chosen to make light of his unsettling hints aboard ship concerning me as Markham's replacement, my fear for Jan's life having rooted out all else. And, since arriving in Albany, I spent hours making inquiries, snooping out bits of truth from falsehood. Oh, not that I expected to find my brothers so easily. First, I had need to decipher the pathways of trade in this land—a land so vast, a land with a reach of eye undreamed of when I slept so soundly in my narrow Hollands bed. Was it only months ago in walking the streets of Amsterdam, I'd thought success assured? Amsterdam is a city of canals with bridges crossing over its waterways, and its bridges lead to named and familiar places! Here, little Albany sits locked in by forests, and to where its rivers might lead, why few besides the savages seem to set out upon to learn. It came upon me, then, that I was only beginning to fathom how unequal to the task was my preparation for this journey of my father's making.

Sunk in so unaccustomed and low-spirited a melancholy, it is striking strange that those brooding moments should seem to manifest themselves right up out of the brush. Like a lean wolf the sallow-skinned ship boy, Sarkey, emerged.

"T'night, Sir, t'night," he whispered as he half skipped, half walked alongside Sir James. But I heard him plainly. Just as plainly, I saw Sir James reach into his pocket. Sarkey plucked what I took to be a stiver out Sir James's hand, mumbled, and jittered off into the fog that tunneled the banks of the Hudson.

Here and there, chalky masts of sailing ships poked through the thick gray mist. Some, large enough to be ocean-going, were moored among the smaller fore-and-aft-rigged sloops. Another day, I would have stood about to watch the activity coming to life alongside the banks. Cattle at the water's edge were being readied for loading on a bark. Giant timbers piled at odd angles were likely destined for the mill at the Normanskill. Would that they ended up in our Naval dockyards in Zaandam and Amsterdam.—There is where the world's most-prized ships are built!

On leaving the river, we walked up Handler's Street in silence, time enough for my gamut of thoughts to leave off self-doubt and grievances, and fix on pride! As though reading my uneven mind, Sir James took my elbow. "Sarkey has cunning. He may prove more useful on land than at sea, and is as loyal as the next man when paid. He grasped my arm harder. I jerked about as his hawk eyes darted up at me.

"I have need of more than a Sarkey's base cunning, Van Doorn. I need an assistant who can look beyond immediate profits. In short,

I need someone able to learn and willing to undergo high risks for high rewards." There was no trace of banter in his deep-chested voice, nor did his penetrating gaze release mine. We stopped; our glances held.

"You are English."

"Yes?"

"You would have me hire out to my enemy!"

"Fah!   Dribble!—Nationalities?   Enemies?   Friends-Kings-Paupers!—We are all men clinging to our own slim fate. Leave such notions to the politicians, Van Doorn, I will make you a Trader—an ancient and honorable profession which throws open the wide world to those who have courage and foresight enough to grasp it. Forget your stodgy notions of patria—pay allegiance to the more fundamental, even nobler, cause. Out there!" he said, arching wide his arm in a theatrical gesture I recognized only too well, "Out there a young man can be a free man, free to roam a waiting continent! My time has passed, but you—once you've satisfied your wandering and stuffed your purse in The Trade—can pluck choicest acreage for token exchange, raise a family and leave riches to your posterity."

My throat felt parched. In all my father's impassioned harangues, never had the word 'free' been spoken, or if so, not to such effect. Sir James' words stirred a wondrous feeling as rare as sunrise on the North Sea. Duty seemed a weary cousin to the heady prospect of the vision set before me.

Yet, call it stubbornness, pride, mistrust—for truly, I did not trust this ponderous interloper who could so calmly signal his adjunct's death at sea. Nor, was I to be swayed from my avowed purpose. My mission in the New World was to find my brothers and to recover my family's fortune. Which would come first, I knew not.

"And you, Sir James though not a young man, are you not a free man?"

He grunted in reply and was slow to answer. "I was once. For too short a time. Now, the rheumatism, a nearly blind eye, and a corpulent body are fettered to softer living. Freedom is there. They could teach you." He pointed toward a stand of oaks, a light wind spreading their yellowed leaves, underneath which, stood four savages. Straight of stance, they were, each wrapped in a blanket of a deep blue or vermilion red. Hard featured and taut-skinned, the color of deer, their sharp eyes looked not at us nor beyond us, just looked our way.

Sir James stopped and beckoned with one hand, palm extended. One savage only advanced.

He came forward with the lordly bearing of a chieftain, a single white feather lofting from the crown of his head. "Tonight?" Sir James said. The savage nodded.

We moved off, my head reeling with half-formed questions. But, within a few short steps Sir James halted, again. This time, in front of a tall step-gabled brick house in the Dutch style, even to its stone steps and a rail, and far grander than any in the close-set rows of neighbors.

The British Factor of Albany must be a person of means; yet, Sir William Grave's daughter, Mistress Mary herself, white-capped and aproned, let us in. We followed the flickering light of the candle she carried up steep, narrow steps of winding stairs (Its efficiency of space another credit my country).

I pondered the need to keep this visit secret from Jan. He would surely be envious, would think it injustice, itself, that I should be so near her, and not himself. Then, too, there was my foolish excuse for going off to buy sugar buns. It seemed that however I turned, I turned on Jan, my truest friend. From now on, I told myself, any scheme involving me, would involve Jan.

Mary Graves, her smile gentle and eyes downcast, left us at the entrance to a room longer by far than its width. Strong light coming through triple-paned windows at the far end, lit on the stout-timbered beams of the ceiling. In partial shadow, highly polished plank slabs made an expansive desk for leather-bound account books. Sir William set down his quill. Before he could rise, a jovial Sir James called out, "Stay, stay," and settled himself in an ornately carved, high-backed armchair, and not unlike the Spanish, covered in garnet-colored leather. He motioned me toward a side chair against the wall with a "Sit, sit." After exchanging greetings with Sir William Graves, I did so.

The Factor lost no time in getting to matters of business. "It's all here." His long slender forefinger pointed to a page in an open ledger. "You've only to look. Each peltrie. Its type, value, and number purchased; all are entered." He paused, then eyed Sir James with a steady look. "You've only to turn back pages to see how prime pelts have dwindled over too few years. Time is short. Soon, we'll overreach the beaver remaining from the Delaware to Fort Good Hope!"

"Then let's act, William. Tonight."

For the third time in so few hours, I'd heard spoken the word 'tonight', though portending what, I had no inkling. I'd only to look at Sir William Graves' unchanged and serious expression to know that he, too, understood, just as Sir James, Sarkey and the white-feathered savage had understood.

"There is danger. Considerable danger." Sir William of the even features passed a hand through his crop of straight, silver hair. "The French have paid informants everywhere. Albany is a stew of treachery.—And not just for fear of another massacre such as occurred at Schenectady this February, past." Sir William, I thought, speaks with a frankness not uncommon to one who pours over figures. "Perhaps you've not heard of it, Sir James," he continued, "you being so newly returned."

Sir James's eyebrows lifted. "You refer, of course, to the Dutch settlement just north of here."

"The very one. A few blacks and Indians were slain as well. " At the word Dutch, I bristled, and would have questioned had Sir James not hurried in."

"Any by name of Van Doorn, Sir William?"

"No, Sir. I would have told you so at dinner when we first met." He of the even, noble-appearing features sent a glance in my direction. "The slain numbered thirty-eight men, ten women, twelve children. And to think among the so-called Christianized savages, were French raiders from Montreal—as bloodthirsty a gang as any Mohawks.

"Captain Schuyler's militia avenged that outrage by attacking La Prairie on the Saint Lawrence, but future raids are sure to center on Albany. The French seek to make divisions among the tribes, bribe or slaughter Indians allied to us, and destroy—meager as it is becoming in these parts—our British advance into the fur trade. Had Albany been attacked and not Schenectady, they might have succeeded." Sir William's tale spelled a tragedy too close in time and place to relegate to history, and I might have asked after those unsuspecting settlers without means of defense had not Sir James merely coughed, and Sir William not hurried on.

"Did you know that Frontenac has returned to Quebec? Our spies tell us he was given orders from Versailles to break the back of the

English colonies. So, he begins by offering a bounty on the scalp of any English! The result here is havoc. Merchants fear to sell grain to the baker, bakers fear to sell flour to citizens, the citizens fear the Indians—the tribes each other—it goes on and on! Dutch merely tolerate the English, English despise the French, and the French spit on everybody—unless it be female or Huron. And all this contrives against honest trade. Madness!" he sighed, heavily, "has crossed the very ocean."

I looked from Sir William to get Sir James's reaction. He sat impassive as though the peroration just heard was nothing new to him. "You'll be protected." His voice, normally a melodious roar, was emotionless. "Mary, too, will be protected." Sir James's unwavering assurance seemed to pour liquid on the other's passion. "She will stay tonight with Amelia. The widow likes the company of another female.—From time to time." But for the wattled jowls that hid his neck, I could almost imagine a sly, smiling, younger version of Sir James playing court when and where it suited him.

"Van Doorn? You will accompany us, tonight." He didn't wait for me to protest or to accept, but must have seen my displeasure at being so ordered. "The matter we talked of will become much clearer," he added by way of explanation. "You'll know tonight your future course. Unless...,"—he stopped long enough to raise an eyebrow over a beady-gray eye—"it takes you longer to decide than I wish—or, one 'other' should not wish it."

His twisted "you wish-I wish-not wish" wasn't lost on me. "If I go," and I spoke forcefully, "Jan goes, too."

Their glances met, then turned back to me. I looked from the one to the other, resolved to hold as firm as the ivory fast against my chest. Sir James sat back. His plump fingers stroked his chins. "That would be the case, Van Doorn," he said with irritating calmness, "if Jan Carpentier were not needed elsewhere. I thought to assign him to guard the ladies, the Widow Spence and Mistress Graves."

Crafty old man! Am I such a simpleton that he can weave the threads of my mind into his own schemes? In one master stroke, he'd reduced me. How could I deprive Jan of a tête-a-tête with the lady of his passion, to go chasing off instead to an unknown place of purported danger and leaving Mary—so it would seem—deprived of his protection!

The place and time of our night's meeting being agreed upon, I rose up at once to depart; and I was clear enough in my head to mask my anger with nonchalance as I took my leave.

Not forever, I told myself as I set off at a brisk pace toward our quarters, stopping only long enough to snatch a quick draught of ale at the Handelaar Tavern, would I heave-to and fro for the Sir Jameses of this world!

Chapter 12.

The Forest

We went upriver by sloop, a quarter moon tippling a silver stream across the black water. All was a-hush on this gentle-seeming night. The sails were darkened with soot as were our faces and hands. The town guard though handsomely bribed, might be better bribed should our presence be discovered. If Sir William Graves was to be believed, the enemy here was the Dutch farmer, English soldier, French spy, roving Mohawk, or restless housewife of any nation.

We plied northward for the better part of an hour, then came ashore on the west bank of the Hudson. The hired sloop put at anchor, and we waded in the last few yards along a sandbar. Two figures stood outlined at the top of the bank. Then, as they strode down toward us a white feather flickered in the moonlight, and I saw that it dressed the head of the same savage as Sir James had words with in Albany. And 'White Feather', too, would be the name I would learn to know him by. But that knowledge came later. They stepped singly, making sounds no more than the whispering of leaves.

Sir William Graves, Sir James and myself, one behind the other, followed them off into a forest of such height the very tree tops moved amid the stars. At first, all that surrounded me occupied my senses—a distant rush of water, creaking branch, falling pine cone, crunch of leaf, or brush grazing my elbow. Sir James's stride seemed no less than Sir William's or my own as though his dismal eyesight and sizeable bulk posed no handicap. As the hours drove on along this midnight land trail, however, his labored breathing betrayed him.

The sound of rushing water mounted steadily as we pushed onward and, as the trail took a southward turn, burst into a roaring clamor. Soon, in flickering moonlight beyond the trees, the ghostly glow of a high and tremulous falls shown itself. I gasped to see so formidable an obstruction to passage. This waterway, I would learn, was known as the "Mohawks' River."

The land trail led us well beyond the falls to a sandy ledge, at which point, we took a short rest while the savages, laying aside branches, I mistook as joined to tree limbs, uncovered a hidden canoe. The canoe, dug out from the trunk of an elm, was the first such craft I'd seen at close range, and the first I'd boarded, and this in the still dark of night. One savage ran it out into the water, climbed in, and knelt in the bow. The savage, White Feather, holding the stern, motioned me in next, Sir William and Sir James taking the middle. Then, hoisting himself on in, and using his paddle, White Feather pushed us out into the current.

Once underway, Sir James must have determined our danger of being discovered to be over. He lit up a pipe and, head back, seemed content to puff and ponder the heavens. I, too, felt an odd peacefulness in the late hour with the lift and dip of the paddles racing us along, water lapping at the sides, and my head nodding to and fro—until an obstacle of rock or sand thwarting our passage, the canoe swerved; yet, overturning was skillfully averted. The moon was fading as the canoe, steered shoreward, and in water reaching over our ankles, we sloshed up onto a low grassy ground. Ahead, blazed a great fire.

Unaccustomed as I was to the company of savages, I could tell that the band of them gathered by the fire were different from any I'd seen since my arrival in the New World. They wore tanned hides and the faces of some, hideously painted, looked most fearsome by firelight. Summoned to the fire, White Feather led Sir James, Sir William and myself to a seated, imposing figure who was clearly the leader of a tribe calling themselves Ojibway. After passing around a pipe with some amount of ceremony, they commenced to speak. I could make nothing of their soft to guttural sounds, so watched the gestures of their hands, intrigued as to whether they be for emphasis or picturing.

Sir William sat in a forward lean as though intent to catch each meaning. Sir James began offering gifts. He handed the leader, whom he addressed as Au-daîg-we-os, a skinning knife with a fine narrow blade and richly carved pommel. It became clear that Sir James had some knowledge of the Iroquois tongue, but chose to bargain back and forth with Audaîgweos through White Feather. White Feather, whom Sir James described as a 'prince among the Iroquois', must have known the tongue of the Ojibway as well as his own from the rolling pace of his speaking.

While I knew no words, I did learn their substance upon hearing Sir James repeat the agreed terms to Sir William. The Factor, acting as clerk, copied down the terms of exchange. At one point, Sir William shifting the ledger from his right to his left knee, I glanced sidewise, and read: 4 brass kettles for 8 made beaver; 10 looking glasses for 8 made beaver; 2 pounds gunpowder for 3 made beaver. And so the listing went. Myself? — I was much affected. After years of my father's tutoring, and although now I was escorted by the English — a detail I hoped he need never learn — I was at last witnessing, in practice! — the conduct of The Trade.

The meeting I thought ended, until Audaîgweos started up from the circle and Sir James held up his hand in a signal for him to wait. Sir James, whispering to Sir William who whispered to me, "Your ivory pendant, — let Sir James have it."

"It stays on my person," I whispered back. "Always."

"As you wish," Sir James, said, and less cautious, added, "Then lift it up and hold it forward."

In the firelight, my gold chain gleamed and the moon-washed ivory shone. I stretched it toward Audaîgweos for his scrutiny as Sir James intended. Again, White Feather translated between Sir James and the leader of the savages. I was half squatting, half kneeling with my hand extended out to show my talisman, when Sir James announced, "Audaîgweos says he has seen such before."

"Not so! There is no other."

"Perhaps the very one." Sir James' curt reply did not deter me.

"Where, then? Ask him where!"

"Calm yourself." Sir James spoke low and even. "Don't persist in putting your thoughts on your face. Not here. Not now."

Was it possible? Here in this wild land among enemies and savages, I would truly encounter a brother? Gregor, Dirck? No, surely it would be Willem the eldest. In my eagerness, I missed some transacting, until hearing Sir James ask Sir William's advice, and the latter answered: "Tell him, it should be the region of Great Lakes."

Shortly, Sir James bent my way, again, and in the same low tone said, "Stand up and move so Audaîgweos can see your face clearly." He interrupted my question with, "Do it."

I took no time to ponder the workings of Sir James's mind,

surrounded by so fearsome a number of waiting savages who doubtless comprehended this ceremony in ways I did not. So, was I a marionette to be dangled, while Sir James shortened or lengthened the strings? My best recourse, in this instance, was to follow and question, later. But, I determined, to act in my own time and inclination.

I arose slowly, spectrally. And, standing, I was supremely conscious that I towered over this ring of expectant seated bodies. I began to move, not toward Audaîgweos, not at first. Instead, I spun counter-wise, arms pressed, my ivory talisman alternating from black to white in the shooting flames while I twirled and faced each seated savage, one-by-one. However brief the moments, the whirl of time now revolved around Pieter Willem Van Doorn the Fourth of Amsterdam in this New World. If Audaîgweos did, indeed, see another wearing my talisman, who knew but others had seen it as well? One or two savages looked me full in the eye, some I could not tell. Most had their eyes half-lowered, a not common habit when staring over fire.

My 'time piece' halted at twelve o'clock when I stood, legs apart, and face-to-face with Audaîgweos's upraised, rock-like countenance. Vermilion gashed each cheekbone. His hair, plaited in two parts, hung down from his high, full-feathered headdress. His eyes glittered. I made a deep, stiff bow and paused, my face near his own in my lowered position. Then, keeping to the same slow even movements, I nodded my own dismissal, passed by Sir James, White Feather, Sir William, and sat down, cross-legged as before.

Talk began anew. I was left in ignorance until all was concluded. This time, I did not ask, but left the question burn on, knowing that candor from Sir James, difficult at any time, was unlikely to come so long as we were in the company of the savages.

We returned as we had come by canoe, portaging, and the long passage through woods to where the sloop lay waiting. Sir James walked heavily, now, and leaned on a stout stick. I chose not to weary him further and practiced holding my tongue. I felt no small satisfaction, when on his own he said, "You performed well. Audaîgweos was pleased."

Still I kept silent. I longed to know of what import a savage's opinion was of me, and more still what it mattered to my finding my brothers! Where had Audaîgweos stumbled upon the pendant of my family for, surely, unless there was no honesty left among men, he had seen it, and at the throat of a Van Doorn and none other.

Sir William whistled for the sloop to lift anchor. The gray light of dawn was in ascent. We had need for haste. Persons of any station, and surely those of importance to the trading of furs, as were Sir James and Sir William Graves, dare not be seen abroad at such an hour without arousing suspicion of illegal trafficking. The temptation to profit being so great, all residents were suspect and more so were mere trespassers in the colonie, such as myself and Jan.

My head was so full of the night's events and new hope for the future, I'd quite left off thinking about Jan and his assignment—one he'd agreed to, I thought, with unbecoming eagerness, and one I had to wait to learn the outcome of since on landing, Sir James urged Sir William to take his rest. "I will trust that younger legs," he said, turning my way, "will accompany me to my lodging."

Chapter 13.

The Proposal

I escorted Sir James to his lodging and, played out from our business up river, would have left for my own, but the hour being late—rather, so early into the new day—I was persuaded to stay the night. "Your lodging, here," Sir James urged upon me, "will convenience our settling matters at hand on the morrow."

I remember dropping into bed to Jan's steady breathing that missed not a beat, and wondered at his wits for providing 'protection'. But not for long. I too slept the sleep of the dead to awake in full sunlight, my companion gone and the village bells ringing noon. I rose quickly, dressed, and descended the creaking, narrow staircase that adjoined the Widow Spence's private quarters.

The door off the hallway led into a pantry. The pantry, steeped in the aroma of cloves from spiced meats strung on ceiling hooks, afforded reason enough to linger. Only, not fragrance, but curiosity stopped me short of flinging open the door that led into the dining room.

Something there was about Sir James's tone of voice,—a warmth that drew one to him; but just as a gloss veneer covers what lies beneath, I'd come to recognize when that smooth-gilded tongue overlaid an interrogation. And I listened.

"You've the look of a Frenchman," I heard him say. "You, of course, speak it?"

"My father was Flemish—from the south of Flanders. I understand French, speak less. My mother's tongue was Dutch. She raised me."

"And English?"

"I learned as needed, along the way."

"And what 'ways' might those be?"

Jan's sardonic laugh spoke more than his words. "What ways I could."

"It is just as well. A tight lip is useful. This business needs your ears and eyes more than your mouth. You will do it?"

"With eagerness!"

The clap was of clasped hands. To what bargain Jan consented was at the moment of less consequence than that Sir James should be at the root of it. He plays cat to our mouse once too often! And, swinging wide the door, I strode to the table where sat the two conspirators.

"What is it you will do, Jan?"

"Ah, he's among the living! Amelia!" Sir James called toward the kitchen. "Bring the surly young bull his compote." He rolled his eyes, his broad tongue circling his liver lips: "The Widow thickens her bread-and-butter pudding with plum, currants, citron, and lemon. There is none better."

"Pudding!" I spat. "That is the business that will fill Jan's ears and eyes and not his mouth?"

"Good, good!" laughed Sir James. "You have humor, too. You're not all solemnity, young Dutchman." This was not the time to vent my temper. I knew it when Jan's lip curled and, in turning, he cast a withering look full upon me.

"I go to Montreal," he said with infuriating deliberateness, arms tight against his chest. "There is no one and nothing to keep me here. My business is with Sir James."

His curt speech, the hard look in his eye, his gaunt angry countenance.—Was this the face of my friend? A thing I could not fathom was amiss between us. I felt at a loss. I knew not which to pursue, first,—the cause of our rift, the manner of his leaving, or my own business with Sir James. And there he sat filing his fingernails with a surgeon's rasp!

"You, Sir James, you will speak plainly now. I wish to know what you've instigated that turns my friend against me. I would know the meaning of last night's rendezvous—what it portends as you wish me to believe—toward the course of my future."

His head bent in deference as those shaded gray eyes lit on me.

"Sit down, Pieter," he said in silken tones empty of the banter usual to his speech—nor had he ever addressed me before by my first name. Soft speaking was another of his tricks! I felt stiff and sat so, vowing to keep my thoughts as veiled as a Turk's and unmoved by the first warm breeze.

He leaned back, hands atop his chest, locking and unlocking his pink sausage fingers. Jan's face wore a look I'd never before witnessed. It was not the flashing anger of the good heart I'd known aboard ship and since. No, a determined, yet mournful look hinged the corners of his mouth and glazed his dark eyes. He stared on past me as though fixated by the glimmering brass andirons set against the hearth wall.

"As you wish!" said Sir James at length. "In plain words, then, I propose to send Jan by land to Montreal to consort with—no, in plain words—to spy on the French. Until spring. Then, he will buy his way into a trading expedition or engage men of his own, to travel from Montreal down the waterways beyond. His destination will be a place the Ojibwa people call Ke-che-ne-gum-eng and the French call Gran Portage. There, God willing, you and he will reunite.

"But, you, Van Doorn, as my personal apprentice, I will send along a different route. A very ancient waterway known as well to White Feather as to the Ojibwa. It is with the Ojibwa, we aspire to establish inland trade, along a route requiring utmost urgency."

Apprentice me to the savages and with Sir James the guild master! I suffered my thoughts in raw silence as he unrolled a drawn map. He pointed to the spot where the mouth of a river joined the River Hudson. "You travel to the interior, beginning here, on the Mohawk," then ran his finger along its length. "From the Mohawk—the river of last night's meeting—to the lake of the Oneida, and thence to wherever Audaîgweos and the Ojibwa choose to winter. The route will be difficult; it will be hazardous. It will be hurried. Travel must be undertaken with all speed—before the rivers freeze,—yet, cautiously. Other tribes encountered enroute may be friendly or hostile to Ojibwa passing through the land and waterways they claim as their own hunting grounds. He paused, poured water into his glass from a pitcher and drank, gesturing for Jan and I to do likewise.

"You will have with you a stock of trade goods to use as gifts—No, in plain words, to use as bribes."

Hands on the table edge, Sir James stretched, leaning back until the chair creaked. I was torn between wanting him to talk on and the rancor I felt for his methods. His eyes, dovelike a moment ago, roved hawkishly from one to the other of us. "Think on this, my young friends."

"Should you succeed in this first stage of your apprenticeships, and should you stay on to prosper in The Trade, you stand every chance of being rich, well-seasoned men before your twentieth birthdays.

Failure is always possible. Always. Winters are long, bitterly cold, and time hangs on the bravest of men as heavy as the wilderness landscape is bleak.

From sounding the death knoll of tolling church bells, his voice all at once lifted. "Rewards come in spring! Rivers unleashing and bountiful, rush on through summer. And, you?—Stretching your unknown muscles and, with each man your comrade—each so dear and so necessary—you'll break your backs in united effort to steady the canoe, plough it, and to shoot all manner of rapids. Many are deadly. Portages, some worn and fragile and others unmade, are always too long, too frequent. For hungry men who've toiled from sunup to sunset, even bad food may be scarce. Still, amid all the grief and bone-weary toil, comes to those sufficiently spirited—" He stopped, pausing again to fasten in turn, the two of us with his gaze.

"Still, amid all that is to be endured," he went on, "comes to those sufficiently spirited a grandeur of sky—of land—of water—a grandeur of all that is natural and magnificent in creation, such as you'll not venture upon elsewhere in your lifetimes. "Of course," he added, teasingly, as though it were an afterthought, "to keep you going forward, there is The Trade."

So contrary were these vistas he sought to reconcile in the name of The Trade, I stared at Sir James as in the century past, I might have looked upon Erasmus as he preached a middleground between warring factions of Catholics and Protestants. But Sir James' was no reformer; he was an engineer! Nor was his oration yet finished.

"To both of you, I say, be ever watchful. Enemies can be thieving savages, prying Jesuits, the opportunist French, and not impossible where you'll travel, Carpentier, English farmers, now bearing arms as Militia." He snorted and swept his hand over the eastern edge of the map.

"Should you stay here in Albany, Van Doorn, to dabble in the fur trade, failure is assured. The good days of mining this region's peltries are well behind us." He sat forward, thrusting his layered chins and hawk-beaked nose full at me. "Now, should you plod westward on your own, you just might succeed! You have the stubbornness—or uncanny luck—of sticking with a thing to make ordinary men quail. So—if, first, you don't lose your fine Dutchman's skull to a tomahawk, a French axe, an English noose or starve or freeze to death,—Yes, you could succeed. But on your own, Van Doorn, it will take you a long lifetime to learn what I have the means to lay before you in a few short years."

Then, just then, in white kerchief, black hair flying loose to the shoulders of her ruffled bodice, Widow Spence spilled out of the kitchen setting a sweet-steaming tureen of fruited custard before me as bewitching as the English's proposal.

"The pox on you, Jamesey!" she cried. "You would turn away these young swains from the colonie before our Mollies can ride them!" From behind, two white arms clasped me round the neck in perfumy softness, and practiced fingers rifled my hair. "Why this fair, blue-eyed David," she prattled, "could have his pick!"

Ever as sprightly, she left off me and ensconced herself on Jan's lap, cooing and stroking his swarthy cheek, "But you, my lean darksome one, could make even this knowing heart tick and totter." For all the widow's unseemly conduct, it was with relief I saw a smile break through Jan's gloom. He shook with mirth.

Sir James guffawed. A rhino of unreserve, he reached out grasped her hand, and drew her away from Jan to his own ponderous lap. "Ah, Amelia," he said, mid his caresses, "you should have the courts of Europe and seraglios of Persia to play out your games. Now, back to your kitchen! Leave us to finish our business. Rather," he added to Jan and me, "let us at last begin it."

I busied myself with my pudding. Intrigued as I was, drawn even to his scheming, I kept to my resolve and held my tongue to better observe the tactics of this grand puppeteer. A quickening, telltale pulsing of Jan's neck told me that he, too, was taken in.

"Our Albany merchants are more and more being forced to turn from furs to supplying grains and timber—massive hardwood—for masts and beams, most certainly. Our good William from Orange has need of ships no less than our Charles and James before him, while Le gran Louie deigns to snap up the British Isles on his way to conquering the very sun.

"In short, Sir William as Factor of Albany and myself on behalf of—expanding

interests—shall we say?—seek far richer sources of furs. To accomplish this, we need friends among the savages. We English conduct friendly trade with Iroquois as do your Dutch merchants. The Mohawk, White Feather,—you saw me speak to him earlier—

belongs now to an inland-dwelling band of Iroquois to the west. His people have long traded with Ojibwa hunters.

"And your trade items..." I started to interject, but Sir James ignored me and ran on.

"We supply knives, awls, hatchets—beads and blankets—and all such things as we can exchange for what the French call castor gras— those most valued peltries of the beaver whose skins are taken in the dead of winter and worn into a fine softness. The Ojibwa exchange furs also with the Ottawa.

"Do you know, young Dutchmen, what the Ottawa do with the furs?"

Entranced, I sat as Sir James paused to lean into a candle. He lit up a thick roll of tobacco and puffed, while his question swirled in my mind. Of The Trade's textual nature, indeed, much I'd learned from my recluse father. But here and now—to hear this practitioner divulging The Trade's very secrets!—I could only draw a breath and acknowledge my ignorance. For as surely as wind powers sails, I knew that Sir James would now speak of the essence of The Trade in the New World. For all that I had been taught, did I comprehend its inner workings—and the particularities as regarded the savages? I did not. Jan, who knew even less than myself, looked at half-mast as though his interest slackened with each new detail Sir James revealed.

"Well, to continue, then," he said, smoke pouring from his enlarged nostrils. "The Ottawa load their canoes with furs in trade from inland Ojibwa and other nations. The skillful Ottawa are accustomed to transport—remember are accustomed, young gentlemen—are accustomed to transport such furs to the French traders in Montreal. Now, for the moment, let us look at one of our most popular British items of trade—the blanket."

Sir James stopped long enough to pin Jan with a schoolmaster's stare, and the latter came alive. "Wool from Yorkshire sheep is shorn, carded and spun in some peasant's cottage and traded for what?—a pot of potatoes? If they've enough, a calf?" He laughed and inhaled, again. "The wool is dyed and woven in a Birmingham mill into a blanket. Shipped across the sea, this selfsame blanket will more than likely end up, not on our good Dutchman's bed! No, now it is customarily found, wrapped around an Iroquois on our eastern shores." He paused, looked squarely at Jan, then rested his eyes on me.

"Could not our British blankets wrap as well around inland Illinois, Missisauga, Huron, Ojibwa, Cree?—Or, whosoever's cache of beaver we can secure in exchange? But to end the circle, then, young gentlemen. Our peltries, from whatever the source, are shipped on to Europe. The Russians make good felters. Then, as is likely, they are fashioned in Paris and, thence? Why our furs, gentlemen, trim the gown of m'lady and crown the head of m'lord in courts from London to Madrid—and Pope and cleric, too."

"What of the Albany trade?" I put in, seizing a chance to break into Sir James treatise. "You do not mention it. Some Albany merchants appear wealthy enough."

"Just so. There are some few. But you, Van Doorn, arrived years too late. Not only are you new to the colony and unlicensed to trade, you are a Dutchman, and subject to British control, are you not?" As he said this, he had the audacity to wink! "The spies of our Albany monopolies are ever watchful. In better years, I might have interceded with our merchants on your behalf. My use for you, now, is elsewhere. Besides, at your age, enterprise in The Trade lies West or to the far North. Do not doubt me."

"Our secretive gathering in the forest, then, was only for me to meet savages that you desire should accompany me."

"Yes, that too. But more to the purpose, Van Doorn, was to see if they and their sachem, Audaîgweos, would accept you."

I ignored Jan's sneer. Even Sir James's rebuke. I was intent on pursuing what for me was the crux of that meeting. "My ivory the sachem claims to have seen, what of that?"

"Chance..." he said, wistfully, "but not quite chance. Little can be learned of your brothers, locally. I am certain their stay here—if here at all—went largely unnoticed except for the scant mention of a Gregor in the Patroon's ledger. But the ivory that you, on occasion, display around your neck,—now that would capture the eye of a native even more so than it did shrewd-eyed Markham's. It is possible that Ojibwa, their ancestors having removed from the area of the Hudson years earlier, would from time to time travel back to their ancient homeland and, while so doing, conduct trade. And trade, certainly, they would with one showing such an ivory! Your eldest brother, perhaps? Your grandfather even."

"You, Sir James, saw Audaîgweos ogling it! Why did you not question him? Could you not learn more?—Or perhaps, in fact," I said with intended irony, "you did think it but a 'sailor's trinket'."

"No!" His head shook vigorously. "Truth-seeking by questioning is the province of solicitors. It is not their way. You wish to learn more? Go with Audaîgweos. See if you can learn more, you young Dutch pup!" But quick to regain his refined calm, he added advice I would not forget. "Give him reason to trust you, Van Doorn, then to instruct you."

Does Sir James in giving 'possible' merit to my ivory as a link to my brothers, do so to entice me into embracing his proposal? I felt no certainty about a man speaking honest truth who could so brazenly plot out another's future, and no kin to him. "You speak with all the earnestness of my father, Sir James, as though I wear the Holy Grail around my neck. You contrive to set me—no son to you—off on a quest of your own making, holding out only maybes, vagaries, and possibilities cloaked with mystery and savages. "

"Yes. Yes, you are right, Van Doorn." And, with a sigh as though he was at last tiring, he reached across to a tarnished silver salver, plucked a ripe plum and, stuffing it whole into his mouth, rolled it around as though uppermost in his mind, was dissecting the pit from its flesh and juices.

My mind was in disarray. I stood up, turned on my heel, and with an uncertain hope, singled out Jan. "My friend, I would talk with you." But, he whom I addressed as friend made no move to leave as I faced him. He sat motionless, dark eyes cold as stones.

The silence wore, until Sir James, his unflappable, gregarious self quite returned after indulging himself in yet another juicy plum, stepped in, urging us to settle matters between us, and to join him at the Handlelaar Tavern on the morrow at three bells.

"Van Doorn...," he said after I had thanked the widow for her artful pudding and started for the door, "your decision. I desire it when we meet. We will not speak of it with others present—merely sign 'ay' or 'nay' over your name. Be circumspect."

With a slight lift of his shaggy brows, Sir James brought our discussion to an end and, in dismissing me, pressed into my hand a scrap of paper separated from the part deemed a map, the same that, only yesterday, I had thrust at him demanding explanation.

"For the time being, Van Doorn," he intoned, seeing me to the front stoop, "this shred of paper serves as our contract."

Chapter 14.

Quarrel Among Friends

A wall of standing logs shot giant arms down the hill from the Fort, surrounding the village of Albany on all sides. Inside the palisade, houses and shops clustered together for safety as a bulwark against marauding savages and a shield against the unending dark wilderness outside the settlement. The East Gate of the stockade gave access to the River Hudson. The river, even though it got its name from an adventurer kinsman of Sir James, pleased me in the knowing that Henry Hudson sailed up its uncharted, winding narrows and rock-lined shores on a stout Dutch East Indies ship manned by stalwart Dutch sailors. Loud prattling Germans in the Handelaar Tavern, I've heard contesting the height of this wide river's rocky shores with the River Rhine of their homeland and its 'castles'. I, myself, know only the flat Rhine delta that floods our Dutch lowlands, and so have no opinion. Of none of this, however, did Jan and I speak as we walked along the Hudson's bank in awkward silence.

A yacht bearing the Van Rensselaer crest was sailing south against the current and straining under a load of commodities. I strained to come up with some means of conversation. "Do you think the Great Patroon's lands stretch the whole of this river, Jan?" Jan made no answer.

"I'm told it flows north up into high mountains. Someday, we should see those mountains. Yes?"

"No."

"The cause of your foul temper, your black mood,—what ails you, Jan?"

His facing straight ahead did nothing to hide his anger. I felt the dark-eyed scowl; nor could I fail to see how rigid was the line down from his neck to the deliberate pacing of those feet in front of me.

Some seconds later, he broke the silence. "Have I tramped these streets at your urging for no reason? Come, come. You're mindless? Wordless? Which is it?" His disdain was like a gag. I fell mute.

"Well? If you would, Speak! After tomorrow, I doubt we'll meet again. Not even, as Sir James contends, in some far off region." Our eyes met, then he looked down to the stones beneath, gave a solid kick, and a stone flew across the marsh grass.

"You are bent on going, then?" He nodded.

"Time past, you and I would have talked over a matter of such importance to us both."

"Time. It changes."

"But you seemed all content to stay here—eager to remain within sight of Mistress Graves, to..."

"YOU? You dare speak of her to me? You go off with Sir James on some night-long prowl with no explanation but that my services are "demanded"—those were your words—to assist Widow Spence and Mistress Graves should trouble arise."

"Yes, so I said. I knew not the nature of my going. I knew only I was to go with the two English, that if our whereabouts was detected, they had reason to fear for the ladies. I was told so little. And of that little I was not to divulge.

"I thought assuring the ladies safety would please you. You pleaded such affection for Mistress Graves."

"My affection. You mock me." His scowl rippled into a look of pain. "My affection pales besides the lady's own."

"Then, Jan!" I said, clutching his sleeve. "Is it not as you wish? Are you so fickle that her affection no longer pleases you?"

"Pleases me? Thick wit!" he shouted, shrugging off my hand. "Are you blind? Dumb? Do you think you can fool me? Your playing dumb aboard ship fell down on me!—I do not forget.

"Nor will I forget, that the lady you sent me to protect pines all for yourself. Her talk was all of you."

"Not so!" We stood, gaping at each other. He could not count the foolish table chatter at the Widow's dinner party. Nor, did he even know if words passed between the girl and myself in the hallway at Sir William Grave's house, and if he did, they were expected politenesses.

"You're wrong, Jan. All wrong!" His unshaven chin jutted up at a ferocious angle. "What makes you slander the lady so?"

"Slander? Is it slander for a lady to show her love?"

"NO! But it is libelous slander that you declare a lady's lover without a wit of certainty. And certainty, you have not!" My heartfelt logic gave me relief. I was quite restored now that the silly nature of Jan's peevishness was out.

"So, you don't deny it and act the part of the un...certain lover."

"Domme ezel! My love is not uncertain—She waits for me all these months.—And she'll wait yet another long year or more! But it is of your love, Jan Carpentier, not mine of which we speak!"

His eyes narrowed. We stood face-to-face. Two wrestlers apprising each other's measure. "The girl in Amsterdam, you spoke of,—you are betrothed?"

"Surely, you knew it!" I had to shout to be heard, only now aware that the town was alive with the jostle and rattle of loaded carts being pushed and others pulled off the pier. I jumped aside as a ruddy, pox-faced drayman plowed centerlong through the crowd heaping curses left and right. "Jan," I said, steering us on to quieter ground, "Kristina and I were infants when our parents promised us."

"And you, Pieter-Willem-Van Doorn-the-Fourth," he sneered, making a mockery out of each syllable,—"you strutting along at my side, can pretend such high honor over your promise, while toying with Mary Graves? An honest lusting, I understand, but you-YOU are a hypocrite! a LIAR" He lunged, gripped tight my collar.

"DWAAS!" I slammed down his arm and squared up. His fist struck my jaw. I shot back; his nose bled. He blasted my right shoulder. I caught him hard in the ribs. We locked. A small crowd started to gather. We were new to the town, about equally matched, and none had cause to choose sides.

"Sla hem dood!" screeched a matron as her little one tossed a mud ball, and scurried behind her ample skirts. Jan and I might have quit but for cries of Clobber! and L'bataille! goading us on.—Oh, no lack of raucous cheers among the garble of Albany tongues.

How long we battered and pummeled each other or how much longer it would have continued, I can only guess. One of us it seemed flung the other into the crowd, and then fists not ours went flying everywhere. Urchins pelted stones to spur on the brawl. The last I remembered was a hammer-like blow to my head.

When sometime later I awoke, a cool hand lay on my forehead. My one eyelid swollen shut, and the other too painful to open, I made out a blurred female form who proved to be none other than the cause of my throbbing head and aching body.

"Where is Jan?" I mumbled.

"He brought you here and left. His wounds, he said, were slight. He would not say the cause of your condition. Perhaps, you will, Sir."

"It is of no matter." I drank deeply from the tankard of water she offered. "As to Jan—I will speak bluntly, Mistress Graves. There is no time to do otherwise.

"Do you care for him?"

She flushed crimson and below the high-collar of her frock, her breasts heaved. "I—I have no answer to make to such a question, Sir. I do not understand why you should ask it." She twisted her slender fingers and blushed, hotly.

"He leaves in the morning," I said, working myself up from the low bench on which I'd been deposited inside her father's house. "I must speak of it.

"Jan thinks—he thinks you and I—that is we—we are verliefd, ah, sommes amoureux. That is, Mistress Graves," I stammered when her brows knit together in puzzlement, "he thinks we regard one another as lovers might.—Oh, it's grossly false, I know! But Jan—he cares for you most deeply. I would not speak for him, except that in his lovesick condition, he mistakes me—his friend—for a scoundrel who would squander your affections.

"Will you set matters straight, Mary Graves?" I pleaded while wondering at my nerve in approaching such delicate emotions of the heart. Yet, between Jan and me, I judged myself to be the more experienced and, not being the object of her heart, could more easily discuss its intimations. It must be said for Mistress Graves, in spite of her maidenly shyness and being pinned to the wall out of my need for directness, she kept her head.

"You, Sir, may tell Jan Carpentier that I do—do not object to his calling upon my father when—that is, should he return this way, again.

"And, you Sir," she said from the entry door, "can find your own way to your lodgings, I trust?"

"Yes, yes, and soon. But wait one moment more. I thank you for your nursing, Mistress Graves. I would thank you more for any inkling of a cause for Jan's misconception. Why should he think you smitten with me, when, most clearly, it is with himself you would be acquainted."

I could gain little from those downcast, thick-lashed eyes or from the hand that flitted across the blue and white tiles of the kitchen wall aside the hearth. I waited, and was rewarded by a smile turning up the corners of her trembling lips, on she vainly sought to stifle.

"You do know something, Mistress Graves. I perceive it on your face."

"Perhaps, Sir, as I think on it, I played your part too well. Her eyes, the color of chicory, came to rest on a linen press that like the tiles, were surely the work of Dutch craftsmen in this English household.

Impatient with her indecision to speak up, I broke into her reverie. "You were saying?"

"As you know, Sir, last evening when he—Jan Carpentier—visited us, Madame Spence and myself, his conversation was all about you. He told how you arranged for his crossing from Amsterdam, about your father's plan in sending you here after your brothers. And, he spoke about your refusal to leave the ship without him,—a strange circumstance, I thought. What was I to do?

"When I asked why he would chose to stay aboard the ship, he gave no sensible reason, but went on exclaiming how you threw yourself into the sea to save a drowning—wastrel, he called him.

"How, Sir, was I to speak of Jan, himself, when each remark turned on you?" She shook her head a little sadly, seemed quite discomforted, and I detained her no
longer.

At last his misunderstanding became clear to me. Poor Jan. I couldn't wait to tell him that his malady was not uncommon. In his state, one could prattle on about a friend, and find it most difficult to speak of matters most touching upon his own person. My poor misled friend! He tormented himself, never sensing that he, not I, prompted Mistress Graves to talk of me. All would yet be well between us! I was all eagerness, itself, to set him straight, see joy scatter the clouds he wore like rings around dark Saturn.

I pondered the meanderings of love but momentarily, having matters of greater importance than the affairs of hearts to consider. I had to make haste to the Handelaar Tavern; already the afternoon bell had rung. I would be late for our meeting with Sir James.

Sun by day and cool winds by night were swiftly turning leaves of the maple, oak, larch, and hickory, all so plentiful in the region. How richly mingled were their golds and crimsons, and how bracing was the autumn air—a portend of a friendship restored! If that were not enough to sooth my aching limbs and speed me along , the course I would decide upon in determining my future lay just ahead.

Chapter 15.

The Banishment

"There he is! Seize him!"

I'd scarce set foot in the Handelaar Tavern, when a pair of ruffians ran up and, one on each side, seized my arms. A scant second I stood dumbfounded. Who were these heavy-handed oafs? Why was I their prey?

A short, beady-eyed and straw-whiskered man approached announcing himself as Constable. He took up a swaggering stance and eyed me head to toe.

"You. You are Pieter Willem Van Doorn, newly arrived in our Colonie?"

"The same."

"So, Van Doorn, I charge you with disturbing of the peace well before the third bell tolled. And, further, forcing God-fearing citizens to stay the ruckus instead of attending to worship."

"Nabbed for fighting?" I laughed, incredulous that so much be made of two Dutch men brawling. "Our quarrel was private! Any who joined, did so by choice!"

"So, you admit to the charges. That's best. A guilty plea may get you by with a fine, spare us space in the jailhouse."

Around the room, patrons, their faces made merry by wine and ale that flowed freely after the Sunday church doors closed, bent their ears to this new distraction as all eyes riveted on my person. I looked from one to another and, at a table in the far corner, whom should I spy sitting by himself but Sir James! My captors tightened their hold as I strained forward to better see that satisfied, cheek-to-jowl leer I beheld on fleshy-faced Sir James. — But, why so? Was not only his eyesight diminished but his hearing, too, that he took me for another? And, Jan? Surely, our little quarrel would not stop his joining us.

"Sir James Blackman!" His triple chins, beaked nose, and furred eyebrows lifted as one, but those hawkish eyes looked not on me. "Sir

James, you will attest to my good conduct. The Constable accuses me falsely, he..."

"I, Van Doorn?" he interrupted, sounding both annoyed and baffled, "I attest to your good conduct, you rabble-rousing young Dutchman! In truth, had the good Constable been less diligent in performing his duty, I would have proceeded him in swearing a complaint against you."

Of the many expressions plying the mobile countenance of Sir James, never had I seen him appear so sanctimonious! Patrons ceased clinking and clanking. Even the barmaid set down her hefty tray of foaming cups to better look on what would follow between us.

"I have a most grievous charge to make, Constable," rang out from that master of pomposity, "I charge this young hoodlum so newly arrived—this same Pieter Van Doorn—has sold liquor to bent-on-evil savages; savages who for a French trinket murdered our neighboring citizens in their beds, and would so do, again!"

"Dik varken! VILE LIES! Curses I spat out, loathing the viper's new skin. What might I expect, when even his usual moderation toward savages had turned. The Constable threatened to muzzle me until, in looking around he observed his constituency. A swarm of squared chins, shaking fists, and flashing eyes, all relishing the spectacle being performed for them. Sir James had only to bring up the slaughter at Schenectady, so fresh in all their minds, to steer the direction of this so-called 'Keeper of the Peace'.

"You swear it, Sir James?"

"I do." He trounced his chair back on its legs, stood, and for all his potbellied girth, swaggered towards me so like a high court magistrate, a laughing sneer caught in my throat. He needed no powdered wig and flowing robe to survey his roomful of vocal jurors. While he'd still a yard to walk, I seized the moment.

"This same Sir James Blackman who accuses me, I would inform the New World, is the same who caused the murder of his own...." I got no further.

"Be still, rapscallion! I have leave to speak."

An arm clamped around my head and mouth until a foul kitchen rag was proffered to silence me. Sir James aside the constable, paused to run his gaze upward as though examining the crossbeams, then began declaiming to the audience on how matters of local government stood in the colonie:

"The British court has jurisdiction over crimes, whether of fraud, such as the short weighing of bread; or over the most serious of crimes—trafficking in guns and liquor with savages! And, as you well know, Constable," he intoned, "the Duke's Laws take precedence over your local Dutch ordinances." He turned a scurrilous look on me, then beamed like a wily fishmonger at the constable. "I'm sure, Your, Honor," he prattled, deferentially, to that miserably petty functionary, "you'll be pleased to turn such a troublesome Dutchman over to me, by virtue of my office as a representative allied to the British Crown. Oh, be assured, we shall see that he is fairly and properly disciplined."

Well I knew, from his own testimony, that Sir James was here for The Trade and ignored politics and civil authority as he chose; but, how convincingly he took on the role of a staunch upholder of the law before this awestruck audience. An answer came forthwith from a tall pole of a man who rose up with the demeanor of a deacon.

"Banishment or hanging's the proscribed punishment for any sinner, man, woman, or child, for any who would fire up savages with liquor in these perilous times!"

"Precisely what I had in mind," said unctuous Sir James, bowing slightly to the deacon and lower to the constable. "Banishment." The constable, if less content with the more lenient sentence being imposed upon me, looked gratified by the obsequious behavior of one so outranking him. However, sly Sir James when speaking had, in raising his head, sent the merest lift of an eyebrow in my direction. Anyone might think he but chided me, further. For me, that raised wink, swifter than the flick of a forked-tongued snake, once again showed Sir James as Master Controller. His accusation, I concluded with an exhaling of my breath, just might be a grand ruse.

"See to it his hands are bound, securely, behind him," barked Sir James. "Leave a length of rope, enough that I can lead the cur in safety to our Magistrate.

"In the meanwhile, good gentlemen—and worthy ladies," this directed with a nod at two painted females sitting archly with their several partners while Sir James reached into his pocket, swung around, and clinked a handful of guilders onto the table where, lately, the Handelaar's manager and owner had seated himself. "For your indulgence, citizens, on this Holy Sunday—the sanctity of which this young heathen, here, hath disrupted, I invite you to partake, one and all, of a full measure at my expense."

Sir James gave me so hard and unexpected a shove, he nearly knocked me off my feet. The tavern door creaked shut. Just so, his pious manner broke and, after rounding the corner of the Handelaar Tavern, and at some little distance, he unleashed me from gag and rope. "Later!" he said, sharply, before two words left my mouth. He hurried me along as fast as his ungainliness was able, past dockside and shops, past Domine Dellius feeding his chickens in the churchyard, then onto Rum Street, where he finally spoke his mind in a low mutter and I listened, closely. "There's no time to lose. Your foolishness on the riverfront called undue attention to the both of you. Fortunately, the authorities were convinced Carpentier's part was in self defense."

"Jan said that? But he struck first!"

"Carpentier said nothing. He knew nothing. He was already gone when the authorities thought to come looking for him at the Widow Spence's. I took his part with the officers, they left, and by now he should be well to the North of here."

"Jan, you say, has already left?"

"I just said so."

"Then, he's gone without knowing how he wronged me, and one other. I must get a message to him. You will arrange it?"

"I will do my utmost. Now, in what time is left, we must complete our business. Your decision?"

Wrongful, evil accusations thrust at me in the Handelaar Tavern windmilled in my head, tilting at the decision I had thought out and resolved upon, well beforehand, and that Sir James now waited to hear.

"You ask, but you know my decision. You plotted it. You threw Audaîgweos before me with little or no certainty of his being a link to my brothers. But, wasn't I raised and tutored to nurture failed dreams as certain hopes? In that regard, Sir James, I begin to see myself as my father's son. As for establishing myself as a trader in furs, I too see that the Albany of today is not the Fort Orange nor Beverwyck of my ancestors.

"But, would I endeavor elsewhere? That much is certain." I swerved away from the hand that rose too soon to clap my shoulder in approval. I continued:

"As if this reasoning was not enough, you, Sir, have just established my reputation here as a smuggler of liquor—a crime for which my sympathies also lie with hanging. No doubt, by banishment, you thought to make a way to secure my decision in lieu of hanging. I tell you, Sir, it was not needed. Nor need I or will I thank you for rescuing me from your farcical 'arrangements'.

"Before leaving, I have two letters for Amsterdam. Will so proficient an 'arranger' as yourself, Sir James, see to them?"

"That, I can promise to do. Captain Von Streppe's ship sails out of Manhattan before month's end. I will see that your missives reach him and travel on his own person. As to your banishment, don't you comprehend the need? It is quicker!—In doing so, I, young hot head, had the quick wit to save you from serving a lengthy jail sentence, the stocks, or both for the far lesser offense which, the Constable, not I, charged you."

Was it possible? Might one think that Sir James' confident,— nay, bombastic—demeanor wore a look of hurt? It was not in me, then, to thank him for the 'quick wit' he so regularly displayed to convenience his schemes. I bid him a hurried goodbye outside the Widow Spence's house.

In retracing my way to my lodging, I considered the urgency of the journey that lay ahead. In part it was to beat the onset of winter and, more so, it was to forward my own pursuits.—A decision made before the latest 'Jamesian' intervention. Jan's leaving with our differences unreconciled, of course, strengthened my resolve. But uppermost was my need and desire to quit this colonie of cheats and snivelers!—and a noose around my neck. All conspired to seal the lid on a decision already hatched. I welcomed a hasty departure! I scrambled to ready my few belongings before quiting the lodging Jan and I had shared behind the Handelaar Tavern.

While changing into clean linen and thrusting a shirt over my head, I felt victim to an unaccustomed gloom. The cold ivory slapped at my bare chest. Uncommonly strange I should be beset by shadowy, wavering spectral thoughts. Consulting fortune tellers or astrologers or witchery was no part of my family history! Ma-ma may have been too frugal or to aware that my father lacked all conviction in anything that used the stars for other than navigation. Only the fogged-in history of the Van Doorn family fortune comprised his past and present.—His future? I knew not. Unbidden, another question came upon me and hovered: Could Destiny feign to direct a course within the personage of another? In another such as a Sir James

Blackman? For surely he had acted the part of Unceasing Interloper in my daily affairs ever since we'd embarked from Amsterdam.

I indulged the shadows in the minutes left to me in this room. And, upon shutting the door, shrugged off such superstitious notions, altogether. Then, stepping out, looking up at me from below was the wan ghost-faced Sarkey, waiting to take me off. I directed my baggage at him down the so-solid steps, and gratified I was to see him leap and lean to the catch, bumbling about to keep his footing. This made far better sport than quizzing Fate.

The Handelaar Tavern was left a stiver poorer, the earlier entertainment I'd provided its patrons being payment enough. I hurried away to bid farewell to Sir William Graves and daughter Mary, then to Sir James and Amelia. No long goodbyes; little was needed not already said. There, too, at my insistence, Sarkey remained. I set out, alone. From a bank above the River Hudson, I cast a furtive backward glance at Albany and its environs. A single glance was enough.

With a brisk stride I headed northward to gain the trail beyond the Great Falls, the same as trod, earlier, with Sir William and Sir James. Where the trail led off into the forest, I would be met by White Feather.

At long last, I could stand or walk alone, breathe in draughts of fresh cool air above, hear the rush of the great river to the right and listen for the echoing call of the loon. So heady a feeling to be on one's own. I surged with renewed sense of purpose and, in a rash of tomfoolery, sang out my appointed self as Bender! Shaper! Driver of my own course!

In the lowering sun I entered a darkening forest floor, its leafy canopy gilded in pale yellowing light. Here lay my Destiny. Let me be on with it!

Chapter 16.

Into The Wilds

The Mohawk River is a varied stretch of more than forty leagues with some 90 rapids intruding upon its slower-moving waters. Countless in-flowing creeks throw canoes into currents and perilous rifts. I kept diligent track of this river in my journal—as it was my first. So, I can also relate that we came upon falls but, thankfully, none so riotous as those high falls, I came to know as the 'Cahoes', close to the river's mouth, only a short distance from the ill-fated village of Schenectady that White Feather called 'place near pines'.

We were gaining on the west, when the boatmen steered us past cliffs high enough to strain this lowlander's gawking neck. Close upon that rocky passage came another gushing falls. So it went. A fast-moving stretch of deep smooth river to speed us forward, then a shallows or an impassable pile of sand or rocks to slow us down, forcing canoes to bear around or be carried over. I survived some forty rapids at the hands of these skilled canoemen before my stomach began to settle into normalcy. I hoped it would remain so for the at least equal number of rapids ahead feeding this river.

I was curious about the savage Mohawk White Feather. I asked him, pointedly, about his "work" for Sir James. Clearly he heard me. His head—clean as a cannonball except for the peculiar strip of center hair left standing upright—turned my way with exacting deliberation. His piercing eyes darted like firelight and gave me a sharp, penetrating look; but from the firm line of his mouth ushered not a word. So, I contented myself with one more of Sir James's brief explanations, this one informing me that White Feather acted the part of "go-between" in securing furs from inland-dwelling tribes of savages.

Now and again, I looked up from the river upon roofed houses, ingeniously fashioned from poles and covered with slabs of bark. Only occasionally, did I see people. Small naked children might run to the bank, shouting I know not what, and once several urchins pelted stones our way. Elders seemed too disinterested to pay us heed, being familiar with dugout traffic on this ancient riverway. Nor was it unusual to see these hollowed-out logs, lying above the river's banks.

Back from the Mohawk's banks, I saw tattered remnants of tall husks scattered over small fields; the husks were left after harvesting a food the savages called maize. Industrious, they must be, these savages, whom I can attest did more than hunt and barter as I'd heard Albany citizens harp on about who, had they the choice, would have worked the natives in their own fields.

Yet, as concerns industry, I found myself intrigued by a peculiar thought along this river. I wondered, if for industriousness, could any one man compare to the beaver? These shiny, brown-furred animals weighing some thirty or more pounds, are models of industry! With four, sharp and curved front teeth, they bore small cuts into a tree until it topples, gnaw off the limbs, and then push or drag the log down little tunnels. Now, I think, these strands of tunnels must be as necessary and useful to these water creatures as canals are to us Hollanders; canals afford us connections among our islands of houses and commerce—as, with slight alterations, tunnels do for beavers.

As we approached, the beavers nearest us dove under water. Further out, I saw one paddling most furiously with a tree limb balanced perfectly across its mouth. It held on as though waiting to drop the limb until we were right in its path, then dove under in good time. Even White Feather seemed amused, or so I interpreted the sideway shift of his mouth. I watched over my shoulder, wondering when the creature would come up for air. We were well past and, when he'd still not surfaced, I concluded that lungs of beavers hold air at least three times longer than the lungs of us humans.

We left the Mohawk River and stole silently along a well-trod footpath through dense forest, two of them ahead of me and three behind so, at least, I was spared their faces—fierce, boldly painted faces that rivaled masks the Iberian Christians flaunt on their Festival of the Dead. One, an Iroquois, left us at a carrying place to turn south. The trail he started off on appeared well traveled. I pointed, asking White Feather to where it led. "Onondaga," he said, lofting his shorn head toward a valley set amid hills.—Strange, when one is all alone, bereft of any familiar face or object to rest the eyes upon, how the mind will seize what one can—even upon a savage—

just to make some human connection. I did so with White Feather, and not only his bearing was erect; his manner, while I could find no fault with it, on this occasion yielded no more than that single word, Onondaga.

The darksome wilderness seemed unending. Daylight shot through with a steady rain making grey apparitions of giant hemlocks, maples, oaks and pines. All around us limbs creaked and branches swayed in some eerie, preternatural dance never before perceived by this lowlander. My eyes and ears were accustomed to sounds of the open sea and strong blowing winds, to repetitive natural rhythms. Wrapped in this forest of discordant moanings and sighings hour upon hour, jangled the mind, and I supposed it enough to cause untutored forest-dwellers seek gods among nature. It took some effort to steady my gloomy thoughts, so kept watch for those trees with the groove of a hatchet notched in their bark that marked the trail.

At every turn, it seemed we scared up quail, fox, deer, or some fog-shrouded creature rustling through the underbrush. The underbrush, padded with the rich decay of unnumbered seasons, forced each shrub and fern to mount the labyrinth in search of light. And, for a moment, I was back outside Amsterdam to a day, when as a small boy, Ma-ma gripped my hand as I strained and stared up through a cloud-shadowed sun at Muiden Castle by the Zuider Zee. That small boy in me yearned to see inside the narrow slits of those tall turrets as in this moment, I longed for space bare of giant trees.

I plodded on, thankful that however my thoughts wandered, at least my deerskin-shod feet kept pace with my unstoppable companions. But, well content I was, when at last, leaving the immense forest behind, we put back on water.

Just beyond the Lake of the Oneida—a long, wide lake with islands and abounding with fishes—we started up another river called 'Oswego'. Somewhere on the Oswego, as nightfall was approaching, White Feather bade the steersman turn for shore. Three of our party stowed the canoe on high ground and covered it over with branches, so skillfully, no sharp-eyed water travelers would spot it. An unnecessary precaution, I myself might have thought, so removed we became from other humans the more we advanced. Yet, not infrequently, on our river journey the savage in the bow lifted his paddle to point out some telltale sign, an unnatural piling of rocks or bent tree limb. Out of their muttering back and forth, I began to pick out the word Huron, it being mentioned often. Later, I put together the cause. They seemed to harbor a spitting hatred for the Huron, it having stemmed from their ancestors' first battle with white men.

Pleased I was, then, to remember something of this from my early reading: On his voyage of 1609 L' Sieur de Champlain with three other Frenchmen, took on as guides, a small force of savages called Hurons and Adirondacks and, together, they ascended into Iroquois country. Here, they were met by a war party of some two hundred Mohawks and, although greatly outnumbered, Champlain's men defeated them. Not surprising! This was those unprepared warriors' first encounter with firepower. I questioned White Feather and, it being one of his more talkative moments, he gave me to understand that his people took their revenge. It came about when, many years later, his people began to trade furs with the Dutch and English for firearms. "My people," said White Feather, "learn to fire gun. Learn well. Kill many many Huron. Others flee far away; some come back to old hunting grounds." So it seemed that because of an occasional random encounter, savages stay ever on the alert, both for their old enemies as well as new ones.

I had expected we would reach the encampment of Audaîgweos by nightfall of the first day, thinking our destination would repeat that earlier trip on the river with Sir William Graves and Sir James. But when evening of a fourth night came, and we halted our march in a place, seemingly inhabited only by black bear and hordes of screeching ravens, I asked after Audaîgweos. White Feather understood, but refused to answer me in English. Instead, he mumbled words in his own tongue, pointed into the forest, and gestured with the five fingers of his one hand by which I presumed I would meet Audaîgweos on the morrow.

Only four days past since departing from Albany? Only four days since Sir James clapped his heavy hand across my shoulders, saying brusquely: "Watch! Observe! Learn their language!" Four days since Jan and I spoke bitter words, not knowing that they were our farewell. And four days since I'd penned a message to him, a hasty note to my father and mother, and a third to Kristina. Had I more time, I would have poured out my thoughts on this venture. Still, I recollected, haste had saved me from explaining by letter the strange and unforeseen circumstances that saw me deployed by the English. Father would view this as traitorous work for the enemy, the same Sir James had made light of. "Let those who have armies and palaces worry about such distinctions," he said, coolly. "You are out to make your fortune!"

Stretched out on my mattress of fragrant cedar boughs spread upon forest floor, I consoled myself with the thought that when I did sail into Amsterdam with jewels tucked carelessly inside my velvet pockets, and a cargo hold of prime beaver pelts bound for the Van Doorn's own warehouse—one I would insist be built—my uneasy deception involving the English would appear bold. Necessary! And all would be forgiven.

Thus far, my fortune was strung only around my neck. And not for the first time, I felt it weighing me down. Memories nagged of glowing promises I'd made to myself and others, promises holding all the brightness of the ignis fatuous that, upon facing the light of day, fade into nothingness. Accustomed as I was, being a lowlander, to damp, chill weather, the onset of these gray rainy days did its part to settle me into dull and gloomy thoughts. The extremes of this country! The eye stops at thick forests of towering trees! In Holland, one looks from open sea to open land with a level eye, and across fertile soil of the polders onto flat plains of sand! Here, I had no high-spirited Jan at my side to argue and fight with and cheer me on.

Yet, in time, our river journeys and forest marches would begin to take on the routine of an established present, and the past seem far off. And of the future? The future kept me dreaming onward. Even the strangeness of these savages ever at my side became less strange as I began to observe differences of features and manners as one does among his own kind. (I must have smiled, then, at whether my estimation of self had sunk low—or my estimation of them had risen.)

Hada—as I came to call Hadakotona, the youngest and most friendly of the lot, bore uncanny semblances of Jan, not so much in the way of bronze skin and dark eyes, but in temperament. He and two others I discerned, rightly, were not of the Iroquois tribe, but were Ojibwa like Audaîgweos. Hada would watch me when I sat at the fire roasting my slab of deer meat, carefully basting it all around to keep the flesh from searing. The savages, themselves, ate the flesh either half-cooked or immersed it in flames until it charred crisp and black. Either way, they clamped teeth into the meat tossing their heads, tearing the flesh off the bones and chewing with lusty satisfaction. About the time they finished, I began. This caused them some merriment. Once, Hada stood up, and grinning like an Eastern dervish, pointed at me and went into a little dance, flapping his arms like a gawky bird. I kept on eating. I ate slowly, savoring each bite of tender venison before using my blade to cut another small piece. I suppose when one is used to eating like a ravenous dog, my deliberations struck them as ludicrous. Hada's antics seemed friendly enough and I took no offense if my behavior gave them simple pleasure. Indeed, it was a relief to detect grins on those painted faces, less hideous after days of rain washed them down.

Most curious was the priest-like reverence they showed a felled bear. Here, the steaks were cut away and the bones hung to dry high above the ground. The bear's nose was lifted up on a pole with the solemnity of the priest who raises up the Eucharist. I began to recognize such ceremonial behavior as distinct from more ordinary, daily activity as my early fear of these savages left me. Besides, embarked as I was in what appeared the very bowels of this foreign land, what choice had I but to do as I was bidden, to watch and observe.

Chapter 17.

The Encampment

Overhead, blue blue sky, a Holland blue sky spread and faded into the water of a lake so wide, so long—it might be a smaller sea but for the margin of sandy shoreline that now and again showed itself coming nearer; that nearness becoming an illusion as yet another and another watery channel appeared, hidden behind clumps of tree-covered rock. I marveled at the sureness with which our steersman followed a course so devious. Is not water, water? Are not trees, trees? Does not one shelf of rocks rise up like any other?

I had hour after hour to posit questions with little else to do but make notes in my journal of whatever might prove of some use, small things, I did not suppose I would ever have cause to do myself. I noted that the canoe we began our journey in, made of red elm bark, was left behind and the slightly larger one we now traveled in was from the bark of the birch tree. Roots of black spruce, soaked in water, made the "watapa" used to seal seams in the canoe. No, I did not expect I would be soaking roots, nor casting about for dried dung to kindle a fire. Savages did this onerous work. Yet, one work I most earnestly wished to learn. Nay, master; I wanted to maneuver our canoe. This skill I needed! In making my request, I even said "gä-snä' gä-o-wo" for 'bark canoe,' but White Feather refused, laughed even, a sound he rarely made. I understood his "other moons" to mean there would be time later. 'Later' smacked of the vague promises parents make to children who, thereby, soon learn to still their hopes. In respect to White Feather's vagaries, however, I would be proved wrong. In time, I began to understand that he spoke little but spoke truth. I listened to his voice undulating from high to low in forceful tones that seized one's attention. This 'warbling' quality to his speaking was present in Iroquois or Ojibwa tongues, while his English lacked expression.

One day when he seemed disposed to be friendly, I asked, "White Feather, teach me your name in your own tongue." He seemed in no hurry to respond as was usual. So, before we would march into the forest, again, I thought to fasten on a kind of leggings provided me I'd not yet worn. Called gisé-ha, they were sewn from strips of deerskin, trimmed with porcupine quills and so wide at the top, I tied the lacings around my waist. The savages, naked except for loin cloths, provided me no models, only grinned and guffawed! I admit they had good reason. These leggings they wore for ceremonies, and secured above the knees fell down to their moccasins.

After this latest of my 'performances' and the laughter having ceased, White Feather reached up and touched the white eagle feather anchored to the narrow band encircling his head. "O-sto-weh´-geh-ant." He spoke most solemnly.

I cannot be certain, but believed it to be his Mohawk name, since never, again, would he repeat it. I render it, now, as best I can recall, and as my understanding grew, marvel that he would utter a sacred name at all, and to a white man. At the time, I thought him a moody savage, open and shut by turns, and wondered how his tongue would wrap around our Dutch language. Holland is a place of refuge for many foreigners and your average Frenchman turns up his nose at learning our 'unintelligible' language and, instead, earns his living teaching French to us Dutch. How contrary are natives of this country! More often than not, my pains to understand their names or words used in certain ceremonies, are met with a cold silence or a rude stare as though I am ignorant to question them. I suppose they attribute to the words, themselves, some mystery or significance.

And so the hours played on. Joyous I felt by morning in the brisk, autumn air—for surely this day would bring us to Audaîgweos and the Ojibwa encampment. Then, back once again on water and the day wearing on, I tired of being solitary companion to my thoughts and grew restless mired low in the middle of a tiny boat none of my countrymen would think fit to hoist a sail to. But, crude as it was, these savages were wont to reef a rag of bark to a pole and skim with the wind! But not this day. For hours we paddled into the wind, following up the eastern shore of that wretched lake with only chunks of tough, stringy meat and pounded berries for nourishment. I accustomed myself to the taste of the pemmican, downing it with clear lake water ladled up into my onagans as the Ojibwa called the wooden cup. White Feather, when not in the stern, would pull from his bundle a clay pipe of sorts. For tobacco, he sometimes drew from his pouch a mixture of small twigs and leaves that, when smoked, smelled of cedar. When we'd first entered this lake—although he lacked a censer of wrought silver for dispersing incense—he scattered this same tobacco over the water and called on the Great Spirit as earnestly as any Christian beseeching divine protection.

Late one day, just as the burnt sun started down, sky and water aflame like the red-gold fringe of a split peach, hope took hold. Passing between small islands, White Feather called "Béka!" to the bow, swerved the canoe, and we headed toward land. In making the drive for shore, I didn't need eyes to feel the muscles of our paddlers quicken. Though savages inured to traveling by canoe, they were as eager as myself to loosen up their legs and walk again like men.

A strange sight met us: Women, young and old, some wearing babes strapped on boards to their backs, and others, stoop-shouldered with gray hair hanging loose. Little ones running about near naked even as the chilly night set in. All gathered along shore like the families of long absent sailors. But where were their men? Where was Audaîgweos? I was not alone in my curiosity. It was clear from the way White Feather leapt from the canoe into thigh-high water, calling out and gesturing, that he, too, sought answers.

"White Feather," I asked, clambering ashore after him, "Where are their men?"

"Gone. Gone to new hunting grounds. May be war." I started to speak, but he held up his right palm, motioning me to be quiet. This, I knew, meant conversation was at end before it began.

Fires were built up, and I presented gifts of bright blue beads and thread. We ate a meal of whitefish staked over coals prepared by women who then waited to eat until we men had finished. While the women's eyes seldom met my own, I could feel their secretive glances. When the meal was finished, we rested. And, again, as on so many a night past and to come, I lay on a soft bed of cedar branches roofed in by stars.

About dawn, I heard a stirring in the camp, straightened my breeches and got up, hastily. Nearby, White Feather, Hada, and the two other canoemen huddled in what was a face-painting rite of warriors. A boy about eight or nine years held a clay vessel of lake water. A leathery-looking woman, whom I later learned was Audaîgweos's wife (by whatever ceremony the heathens deemed marriage) was stretching out a huge shaggy animal skin some Ojibwa called, mashkodé-pijiki and others, 'buffalo'.

"You," White Feather said, pointing at me, then at the camp, "You stay. We go, join Audaîgweos."

"To war? To war against another nation?" My question was simple. I kept my anger in check in spite of his command that I stay behind. He made no answer; I grew insistent. "I will go with you. I can fight." His dark eyes gave me a smoldering look, a long look. Could this savage not understand how eager I was, how eager to fight? To use my wits and limbs in some honest activity?—My heart beat faster than it had in many a day. Still I held, steady, judging it wise to conceal my true feelings.

"You stay," he repeated and, before more could be said, a small, pleasant-faced girl with long plaited hair and child-like manners approached and handed White Feather a quiver of arrows. He fastened it to his beaded waistband, the fringed flap of which held a pouch of war medicine to insure his safety. "An-i-mi-ki," he said, nodding over his shoulder at the child rushing off after completing her errand. "She 'Little Thunder.' Girl-child of Audaîgweos."

I wasn't to be put off. "White Feather, I wish to go with you."

"You stay." Without another word nor glance, he strode off to the canoe like the barbarian prince he supposedly was. The others followed, leaving me behind with their ill assortment of women, children and a few old men.

Never had I felt so abandoned. Never had I such cause! To be stranded among pairs of black, prying eyes searching my person from head to heel, pointing and gesticulating what obscenities I could only imagine as they circled around me, few as high as my shoulder. Whether desperation or need drove me to it, I fled to the lake and plunged into water cold as the North Sea. Such a caterwauling of voices rose up behind me! I swam toward the canoe, lashing through the slap of choppy grayness. The numbing cold would not have stopped me; I would have trailed a mob of drowning Markhams rather than face that red-skinned armada of females chittering on shore! The mind knew, if not the heart, that I was no match for the swift-moving war canoe heading up the bay. Still, dreading what lay behind me, I swam out until, fully spent, then turned back and staggered up on land.

I was met by a blazing fire piled high with branches. Coarse, yet strangely gentle hands pulled off my soaking garments, wrapped me in bearskins. I lay on the ground. A female hand held out a small wooden bowl of a smoky liquid. It smelled of a woody bark and tasted of herbs. Not long after, a calmness like none I'd ever known put me into a deep sleep.

When for the second time that day I awakened, the clouds had lifted. I lay warm and lazy inside the bearskin. Nearby, a woman sat pounding grain, and next to her Audaîgweos's girl child squatted, catching up the grains in a broad, shallow basket.

"An-i-mi-ki," I called. Soft syllables named her, and soft doe eyes looked up at me. I flung a bare arm out from under the bearskin. "Clothes," I said, gesturing the length of my body to make known my meaning. The woman stopped pounding, making signs to the child who took a hesitant step toward me.

"Chi-o-ni-ga-mig A-nish-i-na-be," she began. And with small change in her earnest expression, amazed me, saying, "Big Lake Person Who Swims Like The Wind must wait for dress to dry." Meanwhile, the woman struggled to her feet from her cross-legged position. "Grandmother come back." The child's clear bell-like voice at that time and place, speaking even the bastard English forced on my ears these past months, warmed me to the quick. The old woman shuffled off, and I saw her stoop to lift the flap of a dome-shaped, frame hut covered in wigwass from the same birch they use to cover their canoes. She went inside.

"Who taught you to speak English, Animiki?"

She looked to the side, timidly, but spoke with directness. "Seven snows ago, Black Robe came to us. Like you, Big Lake Person, he come when leaves fall from trees. He stay through frozen snows and leave when rivers run. He teach my father many words. White Feather say, he too learn from Black Robe when he small boy."

"And you remember this Black Robe?" I asked, thinking her to be little more than seven "snows" herself.

"You not learn words when you were five?" she countered.

"Ah," I laughed, "then you are twelve snows, Animiki."

"Years," she corrected with such quickness I could only suppose her possessed of a superior intelligence among her people. I wondered, too, if this daughter of Audaîgweos might also know something of the 'other' ivory that her father claimed to have seen.

(More than once I saw her eyes dart to the pendant exposed by my half-nakedness, and just as quickly glance away when she perceived I watched her.) And, I was remembering something else.

Audaîgweos when we first met, had used Sir William and White Feather to translate as though he himself were uninstructed in English. Did he know too little? Or was it his strategy to listen, while pretending not to understand the foreigner's tongue! Question her further just then I did not, as the woman she called Grandmother was walking toward me, hobbling slightly from foot to foot. A fold of cloth lay over her extended arms. Her face broke into a thousand wrinkles as she smiled, and as she raised the cloth, giving it a shake, I saw it was a kind of tunic and of tanned deer skin. This garment, too, was ornamented with porcupine quills. A crescent of bright feathers were worked across the chest. Animiki nodded. "It fit Big Lake Person."

I felt moved by this unexpected kindness. But, also, I had observed a seemingly gruff manner their men took toward women, at least in public. I bowed my head, slightly, took the garment and slid it over my head. It hung from a single strap across my left shoulder, open down both sides. At least, it draped between my knees when I stood. "Audaîgweos—his wife, does she speak English?" I put to Animiki. The girl merely shrugged. "Then you shall speak for me, Little Thunder, daughter of Audaîgweos."

Chapter 18.

Taming The Wilds

Sir James in his dissertations or, 'disputations', — I was not always in agreement with his arguments, — was fond of making unnatural behaviors among savages appear merely practical. He once justified the odd practice they have of shaving half their heads. "It is not so much they desire to look ferocious," he announced, "as to keep their hair from getting in the way of the bow string. Consider the warrior dead who uses that split second to raise his forearm to sweep his hair back before taking aim."

Then, too, Sir James' indulgence toward the practice of polygamy among savages was of the same degree with which he asserted the right of civilized men abroad to so freely take a native mistress. On that occasion, he reminded me that the harem-mad Moors overran Spain for centuries; and did I think the Spanish yoke, as he put it, girdled only Dutch ships in the long years Spain controlled the Netherlands? Sir James would have it that putting lust aside, more sons were needed than one woman could produce or keep alive for fighting wars on this continent or any other.

As to 'unions' among savages, I had opportunity to question Animiki, she having agreed to escort me to the wigwam of the woman called Na-ga-wa. I wanted to learn the particulars of those relationships closest to Audaîgweos. I thought the question a simple one: "Your grandmother is mother of Audaîgweos?"

She stiffened, stopped, and tilting her head up, turned halfway around. I saw not her full face, only the smoothly rounded, childlike profile, but could not mistake the puzzled expression of that raised eyebrow. "Have many grandmothers. Big Lake Person not have many grandmothers?"

"Two grandmothers." I left it there, not wishing to talk about dead women I'd never known, and refrained from asking this child the count of Audaîgweos' wives. "Nagawa, she is your mother?"

"Nagawa second wife to my father. My mother dead." I might

have offered sympathy to one so young on the loss of her mother, had she not added,"white man sickness kill her."

"What is this whiteman's sickness?" She appeared not to know, but began tapping her fingers to her face. My not unreasonable conclusion was that her mother died of the small pocks, a disease that leaves any who survive this most deadly scourge scarred for life. "Your skin is clear. Your mother's sickness did not touch you nor your father?"

"My mother visit far village."

"You were lucky, Animiki."

"'Luk-key?' What is this 'luk-key,' Big Lake Person?"

"It means, it is good the whiteman's disease did not scar—did no harm to you and your father."

Such pitted sores of the small pocks had disfigured even our Nederland's great defender of Dutch independence, Maurice, Prince of Orange and Nassau. My memory is clear on how, first I'd learned of this disease. In walking with my father along the wharf near a fortress, the Fortress of Schreierstoren, I saw at the top, women, wrapped in rough woolens, standing there weeping as the wind carried their sailors off to sea. Wailing over going to sea struck my boy's mind as foolish and, looking elsewhere, my eyes starred at the gouged eyes and face of a living gargoyle. My father slipped the wretch a coin as we passed.

"Pa-pa, the coin is of lead!"

"Of course. The old sightless one all wrinkled and pocked is one of many beggars. You, Pieter, might wish a silver florin. He does not. He is one of the lucky ones. The plague of 1639 left him alive, while our cemeteries ran out of ground for all the unburied corpses."

I laid to rest this whiteman's disease as Animiki lifted a hand, indicating we were approaching the hut of Nagawa.

She of the leathery skin who yesterday, squatted on the ground with bone in hand, scraping the hide of a buffalo, today squatted, eyes down, sorting and sniffing bits of leaves, dried buds, and poking through a basket of roots.

"You speak English, Nagawa?" I asked, keeping at a polite distance while trying to determine if the girl were needed to translate between us. No sound or look escaped her, nor did she even raise her head.

"Madam Nagawa?" How was I to address this female savage

crouched over her bits and bundles. and wife to the clan's leader." Still as stone she sat. I took a step closer. "Wife of Audaîgweos, speak!" Still she altered neither face nor position. I turned away, swallowing a rising anger at her insolence in refusing to so much as acknowledge my presence.

I sought Animiki's help. She stood to the side, head lowered. But was not a smile making a crescent of her small mouth?

"Animiki, make this woman speak. What manner of behavior is this? Am I mistaken? Is she not the wife of Audaîgweos, your leader?"

"Big Lake Person," she began, meekly, "Nagawa, wife of Audaîgweos, cannot hear, cannot speak." My eyes must have shown surprise. At once, the pitch of her voice changed to instructress. "Wife of Audaîgweos very clever with plants. She has strong manitou."

I took notice then of what I had chosen to ignore, the cleft above the woman's mouth as though the chin were split with a chisel. "Ah, then," I said, giving myself a moment to consider, "if she has strong manitou, she will know where White Feather and your warriors go to fight."

The child smiled with such sweetness, my impatience lessened somewhat. She squatted down in the dirt, setting her necklace of shells a-jingle and addressed the taut-skinned Nagawa. Unskilled though I was in hand signs, I could see 'fighting' was communicated as she clenched her small fists and pushed them out and back, one after the other.

For some minutes, Nagawa continued to poke and sort. I thought her not only mute, but addled in the brain as well. Suddenly, she placed a hand on each bent knee and grunted. She took up the conversation with subtle movements of fingers, hands, and arms. I watched closely for any change in a manner and expression that scarcely altered from the placid gaze she fixed on Animiki. Not once did she look up at me. When concluded, she grunted again, and resumed her work.

Not so, Animiki. That one flew up, spun around, and faced the dark forest as though calling on the eastern sky to impart divine intercession to her words. "Nagawa say Big Lake Person wait. If men not return by first frost, all leave this place before waters freeze." She gave me no chance to question, flashed an elfin smirk and left, half-running toward the dozen or so dome-shaped huts that made up the center of their village.

Ah, well, nothing being so onerous as doing nothing, I left to rest by the lake to reflect upon my choices. A marsh of reeds claimed its share of the shoreline, while water, smooth and dark, faded to liquid silver at the horizon. Overhead, an army of honking geese stormed toward some destination to lay siege to before nightfall. Off to the side at a short distance, deer drank at the water's edge, their figures graceful and black against a lowering sun. I heard, from some far-away place in the overreaching forest, a plaintive bugling like a call of some largesome animal seeking a mate. The wilds of this treacherous country in such moments all had a defined purpose, while I, a mere human, had to sort out my own.

For several days I observed two old men making canoes. They began by laying bow-shaped cedar strips flat on top of an even stretch of ground. These formed the frame. Underneath were spread long lengths of birch bark, the inner rind being the outside of the canoe which, when drawn up and curved, shaped the sides. Planking and ribs made of cedar were then set down inside and all pieces lashed together with split roots. One old man rewarded me with a toothless grin when, in showing my appreciation of his skill, I said, "Grandfather, has wa'wingesiwin." And indeed it was an amazement to see him with nothing more than a crude knife, split a stick of cedar no thicker than two fingers, into thin strips at both ends. These he plunged into a boiling pot to soften, then shape into the arching stem ends of the canoe.

Easy it would be to steal off! Several canoes lay turned over on the bank. And hadn't I watched the maneuvering of such craft for interminable hours since leaving Albany? White Feather's war party when they struck out across the lake were heading in a northerly direction. Animiki's eastward stance in proclaiming the tribe's travel plan, could only mean that a fork, river, or portage must lead east off the lake to the north. Also in my favor, although not much tested, was my rigorous tutoring in navigation which despite Sir James's sneer about ploughing oceans by-the-book must be of some account on these lakes and rivers.

Yet, another choice moved in on me as the soft-shaded night slipped into shore, a plan worthy of Sir James himself! Here among the women and old men (whose shadowy presence as workmen only seemed outside the business of daily activity—existed knowledge. Knowledge no adult Ojibwa, thus far, seemed eager to freely share.

While watching and observing I must do what Sir James bade me do: win their trust. Indeed, hadn't the women shown more aptness for converse than the men? All at once it came to me. I determined then, on that tame, peaceful shoreline that should the Ojibwa warriors not return soon—very soon, I would secure the most able female among them, forcibly if need be, to serve as my guide. I would set out in pursuit of beaver. And, their warriors? I wanted both!

Chapter 19.

The Barter

The next morning, sounds of chattering, laughing females rushing past the wigwam woke me from a deep sleep. Supposing their men to be returning. I hurried out. Animiki, as though expecting to see me fly out beckoned me to follow as she ran on down to the lake. Six pairs of women were pushing out in canoes, only to stop short in the shallow waters. Skilled they were at balancing in the midst of the tall reeds; the one in the bow turning around to face the stern, then each grabbing handfuls of reed stalks to bend over the edges of the canoe.

"What sport is this?" I asked Animiki upon seeing each take up a stick and, strike not at one another, but flail at the tops of the stalks as though swatting flies, only to loose a shower of seeds.

"Ma-no-min." Her eyes brightened like a Dutch child's over an apple dumpling.

Later, I would see the women husk and winnow the grains and, after boiling the grains, I found the manomin to have a wild but pleasing, nut-like flavor. The reeds were woven into baskets of some size and intricacy.

I must say, the females performed other useful work, and lacked all sense of hurry. When weaving baskets, their hands plaited strips of bark or grasses with an easy grace, and must be a more agreeable work than spending their days inside a Leyden linen factory. Also they harvest the sap from maple trees at the end of a cold winter and, upon being offered a bladder skin of the sweet water, my lip smacking set them off into fits of giggles. But, I get ahead of myself. At the time of my first autumn in this strange land, I observed the work of female savages as a poor choice when I longed to be off and doing! By evening of the fourth day encamped in their midst, I resolved this day would be my last.

Through careful questioning of Animiki, I learned that a woman whose name was given to me as "Long Smoke" was skilled on the waterways to the west. She was of a tribe called Ottawa and had married into Animiki's clan. When the child lifted her hand to sign, making a slash across her throat, I grew impatient. "Dead? Long Smoke is dead?"

"No, Big Lake Person," she laughed, "Long Smoke not dead. Her husband take the long sleep. Over there, naméteg." She motioned to an array of tree limbs strung horizontally between poplars. A stocky, square-jawed woman, taller by half a head than the other women here, was stringing fish to dry across the racks.

"This naméteg is a "tree limb?"

"No, na-mé-teg." She spoke as though repeating the word should enlighten me.

"Does Long Smoke speak English?"

Animiki smiled. "She speak English good as you speak Ojibwa." Her words held a reproof not visible in the innocent look she gave me. Had she been Dutch, or even a French or English child, I might have tweaked the shiny braid that fell down her back. But, there was more I desired to learn.

"And does Long Smoke also follow the haunts of the beaver?"

She looked perplexed, and thinking my words beyond the child's comprehension, I asked, "Does Long Smoke know the land of the beaver?" Her smooth forehead creased and her bright eyes narrowed, and so it appeared that such a frown must be a universal sign of puzzlement.

"Come, Animiki. I would talk to Long Smoke."

I stood back to watch her solid, angular body swooping up, one after the other, a whitefish half the length of my arm. Grasping one under its bulging eyes, she wiped the sleek sides down with handfuls of long grass then tossed it across the rack.

"She is drying fish," I said.

Animiki looked radiant at a perception even a blind Hollander would know. "Yes, Big Lake Person. Naméteg same. Dry fish. Fish feed us when waters freeze." She made a sign of greeting to Long Smoke, then spoke by way of introducing me. Long Smoke turned her broad face toward me, lifted her eyes slightly, and looked away.

"Ask, has she traveled to the land of many beaver?" Animiki translated, and gave me back the answer 'yes.' Again, I noticed the puzzled look on the child's face. I picked a stick from the brush and pointed it in the dirt, then handed it to Animiki. "Tell her to draw the route to the land of many beaver."

A savage's face does not flush with such redness as our fair skins, yet Animiki's embarrassment was evident. "What troubles you, Little Thunder?" I asked, gently.

"Big Lake Person know beaver live in waters."

"I wish to know where many beaver live. Many, many beaver. You will ask her." Whatever she uttered, her words to Long Smoke produced the desired effect. I saw the look of interest that flashed in the tall ones' eyes. Then her arm holding the stick pointed in all directions. Her arm still extended, she dropped the stick and drew her palm in toward her chest.

"She say she trade."

"Tell her I have trade goods." Sir James had seen to the stash of knives, beads, sundry other light items, some blankets and a few brass kettles. The spare firearm and powder, he'd warned me to keep. I passed my hands, one in front of the other, making the sign I had learned for 'trade'. A look of undisguised astonishment crossed Animiki's upturned face, but I hearkened at the broad, greedy smile that lit up Long Smoke's blunt features.

I left the two of them, much pleased with myself, having succeeded so well in my first endeavor to conduct trade. For a string of beads or, if need be, a knife or a brass kettle, I would procure a guide! While Audaîgweos and White Feather made war, I would seek out new dwelling places for that finest of all God's furry creatures in The Trade.

The future pockets of this Dutchman fairly jingled as I lay down that night inside a bearskin spread over pine needles and rushes. I turned back the flap of the wigwam to breathe in the air. A sliver of moon in a sky of dancing stars twinkled like the gold coins that lardered my thoughts. Oh, I knew the uncovering of a rich supply of the beaver entailed much work. Besides harvesting. each animal must be skinned, scraped, cleaned, dried, bundled, and shipped! Still, who has not laid back, collapsing the drudgery of attainment into a spare second and, in the fullness of well being, basked in the dream of reward.

Ah, dreams! Under the warmth of the bearskin came a cool touch. Fingertips traced the course of my spine, the small of my back. Crept lower, lingering with feather-light strokes. The face of Kristina smiled on me with desire so sweet so unchaste! I rolled over and feverish with longing, my manliness beginning to rise, I flung off the bearskin. Dreaming? The reek of oily animal fat bent my nostrils—God In Hemel!—alongside me, a greased writhing body made a shushing sound. A rough-skinned hand clamped my mouth. Soft low syllables cooed in my ear, their meaning I could only guess as I, now fully awake, knew this to be a savage female in my bed!— Oh, I knew such things took place—men of all ranks and no rank fall prey to womanly wiles, but HERE? NOW? My mind catapulted as my body feasted. Practiced fingers stroked my limbs, teasingly down, pleasurably close, closer—so close I trembled with excitation!...yet, just so, I trembled in revulsion that the fair one of my dream was this lusting savage. One bare, heavy leg slid up, encircled me like a vise—"Hoer! Teef!" The gold chain at my neck whirled, the ivory slapped skin—her skin as I thrust her off and she, sucking in her breath, hissed, muttered what I took as a curse, and slunk out the way she'd come. As the flap of the wigwam furled back, I glimpsed the square-jawed Long Smoke.

Chapter 20.

The Shunning

Not even a savage would confide such behavior to a mere child! Yet, in the morning when no Little Thunder greeted me outside my wigwam, nor was even in sight as I approached the village fire, I had cause to wonder if Long Smoke had divulged her unseemly dark of night conduct.

Other mornings, a stick laden with a smoking fish was offered me by the woman with a limp and a permanent grin etched across her wide face. But, this morning, their forms shrouded in blankets, each sat with face averted from me. I looked around the fire with growing uneasiness. Hunched on knees or in cross-ankled squats, they bent to the fire's warmth in the chill morning air. Even the noisy children who, once their hunger was satisfied, roved around at will were sent off somewhere. Being born to savage customs was not required. There could be no mistaking the intent. I was being shunned.

But what did these creatures assume to know? What had they been told? Long Smoke, alone, could be the source of such altered behavior. With no Animiki present, I lacked words for putting the true facts before them. Facts. I began to feel as much contempt for myself as for them! Had I sunk so low, I had need to explain myself to these savages, these females! Inwardly reeling, I stormed away, unsure of what I should or should not do or say—or even what I wished or wanted. One need was paramount. I had to find Animiki.

And so, I strode to Nagawa's wigwam, stood apart, and studied it for signs of movement, A central pole lifted from the earthen floor on up through the opening as a brace for securing the support poles that framed-in the circular shelter. A hooped skirting of skins and bark covered the outside against the elements. I drew closer and, sensing someone was within. shuffled in the dirt to announce my presence. "Little Thunder?" I called, softly.

"Do you hear me, Little Thunder?" I spoke more urgently, but no voice answered.

"Your people are angry with me, Little Thunder. I wish you to explain to them.—The Ottawa woman, Long Smoke, came to me unbidden in the middle of the night.—Animiki!" Still no answer came. I continued, hoping that my words were not falling on the deaf ears of Nagawa.

"A young woman in Amsterdam—my country—waits for my return. You must explain to Long Smoke. I wish to trade with her only as my guide. Nothing more,—nothing such as she came seeking inside my wigwam." A faint rustling and murmuring, then Nagawa emerged head first, her long graying hair caught behind and trailing over the neck of her doe skins. Her straight stance when she stood surprised me, it being the first time I saw her upright.

I made a slight bow, spread my hand in sign just above my waist. "A-ni-mi-ki," I mouthed, supposing that the name of her husband's child could be understood from my lips. She reached behind, pulled aside the flap, and made a motion of her arm inside the wigwam. Getting no response, she made a guttural sound and motioned again. Slowly and with eyes lowered, Animiki came forward, chin quivering.

"Little Thunder, you look sad. I am sorry."

Her round dark eyes pinned me hard. Lips and eyelids opened together and, finally, she spoke. "Big Lake Person break promise to Long Smoke. Breaking promise is not our way."

My astonished gasp must have startled her and she looked at me with quickened interest. Nagawa had not moved, but stood calmly by as though studying my every sound and gesture. "I made no promise to Long Smoke," I said, looking from one to the other, straight in the eyes. "I made NO promise, none! I agreed to offer her trade goods in return for guiding me to the land of many beaver. That is all. You were there, Animiki.—You know this is truth," I chided her.

"No, Big Lake Person. You ask Long Smoke to marry you. This is truth."

"I—Marry Long Smoke? " My face must have spoken for me. I could only gape in disbelief, anger welling up from the pit of my stomach.

Unmatched as we were, we stood as combatants, I gazing down on this righteous female David, and she staring up at about the level of my breast. Of a sudden, she whipped around and faced Nagawa. I could not follow the rapid motions of her small hands and arms as she conversed, telling God knows what. When she finished, Nagawa nodded, and this savage waif making so giant an accusation, faced me once again.

"Big Lake Person," she said, solemnly. She paused, but I caught an altered timbre in her trembling young voice, "make the sign of our people for "to marry.""

"I do not know it, Little Thunder, and if I did, would have no cause to use it."

Her small hands passed one in front of the other. Only then did I grasp the enormity of my mistake. I had transmitted the wrong hand signal to Long Smoke. Dumbly, I shook my head. Most grateful I was that no Jan nor Sir James were here to witness my grand stupidity.

"I thought it the symbol for "trade."" Silence.

Her intermittent giggles slapped my sunken spirits. I revived enough to ask, "Animiki, you will make Long Smoke understand?" She communicated again with Nagawa whose mirthful eyes disappeared into her crinkled, web-like skin. Even I could detect the walking motion she made with her hands.

"Nagawa say, Big Lake Person go walk into forest. Come back when sun is high in sky."

Nagawa was wise. Walking among trees was never my habit, and in the New World, only to reach a destination unobtainable by boat or carriage. Carriage?—a convenience of travel scarcely common in the tawdry villages of this land. Thoughts of home, of Holland,—and even, I admit, of that dreary little gehucht on the Hudson—stole into my mind as I trod a path of sorts through trees and more trees! Great and small trunks of conifers and hearty-limbed chestnut trees, oaks, maples—or hickory or ash or elm—I, after all, am not studied in horticulture. One needed no Leeuwenhoek microscope to see that trees, brush and undergrowth were as diverse within the New World's forests as the fish that swarmed in the great ocean.

I tried summoning Kristina's sweet face, and only a fleeting picture could I form, wavering and all too momentary. So distanced I was from warm companionship, my relations with savages seemed to be taking on shapes unacknowledged by my brain. Such a misunderstanding with Long Smoke I supposed would have humor, had I not been the cause. Always, I prided myself that Pieter Van Doorn IV did not equivocate, but spoke his mind. Now it seemed, I had to learn how to speak that which I thought, and think again on that which I thought I knew.

Lower down on the forest slopes, bluish berries, dried and shriveled, hung in clumps. I ranged on higher up in search of finding them less ravaged, and came upon bushes of berries soft and past ripe, but welcome enough, my having had nothing to eat this day. Moving lower down, again, I looked to satisfy my thirst. Water never seemed far away in these parts if one listened.

I was on my knees beside a cold stream before seeing that I was not alone. Downstream, and no more than a dozen yards off, a brownish-black creature stood on all fours, half-in and half-out the water. Its huge paw swept down and up with lightning speed, and a broad fish's flapping silver tail fin was last to disappear inside that gaping mouth. I shrunk back from the water, grateful for a light west wind. Perhaps, being fixated on his meal, I'd nothing to fear. Thus far, however, I had seen only dead bear, and much preferred them so. I walked swiftly along the path on which I'd come, and was ready to return, it being close on noon.

What contrast to the dark forest was the full light of the sun playing on the bright child helping old Nagawa pick through herbs, fungus, plants, and grasses. I say "old" because with her toughened skin and graying hair, Nagawa, like other savage women, appeared older than her years. The pair squatted side-by-side, and Little Thunder looked up at my approach.

"The sun is high," I said, pointing overhead. "I have walked long. I ate berries. Saw a bear. You have talked to Long Smoke?"

Animiki appeared to be seeking permission from Nagawa to speak. The latter nodded and, as both remained seated, I did likewise. I kept my mind calm as I waited, gazing past their figures and their house of stretched skin to the grove of birch trees that parted them from their neighbors. A covey of partridge skittered up out of a patch of yellow grass. Was I beginning to assimilate a savage's sense of unhurried time? I waited for Animiki to answer with all my earlier tension released.

"Nagawa say broken promise is like broken arrow. Arrow can never be same."

"But, I made no such promise." Before I could remonstrate, Nagawa raised a hand to silence words she could not hear. She motioned, giving Animiki leave to speak.

"She say, hand and heart of Big Lake Person do not speak the same. Nagawa, others, say you to leave. Canoe is packed, is ready for you. Nagawa say to follow lake to meet the river. Follow river. Many beaver. Not need Long Smoke." Without another word, Nagawa rose up and turned away. Animiki did likewise, following her inside their wigwam without a backward glance.

I flew to my second banishment with relief and joy! No one stood on shore to bid me goodbye as I stashed the belongings from my tent into the small canoe, pushed out, and leapt inside. Although they kept their bodies hidden, I was certain that some forty pairs of eyes were watching me and, perhaps, eager for me to capsize. Even Little Thunder, who if she'd any sadness upon my leavetaking, had made no sign of it.

Vague clues were better than none at all and, having myself seen the war canoes heading north that miserable day when I'd been left behind, I skimmed up the glassy lake. Soon, it was the encampment that was left far behind. Paddling came easy. No wonder after days on end of observing the skill of White Feather and the Ojibwa canoemen. My spirits lightened all the more as I fell into a rhythm. I followed the shoreline of the lake at a safe distance. Nagawa's direction, "follow lake to meet the river. Follow river. Many beaver" had seemed a straightforward, but on a lake of such immensity, how many rivers fed into it? The further up the Big Lake, the higher the winds swept across to threaten this paper boat.

I would let the winds make my choice for me. A bay lay ahead and into it ran a river. It was the first river to the east. While not at odds with Nagawa's directive, I could only hope it to be the right river. A rock-strewn rapid blocked its entrance, but a short and easy portage took me around.

Once off from the bay and the lake, I stood on the bank and all seemed so serene, so peaceful. I questioned, again, if this could be the river the war party sought. Only creature sounds, the thrumming of frogs, whistling wings of geese. But what of that! Was I expecting savages to engage their enemy in an open field? Announce the charge with a blast of trumpets? Besides, sounds were all too easily swallowed up inside the dense forests that blanketed so much of this country. Should taking this river prove wrong, I risked losing no more than a day's time. If I found nothing else I was, at the very least, certain to come upon the beaver.

Chapter 21.

Drum Beats Off The River

Keeping a sharp eye out for beaver on the river proved my vigilance excessive when, less than a quarter-league upstream at a bend where the river widened, the first of many beaver lodges stood up from the water. The twining of sticks, branches, and thrust-up pole logs that made these mounds of houses were piled and spaced out like fiefdoms. To observe them without disruption, I paddled as slow as would keep the canoe steady against the current. Such riches! One colony, alone, of the furry creatures could easily yield twelve to fifteen skins! Some swam from dens along the riverbank, slapping their flat broad tails in mud.—Mortar for their lodges! Such numbers waiting to be plucked! Even as the dark, elongated shape of the canoe slipped past them, few of the creatures dove in alarm.

On this river, I came upon numbers of muskrat and otter, and a plenitude of fishes. The presence of so many and various fish and birds, hardly surprised me after all I had seen of this country but, being no ornithologist, I was right pleased to distinguish among the birds, the sweet trilling of the missel thrush.—A sound of my homeland here amid wilderness. I paddled onward in this paradise of natural creatures until graying water threatened to sink into shadows and it seemed wise to stop and put up on land.

I caught my supper and, warmed by a small fire, my trout impaled on a stick over coals, I breathed in the taste of fish and forest and felt utter contentment. And, just so, after flattening a space among pine and cedar, and wrapped in a blanket, I bedded down.

Clouds scudded the stars, darkening the moon and sleep was slow to come. Scarcely had I quieted my mind from all that I had witnessed by day, when the howling of wolves shattered my rest. Sounds to excite the spirit until the fullness of sound rising from their bowels ascended to so eerie a pitch, only to start up where another left off, I was beset by uneasiness. My wakeful mind digressed, fixing on the very material of fear—what it was, and what it was not.

As a child, fear was an unspoken thing. A thing felt from the corner of my eye as I shrank from my father's stinging gaze. He seldom put words to his anger. Fear, like words of affection, was a thing to be kept inside. Inside oneself. Inside that room where his heavy heartedness made even an icy rain outside the dank windows seem inviting. Dismissed, I remember speeding from his presence and racing across wet grass taking madcap delight in catching raindrops on my tongue. Then chilled but spirited, I'd be whisked back indoors by Old Kootermann, and Ma-ma would pour me hot tea.

Thinking back on the past (and what had I to do these long days save paddle or, when sleepless, to think) I realized that I came to fear my father less as I grew older, and stood more in awe, in awe not of himself, but of all that he represented as the impassioned link between a once proud merchant family and my own future. Stories of ancestral assets hung in my father's memory and transfixed ma-ma's, only hints of which remained in the household that I knew: Items on a cupboard shelf, such as a solid silver salver and pitcher. The gilded bronze cross encrusted with stones of lapis lazuli that hung forgotten in Ma-ma's wardrobe unless, perhaps, she'd hidden it from being sold. Awe, it seemed, might bind the imagination powerfully even absent of fear or of love.

And on Captain Von Streppe's ship? Was that fear? No, I reasoned that the tremors I'd felt aboard that ship were of a different sort. Cast among men of strong words and action to engage their ambitions had inflamed the rashness of my untried spirit. I was starved for doing! Hadn't I enough of dreaming another's dreary dreams before boarding that ship? My foolhardy scramble for a King's charter that ended in so wrongly imprisoning Jan Carpentier was reckless, fraught with danger, but of fear I'd had none. So, wherein lay my trepidation, now? — surely, not from packs of howling wolves.

My four and a-half gun lay close by my side. Uncharted waters, nearly impenetrable forests, uncounted numbers of unknown savages and wild beasts made one wary, but fearful? No. This night held more, and shy away from finding it and naming it, I could not. I tossed and rearranged my blanket on its damp bed a hundred times as doubts and uncertainties caught at me. I groped to name the effect this strange vast wilderness was having to disrupt my night. At last, when it came to me, it formed a question. Would I never, again, be among my own kind? Yet, even this uncertainty was not quite the embodiment of fear. This present fear seemed unattached to things solid, to persons seen or unseen. And then I knew.

Fear is that utter aloneness of spirit, whether it be in child or in man. And just as the physical sickness I'd fought off on that other sea, this stark loneliness that crept over me was yet another enemy to overcome.

Morning came. And the ghosts of night gone, I covered over the cold ashes from last night's fire wherein smoldered my shredded mattress of needles and branches. I'd observed that White Feather and his men left no trace of their presence; nor did I in my haste to be off. Daylight was short and ice beaded the river's edge, warnings enough that any day, now, the weather would worsen. Ice was a stern reminder of Nagawa's warning that the Ojibwa camp would leave with the first frost, even should their men not be returned.

I stowed away gun and blanket, and scribbled in my journal my reckoning of this river's location, determining it to be North Latitude 43° degrees, and some 15 leagues east from the Big Lake. I removed a day's portion of the pemmican, and duly left tomorrow's inside the pack. Sturdy poplar saplings skirted the river's edge and as another precaution, I hacked one off to look like the gnawing that beavers made. A pole had many uses on a river I'd learned, especially in shallows where paddling scraped up more bottom than water. As I pushed off, ever-present ravens screeched and wheeled overhead, arcing black against the promise of a blue sky.

With each dip and splay of the paddle my nighttime gloom slipped away and new strength drove my arms. In being alone, I admired all the more what primitive skill went into the making of this lightsome bark that could skim water like a ripple blown on a breeze. Of the abundant kinds of waterfowl in this land, the dabbling ducks seemed most plentiful and green-headed drakes were easily spotted. How Sir James' tongue would rove around his jowls in anticipation of a plump roast duck! I needed no companion to load up and fire. But my too hasty shot sent braces of ducks fleeing skyward.

Cheerful thoughts kept me company close unto noon, at which time I entered a narrows strewn with rocks and fallen logs. A pole would not steer me through this morass. The canoe would need to be towed on foot. "Ik schamen!" As I slipped, stubbing toes and bruising an ankle, my curses rang so that on Shrove Tuesday, could

Hannie the washerwoman and Krol the blacksmith but hear, they'd find a new contender for Amsterdam's 'Most Foul Mouth'. In water to my knees, I foundered for a foothold on smooth slime-coated rocks. How like a toddling child did I struggle to steady my legs. Of a sudden, I heard sounds start up to chill my spine more than the cold water. A low, steady drumming turned more insistent, and as though the beating were closer and louder. Savages nearby could be useful, but coming upon me a-wavering and unsteady would put me at sore disadvantage. No time to ponder how far drum beats or oaths loosed in grappling for a footing, carried over water. Besides, what was one voice among what seemed drummers a hundred-fold.

In one quick move, I unwound the coil of hemp stowed in the canoe and tethered it to the bow. Looping one rope end, I slung it neatly over a limb extruding from the shore. It steadied me enough in the water to guide the canoe around and over rocks, and draw it up the river bank. It suffered only slight abrasions, and its soggy contents would dry when under a full sun. For now, I had to overturn the canoe, well-packed, and conceal it under layers of brush, away from predators, savage or animal.

I would scout the area heading north from the upper bank of this river,—a river I thought fitting to call 'The Trout' as any human might upon seeing the great numbers of these fishes marked by dark lines on fin and tail. Before leaving, I listened, again, and thought how like the howls of wolves was the drumming as in beginning low, it welled up, then quieted down only to thrum up again. With my gun and a little food, I started off into the forest.

Chapter 22.

The Execution Tree

Off the river, sounds of drumming were muted among alders, birch, pine, and various other trees and shrubs seeking space in an ever thickening forest. I was following a game trail of sorts, pushing and hacking my way through thicket and brush, wondering if what I took for a path might be multiplied tenfold over on terrain so burgeoning with growth. Ruffed grouse scooted up from the underbrush and, now and again, I spotted mink of a kind larger than those seen, even rarely, in my homeland. A common sight was a white-tailed deer, browsing or skittering off into the forest. Not just common, but voracious, were swarms of flies. Flies everywhere! I walked with a closed mouth and my nostrils pinched.

By mid morning, the forest gave way to a steep hillside thick with shrubs and bramble. Shriveled berries the color of dried blood still clung to vines. To continue north, my only choice was to slash my way up through the thorny brush.

Before seeing it, I smelled the odorous scat of bear. Though ever watchful, I was of a mind that forage being plentiful even in late autumn, my noisy ascent would excite a bear to move off elsewhere. I'd not yet seen a great moose and much wished to know if a hoofed and antlered creature of such size truly was as the annals reported. Once, when questioning him about the region's larger animals, White Feather put up his hands, climbing his fingertips one atop the other to a height of eleven hands. It seems, here too, the size of a fish or height of an animal enlarges to the extent the storyteller perceives his listener to be unknowing.

Ascending to the top of the ridge, I beheld as fair a prospect as any I'd yet seen on this continent. In such a place I could imagine a stout Dutch house, stepped and gabled; the whirling blades of a windmill; a North wind wafting away pesky flies. But, no, I looked down upon an agreeably wide meadow scattered with charred tree stumps and hillocks of red-blue-gold straw flowers.

The far side of the clearing, situated near wide water at its westernmost edge, gave me pause. Movements? I stared, wishing I'd had the good sense to bring my telescope. Here, at the top of the ridge, the drumming carried, clearly, and I could just make out miniature figures moving about. Not of animals, were these, but figures of humans. I could learn nothing at this distance, and began to descend, the drumming growing steadily louder. I moved, slowly, in a low crouching slither among clumps of brush and saplings, my eagerness whetted by caution.

On reaching the meadow, I started across on hands and knees or, when no charred stump presented itself as a shield, slid forward on my stomach. The shadows were deepening, and so, too, my hunger. I'd eaten little this day and the one past. What reception might I find among these savages? How could I know if any white man before me had penetrated this spot of land amid so immense a wilderness. If friendly, it seemed to be the natives' habit to offer food. I had little on my person to give in exchange, whether they were friendly or not.

All at once the drumming stopped as though on command. I was still at some distance, and had good cover in high, prairie-like grasses, the extent of which gave a false illusion of the encampment's closeness. It concealed me well as I crept forward. I made maybe half a league when it seemed the very sky trembled! I fell flat, grappled for my firearm. So sudden, so shrill was their shrieking and caterwauling that blood-thirsty beasts might cower and shiver in fright. I bellied my way through the grass for this was no band of savages I'd yet encountered. Thus far, those I'd met bedecked in paint and feathers bore an alarming appearance, but their manner spoke restraint. But these! Their very sounds incited nightmares. Sounds. 'Only sounds', I reasoned with myself. Yet reason, unaided, might not be the reckoner here. Still, I'd not yet been discovered; I could go back the way I'd come by land, river and lake. My truer, saner voice clamored: No, and No! If every time you come upon the possibility of an enemy, you retreat, you'll never conquer what lies ahead!

Well, then, if sounds were not to deter me, I must go on. My brain was intact enough to know that I must make contact with people I found along the way, whatever the risk. Sir James be dammed! Paddling alone into the hinterland, when blessed with fair weather for reading the heavens along a route not too devious, and supplied with food and arms, was one thing; these cool nights and shorter days bespoke of what, any day now, lay ahead me. As for the future, should I not come upon White Feather, somewhere, I still most urgently desired to reconnoiter with Audaîgweos—somewhere—on the matter of my brothers. Certainly, my relief over quitting their women, Little Thunder excepted, hadn't faltered. And, this band of howling barbarians might, if only out of curiosity, look favorably upon me. With or without Sir James, the scarcity of furs on coastal lands propelled any serious man of The Trade like myself to seek commerce with tribes of the interior. Shrieking or no, I was about to meet some.

The nearer I drew, the more ear-splitting they shrieked! The Wailing Wall of Jerusalem—the Roman Coliseum—the bullring of Barcelona, all reincarnated here in the New World! I snaked forward, close enough now to see the squatting, half-naked bodies of women, some beating on drums and ranged around the fringe of a spacious circle, inside of which I had every reason to believe was their mob of warriors. Wearing ghastly headpieces, whether of fanged wolf or bear or what evil creature—all had the semblance of the grotesque, the ghoulish as they leapt in a frenzied dance, each brandishing a whip or torch. Painted faces and bodies glistened, oily and sweating, and all the while raising cries to splinter the spine and shatter the brain.

Sparse groves of trees would offer me cover. I chose the nearest. Shadowy darkness fed on the light of torches and flames spitting up from a fire heaped high, and around it circled the throbbing bodies of savages. Half crouching and half-standing to better look on, I watched in particular, the movements of the one wearing the shaggy head of a great horned beast. Naked except for loin cloth and ropes of bones rattling down his chest, his oiled body gleamed a whitish bronze. For all his gigantic size, he danced easily, his chest uplifted and head poised like the Indies cobra. A gargantuan form he seemed, leaping in and out of the firelight with one arm hefting a torch, and the other a stiff upraised whip. As though bewitched, I kept up with his advance as he revolved from light into shadow up the circle. I moved stealthily, gauging my steps among the trees to his own.

Upon nearing the far side of the circle, north and west of the clearing, I caught sight of each weaving figure, undulating as though closing in. Were it possible, the Hi-e-E-e-ing pitch reeled higher and louder in a banshee-wailing chorus to numb all senses. At the pivotal point of a triad, high-stepping and stomping, was the Horned Beast. The two on his flanks, paced just ahead of him, and bore torches to lead the long chain of dancers. All wove inward and outward, until skirting a tall, broad sycamore tree, one bearer raised his torch. DEVILS INCARNATE! I beheld White Feather! Hadakotana! their bodies lashed together on either side of the sycamore's trunk! Here was a spectacle so riveting, so terrible, so bestial! Just beyond, hung the hacked and blackened flesh of he who'd been our steersman, his tongue lolling so I could only hope him dead. The grisly fate of the other canoemen, I could but guess. I gaped in horror as the demons flailing barbed whips and torches wove closer, ever closer to White Feather and Hada's pinioned bodies. The excruciating deaths of those deemed most important, White Feather's and Hada's, had been saved for last, and looked near at hand. Surely, the next circling would bring the whip and torches of the three torchbearers down upon White Feather and Hada.

To flee or to act were my choices. I looked about, hurriedly. On one thing alone I could depend: the trance-like gaze of dancers, drummers, and the swaying bodies of onlookers. Their attention stayed fixed in glassy fascination on their diabolical ritual. To move in close, I needed to gain the dark, far side of the sycamore. In a low crouch I began backing my way toward the edge of the encampment. Amid all the mad shrieking and drumming, any noise I made on foot would likely go unnoticed; yet, could I trust that the metal shaft of my gun and its loading would go unnoticed by even one pair of eyes? Still backing up, from somewhere there sprang into my path a snarling cur barring its teeth. A vicious knock to its head with my gun laid it flat before it could lunge.

I crept on close to the execution tree, calmer now, and emboldened by the stark necessity of what I needed to do. The gruesome dance mounted up in a frenzy to rival Dante's ninth-most circle of the damned. I caught the gleam of the Horned Beast rounding south, turning up eastward, in unhurried moves timed to rain down whips and torches upon the last two victims. The moment came; I slipped up behind the execution tree and whispered their names. A faint grunt from one, then the other. I propped my firearm for a moment's retrieval, drew my knife from my legging. I had to work, feverishly, faster than the ghoulish parade; I had to slice through the tightly-braided roots binding the ankles and wrists of White Feather and of Hada.

He neither moved, nor made a sound, but I felt White Feather stiffen as the first torch seared his chest. I thrust my knife into his freed hands, hiding the glint of my blade. So close upon us were the dancers, I felt the wind-snap of a whip crack against Hada's shoulder. He made a sharp intake of breath, but no sound. The chain was weaving ever inward, building up to the fatal end. White Feather slit the ropes tying himself to Hada. Both pretended to be in their lashed state as the Horned Beast rounded North and west, raising his torch higher. Just then, and flying past that demon head, sailed the tin of gunpowder I'd flung at the central fire.

Stones, sticks, and flames rocketed in a blazing conflagration. Dancers and onlookers staggered to a confused halt. I started to raise my gun to confound their amazement, would have, except for White Feather who wisely held back my arm. I needed no urging.

We fled across the meadow. We would break for the hill, make our way up and over the ridge, then lose ourselves in the forest. Hell's own devils would not stay cowed and dazed for long.

Chapter 23.

Escape From The Hurons

Into the black night and across the meadow we fled, a glimmer of white moon slipping in and out of a cloudy sky. My only thought was to put distance between ourselves and the Hurons—for so I would learn to designate that band, and know them as fast allies of New France. On reaching the hillside, I led us, scrambling up and then down with all possible speed until, in the lower reaches of the forest, only at daybreak could I have hoped to penetrate such a maze and retrace my route.

White Feather caught my hesitation. "Leave river by narrows?"

"Yes, rocky, some shallow narrows."

He spoke to Hada, then both started off in the dark as though treading a sunlit path. I ran, straining to keep up with the two figures who hurtled on ahead making no more sound than the snap of a twig. Such a pace on a well-trampled path known to them, cut our return by half of what it had taken me, by daylight, on a little used game trail. We heard the rush of the river and, within minutes, Hada came upon the canoe I'd taken pains to conceal. Surprised by his good fortune, I said as much.

"Find canoe easy by narrows, by rapids. For enemy, easy too." White Feather spoke with his usual directness. I took his censure without comment. I felt satisfied, that had I concealed the canoe in some secluded spot, it wouldn't have been so easily found in the dark. Every school child knows Aesop's tale of fox and stork, whereby those who try to trick others can expect to be ensnared, themselves. I kept silent until White Feather told Hada to take the bow, and assigned me the middle.

"Wait—" I clutched the bow, preventing Hada from moving it out and leaping inside. "We can't paddle out from here. I had to walk it in among the rocks."

"You want, you walk. We paddle."

This, too, had the tenor of a rebuke and, indeed, I was learning restraint. "Ah, you must mean the river will be open water on our way to rejoin Audaîgweos and his war party?"

"No. First, get women, children, old ones. Then travel to Audaîgweos. To winter home."

"Impossible!" I said. "That cannot be.—You would give the enemies we've just made, a second chance to slaughter us, your women and children, too!" I was not about to leave the Hurons free to attack us,—let alone plunder my only stash of trade goods.

"Enemy go. Return to own hunting grounds."

How could he speak with such irritating calmness when their own men had been hacked to pieces! "They nearly burned you both alive!" I shouted, "We'll not go on to Audaîgweos for reinforcements, come back and take revenge? Kill your enemies to protect your own people?"

In the momentary silence, I sensed White Feather's chagrin. "Sand Hair, you saw Hadakotana, me, three others when leave Big Lake. We go find Audaîgweos. He camp long, long way from here. By Great Sea. Huron old old enemy. They want hunting grounds by Great Sea. We join Audaîgweos, fight enemy. Fight done. Audaîgweos, and others stay.

"Same five, we leave, again. Go back get families at Big Lake. On way, we make camp. Six Huron come. Not all Huron enemy. Some friendly. We offer food. They eat. They leave.

"Morning come. Six Huron back by camp."

White Feather gave a deep sigh, and his voice shook, caught in a long cry of remembrance. "They feed us. We thank, we eat. Get up to leave. Not know our canoe gone. Huron laugh. Signal. More, many more Huron come. We only five.—We not carry white man fire power, Sand Hair."

"Why do you not carry a gun, White Feather?"

"Gun not always good. I can make arrow. Break arrow, I make new one. Arrow not need powder to kill. I cannot make gun. For gun, must trade.

"Winter come soon, Sand Hair. Winter, we trap many many furs on land by Great Sea. In spring, we trade, we revenge enemies when time come. Now not time."

It was true that taken unawares an arrow could fly from a bow before I could load my gun and aim. But, it was also true, that if I were lying in ambush to await an enemy, I'd sooner have a loaded gun!

I raised up my four and a-half. The metal of the stock reflected dimly in the moonlight, and Hada's eyes flashed. I could not understand Hada's rapid speech, but heard his agitation. White Feather's assent showed in the swoop of the white eagle feather that glimmered down then up.

"Hadakotana make good plan. He say you, Sand Hair, you go back. Get women. We keep gun. Make sure enemy gone. You come back with women, then all travel to winter camp."

"NO! You just told me you do not use a gun. You could fire wrong, and kill yourself!" This last exaggerated the danger since, doubtless, White Feather not only knew of firearms from his dealings with the British in Albany, but had used them to assess their shortcomings.—I, myself, had no intention of returning to their Big Lake encampment! We fell into a stubborn silence, quiet save for the river current, the rustle of leaves. I broke the impasse.

"Sir James—or I myself will trade you guns for your winter furs." Still they made no reply. "I will not go back." I felt them tense. At once I realized that, because I'd rescued them, they would think I was making demands.

"White Feather—Hadakotana, listen. Nagawa made me leave your Big Lake camp." I sought words, carefully, to put a charitable face on the ridiculous behavior of their women. "Nagawa made me leave after a bad misunderstanding between me and the woman you call Long Smoke."

White Feather grunted as though clearing his throat. "Long Smoke, she want to marry you."

"Yes—how did you..." I broke off, incredulous! Could there be truth to seafarer tales, tales of magical powers of discernment among certain far off tribes of savages? Could White Feather be one of these legendary sachems?

"Long Smoke without man. She happy to marry even white man." He turned to Hada to confer, again. That ungrateful savage didn't grunt, he chuckled! It was my turn to bristle, but already the waning moon was far to the west.

"Hadakotana asks if you are "priest." Live as black robes. Live without women."

"I am not a priest, nor a black robe. And, I will not go back for your women."

"Sand Hair," White Feather said, quite gently, using that peculiar manner of addressing me, yet again, "I go get women. Back by new moon. You go with Hadakotana. Keep gun. You will see, enemy gone."

My thoughts took in White Feather's concern for a tribe not of his own birth while I recovered from the canoe, the separate satchel I kept with extra gun powder, light provisioning, and my journal. Too, I recollected the cold nights of this last moon and Nagawa's insistence that they would leave before the waters freeze had their men not returned. White Feather was proof that the better actions of their leaders were not undertaken on mere impulse, but that the wandering of the tribes took planning, and knowledge of all things natural to better follow the seasons.

Hada and I stood and watched White Feather zigzag among moon-splattered rocks and water, I marveling at such skill, until a sliver of the canoe's prow swung wide and bobbed upward in a run for the river channel proper, and the barely perceptible outline of White Feather faded in the race back to the bay off the Big Lake away to the south.

"Hada, I must sleep," I said, determining that henceforth motions I made with hands and body would be matched by words that would enlarge our communication. I felt more weary than ever I'd known, more tired even then hungry. Some who preceded me to this continent extol the extraordinary endurance of the savages,— even of their women. At that moment, I knew only my own need and cared not a whit for appearances.

Nor was I alone. We two settled into a hastily made shelter of boughs and branches, and with a single blanket. Mine.—As for touting the savage's vast powers of endurance, Hada, the first to recline, rolled over claiming all but the slim edge of my blanket. I endured his hogishness, and the twiddle and dee of his snoring until my own comfort demanded satisfaction, and I took it with a hard-driving elbow. He stirred and, since I've no recollection of a second spate of snoring, I must have slept.

What darkness had obscured, dawn revealed in sickening clarity. Gashes from the thongs securing his wrists and ankles had left his skin raw and purplish with dried blood. Hada's upper chest and shoulder where torches had seared the flesh, were a crisscrossed welter of pus and sores. I had not yet learned—nor if I had, would I have accepted the notion that such barbarous torture, as I'd witnessed, was to allow one's victims to prove their bravery. I watched him as he squatted over a low fire in a pit, dug deep to hold the smoke. In it, he'd dropped the split-off half of a sizable river stone, the middle rounded out enough to boil a root of some kind. I watched, curious about the manner of poultice he could make to cover even a tenth of his wounds. Instead of a poultice, he took up the stone bowl by its cooler edges, blew on the boiled root, and guzzled it down to the dregs like any peasant his bier. He belched like one, too.

I was ravenous. No dried lump of pemmican, for me. I stood up and, pointing to the river, made a wavy motion with my hands shaping the body of a fish, a generous sized fish; one I intended to catch myself. Hada, quick to comprehend, grunted assent. He himself got up then, painful and stiff as it must have been for him to stand. Perhaps, his need was to accompany me or to relieve himself, I thought. Instead, he broke off a long, straight tree branch and began sharpening the end with the edge of a stone. I, certain to learn something new, watched awhile, then handed him my knife to get on with it, faster. He turned a well-pleased look upon me, and his whittling was completed in no time. Then, the lout slipped my knife into his waist belt!

I thrust out my hand. His eyes flashed in anger. So did mine. "Give it back!" I demanded and moved in closer. After some moments, he seemed to accept that I would not give up my knife—the same I'd used to save his ungrateful skull. He made no further ugly sounds, and tossed the knife my way. Branch in hand, he slipped in among the rocks and stood in icy water up to his calves. Propitious for fishing seemed the early morning light and, before long, he'd speared three small trout. He flared up the embers of his small fire, and cooked the fish over the smoking coals. We feasted, deliciously, if not plentifully.

The not inconsiderable skill Hada had shown in appeasing my hunger did much in my mind to offset his churlish behavior. The incident of the knife, however, served as a useful warning to be ever on guard around one who returned favors in so oafish a manner. And, were it not for White Feather's apparent sanctioning of my presence, would he have relinquished the knife so easily? All this along with last night's scene of carnage, set me to wondering what more of these savages' unnerving strangeness I would yet encounter in the months ahead.

Chapter 24.

Travel To The Interior

Stiff-limbed and weary from so little sleep, we started back for the camp of the Hurons in the chill light of dawn, treading a route Hadakotana led off on. It angled decidedly west, not north. I beckoned him to stop, and breaking off a stick amid the thick entanglement of trees and brush, drew a line east to west. I pointed to the river we'd just left behind, drew a south to north line, and an elongated area for the Big Lake. Hada snatched my stick and pointed, exactly, where I thought we should not go, one which to continue on would take us directly into the Huron encampment, sidestepping any protection the wide meadow had offered.

"Huron!" I objected.

One swarthy-cheek raised in a grin and his obsidian eyes narrowed while, to sign, he bent one finger and pulled it down. Contempt? No, Hada's manner was like a schoolmaster patting the head of the classroom dunce who'd managed to give a correct answer.

And, he being a native to this country, I obliged and we trudged on parallel to the Big Lake, catching a rare glimpse of it only where the terrain rose, sufficiently, and trees parted. I lacked words to make Hada understand that had I paddled up the shore of the lake to the encampment on the bay, as they had done, instead of going on foot in a diagonal direction off the river, he and White Feather would now be smoldering ashes and burned flesh!—I knew for certain that when coming up the lake a day earlier, had my ears taken in the eerie drumming and my eyes the fiendish gyrations of the Hurons, I'd have whipped back around, and taken safety on land, waited out the winds before venturing up that lake; and I would have crossed its middle, not canoed along its margin.

How was it that I'd come to misunderstand Animiki's words and signs about the route the Ojibwa men had taken. Or, had I been misled through her by Nagawa as to the river. However that was, it was past. For the future, I'd attend better to Sir James' command to "watch and observe." I had much to learn about the ways of these people as well as the twists and turns of lakes and rivers. I even began to question whether navigating the immense ocean could be any more devious than these inland waterways.

Hada, not weighed down by a pack and a gun slung lengthwise across his shoulders, was first to reach the top of the ridge. He leaned forward gazing out, his body angled in imitation of a ridge-pole pine. As I approached, he closed his fist, swung it in and out, making a clear enough signal.

"Gone?"

"Gone."

My thoughts were at baleful odds with the peaceful lake and meadow I once again looked down upon. Incredulous! this manner of warfare among the savages. The torture exacted upon their enemies must have satisfied the Huron's blood lust for the time being. Or, perhaps, being a hinterland tribe less exposed to European gunpowder than their Eastern brethren, they were indeed bedeviled by my display of pyromancy, and had fled. Either way, such half-hearted methods of warring were baffling. White Feather's postponement of revenging his enemies was, I supposed, at least practical. Practical, too, was our cautious descent of the ridge as we advanced nearer the encampment; we could not be certain that all of the enemy had fled. Still, no way could their numbers, which without their women I estimated to be in the forties, stay hidden in so open a landscape, even should they be stretched out on their bellies in the long grass.

"Gone," I whispered, surveying the field.

Hada pointed to indentations left in the wet grass along the bank where their canoes had lain, ones that a light afternoon wind would erase. "Gone," he repeated for a second time. Pleased I was for evidence that we had one solid English word between us. I desired to know 'gone' in his language. He made a short clucking sound, and laughed outright at my attempt to repeat it.

Not a trace of them on the site—not even poles such as they used to tow and construct their folded-down houses. What they left behind was unspeakable, all the more so in broad daylight. Strung up from their execution tree dangled the charred remains of the three Ojibwa. The only recognizable flesh was of fingers, chopped off and tossed about the ground before the demons torched the bodies.

High, sorrowful keening noises poured from Hada's throat. Sickened and saddened, I fled to the water's edge to wretch and keep from further desecrating the ground of his dead. In a short while, I saw him set about breaking through the thongs to release what flesh yet clung to bone. With a trembling hand, I offered him my knife, again, and my assistance. He pointed to a space of ground and reached out his arms, letting me know that a pit should be dug. I obliged, using a sharp-edged rock to commence the digging. I scraped through trampled grass and raised enough dirt to form a long and wide, shallow grave.

Hada flashed a look around the camp and stomped about much agitated. At first, I thought this some dance, an extension of their rite of burial. Suddenly, he placed a fist at each of his shoulders then pulled down and around himself. I comprehended his need, fetched my pack, and offered him my blanket. A startled look came into the deep-set dark eyes, and the high cheekbones quivered as though he were uncertain. Coming to some resolution inside that savage head, he accepted my white man's blanket, and with great reverence began wrapping the remains.

I stood in silence as he interred the remains, all the while keeping up a singsong chant, then ripping off strips of bark to lay across the top of the grave. He propped earth all around, and drove a tree limb down at each of four corners as one would place posts. It was their custom to come back after a season or more to raise and clean the bones for reburial and leave necklaces, furs, foodstuffs, and other valuables for the spirits of the dead. Whole villages gathered from long distances to attend such ceremonies, and the feasting and dancing went long into the night. Such knowledge came to me only later, as would the reason for Hada's hesitation in accepting my blanket. A blanket made a poor substitute for a shroud of furs; it would be replaced at the time of their traditional burial ceremony. Observing Hada that day taught me something of a savage's sensibility concerning death, and how in this regard his resembled our own. No matter how a death was inflicted or a burial enacted, a grieving heart felt the same pain.

I had occasion to teach as well. Leaving the burial behind us, and supposing Hada as needy as myself, I leaned forward over my pack to share with him my ration of pemmican. I caught the gleam in his eyes as he, too, leaned forward. He showed an out-of-the-ordinary curiosity as his hand reached toward my chest. Glancing down, I saw that my talisman had worked itself part way out of my shirt.

I realized in drawing it forth that the weighty ancestral significance accorded this talisman had quite left me these weeks past. Strange that here, in a place full of the awful stench of death, Hada seemed so affected.

"Ivory," I said, holding it forth for him to admire. "Ship. My grandfather's ship." Conveying the idea of a ship captain was futile when the very idea of so stout a vessel as a ship, itself, might lie outside his range of knowledge; but teach him the idea of 'ship' I would! Jumping up, and standing on shore, I swung my ivory in and out over the water, echoing "Chi-o-ni-ga-mig," for the name "Big Lake" given me by Animiki, and hoping it also stood for a sea of 'big water'.

My efforts were rewarded. Hada's eyes sparked as he leapt up. In a few quick pulls, he unplaited his long hair (which if to fan out was his intention, did not happen as it was too greasy and unkempt). "Chi-o-ni-ga-mig," he chanted along with a garble of other syllables. He raised his elbows, making a triangle of his arms and brought his hands together above his head. Gracefully, most gracefully, his muscular body swayed, moving up and down in imitation of the play of a ship under sail.

"Good, good! Bon, Bon!" I cheered him on, knowing that many French words crept in among the Northern tribes. This teaching game held so much promise, at one point, I held up my hand signaling him to stop. I paused a few seconds, before resuming our charade. Then, throwing back my head, I made a howling "Ow-oooo" and spoke, "wolf."

"Wool-fa," he repeated, then he himself howled, and said for my benefit the word "ma-i-gan."

In such manner we disported ourselves until mid afternoon, when to our great relief we spotted them. And they us. Chatter and laughter rose over the water upon their sighting Hada and me on shore. Eight craft in all came on, bearing White Feather, the Ojibwa women, children, and old men. Quite a festive party were these savages wrapped in red or dark blue blankets, their line of canoes parting the water neatly as they made for shore. Their manner told me I was once again accepted among them. As well I should, having saved the lives of two of their principals. Spoken expressions of gratitude for this and other favors I'd done on their behalf did not appear their custom.

Hadakotana nodded toward the grave site, and spoke to White Feather. That was, at the time, the sum of attention paid to the burial of their late comrades. Hada then rejoined his family.

I was standing on shore in some uncertainty about my next move, or theirs, when Nagawa stepped forward, handed me her paddle, and motioned me to take her place in the bow. This circumstance pleased me much. I understood it to be her way of honoring me. No spoken words could have rewarded me more. She and Animiki hunkered down in the middle, the girl smiling so, her star-bright eyes shown as narrowed slits. White Feather shoved us off, taking the stern.

And none too soon with an overcast sky, and each day of dampness turning the air colder. At last! I thought with a happy heart. My paddle drove itself, so eager I was to set off for their winter encampment and, at last see Audaîgweos from whom, —after weeks of what seemed half a lifetime, —I was certain to discover what was known by the Ojibwa of my brothers.

Chapter 25.

Land of Rivers and Great Lakes

We were beginning our traverse of the most wondrous body of water to meet my eyes since quitting the Atlantic. The River Mohawk, the Oneida Country, and the bay on the southeast shore of the Big Lake all lay behind us. The chill air so spurred us on, my paddle fell of itself into the rhythm of White Feather's rapid even strokes. From the bay, I had not grasped the true breadth of this inland sea, nor did my rag of a map read true. I felt a rush of excitement. A detail, one I had thought useless when bent over a strange French text, now formed a picture in my mind: The 'Great Lake of the Entouhonorans' recorded in sieur de Champlain's Les Voyages de la Nouvelle France Occidentale dicte Canada. This could be it, and I would know, if with my own eyes I saw a channel flowing north—the river Saint Lawrence—the same Jacques Cartier a century earlier, named Rivi'ere de Canada.

When asked the name of this lake, White Feather said 'Te-car-ne-o-di'. I supposed the Ojibwa name something different. Naming things seemed to hold significances among these people well beyond my understanding. They were not mere labels to convenience travel or trade.

As the hour wore on, sudden wind gusts came at us with the familiar unpredictability of winds off the North Sea. They hit like a winter cold, and I wondered if this deep wide water ever froze as did lakes and canals during many a Holland winter. In my country frozen ice called for rejoicing! Upon sharpening the long, curved metal blades of our wooden skates, we Hollanders, young and old, left off our duties and took to the ice!—Stadholder and guildsman, artisan, inn-keeper, housewife, student. Skating was sport my father did not begrudge us. When I was about four or five, he could still move about freely, and a happy memory is of our skating all the way to Zaandam all sweatered and mittened and scarves flying. But upon our return, Ma-ma fell hard on the ice and could only hobble. Father borrowed, from some house along the Nordzeekanal, a sturdy chair with runners for her to sit in, and with the two of us skating behind, we pushed Ma-ma back to Amsterdam. I smile to think on it. There were times, Kristina and I skated together. On whose arm might her firm hand be clinging to, now, her blue cape set a-swirl in such winds—"Ai,ee!"—the canoe swerving windward, as one our bodies shifted lee. I adjusted, pushing down and forward though, well I knew, it was White Feather who steadied the canoe and turned us about. No rebuke?—No savage so much as murmured. How different was this. My inattention had nearly capsized us, and censure was all my own as we took shelter for the night on land.

The winds calmed by mid morning on another gray but pleasant enough day, and we set off once again. Before noon, White Feather called attention to the northeast, pointing his paddle to moving black dots dissecting the horizon. Now I was certain. The channel, itself, lay too distant for sighting but not the parting of adjacent land. As the canoes came on, and if our flotillas stayed on course, our paths would converge like geese in flight. White Feather quickened our pace to put us somewhat beyond the widest reach of the lake when we met up.

To encounter other humans of whatever kind made my heart beat faster. The canoes drew ever closer. My blood surged to discern, hunched in the middle of their lead canoe the bent figure of a man wrapped in tawny furs. He was a bearded man. Something silver glinted on his chest that when we drew nearer took the shape of a large cross. The symbol assured me of his mother tongue, and I hailed him across the vapid gray dividing us. "Connaissez-vous ce re'gion?"

"Jusqu'ici—chacun pour soi et Dieu pour tous!" His voice rolled back at me in tones to bedazzle the royal flock of Notre Dame. In the brief time we stilled our pace, the savages, too, being eager to exchange news, I learned he was Jean-Baptiste of the Order of Jesuits; that his congregation was the uncounted numbers of heathens from the land of the Ottawa to the land of the Erie. Having visited his Compagnie de Jésus in Montreal, he'd only just left Fort Frontenac. "Built of stone, overlooking the rivers Ste. Lawrence and Cataraqui," he added, pointedly. Although all was in French, I observed White Feather stiffen noticeably at the mention of 'Frontenac.' Jean-

Baptiste went on to say he'd engaged a small band of Ottawa to carry him to Montreal, and they were now returning him to his Mission of St. Jacques in the south, that it lay in land of the Seneca. He expressed curiosity at my manning the bow of our canoe. Not wishing to be indelicate in light of his own prolonged inactivity as passenger, I said only that such was my choice and voiced what was uppermost in my mind:

"Avez-vous recontré une personne par nom de Van Doorn de Hollande?"

"Van Doorn? Non. Mais, un voyageur de la Hollande nom de Carpentier..."

"Jan? Jan Carpentier!" Much agitated, I strove to paddle and hold my own with White Feather as our parties diverged. The savages parleyed as often in sign as in words from their similar languages. I supposed that White Feather held back from these exchanges because he was of the Iroquois nation. Animiki seemed bent on catching what passed between the priest and me, more so than her own people's. This did not surprise me. The partiality she showed me was as useful as it seemed childlike. My last words to Jean-Baptiste were to discover the time and place of his meeting Jan.

"Apres' de Montreal...," and whatever else he said faded out of range as our canoe, keeping to the lead, headed west toward what appeared to be another, though narrower channel. The three canoes of the Ottawa sped South with the first white man I'd laid eyes on since my enforced departure from Albany. However randomly such chance encounters occurred, they seemed preordained in this land of so few destinations with short months of travel and primitive ways of getting to and fro.

"White Feather, you know Fort Frontenac?" No answer was forthcoming. I looked back. A vicious, cruel face it was, transforming its usual even expression, nostrils vibrating and his whole manner, agitated. At that moment, tales entered my head of how Iroquois were known to cut off hands, draw out sinews from the flesh and twist them around sticks and exult in their victims' agonized cries. They did this, it was presumed, to work themselves up for battle.

I looked back a second time. Both Nagawa and Animiki sat rigid, eyes downcast. White Feather stirred, his lowered eyes darted at me as though I were a part of whatever dark abyss he hadn't yet shaken off. His words came, slowly, grating and rasp-like.

"Not many snows past, Hau-de-no-sau-nee—You call us
Iroquois.—Hau-de-no-sau-nee men, women, children live on shore
of lake. This lake. They hunt, fish, play games with French soldiers
at Fort Frontenac. French say come feast at Fort Frontenac. When
come, soldiers take Hau-de-no-sau-nee men. Put on ships. Make
slaves, send to French Father. Also, soldiers trick Onondagas of
Thousand Islands. Make prisoners. Soldiers burn Seneca towns,
burn corn—burn winter food."

Such a woeful tale had me mumbling over my shoulder to White
Feather some inadequacy like my heart is sorry for this injustice.
Truly, I felt sorrow even as I pondered what evil might have provoked
the French to commit such outrage.

Pulling closer into shore, a welcome diversion met us: bogs of a
red berry they called mash-ki-gi-min. All the marsh was red ripe.
I withdrew from my satchel a small parcel of beads for Animiki to
trade. In return, over the side of the canoe came a large woven sackful
of the hardest, most bitter tasting berries God ever blessed upon
this earth. I spat out a mouthful. Animiki hid her face and tittered.
Later along the way, Nagawa pounded them into a mixture with
dried venison, and I found these berries added a tart, rich flavor.

Then began long days, one after another of long portages. Portages
of a league and more were common. So numerous, they were, my
journal holds but scant references. One entry will suffice for all:

"Another day of unremitting drudgery. Up and down well-worn
footpaths strung one to the next by some devilish scheme of rock and
mud puddle or slow water more suited to poling than conveyance.
A weary sameness enwrapped each portage be it linked to brook-
stream-marsh-lake—river, rapids or shallows."

In one of his more talkative moments, White Feather told me
about these Wa-a-gwen'ne-yuh, these 'footpaths of the ancestors'.
They were ancient routes of travel, and used both for peaceful trade
among tribes and to make war on their enemies. Still, in fairness,
let it be said that between portages, more was to be seen from the
waterways than a next portage. Now and again fair stretches of
cultivated land and small villages were visible. I counted as many as
nine. Two villages had been burned to the ground. At one, a ghastly
row of dried skulls, perched up on charred pikes, stared back at
us from out their hollow sockets. Evidence of massacre to all who
passed.

"Huron?"

That quizzical lift of his granite forehead meant that White Feather found my questioning tiresome. "Not Huron. Wyandot."

By means other than White Feather, I would come to learn that the Huron in these parts became known as Wyandot after being defeated and abandoning their eastern hunting grounds.—Ahh, from all I see of this land, I sometimes think my country fortunate to lie on lowlands; our seas and sands and canals make walls to halt the advance of surprise invaders.

Some diversions did occur on portages. All members of the party, young and old, carried some rag-tag possession, even to the three women with babes in cradleboards strapped to their backs. The infant savages scarcely cried, seeming well content to nurse at their mother's breasts or bounce behind at their backs. While still an object of curiosity, I was no longer a stranger, and acquainted myself mostly with children for whom games easily replaced words. When travel together permitted; that is when I was not wearing the canoe on my head, small ones scrambled to walk in front, aside, or behind me. They were quick to learn a new Dutch word or two.

"Hoofd," I'd say, pointing to my head, and wait for one of them to smirk and point to his own head.

A boy, his hair trailing over his ears and too short to braid, spoke out,

"Is-te-gwen." He looked well satisfied when I repeated the word with a tap to his forehead with my knuckle. I asked Animiki the child's name and received a most curious answer. "Boy not have name."

On further questioning, I learned his father was one of the warriors slain by the Huron. "The boy has no name because his father is dead?"

"No. Big Lake Person, child have name when name given him. It big day. Maybe you see." She gave me the smile of a child coming upon a cupboard full of apple tarts.

So much lay hidden about these people—this land! I watched, I observed as Sir James cautioned me to do. I kept alert, striving to learn their language. Yet by what in my upbringing was I to measure so much that remained unknown.

At some villages, cabins were set back in woods behind patches of cleared land for growing maize, remnants from the harvest scattered on the ground. Screeching, friendly-faced children would come tearing out of nowhere and run along the shore to hail our passing. The mornings being cold with frost, I'd taken to wearing a fur cap, but with or without it, young and old alike set me apart to stare and gape at. I did not mind. I was quite certain, though, that manifestations like these would not fall easily on dark haired, swarthy skinned Jan Carpentier! I much regretted the falling out between Jan and me. The chance meeting with the priest whereby I learned that the hardnekkige gek Jan had made it to Montreal, unharmed, now added a modicum of possibility to the converging of our two so different paths.

I began even to think back on Sir James with a certain fondness. Weeks with savages could play games with one's mind! Seeing only black hair, plaited or hanging loose—hair black as the infernal ravens cawing overhead. Seeing all those darksome faces with not a flaxen strand or fair-skin or one blue eye among them. Uncapped, my own hair now met my shoulders. I found myself clutching it to discern if it still be light or dark.

At one settlement, this in the fertile land of Huronia, I traded a small string of wampum for a quantity of the 'potato' sufficient for all our party. The potato, a pale orange-fleshed root, is very sweet to the taste when roasted. At another village I traded for deerskin leggings. Now, I thought it a simple exchange until, to my amazed eyes, the male savages near by began leaping around making obscene anal gestures, and cackling like an army of crows. Had I been one of them, I would have wilted under the enormity of shame heaped upon breakers of a custom. As it was, the intended indignity fired up my determination to learn to speak their language! Many chores fell to their women, and of course I'd observed women making clothing for members of the tribe. Had I only the language to explain, I would have told them that in my country, a woman could be a seamstress, a man could be a tailor! And, neither would be looked down upon! Nor insulted unless their work be shoddy.

Our daily journeying hurried us along in a non-ending dullness that drained energy and left strength for little else. Unless forced by driving wind and torrential rains, we stopped on land only to portage and mend canoes,—another work the women did while we, who'd bent at the paddle, took our rest. Now and again, a glance over my shoulder caught small hand movements of Animiki, whether she prayed to a god of storm or calm, I'd not know. The child's sweetness was a grace in this wild land. Her little humming sounds could cheer a gray day. Scant speech passed among any of us, the sameness of the hours broken, daily, by the ever silent Nagawa who distributed chunks of pemmican and dried fish as we paddled, this followed by our drawing on a pipe. Nor was I alone at the paddle in jerking myself awake from minutes of stolen sleep.

It was some time after departing the Great Lake of the Entouhonorans, and we were nearing the end of the chain of lakes and burdensome portages, that White Feather instructed me to darken my face and hair with soot from the coals of our fires. When portaging, I was ordered to "wear canoe like hat." They had enemies in these parts, and although the lateness of the season was in our favor, we need be ever watchful. I took this to mean that my presence would be deemed a liability in the event of a skirmish—in spite of how well I'd acquitted myself when he and Hada were strung to a tree. Then, as the days passed and no incident occurred, I decided White Feather's cautions were invented to keep me toiling, instead of taking out time for trading.

The woods, as we traveled further into the hinterland held an increasing abundance of game, black bear and deer as well as smaller animals. My fingers itched, I needed practice. But easy game stopped us rarely, and this only to maintain our meager nourishment as we pressed on.

One day, we came upon a wide lake, one I gauged to be some twenty-five leagues in circumference, the largest since leaving the Great Lake. At the strait on the far end, we were forced to halt by a large number of stakes set up to discourage further passage. These inhabitants could net a vast number of fish by means of entrapment and, though they did not appear warlike, we were clearly expected to reward them for allowing us to pass into a smaller, adjoining lake that lay ahead. White Feather always left it to the Ojibwa women to haggle, but this time it fell to Long Smoke. I must accord to her her due. She understood their language best, and we left without incident.

By late morning of the twenty-fifth day after our meeting with the Jesuit, and having made a portage most memorable for its length of three leagues, we arrived at the lower span of a river flowing north and west. We made ready to descend, and took shelter on land for the night.

Did elephants trumpet? Did chariots leap? Why, no blast of horns? On that dull gray day in late afternoon, I inhaled the sharp, clear, penetrating scent of fresh water! It was 26 November. We came off that final portage and put back on water with White Feather steering us through a surround of islets, each canoe skimming and each pair of eyes alert for shoals. Within sight was a large bay, an immense bay! perhaps the very one the sieur de Champlain called Mer Douche. But if so, its waters were in no way gentle and, should I be a namer of places would choose words to encompass its true condition. No matter! Scarcely could I contain my excitation to see this journey ending, and even White Feather's lips drew back in what for him passed as a smile and, upon reaching open water, we had only to round a distance of the bay, not far, and speed us landward.

My reckoning fixed the date of our arrival as the feast day of my patron, Saint Pieter of Alexandria, chosen over the Cyrene fisherman Peter, because of the former's store of worldly knowledge. "Your patron was not chosen for you," said my father, "but for your grandfather." Just so, each Feast Day, I added on another year, and none surpassed in new knowledge these six months and more days, since I had left the Old World for the New.

My sense of purpose, I admit, had languished over the long weeks of struggling to stretch body and mind and wrestle the tedium and ordeals of each day. But, now, with our arrival at hand I was swept up with renewed purpose. I exploded with purpose! I was on the very verge of discovery! Did not a lodestone lead the Asian shepherd, and does not the lodestone guide ships at sea? Just so! a lodestone swung from my gold chain and would lead me. Lead on to the business of The Trade! To Brothers! In the words of Jean-Baptiste, I was about to sally forth with a new song on my lips: "Each man for himself and God for all!"

Chapter 26.

Arrival At Winter Camp

We poled through the soggy marsh of cattails and tall swamp grass, one last test for bone sore, hungry bodies eager for solid earth. But, we'd arrived!

The Ojibwa camp seemed all astir with the largest gathering of their people I'd yet seen. They took little notice of their newly arrived kin and, except for a hard stare, even less of me. Welcoming be damned! Roast quail or venison, stewed porcupine—I'd even trade an arm for a heap of fresh herring from the North Sea! I craved fresh food to larder my insides lined these months with little else than dried meat, roots and berries.

Among all the comings and goings, I watched in particular a group of men busy at scraping out a hole of some length and depth. Animiki came by, carrying a satchel of bird feathers she'd collected at various stopping places. I asked what the men were doing. "Pots?" she asked, hesitantly. No, pit—they dig pit for to cook." A fire pit still in the making did little to satisfy the gnawing inside my belly.

She followed me or I her to the middle of the clearing. Here, children ran back and forth piling up sticks and branches high enough to ignite the whole village. Women stood at the flaps of their wigwams swishing branches to clear their dirt floors before spreading fresh cedar boughs, and their young offspring ran the discards off to the fuel pile.

Something out of the ordinary was afoot, and Animiki assured me this was so. "Totem of Loon make ready for big feast. Many clans come." Then she hurried off, no doubt anticipating more questions that were sure to follow had she stayed.

Somewhat later, I observed another strange custom. Not for the first time was I with savages when, removing our clothes, we rolled in mud or clay to lather our bodies, then bathed in a river or lake. But on this occasion, cleansing one's self seemed not the outcome. A game was made as whole families romped and splashed, dousing one another playfully with water, and then with mud. I watched without knowing if it be all for fun. For all I knew, flinging balls of mud could be yet another earthy thing they honored.

I fended for myself at mid evening when it became evident the fire pit, and none other would be lit for a meal that night. The savages were fasting but I was not! I took myself to a full-flowing stream nearby. After several attempts at dipping a funnel-shaped reed basket, I snared six, fine small trout, and started a fire. Sizzling them over coals until their juices spurted made so sweet and succulent a feast I soon felt whole again. A rising sense of gratitude for this plenty caught hold of me. I spoke no words. Thoughts must suffice for the Creator hearing human heart beats.

Late in afternoon of the second day, Hadakotana invited me to accompany the young men on a hunt. I accepted, readily. Tobacco and prayers were offered for our success. I would have added thanks that, this time, we were leaving on foot without facing a portage or river ahead.

We ranged through the woods in pairs, fanning out at intervals with some of those in front knocking wood sticks together to drive the deer before us. Against an orange sky, bare branches of trees stuck up like towering black candelabra. We started up a ridge when, having ascended about halfway, I turned and looked below. Something off to the side of the hill had caught my eye. I motioned Hada to stop and he and I fell back from the others. Gazing at what could be seen from that angle, resembled mounds of entangled brush such as beavers construct, only this was somehow different and, besides, had no water source nearby. Hada seemed as curious as myself, and we cut across the hill and down, then circled in at ground level.

Hidden under the layering of brush emerged a squat hut dug into the hillside. And above the hut's bolted door was a lintel! "Waiâbishkiwed!" flew out of my mouth, Ojibwa words, I knew not I had. Hada's face bore a wide grin of satisfaction. I thought him acknowledging my surprising agility in using his tongue to declare 'white man lives here'; until on approaching the hut, he struck out a foot to break in the door.

"KA!" My shout deflected his foot long enough for me to make a fist, nudge him aside, and knock on the door. This gentlemanly manner of announcing one's self set him off into gales of laughter and slapping his thighs. Of course I expected no answer from knocking, and got none; whereupon Hada made fists of both his hands, and pounded so hard that the heavy slab door rattled. It was my turn to laugh. So superstitious they are, he seemed to think knocking with one's fists was a new kind of magic. Getting no results, he thrust his arms out in front of his chest and would have propelled all his weight against the door had I not intervened.

"No! Kawessa mika! That won't do. We go back to the hunt."

All in all, I was more than pleased to find my Ojibwa equal to sudden, overriding needs and, then, to discover this hut! I'd been adamant that the hut be left undisturbed. Winter camp was less than half a day's journey and at a later time I would return. And return, again and again, until I found it occupied. I felt utmost certainty that a white man had built the hut. The green branches covering it over had not yet seen a winter, reason enough to be hopeful of encountering the hut's inhabitant. For many a night to come, my mind would play on its occupant. Ah, dream on, I told myself, play at self delusion. Yet, however earnestly I would chide myself over my too frequent flights of fancy, hope clung on with the ferocity of barnacles to a ship's bottom that fate would turn up a brother.

We retraced our steps, starting up the ridge and moving at a fair pace when, this time, Hada stopped short. He sniffed the air, lowered head and shoulders, and crept down the far side of the ridge west, then into the woods. I stole behind him. I followed his hunched back and the jagged outline of his upraised bow arm with a quickened heartbeat, eager to discover what he perceived at this dusky hour. Almost at one with the zing of his arrow I heard it—SAW it! A mammoth creature bellowed in rage, its huge eyes rolled and glazed over, its enormous nostrils quaked. I whipped a powder charge to my gun and took aim. Hada was quicker; he let fly a second arrow. A third arrow felled the giant creature in a thunderous spasm that shook the very earth. This was the fabled moose. I marveled. Its enormous antlers spread out like fingered palms in a span wider than the tallest man.

I marveled, too, at Hada and proffered my hand. He took it. Eye to eye we stood and, for a moment, strength emanated from that hand and arm as though the proud deeds of his savage heritage came surging through it.

He twittered a series of short bird calls. In little time, two hunters of our party ran up to help lay out the beast. Steaks, the tongue, entrails, sinews, bone—all parts were valued, and all would be used. Later, women of the village would cure its vast hide. For a tool, they'd split a leg bone of the moose with a rock, and work over the hide by soaking. and scraping it with the sharp-edged bone. It being tougher than deer, the hide of moose was favored for making their moccasins.

More than once after arriving at Winter camp, I had asked after Audaîgweos. Vague answers came from both White Feather and Animiki—even from Hada who usually provided a straight answer (even the wrong one) to any riddle. Audaîgweos, it seemed, was here. But was not here. I asked again, and after much urging, Animiki came up with words. "Audaîgweos make self ready for Midéwewiwin. He pray."

Her answer fell short of my understanding. "What is this Midéwewiwin?"

She paused in obvious discomfort. She'd satisfied at least some of my questioning, in that I knew about praying. I should have been content, I suppose, but wasn't.

"Yes, Audaîgweos prays. This Midéwewiwin. Tell me its meaning."

A long delay, then those dark eyes turned fierce. "Grand Medicine," she whispered.

About some things the savages seem unable or unwilling to communicate. Midéwewiwin was most certain to be a ceremony; but beyond grand medicine, she refused to say more, standing mute and stubborn, lips in a firm line, staring at the ground. To hide my annoyance, I moved off.

For three days while Audaîgweos had absented himself from all preparations going on around the camp, various clans from afar were continuing to arrive and to assemble their temporary homes. Named for the Crane or Fish, Fox or Bear or other common animals, the men of the clans looked and walked handsomely, striding forth wrapped in red or blue wool blankets, commodities I discovered were bartered in trade with tribes far to the north. Women wore deer skins, heavily fringed and trimmed with many-colored beads and quills. The women, I thought in spite of their costumes, looked less comely of stance and feature than their men. Many had their faces garishly painted for the occasion. Still, let it be said that such apparitions in red, ochre, black repelled me little more than the custom of some French women who whitened their faces with a ghostly-looking powder and clotted their cheeks in beet-red rouge.

Late the afternoon of the fourth day, I followed as, en masse, all the clans one after the next, and from eldest to youngest,—obeying some signal unbeknownst to me,—paraded toward their newly built Long House (aided, I might add, by the axe I had provided in return for my shelter.) And outside the Long House we waited. Surely, now, and soon Audaîgweos must show himself. And soon he did.

The Ogima of the Loon Clan appeared in grand ceremonial manner. His walk was in a step-pause rhythm down the path to the Long House, forceful, but not ostentatious. His gaze straight ahead, his deep-set eyes revealing nothing. Resplendent he was in trailing skins of river otter, the rich, dark brown tapered tails swaying along the calves of his fringed leggings. Across his chest, draped a rainbow mantle of beads, feathers and quills on a body not overly tall but substantial and erect. The richly embroidered mantle bore a fine design of leaves and flowers. It had not the intricacy of tapestries produced in Arras or Tournai, but in its own simple way had a most pleasing display of naturalness. A flourish of egret feathers leapt from the crown of Audaîgweos's head, his gray-black hair bound in one thick braid hung halfway down his back. All followed into the Long House, arranging ourselves on either side of the center aisle.

Audaîgweos summoned the elders of each clan, and each sat cross-legged in a circle to smoke the pipe and pray to the Great Spirit. No ordinary pipe was this; it had a bowl and elbow fashioned of grey stone from which was drawn for passing around the council, a long upright stem wrapped in quills with tail feathers of the pheasant.

After some time, Audaîgweos began to speak. In words pulsating out, half spoken, half chanted, he began by welcoming his brothers to the Loon Clan's winter home on the shore of Kitchigami, a word that designated a large lake. Much of his oration I missed; yet, if such be possible I felt I grasped its essence. Many times he spoke of Kitche Manitou, the Creator. Nor, could I miss the sweep of his arm as he invoked Father Sky and Earth Mother.

I don't call myself a religious man, raised as I was by an austere father with strict Calvinist morals more of habit than of spirit, and whose overriding faith was lodged in The Trade. Yet something powerful stirred within my breast by what I heard and saw that night. My eyes opened wider and my ears listened harder; and I wondered with what success Jean-Baptiste could bring to untamed men, entrenched in primitive ritual and tradition of the clans, his gospel of One True God, a gospel entwined in this wilderness with that other doctrine of Chacun pour soi et Dieu pour tous! That doctrine I myself espoused, one it would be foolhardy to disavow if The Trade were to prosper.

Chapter 27.

Growing Horns

True, the savages had fasted for some days so were primed for a ceremonial feast. Still, how could they devour a shank of one large animal,—moose, bear, deer,—and then chomp down on another and another. Their gastronomy would test even lusty Sir James! Though, unlike him, savages appeared to gorge themselves only rarely and were taut-bellied. We Dutch are not known as mere peckers of food and drink, but the economy of my parents' household made these ceremonial heapings of meats seem fitting board for kings and emperors.

After the feasting and passing of the pipe, the old ones told stories. They half-sang them in throaty quivers that chilled my spine. Then, gradually, my ears grew accustomed to wild sounds, and I counted them no wilder than the wildness all around us. The clan elders were seated in a large half-circle on either side of Audaîgweos, at the far end of the Long House, each clan distinguishable by dress rather than location. White Feather sat near the entrance to the Long House, apart from the elders. I sat next to him and, during a lull, asked about the stories. White Feather called them 'songs', songs to teach about when earth was new, their great battles and ancient enemies.

I wanted to satisfy my curiosity about those ancient enemies. He himself was an Iroquois, Long Smoke an Ottawa, and both were living among the Ojibwa, at least for now. And there were the Huron. But White Feather averted his head so that I saw only the intensity of his stony profile, straight back, and rigid shoulders. I was forgotten, his attention, elsewhere. So I sorted out for myself, concluding that ancient enemies entered perpetuity on both sides of the ocean. Tribes of Vandals and Visigoths, Angles, Jutes, and Saxons, barbarians of the Roman Empire—all had made war, then co-mingled with the populace they'd overrun and, over the eons, as here, their stories as conquering warriors continued to be passed on down. Then the thought struck me. Did White Feather ignore those questions he thought this white man ought to answer for himself? — A wise method, and so unlike the withering glance of a father to signify his son a dunce. A deaf ear, a quiet tongue and a closed eye cast no blame, no shame.

White Feather barely stirred as the voices among the clan elders rose and fell. Mostly, I could not judge his interest or disinterest, and yet one audible recounting, spoken just above a whisper, allowed me to be a listener to his own bit of history:

"In ancient time, Iroquois weak. They work, work hard. Make Iroquois strong. More strong than all others. Then make many enemies."

Surely, he was affirming what I would later learn. His Mohawk ancestors along with other Iroquois nations had slain whole villages of Algonquin tribes, and those who escaped were forced to flee westward from their ancestral homes in the East. And here sat White Feather, sitting among descendants of those who had fled and, now, went on and on about long-ago victories. I had the good sense to remain quiet. I wondered if White Feather was even aware that he'd spoken aloud, so turned inward was his demeanor. Yes, White Feather chose his own time to talk and to whom. For me these occasions were all too rare. When he did speak, it was best for me to keep silent and just listen. So be it. Left to my own, I could better watch and observe.

The Ojibwa ceremonies and celebrations would last through the evening of the third day. As on the first night on this, the second, I tried to be invisible while the elders ran on with their stories. As one finished, another came up and struck a war club, signaling readiness to speak about his exploits. Details were lost to me, but I caught enough to know that they told many a bloody tale of victims, tortures, and slayings.

The moon must have risen overhead by the time the last elder finished. In the pause that followed, how curious it looked to see Animiki steal up close behind and approach her father. Like other females present, young and old, vermilion slashed her cheeks and, in the firelight, her dark pupils flashed against the whites of her eyes. She leaned close in to Audaîgweos and whispered in his ear. I surmised the content when, shortly thereafter, he beckoned to me, announcing that the wákomind among them sing "song from across far waters." I groaned, inwardly, that I'd ever given cause to prompt such a request. The one song I knew from my childhood was a silly Dutch schoolboy verse I had sung once to the Ojibwa children, and Animiki remembered. To refuse a request from Audaîgweos, himself, might be an irreparable insult. Anyway, few among them understood English let alone Dutch. Not even White Feather, having lived in Albany, knew Dutch. So, trusting that a brave face and stalwart stance might hide my discomfort, I strode up to the center. Lacking the round and high-ruffled white collar, black garb and leather boots of a Rembrandt musketeer, I nevertheless mimed the red sashed Captain of the Guard and, hand extended, sang out lustily, finishing my performance with a bow. Feathered headdresses of the elders nodded, solemnly, in a faint show of politeness amid the smirks and gestures of more honest young braves who were astute enough to know my singing made poor song.

On the final night, Audaîgweos summoned me to join the men in passing the pipe. The smoke stimulated my tongue and I found myself speaking freely, coupling my smattering of Ojibwa with what English Audaîgweos could offer. In this benign atmosphere of pungent aromas, and a light head, I asked him if the hut of a white man at a half-day's distance was known to him, supposing that this knowledge would be conveyed to him by Hadakotana.

"Many many huts," Audaîgweos said, swinging his arms with sudden force eastward. He made a circle of his arms, then, and raising the forefinger of one hand added more softly: "Here, one hut." A faraway look came into his eyes. And, suddenly, his hands came together about a bread-loaf apart; and he moved them in rapid succession, saying, "Some day, may be many many huts, here and here."

Had he mistaken my question? In the silence that followed, and in seeing the serious composure of his features, it came to me that I had provoked a deeper question, and one quite preposterous. I shook my head slowly to indicate disagreement and ventured my opinion. "I do not believe many of my people would choose to stay in so big and so wild a land."

At this, one side of his mouth worked into the universal half-smile of one unwilling to relinquish a strong opinion. The obsidian cast of his eyes hardened and fixed on me, warily.

"Many winters past, Great Dreamer of my people speak. Say

White Spirits come with the Rising Sun. First bring gifts to my people; we have stone axe. They make presents of iron axe, sharp knife. Glass beads. Cloth. This much has happened.

Next, Great Dreamer say they bring us fire-arm. This too has happened.

Great Dreamer say they bring fire-water. I was young boy; I see this happen. Great Dreamer say White Spirits will come like sand on shore of Big Water and sweep away our hunting grounds. Our hunting grounds gift from Kitchi Manitou."

My face must have shown my astonishment as I started to protest, and Audaîgweos raised a hand to silence me. He continued speaking with the same softness like the sound of clinking pebbles. "You say your people not stay here. Not in this wild land, you say. You not speak truth. You here, Yellow Hair!"

Before answering, I showed my appreciation for the turn of his argument with a vigorous smile and nod. I'd been among them long enough to know that in company with savages, one ought not press points one upon the other, but draw them out slowly. After a sufficient lapse of time, I said, "This is true. I come to find furs. When the time comes, I will trade for them. Just like my grandfather and three older brothers before me. We, come like other white men. For furs we bring you blankets, knives..."

"Ataia´! White men come for furs.—Listen, Yellow Hair." I marveled at the tone of command Audaîgweos conveyed in so unaltered a voice. His position, still seated, took on that of a storyteller, erect, with a hand on each knee. He began in a half chant:

"Once, long long ago, long before white man come, our people live by Great Salt Sea. Ojibwa, Ottawa, Potawatomie—others. We fight as one against our enemy, Naud-o-waig, later call 'Iroquois' nations. Our enemy lose. Many years we travel Great River and Great Chain of Lakes in peace. White man come; we trade. Many of our people fall sick. Many die. Our homes move, move to new hunting grounds. All winter we hunt. In spring, our canoes carry many furs, but never enough furs for white man! Our homes move again, far from Great River and Great Salt Sea. We make many enemies for furs." His eyes glazed over as he spoke, the words pouring out in a sing-song. "Our people. they come to want white man's things. Young men want fire-arm from white man." Suddenly, his manner shifted; his head whipped around and he confronted me, directly. "All this happen! You say Great Dreamer not speak truth?" I answered him as earnestly as I could find the wit to do so.

"White men come to trade. This is true, Audaîgweos. But, I think most men who come will not stay. They have families. Our women are not like your women. They do not carry such heavy loads as your women carry. They do not scrape furs and gum canoes. Our women spin and weave, they plant gardens, harvest vegetables, salt meats—and stay in homes. They do not know the ways of your women. Your women very strong.

"—I think to live in your country, our men and our women must learn your ways to live here." At this, Audaîgweos's burnt-leather face bent toward me. He looked into my eyes, making a satisfied sound I took to mean he was pleased.

"When we meet first time, you are as kitagâkons—young spotted deer. Now, I think maybe someday you grow horns, horns like the mashkodé-pijiki." I learned he meant the horns of the buffalo, an animal who prefers grasslands to the forests. Audaîgweos stopped speaking, then, and the leader of the Fox Clan, a big man with a rope of animal teeth and claws jangling on his chest, strode up and stood before the Ogima.

"Makogânj," Audaîgweos said, addressing him as 'Bear Claw'.

I was not included in the conversation between the Fox and Loon Clan leaders, nor could I understand the details of what was being said about their people and the winter ahead. Besides, my head was pounding. I'd had too much of everything—and everything so strange. Too much food, too much smoke, and too much infernal drumming. Nonetheless, I had acted the better part of my orders from Sir James by watching and observing, and it was long enough. I slipped away, quietly.

Scarcely had my shadow fallen past the fire-lit doorway of the Long House, when several young men ran up to me, Hadakotana among them. At Hada's insistence, a wejinigewînini, or painter, blackened my face and urged me to dress like one of them. Good nature and curiosity supplanted my aching head. I agreed, and let them decorate my face with a foul smelling, oily substance of animal fat and plant dyes, accompanied by encouraging grunts and 'hi-yas.' They threw a beaver robe over me, calling, "Ondáshán!"

I followed. Dumbly, at first, as I began stomping around the great fire circle, imitating as best I could the quick stepping Nikkutew, a relative of Hadakotana's. Nikkutew's feet flew up-down, and in-out with abandon. I felt clumsy as a ship in irons. As time passed, and little-by-little my legs loosened, my feet began to move with a lightness I'd not felt before, nor since. The singers' high notes pierced the top of my head and their low notes thumped in my groin. The feeling could only be likened to aboard ship when, with a full wind shivering the sails, one exults in the feeling of being washed clean, through and through, stem to stern. Maybe that is how the soul speaks. I know that as the drums beat on, my limbs seemed one with the sparks of firelight flitting from earth to sky.

The long night ended only as daylight began. A light rain was fast turning to snow. I crawled into my wigwam, too heated to feel the cold, too exhausted to care.

Chapter 28.

The Long Winter

All else throughout that long winter of falling snow was eclipsed by a most singular event, and occurred some time after the clans had made their departure. Their leave—taking was hastened by a lowering blanket of storm clouds, after which, a fortnight of heavy blowing snow and days of thick fog kept me from straying outside the encampment. With each delay my agitation mounted for I was bent on revisiting the hut of the foreigner. And delays there were:

One blustery afternoon, I heard drumming and ventured out to investigate, stopping at the Long House from whence came the sounds. White Feather, who sat nearest the opening, saw me approach and immediately came out. "You stay," he said. "You wait." It was not my intention to enter uninvited, only to look inside. But as time passed, and sheltered from the wind between the Long House and towering evergreens, I swallowed my chagrin at waiting once again in this strange world of savages, and waited with the outward show of obedience drilled into me as a child. So, prevented from watching what went on inside, I observed the outer structure of the Long House. Close-fitting poles, one lashed to the next, held fast the length of its high walls. A narrow air space between walls and roof let in light and emitted smoke. Covering all, a slanted roof, tightly woven of sturdy reeds and dried grasses, was anchored to the walls, midway, and at the corners of the walls. Sooner than expected, White Feather came outside, again, this time motioning me to enter, but "No speak."

Only males were assembled inside the Long House, or Council. Some beat on kettle-shaped wooden drums encased in skin, their solemn faces in accord with the belief that sounds made by drums were sacred and could be understood only by the Great Spirit. The drone of drums went on and on and on. Each drummer seemed so single-mindedly intent that, not unlikely, an enemy could have felled them one-by-one without their neighbors being the wiser. I wished only for the ceremonies to end. Unattuned to accepting the superstitions of this or that practice—be it of a god or of a devil, I struggled to keep from dozing off. Thankfully, before a display of such weakness could occur, to my well-disguised relief, I was ordered to leave.

Clearly, what those secret rites to come might be, were to be revealed only among clan initiates. Of course, denying my presence also negated Sir James's dictate to "watch and observe." Anyway, that certain of their ceremonies and what transpired, therein, be forbidden to onlookers distressed me no more than were I refused admittance to secret affairs of Amsterdam magistrates and shipping magnates.

The bad weather persisted. White Feather promised a ningekide would come, but Saint Nicholas Day passed, and the New Year passed, and the scant fluctuation in temperature did not produce a thaw. Those Holy Days celebrated in Christian lands being of no account to the natives, here, I scarce noted them but to reckon the dates in my journal, and recall childhood memories of my mother flitting about strewing balsam branches and lighting tapers to cheer our dreary household. She always waited until Father slept before shaking me awake. Then, to her sweetly sung refrain—"Apples from Orange! Apples from Trees!"—I'd slip down the steps of my sleeping cupboard to set out my small klompen which, that same night, Saint Nicholas and his helper Swarte Piet would fill with sugar-candy. And in the small hours of the morning, before being summoned to our meal of warm milk, bread and cheese, I took care to conceal the sweets under my bed cover. Perhaps Father overlooked this stealthy gifting from wife to son, choosing not to interfere, thereby, permitting this little joy to offset his customary distance when not engaged in tutoring me.

Far from the thaw that White Feather forecast, the bitterest of cold set in. All the better for them. Their food stocks were worsening, and the freeze hardened the snow pack and froze the great lake to a distance of a quarter-league or more. Shards of ice piled up like miniature glass glaciers along the edge of the black, open water. Close off shore, both their men and women set about breaking holes through the bay's thicker ice to fish. Of all the varieties, most favored for taste were the large white fishes. Smoked over low coals, they made a nourishing and welcome change of diet. Moreover, thrusting a spear, fashioned from a bone tip tied to a hardwood shaft, and snaring a fish for one's supper made fine sport in the long gray days. On occasion, at night, a torch was suspended over an ice hole and attracted a pike or better, the grandly armored, bony-plated sturgeon. Another diversion (and of most interest to me) during that long winter came when the Ojibwa snared beaver. This they did by using small, deadfall traps or even digging the creatures out of their lodges. Roasted beaver meat was tender and juicy and made a fine meal. But finest of all was that warm, lush and so highly valued winter fur. I'd seen none finer. How my desire ignited to get on with The Trade!

A morning came when I awoke to a most perfect silence. No wind battered my wigwass walls nor even swayed the holding poles. I stuck my head out to discover calm, cold air, but the sky!—Ah, the sky was clear and of that utter blueness to swell the lungs and make all things possible. The very morning to reconnoiter the foreigner's hut. I hailed Hadakotana, and found him as eager to be gone as myself.

It was my first time to walk any long distance on agim, though I had seen Ojibwa hunters dance in their snowshoes while waving short spears and clubs to thank Kitche Manitou for the snow that made an animal's tracks easier to follow. These quaint shoes were cleverly made by soaking large strips of ash, curving and binding the ends together, and then lashing the frame tight with crossed strings of deer or moose hide. Hada and I skirted the edge of the forest with me trying to keep astride of him as I shuffled along in my long skin coat. Had I known the body worked up such heat from working one's legs spread so wide apart, I'd have worn but a shirt and leggings as he did. But, turn the globe on its heel! Hada, then, would surely be panting to keep abreast of me in skating the frozen Amstel.

Of a sudden, Hada stopped and threw his arm out to stay my movements. His nostrils pinched in and out in sniffing the air. He leaned an ear up against a tree. I listened and, at first, heard nothing. Then, all at once, a full rushing sound and in seconds, a herd of caribou loped out of the woods, crossed the clearing, and fled up the ridge. A wondrous sight, some fifty beasts with flashing antlers and hooves in flight. When they'd past we continued on as we had, crossing over the multitude of heart-shaped hoof prints left in the snow.

Coming out of the trees, we glided across what in summer would be a tall-grass meadow of about four leagues. This day, my collar of fur served to helmet my head against the sharp North wind that swept down on us from the ridge. We trudged parallel to the ridge, moving eastward, and watching for some sign of the foreigner's hut amid all the whiteness. I was first to spot, sticking up part way above the snow, an iron trap. Only stiff, stringy entrails remained attached. To the far side of the trap, aligned to the ridge, faint traces of human tracks dented the snow. I was all for following them, but Hadakotana held my arm. He was insistent that we fall back and continue on inside the border of trees, south of the ridge. If not for the mission I'd set us upon, Hada might be dressing down a caribou, and so I gave way to his wishes. As we backed away, he erased the markings of our snowshoes with a tree branch until all trace of them disappeared. My impatience was mounting! Here, when we had new evidence of the hut being inhabited—and with every likelihood it being by a bosloper or, at least, a coureurs-de-bois or foreigner of some sort—Hada's primitive instincts of secrecy bade us adhere to such extreme precautions. I yearned only to meet the hut dweller. My reasoning mind said to pin no hopes on the foreigner should one indeed be present; but, my heart beat quickened.—It had been some time since the tug of my family talisman fueled my spirit with such anticipation.

Back into the shelter of trees, we went, our progress slowed in side-stepping tangled brush and trees that lay uprooted at sharp dark angles in the pristine snow. When the wind blew, a tinkling of frozen branches rained down showers of ice. I was in awe of this frenzied landscape, and wondered how it was a white man could be in these parts and Audaîgweos's people, so alert to every movement of man or beast, not know it. I thought, too, on how Audaîgweos had failed to satisfy my question by turning it into one of his own as he'd asked, "Why you, here, Yellow Hair?" then went on about the predictions of their Great Dreamer. In fairness, his people had much to do to set up their new winter camp. With the steady snows, cold, and their paramount need being to trap and hunt, it was possible Hada and I were the very first to come upon the hut. After all, the hut was skillfully designed not to be seen. Some, like Jan Carpentier would deem this effort a futile hope. Not I. My doubts eased and my assurance grew in contemplating the benefits of wetting natural curiosity to an iron purpose; I would search out all signs of my brothers,—even to exploring a heap of sticks to uncover a hut!

Only screeching ravens and the schuss of our snowshoes shattered the stillness as we pushed on. The day's light lay full upon us with the sun moving in and out of a leaden sky. Well-screened by the cover of trees, at Hada's insistence, I endured a painfully sore neck from the constant strain of looking north to espy the hut, while my body strained onward, east.

At length, roofed under snow-laden branches, a wood crosspiece showed itself. I must admit that Hada's maneuvering had proved right for a better reason than caution. If we'd approached directly along the ridge, we might easily have passed on by, so cleverly was the hut disguised in the snowy hillside.

Suddenly, Hada started a howl deep in his throat, and I bade him stop. "Make like wolf," he protested. "Maiâginini come out."

"No! Stay back. First, I meet foreigner, alone." I had savored this moment far too long to be dissuaded. Nor could I hope to explain to this savage whom I thought of as "friend" why, at this pivotal moment, I desired to meet the hut's occupant by myself. Hada tossed his head in the angry arrogance he'd displayed when I made him give back my knife. Much had passed between us since, and I did not want to lose his friendship; indeed, I depended upon it.

"Maiâginini may have firearm. You stay and watch for me." He studied me one long moment with narrowed eyes before tossing his head in consent.

I strode out from the shelter of the trees and crossed the meadow, made straight for the door, and knocked. I knocked louder. I pounded. Did I hear a stirring? A creaking as of a man rising up from a cot? I stepped back a goodly pace for the hut had no window from which to take the measure of intruders. One click of the bolt and the door burst open. I was ready. The same instant as the glint of the rifle leapt across the dim space, my arm shot straight out from my shoulder, warning Hadakotana against letting loose an arrow should he presume to do so.

Clad from the neck down in fur, the foreigner stood hunched in the doorway. He was too tall to stand upright inside his enclosure. I made not a sound, terrified that I make the wrong sound. This hulking stranger—was he Dutch?—or French, English, Russian? Surely his was not the face of a brother. He took a step forward, focusing slitted eyes against the light to see who disturbed his rest. He brought his head out the doorway and then, as they opened, I beheld the eyes. Eyes eerily like those coal dark eyes that stuck in my memory. But these eyes were brighter. This face was weathered with a coarse, full beard and this head sprouted shocks of wild gray-black hair.

My tongue locked in my throat, no partner to my racing brain. Of an instant I vowed not to declare myself brother—should he be brother. Had long months among the wildness of this land and its inhabitants ravaged me of all civilized emotion—despoiled the dream I'd so much longed for and now hung back from declaring?

Something there was about this stranger—for brother were I to call him so, he'd not know. Not know that he had a third brother, a mere half-brother; not know that one such as I even walked the earth!—Something there was about this great bear-man served to warn me he'd not harbor a fool—nor a foolish lad—for surely he would deem me such were I to proclaim him brother, me with the face of my mother, not his mother, and nothing like the face of our father, if our father. I knew only, and with utmost certainty, I should not seek to bind our relation—should it prove to be so—upon familiarity with a "sailor's trinket" as Sir James once called my family talisman. Thus, to conceal myself until I could choose the moment, I greeted him with profuse "good day-ing" and "Sir-ing" as though I were addressing the Baron Noblesse of this unknown land.

"Speak! Why do you come here? From whence?"—His voice, surprisingly unlike his appearance, was no more than a sustained whisper, thin and ghostlike.

"I have come lately out of Albany, the River Mohawk by way of the Oneida country, and then by way of the Great Lake of the Entouhonorans, so named by sieur de Champla..."

"Yes, yes, you mean the Ontario Sea. Go on."

"...then by means of a labyrinth of interior portages and waterways to the great bay called 'Mer Douche'..."

"Yes, and the land called "Huronia" and on to the bay! Do you intend this to be a lesson in geography, lad? From whence do you come here this day?"

I strove to not be put off by his irritation as I roamed my mind for words to calm him. "I lodge with savages encamped some four leagues to the south of here. You do know the bay?"

"I know the bay, of course. I know not that Ojibwa encamp there."

"They came to winter," I said, perplexed at his naming the tribe while claiming not to know of their presence.

"Hmmm. Then that is possible. And how do you happen upon my house?"

"In hunting along the ridge before the snow fell, I looked down on what at first seemed the shelter of a beaver, but I saw no water nearby. I became all the more curious, upon discovering it to be a man-built hut, and with a lintel carved above the door."

A glimmer of a smile parted the suspicion in his eyes. "Waiting the hours goes slowly once I have set my traps. I whittle. — It is a good lintel?"

"A very good lintel!" I paused, wondering at this sudden turn of good humor, and hoping he would venture more, but he did not.

"It is like lintels I've seen elsewhere." Still he said nothing.

"I believe it very like lintels to be seen in Amsterdam."

"Ah. You speak Nederlands?" I nodded. "Why do you speak to me in English?" The massive head leaned close, and his were not the first set of eyes that dared me speak truth.

"Do you wish me to speak in French?"

"I care not that you speak at all!" His harsh throaty whisper rose to a strangled roar. "Why do you come here? Speak! Do you require a draught of sterke to state your business?"

The word "business" had a calming effect on me, it being business, after all, that sent the both of us to this continent, however many years apart.

"My name," I said, without a quiver of hesitation, "is Peter Dorn."

Chapter 29.

The Hut And The "Bear"

"Call in your Ojibwa servant." For the second time he used the name of the tribe. This time my face must have shown surprise.

"You did not make those." He pointed to my snowshoes. "Nor did the Micmac-Iroquois-Wyandot-Cree-Ottawa or Potawatomie. Nor, I suspect did you come here unaided."

"Hada, ondáshán!" My voice shattered the cold stillness like the hammer of the smithy striking the anvil. It gave me courage. "Hadakotana, you surmise correctly, is Ojibwa. He is not my servant."

"You speak their tongue?"

"Some. I learn."

His gaze as he stepped clear of the hut fixed not on me but on Hada. Against the light, Hada's shadowy figure skimmed across the crusted snow with the swiftness of an antelope, made straight for us, then stopped short. He paid the Bear-man back stare-for-stare with that sharp, penetrating look I'd come to know. He approved at least the Bear's dress, side-stepping around to openly admire the finely dressed robe of buffalo. His interest was more than complimentary. He wanted to know from whence it came, how it was gotten, and seemed well pleased on being told the robe was bought for one pâshkisigan, a type of gun used in the trade.

Still, he persisted. His true interest not being the robe, his real question emerged. "Amikobiwai, Anin minik?"

"Maybe, twelve made beaver," I said, estimating a trade gun to be worth more in the hinterland, than along the Atlantic.

"Niá!"

At Hada's exclamation the Bear-man shrugged, turning his sharp-eyed appraisal from me to Hada, speaking to him in Ojibwa, "É", yes, it is so.

The Bear-man's backing me up gave me no small satisfaction!— until, Hada continuing to meddle in his surly way asked about the pinâakatewan. I put him off. "Mi minik!" Enough for now! Hada, of course couldn't know the cause of my impatience, and I'd deal with that later. I had more urgent matters to discuss than powder horns. and I wasted no time. "Your name, Sir," I said to the Bear-man, "how am I to address you?"

His laughter was unexpected and the throaty sounds, jarring. Yet, he seemed not unfriendly as he pinned me with one eye while the other roved on its own. If his high nasal whispering suggested weakness—a sinusitis or malady of the sort—it was eclipsed by the forthrightness of his manner and presence. "Names, ah names," he began. "The Ottawa know me by occupation for a trader in pelts and, more lately, for a trapper. To my face, they call me, "brother." As for the British, given the opportunity—Ah, the British would hang me tomorrow and wish it were yesterday; they call me names not to my liking. Only the French call me by my Christian name, as may you. My name is "Gregor. Gregor Van Doorn."

He was Gregor! mijn broeder, Gregor.—My limbs went weak. Stupidly, I nodded acknowledgement and, in bending down, mumbled something about the tightness of my snowshoes. I stayed bent over as I fumbled with the laces, my brain swimming to comprehend the mangled thoughts crowding my mind. The revelations this Bear-man—my brother—had just disclosed were souring the triumph I ought to feel. That this brother—even a half-brother—should inform me, the eyes and ears for Sir Richard Blackman James, that the British want to hang him! Why? Was this Gregor—this brother—partner of the French-led western tribes who burned villages of the Seneca, throwing the whole of the Iroquois league into an uproar? Might he have bargained his knowledge of the interior to help Frenchmen capture the twenty trade canoes of Albany merchants? A Dutchman had captained that trading venture with Iroquois guides, and the loss of so rich a cargo to the French at a place called Mackinac was much discussed in Albany.

One snowshoe unstrung, I retied the thongs and started on the other, shadowed by talk in the Handelaar Tavern of the ghastly revenge wreaked on a French settlement, its citizens butchered in the dead of night by the Iroquois. Here and now, in this place, would my long lost brother come to know me not as brother but as one girdled to the Ojibwa, enemies of tribes allied to New France?

Vervloekten! I must not let the worst, most dire, most unlikely thoughts crowd out my joy at discovering a brother! I straightened up and forced a handshake on Gregor Van Doorn. Even as that one's hand, rough as tree bark, encased my own, I had a gnawing recognition of my own unraveling loyalties, loyalties—to father, to country—to the avowed purpose of my coming to the New World and making my way in the fur trade in spite of the English monopoly.

Strange, after my fierce longing to behold a brother, at the moment of having one, I craved solitude. Solitude to think.

"Hadakotana and I need all the daylight left if we are to reach our encampment by nightfall," I said. And this being no idle pretense, I bade a polite but hurried farewell to Gregor Van Doorn, asking leave to call on him, again.

Some few days would pass before I returned to his hut. In the interim, I sought out Animiki to find out all she might know, or would tell me, about the plans of her people come spring.

"Big Lake Person travel with us?"

"Travel where with your people, Little One?" To my surprise I had never called her 'little one' before, and thought it suited one who scarcely stood to the height of my chest.

The brown, doe eyes looking up at me seemed lacking in their usual warmth.

"Do not see the many furs our hunters bring? Do not see our women grease and scrape off much flesh? Do not see me, the bone of elk strapped to my arm, make hide grow soft and dry?"

In truth, I had paid scant attention to the work of the females. But to rid her voice of its sharpness and bring a smile back into her eyes, I made a slight prevarication as though shocked that she'd think me so unaware.—I did, of course, know the Ojibwa had taken many furs! I'd made it my business to observe their use of snares and deadfalls—any means of entrapment—as well as the results!

"But where? Where will you trade all your furs? I have seen you and the women labor over furs many days, Animiki. Many furs of marten, otter, lynx, wolf, as well as beaver skins. Where is the place you trade?"

"We travel when sun warms the waters. You travel with, you see place of trade."

Her behavior seemed passing strange for one of her usually gentle disposition. Were she older or a white woman, I might have judged her quick words and hasty departure to be a show of momentary foul temper. As it was, more pressing matters occupied my thoughts than the vagaries of one small savage.

Chapter 30.

The Visit

Long Smoke sauntered by carrying a basket woven of linden bark filled with fresh fish. She stood, defiantly, blocking my path. Since that day of our first dull-brained debacle, we'd not exchanged a word and, for my part, none would be spoken. "Trade," she said, curtly.

I hesitated only a moment. The sky was clear as any I'd seen in days. With good fortune a calm night and clear day would follow, and I would be off. "Wait, here," I said with equal curtness and, disappearing inside my wigwam, I came out holding up a shiny metal comb. A glint lit up her eyes. We traded, and to my relief and satisfaction, she turned on her heel and hurried off. To my way of thinking, the exchange buried fault on both sides, and the incident was erased. Did it signify the same to the savage mind? I do not know. The supposition seems reasonable. No safety latches protect one's wigwam nor possessions therein. Trust among clan members supports bartering, else thievery steps in. Allowances were not made for one like myself, a tolerated guest.

I left the encampment at the crack of dawn before others had stirred. In particular, Hadakotana. I wanted to be alone, to reach Gregor's hut before he himself might be gone, hunting, or seeing to his traps. At sunrise, a brilliant orange glow spread over the breadth of the land. In the freshness of morning, I could glide across still-frozen snow. But, without a cold wind and harnessed to snowshoes, I would, soon enough, be sloughing through heavy, wet snow. So I took full advantage of the hour or so left, and sped along, profiting from having studied how Hada used his legs. The method was not too unlike a skater's. One could race along in laps when the terrain permitted, making a goodly distance in a short time. —Ah! Certain it was, I reached the hut in record time, and in spirits as buoyant as when sailing with the wind.

This time at my knocking, he seemed not displeased to see me, especially when I pulled off my pack, and presented him with the basket of fish I'd taken precautions to harden down in snow the night before.

"Come, come inside." His hissing syllables fell on my ears as an echo, an echo of a once sonorous voice. His big splayed feet were bare and calloused, and he wore a coarse, loose-fitting shirt over deerskin leggings. His buffalo robe hung from a peg aside the door. "Come, come. Sit."

To sit was necessary, lest both of us stand with bent heads and slumped shoulders. He motioned me to the lone table, one hewn from maple and crude, save for its well—planed surface rubbed to a honey-tone smoothness. We sat on squat benches, one on either side of the table. The door, left ajar and backed up against a narrow cot and shelf, allowed air and sunlight to do battle with the stale smell of the room. I complimented him on his furnishings—he being ignorant of my deprivation these many months.

"So," he said, one bushy eyebrow upraised, while pouring two thimbles of a rich, amber-colored brandy. "Prosh!"

"And to you." I wished our converse to be in English until such time as I chose to reveal myself to him; and to assure myself of that time, I had to know if on his travels, by chance he'd met Jan Carpentier.

He scratched at his beard, shook his great shaggy head, and mumbled, "No."

"Ah!" I sipped with the gusto of a Sir James, teasing the brandy over my tongue and letting it glide down my gullet. Had he met Jan, this brother would be playing a more sly game than I myself, for surely Jan would have told him of me.

"You may know the Jesuit father, Jean Baptiste?" I asked with the easy manner of a drawing room loller tossing out names at random.

"The same Jean Baptiste that missionaries among the Ottawa? If so, he is by reputation a hardy soul at work among a dwindling tribe."

"How is that?" I leaned in closer so not to miss his words.

"The savages always had enough wars of their own. But close on a hundred years, now, England and France in their mad lust for furs—the "gold" they covet to wage their merry wars at home—have split the tribes in twos and sixes." He sucked in a deep breath, then continued. "For over thirty years, these hands helped first the Dutch, then the English, then the French. Now I work alone." His hands, like paws carved of walnut-bark, spilled out in front of him, and I saw the left hand shy of two fingers above the knuckles. I exhaled easier, greatly relieved to learn he now worked alone. Gregor, misjudging the cause of my sighing, assured me the pain of his affliction was long past.

"A savage found them a "dish" much to his liking." He tweaked the puckered joints. "I have eight left thanks to a Friendly who sank a bullet into the Iroquois's shaved skull.

"Not long thereafter, I thought I would like the Huron—those who still remained—better than the Iroquois, and went North to engage with their allies, the French." A weary look came into his eyes. "Wars at home boil up blood clear across the Atlantic."

"You speak like Audaîgweos, the Ojibwa's captain. He has it in his head that some day white men will rule all this wild land." Maybe, the ridicule in my voice stopped him short for Gregor apprised me, solemnly.

"I wish to meet your Audaîgweos."

"Then you shall!" My sudden enthusiasm seemed to unsettle him. He gave me an even sharper look, but I was not to be restrained from enlarging upon so safe an arena of conversation. "Audaîgweos, he is like a prince among the savages. As good as one could expect to meet but for White Feather. The Ogima has the respect of all his clans." I rattled on about his praiseworthy conduct in having all his people conducted to their new hunting grounds. The ambush by the Huron. The killings, and a brief rendition of my part in rescuing White Feather and Hadakotana.—All this to disguise the cause of my rising joyousness that this brother, whatever his past alliances, now seemed free of them.—Was this the moment to declare him to be my own brother? Still I held back, and Gregor leaned forward across the table, so close we could have butted our foreheads.

"How is it you came to travel with the Ojibwa, and so far? You are too young to be a Jesuit, too young to be an experienced trader. And, too inexperienced in matters of alliances, I presume, to be serviceable to and among the various nations."

"A friend—a friend of the Factor of Albany—made my arrangements. He was anxious to engage my—my facility with languages so useful to The Trade, and I myself am eager to learn much more about the interior of this North America."

"Which Albany? Surely not the Fort on the Bay. You must mean that on the River Hudson."

"The same." We settled into an uncomfortable silence. He, seeming to examine the measure of my words, and I questioning how much to reveal of my purposes, not knowing, as Sir James would have said, his friends or his enemies in spite of his working 'alone' as he put it. "You've been to this other Fort Albany?"

"I have. You know it remains under French control."

"I do not know the Albany to the north—nor any of the country of New France. For that matter, how does one learn where one steps, or on whose country one walks in a land without bridges or buildings, no canals—no beschaafde bevolking..."

"You!—You not only speak Dutch, you are Dutch, I knew it!" My unintended lapse into the mother tongue spurred him on. "Who are you?" he demanded.

Those eyes, I swear if the door were shut against the bright sunshine without, those deep set eyes would have burned just as fervidly in the dark. Yet his face was not the stern taskmaster's of our common father. I liked this face.

"You call yourself Peter Dorn." I nodded.

"Strange, is it not, our names?"

"How so?" Still I chose to appear dense in the expectation, that were the revelation to come slowly, he'd be the more ready to accept the truth when the time came.

He made a heavy sigh, drumming the fingers of his good hand on the table. "My younger brother Dirck was much like you, but also a good many years older than yourself. How I long to know if he sailed from the parental home in Amsterdam. Doubtless, like myself, Dirck would follow The Trade; yet the certainty of his leaving I know not." He paused in his reverie, tugging at his beard. "In 1644, two years before I arrived, Pieter Stuyvesant surrendered New Nederland to the English, renamed New York; but that was of no account to our merchants back home so long as their furs kept coming. When our ship reached New Amsterdam, rather New York, I went straight up the Hudson to Rensselaerswyck—my grandfather was well known to Kiliaen van Rensselaer—but as time went on I found the old Patroon's colonie no place for a free trader. Nor could I stomach what was once Beverwyck—now Albany—with its Dutch housemaids and Dutch shopkeepers and English overseers."

"And your older brother? Did you learn of him?" Again, he looked at me with suspicion.

"Would that I did not! I learned that a Dutchman of my look and size was slain by a rampaging Mohawk in a drunken frenzy. My elder brother, Willem, I knew to be more fond of drink than of an honest day's work. Some said he was caught trading liquor to the savages. Yet of his arrest, the Colonie produced no record. But, Peter Dorn,—how is it you knew I had an older brother?"

"Why, you—you spoke of Dirck as "younger brother" implying you had...."

"Yes, yes, I see."

"This Dirck, you say he and I share a likeness?"

"Perhaps, perhaps not. I thought of him when I first laid eyes on you, yet too many years cloud the memory. But I talk much, and you—you are close-mouthed, my young friend." At this I could hardly contain a smile, thinking back on the many many times Jan and Sir James had warned me to curb my tongue.

"It was not always so, Gregor Van Doorn. I have a great need to be instructed by one like yourself, one of my own countrymen who has survived these many years on this untamed continent. But say, did you never wish to return to Amsterdam? To your home?"

"The years pass quickly, and with each, the wish to go back to a life—one I remember with not so great a fondness—weakens. So how is it with you? You have become attuned to the savages?" Once, again, he refilled my thimble.

"Like you, my Amsterdam connections to the New World, if ever they held promise, proved worthless to me. Aboard ship, I fell in with of all persons, an Englishman who seemed, the more I knew him, to bear scant allegiance to his mother country—at least less so than seems common. He singled me out for favors not, to be sure, without recompense! Earlier, I spoke of Sir James Blackman's friend—one Sir William Graves, Factor of Albany. The Factor is in poor business straights and seeks new sources of furs.

"—But, Gregor...Van Doorn,"—I looked him full in the eye, "I do not wish you to think me tight-lipped on matters of a more close nature." I raised my cup, slowly drained the brandy, then more slowly reached inside my shirt. Our eyes locked. In one swift motion, I withdrew the gold chain, whipped it over my head, and set before him our ancestral ivory, Der Vogel de Nederland.

Chapter 31.

The Acknowledgment

"God in Hemel!" He snatched up the ivory, catching the gold chain in the frayed cuff of his woolen shirt. He held it in his palm, bent close and squinted as a jeweler might the facets of a diamond. "God in Hemel," he whispered, again, the stubs of his maimed hand boring into my wrist. "The ship faces West."

"Loosen your grip, Gregor Van Doorn," I said, ignoring his dull observation. "I have much to tell you. — Ah,...more brandewijn if you will."

"Ja." His three-fingered hand seemed as accustomed to refilling cups as the good hand that clutched the ivory while, in stony silence, he kept eying me with a mistrust unbecoming a brother. 'Brother' was a fact he was about to learn for I had determined to speak plainly.

Yet, still, I continued sipping and swilling the brandy, drawing out the seconds as if unleashing an eighth day of creation, the sweet fumes of liquor blunting the rank smells inside the hut. I'd not bathed in some weeks, and my nose assured me that for Gregor, bathing might stretch back to a warm day in October, even September. — In truth, these small matters were unseating my resolved intent! The moment I'd longed for lay upon me and, of the hundred ways my mind had replayed it, I knew not how to begin! Never had I envisaged the aged exterior, the gruffness of this old man before me, his gnawing impatience as I hemmed and hawed, his mouth and jaw slanted into the bearded cheek he pawed at with two stubs.

I steadied myself, set down the empty cup, looked up and, however poorly, began: "The Groote Kerk of Amsterdam, I was baptized there, Gregor. Baptized, like all the family." His eyes stayed fixed on me, yielding nothing.

"I was named for Pieter Willem Van Doorn the First, — our paternal grandfather. — No, wait, hold!" Gregor's eyes flashed dark fire and his grappling stubs solidly clenched my arm. "Let me finish—"

Again he obliged, and finish I did. I recounted the death of his mother and remarriage of our father to my mother, the loss of our grandfather, Pieter Willem I at sea in 1647, and all the family history as it had been drilled into my head. I named eldest brother Willem II, and the year of his sailing, then added: "Yourself, sailed in 1666."

His agitation mounted with each new revelation. The purplish veins of his neck pulsated as though about to burst. "Dirck—," I hesitated upon seeing him wince, his expression softening.

"Dirck...," he mouthed in a cascading whisper. He reached out his good hand seeming unaware that he'd tapped my own like one might a child's. What else might so shake a man such as Gregor, one so hardened in body and mind, if not that, here in the interior wilds of North America, an unknown brother should thrust himself into his presence and speak to him of his beloved brother, Dirck. I kept silent, drawn in by the faraway look in his eyes.

He went back to fondling the ivory, turning it from side to side in the waning light. His hand shook so. What significance such an object might hold for him beyond our kinship, had not once crossed my mind. His whole self seemed bound up in what I had come, little by little, to regard as a family trinket—a curiously clever trinket to be much treasured but, nonetheless, an ivory without portend. Why did it so engage his mind? Why, instead, did he not acknowledge me, his living, breathing brother, here and present!

I grew calmer with the thought that, unlike me, he had known what it was to have brothers. Moreover, the strong drink was making my head swim. And, the silence. Silence and silent. Silent except for the clicking of his remaining teeth was my new found brother. Wordless.

At long last, I tired of watching him wallow in his thoughts with less regard for me than for catching at a fly and snapping it in two. I rocked back the bench and started to rise. Only then did his eyes refocus. "Oud gek, Oud gek!" he hissed, leaning back and forth. "Old fool, old fool," he repeated a second time, then slammed his fist on the table. When, finally, he roused himself to look at me, those fiery eyes seemed not unfriendly.

What an ocean of time a look can encompass in crossing so small a table. His lips groped to form a thought known only to himself. At last he got up and stood hunched in the doorway.

"Fool he may be, Pieter..." The deep long sigh he emitted in pausing over my name did not end there, but seemed to resonate across from meadow to forest. "Ja, fool he may be—yet, were our father but an ordinary man, not you, Pieter, nor I would be here in this New World."

I'd listened, snatching at each soft-spoken word and, then, like a new morning I sprang up; and with both arms lofted and spread wide, I clasped him around. "Gregor—" I clenched his shoulders easing us both out the door, outside where we could stand tall and I could gaze in full light at his face. It was a good, hardy Dutch face weathered as any seaman's by years of braving all manner of diverse elements. I could imagine that face as a young face—had he been accustomed to the life of a wealthy burgher, a face set off by a high ruff collar and velvet doublet, a fur-lined cloak with slashed sleeves. But, no, here stood rough clad, bristle-bearded brother Gregor, in oh so solid a flesh. And just so we stood. Entrenched.

Years later, I would recognize that embrace as the moment the heavy burden of my embittered, half-crazed father slid off me, not in hatred, not in anger; no; I would come to acknowledge his mad obsession with a measure of love and a full measure of gratitude.

"So! let me look at you, Pieter." He pushed me out at arms length. "Dirck, yes. Most, you resemble light-haired Dirck. I even was struck by such a thought when first we met, although his fair hair must have darkened more like your own since I last laid eyes on him. Dirck, I always called klein broeder. Well!"—His jocular whisper came with a clout to my back—"You shall be "little brother" now, Pieter, or 'Peter', as you wish."—This last he said shoving a well-made fist into my forearm. "And if by some ill chance we should be off on separate journeys, be assured that I am much, much gladdened for having met you, brother."

Brother. I had no words. Not before nor since have words so caught in my throat or moistened my eyes as did his uttering this one simple word of acknowledgment. Brother.

Over a light supper of poorly fried fish—this brother of mine was not skilled in culinary art—our talk came not so easy. Our display of such heartfelt emotion laid on me, and I supposed on him, a restraint of sorts. After all, apart from blood, we were as strangers, and our politics open to question as regarded his French leanings and, so it would appear, the British in regard to mine. Once the despised enemy, I could no longer deny my having a—yes, a fondness for that round rogue Sir James, nor even for his unmated Albany 'widow'. At length, Gregor spread furs on the floor for me and I laid down, for I'd been adamant in refusing to take over his cot.

Sleep that night was fitful. True, I had much to think on, pumped up as I was in pride and satisfaction at having both found and been accepted by my ouderdom broeder, Gregor. Moreover, by morning, he would return with me to the Ojibwa encampment to meet Audaîgweos and, after that? I did not know. But turning over these thoughts in my mind would not long have kept me wakeful. No, it was Gregor, himself. Once settled into his cot, he tossed and turned and snorted and honked and droned on nearly to daylight.

I acted with unaccustomed restraint, sparing him a solid knock where ere it should land, convincing myself that one sleepless night ought to be tolerable for the sake of bedding down on the hut's floor with my own brother.

Chapter 32.

The Welcome

We ate a gruel of some sort, a tasty mixture of grains, berries and honey and, warmed by a thimble of brandy, set off while the snow was still hard, and could make time drawing Gregor's sledge. The sledge was packed with his winter catch of shorttail weasels and, he instructed me, other weasel family members: minks and martens. Raccoon skins and, lastly, those well-cured bear hides emerged from the hut to complete his catch. Traps were strapped to the sides, like the one I'd seen to the west of the hut. "That one's been scrubbed up since you last saw it."

"Ja," he said with a slap to my back and a chortle, "I left it behind hoping to catch a curious 'broeder' in it."

"And, you did! I hope you're as good at catching beavers!" At this, a slight smile etched his face, but one I thought more moody than merry.

The sledge, itself, a sturdy construction Gregor'd made to suit his own needs, in no way resembled the large carved sleighs with upturned ends and smooth runners designed to be pulled by horses. The bed of Gregor's sledge was about the size of a small cart, but did have a pair of well-planed runners to ride the snow, and could be pulled by a single man. But, now, he had my help. Each of us gripping the tow rope, we snowshoed side-by-side, drawing the sledge behind us.

Sometime later that morning, but still below the ridge, and at some distance from it, Gregor ordered a stop, and took a few steps to the side. Fresh tracks marked the snow. "An old and hungry black bear," he said with pleasure. I know this bear."

Now, having seen any number of tracks throughout the winter I, too, would recognize these as bear. And, with scarce vegetation to be had, until into spring, I too would conclude it a hungry bear. "But," I asked, "what tells you it is an 'old' bear?"

"Observe the foot prints more closely. Their size show it to be full grown and, moreover, the wobble indicates a bear not so steady on its feet as when younger. Note, also, Pieter that the front footprints are weighted to the outside; if to the inside, we'd have us a female."

"Ah, Gregor, so much I can learn from you. Doubtless, you know as well all there is about the ways of the beaver."

"I do. Although, for some years, now, I've left them alone. For the tribes."

I did not ask more. I wasn't sure I wanted to know more about some kind of generosity on his part that made beavers the province of savages in The Trade.

We'd no sooner reached the Ojibwa surround, when the boy-without-a-name spotted us and came running up. The suspicious glance he lit on Gregor turned to fox-like eagerness when it caught the heaped sledge we had in tow. The boy stood in a proud stance, small back straight with legs apart and stiff as sticks. "Big Lake Person, Nind ijinikas!" he announced, wanting me to know he'd been given a name, 'strong name like father'.

Others of the clan, old and young, having gathered around us, stared at the bearded stranger by my side more than at the sledge. I spotted Animiki crossing up from the water's edge, bare of foot, and hands clutching fist fulls of tender green shoots wet with morning frost, the first offerings of the coming spring.

I beckoned her over. "How am I to understand the name of this oshkiabinodji?" I asked of her, while making a friendly salute to the boy at my side. His sharp intake of breath betrayed satisfaction at being singled out as 'young man'. She, lips puckered in a tight bow, looked obstinately at the ground. This was not the first time I'd encountered a native reluctance to utter a name. I kept silent in expectation that, if I did so, she would reply in some fashion. After all, wasn't I about to declare the white stranger who'd returned with me to their camp 'brother', and in so doing, name him?

Time seemed to be the savages ever present commodity, and idle words not their custom. But, in her own time, Animiki's eyelids did lift and her lips did part.

"He named Eye-Of-Flying Crane." She faced me with an elfin lift of her eyebrow. "Big Lake Person, know what mean?" she challenged. I had a fair idea, but through prior encounters with this forest nymph of varying moods, I knew that more was to be gained from her translations than from my interpretations. I played dumb.

"Name mean, boy grow to see big plenty. See 'much', you say?" Not waiting for me to confirm, her manner stiffened. Plainly, she was seeking words, and soon I understood, more or less, that my presence being forbidden at the boy's naming ceremony, it was just as well I had absented myself these last two days. I stifled a smile that her sincerity cost her such effort as she, bending to retrieve her morning pickings, hurried off. In the meantime, Gregor had gained Eye-Of-Flying Crane's affection by presenting him with a slim knife, one better for whittling wood than for serious undertakings as I would come to learn.

My enthusiasm in presenting my brother to Audaîgweos was more than matched by the latter's unabashed pleasure at Gregor's gifts. His lordly demeanor of chieftain displayed a boyish greed as he admired the iron trap and Gregor's demonstration of its workings.—Indeed, Gregor in responding to the crowd's excited gasps overacted the part of trapper for, in showing how the tightly coiled spring snapped open and shut to instantly kill muskrat or beaver, he narrowly missed losing a third finger!—This brother of mine, I would discover, was as practiced as any savage in a display of outward bragging and, likewise, could disguise any signs of inner alarm. Audaîgweos made him a gracious welcome and, as days passed, others of the Ojibwa followed his example in bestowing courtesies upon him.

Late one afternoon, we were summoned to the wigwam Audaîgweos shared with Nagawa and Animiki, but without his wife and daughter present. Once again, I was awed by the imposing figure of this Ogimá of the Loon Clan. He sat cross-legged on a bearskin, his broad, hairless chest greased to a shine and covered with ropes of polished bone and turtle shell. His upper body reclined, slightly, as he drew deeply on a pipe of an elbow shape, a slow funnel of smoke coming out his mouth. Trade tobacco, they knew from gifts or exchanges but this tobacco, concocted from the bark of red osiers and autumn-red leaves of sumac, gave off a mild, sweet smell. Audaîgweos passed the pipe to Gregor seated at his left, after which it came to me. Now, only once had I visited a place of worship of the Papists, and that the Cathedral of Utrecht—a cathedral still in possession of its nave and tombs, altars and ritual vessels—I think the intent of the burnt offering of priests in expelling incense from a thurible to be not so different from the intent of savages in smoking and passing of the pipe. The calm pleasantness I felt on this occasion was no doubt aided by the intimacy of our small, congenial number, where I, who sat nearest the flap of the wigwam had only to open it the width of my hand to let in a stream of cooling fresh air.

Upon returning the pipe to him, Audaîgweos showered upon us a litany of polite sentiments. Gregor and I made pains to return his effusive compliments by extending wishes for the prosperity of himself and his people.—Rather, I was pained. Adulations fairly flowed out of Gregor's mouth. My growing stock of rudimentary words was still shy of lofty phrases.

The greetings over, Audaîgweos pointed to my neck. He wanted to see my nábikawágan.—Certain it was, he recollected my refusal to relinquish my ivory on the night of my 'initiation', that occasion of our first meeting instigated by Sir James on behalf of Sir William Graves. This time, I obliged by laying it across his extended palm.

"You," he said, pointing next to Gregor, "show nábikawágan."

"No," Gregor nodded, shaking his head, "I cannot. There was one other, but I was not given it. The other nábikawágan left my country with our father's eldest son, Willem."

A second talisman? Always, I had thought mine to be a singular object! I had apprised Gregor of the meeting on the Mohawk River when I'd made showy rotations around the campfire, and of Audaîgweos intimating he'd seen my ivory before. I watched, now, as my brother made a hand sign and circled his own neck, asking Audaîgweos around whose neck he had seen such an ivory before.

Scarcely altering his squatting position, Audaîgweos held up one hand and, with his other hand clutched, not one, but two fingers. "One time I see nábikawágan on dress of white man. I was young. Small boy. White man big like you, hair on face like you. Not dress like you.—Or you," he said, gesturing at me. "White man wear hat. Big hat. Color of night sky."

"Where? Where was this?" Gregor's voice, soft and whispery as usual, held a quiet trace of urgency. We had no need to question one another to perceive the other's thought.

"Far. Far away. My people bring winter furs to shore of Great Water. Great Water home of whale and many fish. We know white man want our furs. My father teach me to look with my eyes closed, yet see into white man's eyes.

"White man offer us tobacco and wampum beads. My father say he want more. Big Hat laugh. He take off nábikawágan and hold up for my father to see. When my father reach out hand, Big Hat put nábikawágan back around own neck. My father angry. Refuse to trade with Big Hat. Then Big Hat signal. Men of Big Hat bring many warm blankets. My father trade furs for tobacco, beads, and many many warm blankets." The smile that crossed Audaîgweos's face did not escape us as he spoke of his father's shrewdness at besting Big Hat in the trading.

"The man with the Big Hat, Audaîgweos, did he come on a ship? A ship like this?" I pointed to the image of *Der Vogel de Nederlands*. The old leather face looked from me to Gregor.

"Enh-enh," he nodded. "Ship same. Face same way."

Astonished, I demanded to know why he had not spoken of this before. Why he had withheld this knowledge from me. Did he think our attachments to family less than their own?

Audaîgweos grinned, broadly. "Time to speak of Big Hat is now. Now when brother come."

"When brother come! You knew of Gregor? All this time you knew of my brother, Gregor?" Dumbfounded, I fought to control my ire at his duplicity.

"Not know brother, Mashkodé-pijiki," he said, calling me again by name of the horned buffalo. Know brother, now, when brother come. He reached out and drew back the flap of the wigwam. "Look. Young onimik," he said, pointing to a spruce sapling. "One day, young onimik will look old like Grandfather." This time, his hand pointed toward the tall, sweeping spruce tree near the sapling.

The lesson took and I regretted misjudging him. Audaîgweos was not one to deny hope or spread it falsely. It was at least certain that at eighteen, I did not resemble Willem nor Gregor but, perhaps, would one day look like our grandfather, whom Audaîgweos remembered as Big Hat. Gregor clutched two fingers as we'd seen Audaîgweos do, asking him if there was a second time that he saw the ivory. His answer was unsatisfactory. "In dream" was as much as he would say, signaling that our talk was ended. We thanked him, then departed from his wigwam.

The last shreds of the lowered sun stretched out in darkening hues of red and purple across the great bay. We stood, companionably, my brother and I, looking toward the horizon where the ice sheet lay still visible. Water ran free along the shoreline, for now, but a strong gale would surely drive the ice sheet landward. But another matter was uppermost in my mind.

"What of this other ivory, Gregor, you said was given our eldest brother? I knew not of it."

"You heard Audaîgweos when he said 'ship same, face same way'. The ivory our father gave Willem as the eldest, faced east, the direction of Grandfather's earlier travels to the Spice Islands. Yours is west-facing, Pieter, and is the same as our grandfather wore on every later voyage save one, and that his last."

"Ah, Gregor, and I thought your brain addled upon seeing our family talisman, again, that you should mutter the ship faces west."

"Not yet so addled, klein broeder. I've no doubt that our grandfather commissioned the second ivory from a shipmate among his own hands, perhaps a clever tooler, ship carpenter, or surgeon. He was a tall, powerful looking Dutchman, was our grandfather, Pieter; nobody trifled with him on or off the ship. For all his size, he'd rove up and down the mast like any sailor. Often as not, he took upon himself the first watch to be alone when Venus lowered on the horizon. He once told me that the study of planets and stars when darkest night covered the ocean was an occupation he followed from his boyhood. I like to think he envisioned himself on a return from the islands—Ambon or Melaka—as setting off in a direction he'd not yet sailed, a new voyage even as the world itself was expanding in The Trade. Does it not seem so to you, Pieter, that he would desire a new likeness of his ship? One carved to mirror the new direction Der Vogel de Nederland was to take him?"

"Had I only but known him!"

I remember well my outburst. I was unaccustomed to letting out words to match my feelings of deprivation, feelings felt so keenly. Grandfather was the icon adorning the altar of our family and, I alone, had no visible memory to reverence. "Gregor," I said on regaining my composure, "is it not strange that Father made no mention to me of this being the second ivory, especially his having given it to me?"

"Why strange with so strange a father? Put it to rest, Pieter."

Very soon, I would have no choice but to leave off wrestling over matters past or present; such ruminations needed a more idle mind and body than the days ahead afforded. The time for leaving Winter Camp was fast upon us, and pressing occupations engaged Gregor and me. The loading of his store of furs that we'd transported from his inland hut had been done in haste, and would need careful rebundling. Mending of clothing, repairs to equipment, seeing to adequate supplies of food—much hard work needed our attention.

My pondering, however, did not always cease when I fell abed at night. Before giving way to sleep, my mind often dwelt on Andrew Markham's claim to having seen my pendant in Portsmouth, the observing of which Sir James had dismissed as 'poppycock'. But if true, Markham could only have seen the ivory given to Willem, and on my eldest brother's living person or, if, as presumed, Willem was dead; then, God forbid, the ivory must have been wrested from his body by foul means or simple avarice and traded and transported to Portsmouth.

One night, feeling foolish over so futile a waste of good sleep, I laughed, outright, as one might do when the mind is active and twists about with this or that thought to keep sleep hovering at the mind's edge. Gregor grunted and rolled over, inquiring into the reason for my mirth.

"It occurs to me to let the dead sleep without regret, that Andrew Markham sleeps in his watery shroud all the better without his having known."

"Having known what? Come, come. I hope you disturb my slumber for better cause than mouthing a riddle."

"Don't you see? Markham died without knowing that a savage Ojibwa Ogimá here in the hinterland has powers of mind far superior to his own. Think on it, Gregor. Audaîgweos, when he was but a child marks the orientation of a ship carved in ivory and Audaîgweos, who has never even sailed on a ship, still, all these many years later, remembers that it faced 'West'."

"Ach, you have a good heart. Also, you have a roving imagination. Now, for the health of our bodies and a night's peace, klein broeder, you will put both to rest."

Chapter 33.

Spring Breakup

Ice on the Bay of the Huron broke cracking and booming into a fine, if belated, spring. Shards exceeding the height of a man thrust up along the shore toppling and transforming it into castles of jagged spires. Just as the ice was sufficiently melted or was blown far enough out to sea, the whole encampment made preparations for departure, and with myself and my brother among them.

Birch bark canoes, refitted or newly built, straddled shore and water, and were being loaded with bundled skins of many prime beaver; and also wolf, marten, and otter were in plenty. Gregor and I had earlier bartered for a canoe from Nuganash, an old and toothless Ojibwa named for his success as a boy 'hunter'. Though not new, its bark the color of yellowed parchment was well sealed. Moreover, the canoe was larger than most, and so pieced out in its mid section and around its higher curved ends. "A good sign," said Gregor.

"Yes, and the rib tips are well fitted and its lashings pliant and snug," I added. So, well satisfied with our observations, we had us a vessel in trade for one looking glass, a half measure of beads, and Gregor's spare awl.

We were making a final check for the stitching of each seam and gore before loading, when Animiki, with scarcely a sideways glance, walked on by. "Why is Little Thunder so quiet?" I asked, and stepping toward her, made a friendly gesture of patting the top of her head. She recoiled from my touch as though I'd slapped her.

"Animiki—I meant no harm."

"Big Lake Person touch small dog. Same way."

I laughed good-naturedly at her rude retort as she padded on down the shore, her shoulders crimped by the bundle humping her back as she headed toward Audaîgweos. He, standing alongside White Feather at the water's edge, seemed to be overseeing the work, allocating their bundles of furs and supplies women and children dropped off for the men who were loading canoes. I went back to placing poles down the length of our canoe to guard its bottom. Of course, the brief exchange between Little Thunder and myself had not gone unnoticed.

"You made her feel insignificant."

"What? You side with the little wretch!"

"You hold out a scrap, klein broeder, but that one, I think, is wanting the whole bone."

"What nonsense, Gregor, this talk of dogs and bones. I've never mistreated her. If anything, I've treated her with special fondness."

"Fondness for a child, no?"

"No—Yes! Of course, child. What else?"

"What else, indeed," he whispered, averting his grinning face while setting-to the stowing of his bundled furs inside our canoe. In answer, I wrested a bundle of provisions and made as though to doff it atop his head. At this, one bushy eyebrow rose up. "I am right, I believe."

For so short a time, a brother, and already he'd become fond of needling me,—while, the fickle ways of one small Savage perplexed me more than did her elders! But having had a stint at finding my own way in unknown country, I was not eager to repeat going it, alone; my brother's jesting I could easily ignore or return in kind.

We would travel light, having only Gregor's cache of furs, our shared provisions, and our own belongings to stow. Thus, we made known to the males working nearby—rather Gregor did as my elder—that we had an excess of space in our canoe, and could lessen their burden by taking on some of their bundles or an extra passenger. His remarks drew all of their attention. One swarthy face after the other looked at us and then to one another. Yet not one of them replied. Had they chosen not to understand? Gregor's knowledge of their language, in many ways, bested my own. When an Ojibwa word missed its mark, he'd speak in the Ottawa tongue, or some other. Roundabout or no answers at all were common among Savages, still I was curious enough about what Gregor would make of so perplexing a circumstance to ask him.

"Mistrust, perhaps,—or uncertainty."

"Or," I said, "they are showing themselves off to be the independent creatures they are!"

"Not dependent on us, yes."

Gregor was right. They did depend on one another. And wasn't it the same elsewhere, though on a monumentally different scale than in this wild land? Why, each town in my country reveled in its independence! This was displayed for all to see in the building of our town halls, each town trying to outdo the other in its architectural efforts. Amsterdam's massive stone palace of a hall had no rival. Not even Dordrecht's nor Gouda's much celebrated edifices; although, assuredly, the citizenry of each would argue the winning merits of its own.

All in camp on the Bay of the Huron were to leave with the understanding that, if separated, we would come together at the place Audaîgweos called Bow-e-ting, the same meeting of waters that French traders and priests called Sault Ste. Marie. I supposed this arrangement to be because of the falls and rapids to be encountered, and Audaîgweos had concern for our safety. Upon expressing this, Gregor gave me a pained look.

"The Ojibwa refused to share our transport, no? They may suppose that we, with our light skins who speak French. think we can out-haggle them over the best price for made-beaver. They may suppose that our craft being swifter, we will reach the fort at Sault Ste. Marie ahead of them. They may suppose we have a change of heart, and that we sell all the furs — theirs, if we carried any, as well as our own; then take ourselves north instead of west to Gran Portage.

"And, most likely of all, Pieter," — Gregor raised up from securing the last of our belongings, and made sure he had my attention. "More than likely, the Ojibwa may suppose us to capsize and drown. For them, carrying their own is a matter of protecting their own."

"Hah! you underestimate Audaîgweos's shrewdness, Gregor, as well as his trust."

"No. Quite the contrary. I am familiar with dealings of the French, the English, the Savages and, I might add, the Dutch. In matters of trade, I have learned to trust none of them farther than my eyeball. Nor should you, Pieter. Nor, should Audaîgweos." I felt he wronged Audaîgweos with his supposing this and supposing that, but of the others I felt less sure, less sure even of Hadakotana whose nature swung in unsteady rhythms as did Animiki's.

A brisk, chill dawn on the day of departure turned as the fog lifted, unfolding a morning radiant with promise. The very air breathed excitement as, one-by-one, we took our places and sped into formation. Our flotilla of fifteen canoes traveled west by northwest upon leaving the bay of the the Huron; only, on this voyage with myself at the bow, my own brother steered from the stern.

Ahead of us, Ojibwa men knelt fore and aft with women and children huddling between them, blanketed like so many bundles. From a distance, they appeared as bright red and blue splotches moving through sunlit water. Time seemed stilled. And, heady thoughts took advantage, teasing my brain as we paddled onward in calm water.

My spirits soared to think that I, the fourth and youngest of my father's sons, might yet succeed on all counts! Hadn't I already discovered one brother? What was to stop me from securing a fortune in furs? From returning in triumph to Amsterdam, clicking along the cobblestones and rounding up and over the canal Centraal in the festooned carriage of Burgemeester Van Laer. We'd ride right up to the Halls of Trade! with dignitaries plying me with questions, seeking my counsel, merchants begging my services....

The fine picture of myself dissolved as quickly as a foolish dream. Gregor, whose voice was husky at best in conversation, all at once began raising up such a racket! It staggered belief at how, on water, his normal whispering now echoed like a solid, if not a perfect, basso profundo. Nor would this be a one-time performance. At times as a starter, he'd let out one of those lully-loo, lully-loo madrigals. More often, he'd begin with a lusty sea chantey. Then, I'd join him as we drove our canoe with all the fervor of seaman breasting the North Atlantic. The Savages, who had chants of their own, took to this Waiâbishkiwed, this white-man brother of mine. And, Gregor seemed as at home with them as with me, his own brother, and full content.

As for me, my blood rushed to the promise of reward as I anticipated the end of what Sir James called my apprenticeship. Why, not many days away, lay Sault Ste. Marie and, then, after more days, we'd come to the lake our Ojibwa were fond of calling Kitchigami, the same Gregor said was reported to be the greatest of all these great lakes.

We paddled, harmoniously, in the early days. But as hours and days churned on, we sang less and, more often kept silent. Indeed, we had cause to be silent. For a sudden encounter with a series of narrows, riddled with fast-moving currents, forced upon us instant mastery of hidden undertows, else we perish in our paper boat. A different circumstance of that stretch came as we we rounded a mass of rocks,—a most particular point of rocks, rocks assaulted by unceasing swells, water pitching and tumbling all about. With each fresh battering the rocks moaned and sighed so as to shatter a man's wits. No sweet singing sirens of Odysseus, these! No,— whitened knuckles gripped my paddle; and full glad I was when, the strangeness of that eerie sound fell behind us, and we made a traverse; whereupon, a narrow strait swept us into the long channel we would follow to our next destination.

Interminable destinations. As one succeeded another, I came to expect that Gregor was sure to enlighten me, about one thing or another, before we would reach a next stop. Always he began with "Did you know, Pieter..." Upon this opening query of sorts I, facing forward, need give but the merest shake of my head. And, always it was enough to set him going, interrupted only by him asking, Could I hear? Was I listening? A 'yes' ringing back over my shoulder his instruction, on one such day, began:

"Did you know, Pieter, that twenty years, ago—it was the year 1671, a great assembly took place at the Sault Ste. Marie? Whole bands of tribes, Ojibwa and Cree from the west, Assiniboin from the far north, even Foxes from the lands of the Ohio and Illinois—They all came. They came and put the totems of their clans—those are their seals, you know—to a royal proclamation. Now, the proclamation was read on the site of the Falls of Ste. Marie and, be assured, such was done with much fanfare. Do you know what that proclamation was, klein broeder?"

"No."

"The tribes came bedecked in their feathered bonnets and best blankets. They, stood alongside white traders dressed in fringed deerskins who set their shells a-clanking like the Savages, themselves.—Now, don't you suppose that this gathering by the Falls of St. Mary must be very fine as the representatives of the French king descended upon them? Those French heads, held aloft in long curled wigs, embroidered doublets swelling their chests, and velvet cloaks trailing their breaches; they must have stunned the Savages, no? Of course, black-robed priests led the procession, carrying upraised crosses and singing the Te Deum. But do you know about the proclamation, itself, Pieter?"

"No."

"At that meeting all the lands draining from these great lakes—the one we just left and the one greater than this we'll enter, next. Imagine, Pieter,—all these vast lands were sealed over to the protection of His Royal Majesty, the King of France. Now, this, klein broeder, took place only one year after another Royal Majesty, Charles II of England, claimed the land and sea called Hudson Bay and all the rivers flowing into it!" Gregor made a deep sigh as his paddle drove in deeper. "Now, can you begin to see why we Nederlanders who dare to tread the waterways of the Trade must exercise circumspection."

At this, my mind rove back to the sham Charter I had confiscated aboard ship, provoking such rueful consequences. My brother was unaware of my misdeed, and I wished to know about this need for circumspection in this hinterland. "Do we Nederlanders not have an advantage, Gregor? We are not so well known for penetrating beyond the coastal settlements of this land as are the French and British."

"True. Yet, we may be caught between their wars as are the Savages."

I said nothing more. I had nothing to add to Gregor's gloomy prognostication. I had no natural ties to France and none to England, but did think he overstated the Dutch position vis a vis The Trade to rank us with the Savages. Still, I don't deny that the inglorious welcome accorded myself and Jan by our countrymen along the River Hudson added fuel to his charge. And, as I considered further that our own Fatherland sent its sons off to the New World, leaving them to fend for themselves as with my three brothers,—my own venture I looked upon as a more 'private' undertaking; I told myself to be content: Whose loyalty I would uphold, only the future would reveal, and I would always be a Nederlander.

Yet, I was not content. Why should I wrestle over confused loyalties to nations, to territories, to trading interests? Was a spectral Sir James prompting my thoughts? Gregor's lectures? No! So, enough of these old men!—my father, Sir James, and now Gregor. I fingered my tailsman, relieved and laughing so, I slammed my paddle stroke.

"You are mirthful, klein broeder! It becomes you, and gives me a bath."

"Ah, Gregor, It was nothing. I'll take more care not to wash you with my mirth."

But it was something. I would come to look back upon this being the time when my resolve shaped of itself: Loyalty was mine, and my own to bestow. I would tender allegiance—to The Trade—where and when it was deserved.

Chapter 34.

Arrival at Sault Ste. Marie

Out beyond the great bay and moving in a westerly direction, the Ojibwa flotilla kept to the mainland side of a chain of small islets and barren extrusions of rocks that formed a natural breakwater. Being the fifteenth and last in the long line of canoes, Gregor and I, dutifully, kept pace to keep them in sight. My muscles grown lax over the winter felt the pull, longing at times for a third to spell us at the paddle, but such discomfort would lessen—and others take its place—as league upon league, we followed up the margin of this sheltered waterway. The low coastline and ashen hills had a mild look that gentled one's spirits. But almost daily, a temperate westerly pushing at us by morning, whipped into a squall by mid afternoon forcing all shoreward until the storm would abate.

On one most memorable afternoon, the winds struck with such sudden force our canoe turned halfway around and was haplessly riding a current driving us straight toward a shallow, rocky cove. Instinct sent both of us leaping over the side. I grappled to hold the bow with Gregor trying to steady the stern as the canoe, hit by cutting crosswinds, shifted about like a child's toy on a string. Fighting for footholds on moss-covered stones wedged between sharp-edged rocks, surely, only the grace of our Maker kept us from being overturned and our craft dashed to pieces as we strove to beach the canoe inside the cove. The cove, one of those many islets demarcating the channel, lay hidden at an angle with no chance of sighting our Ojibwa companions.—In the midst of salvation, does one fret over a temporary parting, a deluge that soaks the body through and through, and when thoroughly chilled is pelted with hail?

Rain and hail ended, but strong winds raged on into the night and, when morning came, fog made land, sky and water all one. We pushed off as soon as the fog began to lift, expecting to discern below the ascending gray mist, moving shadows of canoes in the distance.

Had any been within a quarter of a league. we would have sighted them. Failing to do so, assured me that for the time being we were separated from those who knew these waters best for, on asking Gregor what lay ahead by way of stopping places or landmarks, he said, calmly, "Little better than hearsay, klein broeder, but little is more than none."

"We should come upon them by noonday," I said. "It is certain that in our lighter-laden canoe we will do so." Gregor made no answer. "Often we slowed, I added, just to keep from overtaking them." His uncustomary silence drove me to persist. "Gregor," I called out, expectantly, "we may even be first to reach the Sault Ste. Marie!" I glanced back at him, then, and the one eye I could see of that craggy profile seemed to be studying the shore.

"Maybe, yes. Maybe, no."

His response while not surly, did not encourage me to venture more of my opinions. Anyway, his generally affable spirits often took most of the morning to rise up, but then would last through early evening. To be uncommunicative at times was his right; his bodily humors dictated his predictability even as my own humors accorded me the more venturesome a spirit. Of course, he was my elder by twenty-four years and was slowing down some. Yet, how gratifying that, unlike our common Father, good humors marked the lion's share of my brother's waking hours.

In threading the channel between rock and shore, one that widened and narrowed and twisted by turns, demanded constant vigilance. Especially, from myself in the bow, my eyes straining minute on minute to detect any sign of reef or shoal.—Such an unequal match, a paper boat against the treachery that lurked under so benign an appearing surface. Other dangers loomed from rocky pinnacles that jutted up from the seabed, sending out the devil's own whirlpools, ones that frothed and surged and, should we stray too near, would churn us about like the disk of a grindstone. Then again, the channel as fickle as a nightmare slipping into a soothing dream, would set before us a stretch of serenely placid water.

One such blessed relief came about just as a fortuitous sun broke through gilding wavelets of clear water, and exposing from its base on upward, a sheer granite cliff. Etched in burnt reddish colors, where eagles nested in its rock face, we gapped at outlandishly drawn figures, primitive figures whether human or animal and, one in particular, that for all the world looked to be a tortoise.

"Clan symbols," Gregor said. My mind pictured some ancient artisan swinging across the rock, suspended on a length of twisted vines to serve for scaffolding.

Nearing noon some days after our abrupt parting from the flotilla, I sought Gregor's attention, pointing out hazy movements on the shore at some distance ahead. "Terugkeren! Back, back!" he shouted—It took but a moment's distraction to send us spinning. In the same instant, I made a shield of my paddle and, straining every muscle, backed us off from the reach of the swirling vortex. (Though, in truth, it was Gregor's mastery in the stern that cleared us just shy of its sweep.)

By God's grace, we had escaped another danger just in time to be thrown into the next! We were set now, closer shoreward, close enough to make out the painted faces of savages hieing into canoes. I mistrusted the look of them. "Sooner our cargo be swamped than plundered! This is Huron country, is it not?"

A rod further, Gregor whispered, "Ready your arm.—Ottawa."

I bent to uncover my long gun. Just as I was in the act of snatching it up, I felt a burning, a stinging kiss of fire. An arrowhead had lodged into my shoulder. Another grazed my skull and hit the water. Gregor, fully occupied in manning our canoe unaided, was steering us with all possible speed to the far side of the channel.

I kept down, raised up the barrel, took aim and shot among the six canoes shoving off from shore, hoping to create a show of force more than to kill. The ball struck, splintering one canoe skyward and setting its screeching neighbors racing toward us like foaming dogs. I reloaded. We having cargo, and they without, gave us little chance to outrun them in a chase. I blasted a second, then a third. More bodies now floundered in the water than drove their canoes. Gregor, meanwhile, having put us across to the barrier rocks on the far side of the channel, we made a dash for an opening that would put us into the strait, and out of the channel.

Gaining the open water of the Lake of the Huron uplifted my spirits, doing its part to somewhat dull my throbbing shoulder. When I had breath enough to speak, I ventured my opinion that this lake must be Champlain's mer de l'Eau Douce. I felt confirmed, because beyond the barrier rocks we were met with a fair east wind. We lost not a second raising a sail in hopes of heading off a squall; still, we hugged the shoreline as close as we dared.

"We'll rest as soon as we reach a farther island, Pieter."

"Rest? You think to prepare ourselves against an attack?"

"If need be."

As he was wont to do, Gregor was always ready upon any affair, small or large, to impress upon my mind how things stood in this country. He did so within the hour, after determining that for the time being, we were not being pursued. I doubted that a pursuit, if it came at all, would be from that band of shaken Ottawa, and said so. Gregor shrugged.

"Do you know, Pieter, why the Ottawa figure us for their enemies?"

"No."

"Why should they not? The Ottawa control the trading of furs through their bartering with interior tribes, and then transporting the furs on to Canada, to trade with the French. Why should they welcome us who interrupt this traffic? Ach," he sighed as he continued, "there's no shortage of enemies here or elsewhere." During a long pause I imagined he was considering how to explain such a web of alliances,—nor was I disappointed.

"Christianized Iroquois to the north stick with the French,—the Jesuits converted them and so what's left of them are treated as allies. Now, the eastern Iroquois—and that's most of them—hold an animosity of long standing against both their separated brethren and against the French.—Any peace among the Six Nations and the French is of short duration! Besides, the eastern Iroquois are supplied by the English and our Dutch, neither of whom—there is ample evidence to believe—discourage the terrorizing of mutual enemies by the Six Nations.

"And the Ojibwa?"

"The Ojibwa act the part of neutrals, and are friendly for now— and will be if they can be supplied with weapons and powder to keep their enemies at bay. More and more, the Ojibwa furs wend their way up to traders at the bay of Hudson.—Now, that's a broad land for you, Pieter, with a bay leading right on into the Atlantic."

"So, just whom do you side with, Gregor, savages allied to the French or to the English?" I awaited his answer with some trepidation.

Between rope and sail I could see his lips and jaw rotating as though studying the question.

"I take my own side, klein broeder. And to survive into a twentieth year, you'd best know the factions you are up against before pitting Peter against Pierre!" I smiled inwardly that his advice should so echo Sir James's: Know when to trust one's friends, and when one's enemies. Yet, when one is heavy into the fray of a skirmish occupying both mind and body, I knew full well that such niceties of reasoning felled one's intentions like ripe apples blown from the tree.

We were in no immediate danger. I was reluctant to slacken our pace to rest when we had calm, fast waters and a clear enough sky with the sun showing in and out of the clouds. "Let us forego stopping to rest, and make all possible haste," I urged, leaning hard into the paddle should he need proof of my readiness.

"No, Pieter. We stop just ahead. I will tend your shoulder. Tomorrow, we take the river that leads to the rapids of Saint Mary's Falls. These falls bury strong men by the score. We are only two. Besides, we face, also, a portage a third of a league." He was adamant, he was in the stern, and by the time we reached the island and beached, I admit to feeling myself well satisfied to quit the canoe as I was becoming feverish and chilled by turns.—And, I hoped, most profoundly, that Gregor could show more skill as surgeon than he did in barbering his unruly head of hair.

Gregor drew out his knife; I tried not to grimace and failed. He lost no time grasping the shoulder of my deerskin shirt, then slitting it. From his pouch, he drew out a flask. "Drink," he said, hefting his best French brandy my way. I sucked it down like mother's milk. He pointed me to a stout tree trunk, saying, "Embrace it as you would a woman," as one dark rheumy eye narrowed with a sly grin. I had yet to ask my brother what he knew of the female sex. Just then I did not indulge my curiosity, only fervently clenched my teeth while his fingers felt around the arrowhead, then slit my skin to probe for its barbed tip. My flesh raged like hot fire as he dug it out, and for certain I knew Gregor Van Doorn of Amsterdam and the New World made a better barber!

Drink and fever would put me into a deep sleep, sparing me any lingering thought of avenging Ottawa, who, thanks be to God, did not show that night. Nor was there any sight of them or any other savages when we continued up the lake in the morning.

No, our visitors, as the sun unfurled the horizon that morning, announced themselves first, in a high whining tremolo rising from the south. Then, a deafening quiver of wings shaking overhead darkened the very sky. The flight of geese in the design and swiftness of nature's arrow, in mere seconds, seemed gathered overhead in their untold numbers, yawping and honking and, just as quickly, faded off into the distant north. Such seasonal displays of flight may seem no matter to remark upon, unless one's self be that speck on open water who gazes upward, sees and hears, nay feels! those magnificent frigate birds that scour the limitless ocean—or gazes up at a multitude of wild geese with wings flapping as fast as heart beats in crossing a great broad lake.

Later in the day on the St. Mary's River, we heard a bellowing sound that began as a low roll, then built steadily into a rampaging, roaring thunder transforming into Sound Incarnate. All sound, so as no other sound was heard, sound that quelled all thought inside one's head. All whiteness, too, was that Eternal Engine pumping torrents of snowy water into plunging cascades, over and over and over again in ageless repetitions. How could one know if awe beguiled we two mortal brothers, or if mere necessity drove us as far as men dared; for at the last moment of choice, we swerved like a sickle to bypass those tumultuous waters bearing so gentle a name, Ste. Marie.

Nearby, savages lived in scattered, lodge-type dwellings, and seemed friendly enough. Perhaps, unlike some, this was because their land afforded good soil for growing their maize, and they had large ranging forests to hunt in on both sides of the river. To the south was the mission site of which Gregor had spoken, where twenty years earlier—almost to the day—tribes had ceded land to the French with rituals before a wooden cross and formal ceremony before a post marking the rule of the French King. (Both cross and post, Gregor told me, were said to have vanished as soon as the French dignitaries had taken their leave of the assembled tribes.)

I looked on at the confluence of these frothing, mad-met waters, at the tall-masted forests abounding with furs for the taking; one would respect the vision of any man who claimed it. But it was Robert Cavalier, Sieur de La Salle who claimed it for Louis XIV. The lunatic French king, I thought, must be not a wit wiser than our

Dutch patroons to let his army of coureurs de bois wage his fur wars, wearing animal skins and subsisting little better than the poorest of the patroon's peasants.—I found myself, as my journeying into the interior persisted, tending to rail on inside my head over this or that matter. After all, when no frightful dangers threatened, one was captive to endless hours of boredom in a canoe. Such grave disputes ceased to feed my head when, finally, we shored up, hid the canoe, and once again set foot on land.

There, along the marshy start of an uphill foot trail, another enemy manifested itself as visibly as any blood-thirsty royal army. Mosquitoes swarmed and attacked, full force! Heads bowed and arms bound around our packs, we plodded on up that hill, chins buried in our necks. The mosquitoes, preferring the damp bottom land kept with us, until about midway on the trail, they gave quarter to a fierce armada of black flies. The trail, we expected, would lead us to the Fort of Ste. Marie.

Gregor, in front of me, tilted his head back at me to ask, "How-is-your-French?" His lips formed a narrow slit to keep from being the receptor of a mouthful of filthy swarming pests. If, I wasn't doing the same, I would have laughed at the picture he made, his buffalo robe riding high, and the weight of his pack shifting as he entombed what flies he could between cheek and shoulder.

"Equal-to-the-trade, my French. More-should-it-be-needed."

As my mind was cursing those damnable flies, my attention caught on the figure of Gregor. Would any think us brothers, I wondered. My own crop of hair hung closer to my shoulders than my ears, nor had I arrived on this continent so fully bearded. No matter, we were close to reaching the higher part of the hill. There, a welcome breeze fanning the trees was keeping flies to more tolerable numbers, and I asked what I'd refrained from asking before: "Do you question my facility in French, our having shared the same father?"

"Lay a caution on that facility, Pieter. Speak as little as possible, and speak only in French."

Ah, New World entanglements; they were muddling my brain as much as did the Old World's. I better understood, now, why Sir James dismissed politics with a shrug of his fur-greedy shoulders. And, not for the first time, did I recall the words of the French priest, Jean Baptiste. His maxim "Each man for himself and God for all," to my way of thinking, bespoke the practical mercantile mind more than it did the religiously zealous.

Chapter 35.

The Mission Priest

Situated a short way beyond the hill, Gregor and I came upon the Mission of Sault Ste. Marie, a squat building sided in bark. It was a French enclave now some twenty-three years, but bore remnants of a stockade. Audaîgweos had referred to priests who came among the Ojibwa as "men of the waving cross."

No waving cross was in the hand of this priest at Ste. Marie. Like an earthbound scavenger clawing at the dirt was this priest with unshorn white hair bent low over a hoe, his wide sleeves tied back, black skirts buoyed up and flapping in the breeze. Humped over and intent he was, toiling in his patch of garden.

We hailed and approached closer. He raised stiffly. The face of an aged man turned toward us with a body still able in spite of advanced years. He peered at us through watery, pale blue eyes that, once they took us in, brightened in welcome. For all its trembling, the palsied hand he thrust out to us each in turn felt hard as stone. He introduced himself as Charles Albanel of France and the Order of Jesuits, here to serve the Mission of Ste. Marie.

"And we are the brothers Van Doorn come from Amsterdam. Our business is at the Fort." Gregor's French, though quite proper was too soft and whispery for an old man whose hearing seemed not so keen.

I broke in to say, "We supposed the Fort to be close by."—We knew this to be so, it being the practice of the French to keep a confessor at hand to cleanse the immortal souls of their own people, be they officials, soldiers or traders; their greater calling be to convert heathen tribes for God, thereby making them allies in New France. Gregor's eyebrows shifted, but he said nothing. Nothing was needed for me to know I'd said enough,—our sudden, but close daily confinement had bridged many lost years of understanding.

"To the north lies the Fort." The priest made a sweeping gesture of his arm off toward another wooded hillside. "The distance, it is not so great over the land, but travel to there should you wish by water, you must surmount currents and rapids most deadly, most robust.

"You will rest after your tiring journey? You will sup with me? No bubbling sauces, mind you. Little more than whitefish and bread.— Better for the stomach these plain foods in my declining years." Eagerness for our company shone on his face as he led us around to the rear of his small church and then to a smaller cabin, talking and gesticulating with outstretched palms, his elbows tucked close as I have observed sufferers of the rheumatism to do.

"You will honor me with what news may pass between our countries, yes?" His invitation being so sincere and our desire for an honest meal its equal, we accepted at once.

A small group of natives had gathered around as we spoke. 'Pére Charles,' as he bade us call him, appointed several females to fetch the supplies and provisions still left in our canoe, while two broad-backed young males who left with them were to bring up the vessel, sparing us the need to recover it, ourselves, before rejoining our host. Thanks to Gregor's largess, we would be able to bestow gifts of thanks to secure our safety among these savages whom Pére Charles selected to escort us on the morrow.

Seated at a small table with Pére Charles at the head, myself to his left, and Gregor on his right (and with no wind to blow away my brother's words) the priest and my brother went back and forth about their travels in the New World. I had stories of my own to tell, but held back and listened. Conversation stopped when a pock-marked servant came in to serve up the meal. Her unabashed deference toward the priest bespoke her baptism. The broth of fish and herbs had fine flavor, and, together with a dark bread crusty with thyme and caraway seeds, made a hardy meal. For a time, only the clink of spoons busied us, and my eyes roved from my soup to the lit candle centered upon the table. Soon enough, they flitted back and forth from my brother to our host. The old priest had not a spare ounce of flesh; his translucent skin stretched smooth over his cheek bones, crinkling only when he smiled. Nor did advanced years seem to diminish his presence as an excellent host.

"Your reputation is not entirely unknown to me, Pére Charles..." Gregor's words were barely uttered when his hand flew to his throat and he began gagging and gurgling. I rose up, ready to pound his back. But he, as though well-practiced, threw back his head and, reaching down two fingers, neatly extracted a fish bone from his throat. He made a slight gesture of apology, sputtered a bit and continued. "You were an emissary, I believe, for quelling Iroquois tribes, Mohawks and Oneidas. Is that not so?"

"Oui. And, you, Monsieur Van Doorn, you were quartered where at this time?"

"I was in or around the environs of Albany two years, until 1666. We Dutch having been subject to British rule by then, two years, I was not impartial to intercepting furs from more than one Frenchman who chanced to wander in among a band of Mohawks; furs exchanged in forfeit for lives."

"Ah, and so, a free merchant you were." At Gregor's nod the priest went on. "I was, what you say, an emissary; an emissary on certain occasions with my nation's military excursions, that is, I was a bearer of words. Now, I make you a riddle: Words and the fighting,—can you say which comes first, the war or the words?" Gregor and I stayed mute. Indeed, I doubt Pére Charles expected us to respond. He, having finished his scant portions of fish and bread before us— ours being thrice the size of his own—he sat back with the callused fingers of one hand folded over the other. For a long moment, his eyes seemed locked on the ceiling; assuredly, his thoughts were not on the mold-stained rafters as he traveled back in time:

"I made the long march with Alexandré Tracy—the Marquis was sixty-three then, when we left Quebec. And I was but a young man—in my fiftieth year," he said, with a wink in my direction. His drift into humor was brief, and he droned on without stopping, transfixed by memories about the French campaign to storm the castles of the Mohawks and break up the Iroquois strongholds. My thoughts turned to White Feather, who would have been a child of, perhaps, three or four years, when Tracy's army—some thirteen hundred strong left Quebec. But Pére Charles was the first from whom I learned how the French army marched south, and from Lake Champlain moved on into the Valley of the Hudson, hauling cannons and sounding their drums.

"We learned too late; we underestimated our enemy. These spies of the Mohawk, they follow our movements long before we reach their castles. They see our French cannons and as we advance, the savages—they are not deaf!—they hear our drums rolling, all the more clamorous as we advance, and so, non marveille that the savages they all flee! They leave their wooden castles by the Mohawk River and all their strongly-built palisades they leave, making no defense. The Marquis Tracy, he give his soldiers orders to burn each deserted village." At this, the priest's white head moved from side-to-side but, whether from disapproval or no, I could not determine. It was from White Feather I learned that while the Mohawks fled before Tracy's well-armed soldiers could find them, that their burned-out villages and crops left them with no grain for winter, so large numbers of his people died from starvation.

Father Albanel's summation went differently. "Long years of peace follow after the Iroquois retreat, and many of the heathen, I baptize."

"But, surely," Gregor intervened, "God's work was not without interruption, Pére Charles. Were you not, yourself, imprisoned by the British?"

"Oui, you know that, too. Two years they hold me captive in London.—As though myself, a humble priest should have much influence in the politics between England and France. Still, God's work took a strange turn. In London, I persuaded Sieur Pierre Radisson—'certainement', you know of our famous adventurer; I persuade him—remember he was a man of France; that he should cease to render services to the British at the Bay of Hudson. And, at least for a time, he did so, but poor Monsieur Radisson, his political loyalties were inconstant."

Now, I listened up! Sir James had spoken so emphatically, and I, being so eager to hear all, had paid strictest attention at the Widow Spence's when he intimated to Sir William Graves that it would serve the interests of The Company to have their French conspirator well paid; that his facility in treating with the Indians was deemed indispensable to The Company's interests at the Bay.

"Some thought is fast upon you, my young marchand de fourrure?" Pére Albanel looked at me, questioningly. And he was right. I was filled with the thought that Sir James's 'conspirator' might be this same adventurer 'Radisson' of whom Pére Albanel spoke.

"That is so, Pére Charles. I was thinking that for so vast and wild a country as is this North America, those men like your so adventurous Sieur Radisson—who play across it—there cannot be so many of them."

"Perhaps it is your desire to be one of them—a player?"

Did he mistake my meaning? Was this wily old priest suggesting I join the French or was he merely acknowledging what he took to be a young man's dream. "My meaning was this," I added. "Some names stand out. Like the French Cartier, the British navigator Henry Hudson—who, before discovering the Great Bay named for him that you spoke of, explored the River Hudson for our Dutch Amsterdam Company in the Halve Maen. Of course, there are also the voyages of your famous Champlain, and..."

"It grows late, klein broeder. Let us leave off with this history before our good host tires of us. We will leave early for the Fort, Pére Charles."

For once I was glad that Gregor took charge, my being none to certain where next to take myself in launching further this discussion about players. Besides, the French priest, even if he knew, was not likely to satisfy my suspicion that this Radisson whom he had advised, perhaps aided, was once again playing the side of the British.

Gregor made our host a generous present of brandy, and arranged for natives to transport our belongings to the Fort where Gregor and I would go on foot come morning. Pére Albanel led us to our lodgings, blessed us and, after bidding him a fond goodnight; at long last we collapsed on two well-made cots to sleep the sleep of the dead.

Chapter 36.

The Great Carrying Place

"Oui, Messieurs, they come but they do not trade. Only one young man of them, I give fusil de chasse for seven made-beaver. One tall sauvage, he not look like others, he speak in Anglais. He ask after two white men. When I say none stop these many days, he tell others. Much talk there is among them. I not understand. Soon, they all leave, go Le Gran Portage."

"The tall one, did he wear a white feather?"

"One did, oui, Monsieur, oui."

In this way, we learned from the trader at the Fort of Sault Ste. Marie that our company of Ojibwa, along with White Feather, had come, and gone on without waiting for us to arrive. For two woolen blankets, a quid of tobacco, two traps, and a brass kettle, we had, earlier that morning, secured the services of two of Father Albanel's Indians. "They assist you," the good priest told us, "in the long portage from the Sault to as far as the southeast bay of Le Gran Lac."

So, with the trade goods mentioned, we also parted with the canoe that had serviced us since leaving Georgian Bay. Indians at the Fort Ste Marie would repair damage to the joining of its gunwales and reuse it. In exchange, Gregor and I would now set off with a newer, three-fathom canoe to face the long stretch of big waters that lay ahead.

"They must believe we capsized and drowned," I said, upon our leaving the stockade. "And all because we stayed the night on that out-of-the-way infernal islet!"

"Perhaps," Gregor said, indifferently. "Your shoulder is healing?"

"It heals." At the moment I felt little gratitude to my brother for his overly cautious administrations that caused us to miss our rendezvous. Besides, even with a second and third brandy, I'd scarcely slept, and having listened to him snoring the night long, I was out of sorts with him, altogether.

"They could not know of our skirmish with the Ottawa, Pieter," he said, softly, nor of our laying over on the island at night.—Here, carry these, I beg." He handed me our paddles, and he having the lion's share of our purchases, I took them without answer.

He tried another tactic, thinking I suppose, to assuage my disappointment.   "Consider this, klein broeder. They may have concluded, that having found me, you had no need to stay with them, to learn their ways. Instead, would it not seem most natural to keep company with your brother? Necessity draws them further into the interior while, for me, curiosity alone leads me to Le Gran Portage, far away from my destination.—And, of course, for the pleasure of your company." Sarcasm being not habitual with Gregor, I accepted his last remark at least as half truth; it served his purpose. I opened my mouth to apologize for my ill humor, but he was quicker.

"Tell me, Pieter. Walk with the Loon Clan a minute, and tell me this: Why should two white men such as us travel so far from home?" I made no answer, certain a sermon in the guise of a question was forthcoming. "Well might they wonder, Klein Broeder! They are not fools to think we spy on them to discover new hunting grounds.— Ach, and it is true enough."

My own behavior I thought more complicated than my brothers, since my journeying with White Feather and the Loon Clan was hardly my own doing, even if my desire for furs was as Gregor said.

"Now, how might their procuring of a gun play into that, Pieter?"

"It plays not at all," I said with finality, hoping that a short answer would satisfy.

"How so?"

"You were there, Gregor! You heard Hadakotana, his aching for a firearm is no secret. No, I say, White Feather—Audaîgweos—Hada—Animiki—they know me better than to think I would cross them. Sir James, after all, made a bargain with the Ojibwa. White Feather, himself, acted as his intermediary. They agreed to take me with them into the interior. And I still trust them to fulfill that bargain."

"They bargained to take you, Pieter, but not me."

"You are my brother!"

Yet, even as I gave assurances of their trust, I felt tremors of doubt as I looked out over the placid village and beyond. A lean savage, naked but for a loin cloth, leaned out from a rock ledge holding a spear longer than himself. Whitefish—scores of them—

leapt in the raging waters below. Not just fish, but game was plentiful in this ancestral homeland of Ojibwa peoples.—And it was so for generations, Audaîgweos would have me understand,—"until white men come." But to me it seemed one could spot game or fowl or fish wherever one trod, and would forever in this land overflowing with forests and water. Yet, Audaîgweos seemed to believe that nature's wealth of sustenance would be declining. Still and all, savages were eager to trade all and anything for goods we white men provided! Then again, a general uneasiness was borne out by their people moving further inland.

I, too, had reason to feel uneasy. I recalled Hada's sullen expression on the day we departed the winter encampment, and of Little Thunder's turn of behavior. Long Smoke, who had imagined herself grievously wronged by me, would surely see herself avenged if I met with mishap. To the likes of the Loon Clan, old injuries stuck like fresh burrs to the flesh from all I'd observed. Would they think themselves avenging a past wrong if two less white men failed at penetrating the interior? A fine Christian sentiment it was 'to turn the other cheek,' but revenge was and is the common code among the mass of humankind and, among the savages, taken to exacting heights. Somewhat shaken by my doubts, I was left with an uncertainty whether those many politenesses the clan showed to our face, would be tendered to our backs.

"What do you really know of the girl, Pieter?" His question came at me, unawares and I wondered to where he was leading.

"Animiki? She befriended me, taking my part as translator, interpreter—and she seemed willing—perceptive even, yes, perceptive about my needs for, say leggings or moccasins—such things. And, to show my gratitude, I'd make her a gift of a needle or comb—some small token in return."

Gregor's thick eyebrows bunched together hid the bridge of his nose, but not the quizzical look that sat on his face. Lest he draw me out further, and I wanting for sometime to question him about his own concourse with women, I turned our conversation to himself. "You've never spoken of Matilde, your mother, or...

"I have a wife."

I gaped in astonishment. "You've not told me before! Why? Do I have nephews and nieces, too?—You've not been back to Holland,—is that not so, Gregor?—Ah, but you were some years in the colonies."

I ran on foolishly, unwilling or unable to accept the true meaning behind those steady, unyielding words and the level glance he laid upon me. Some moments it took until, my emotions having wound down like steps of a spiral, I could speak in a settled tone. "She is of the country, then, my schoonzuster?"

"Ah, klein broeder." There was fondness in his whisper. "You do learn. Yes. my Marta, as I call her, is Cree. She would give me four babies, but just one lived past its first year. Knute is now five years, and a strong fine lad."

"Why are you alone, Gregor, don't you miss them?"

"I miss them. Our home is to the north of Georgian Bay. For some winters I have come down to set my traps. I set them at some distance from the Cree villages and in this way do not take what should be theirs alone. I am kept away most of the winter, and so I built myself a little shelter—the hut where my klein broeder found me. His deep set eyes held warmth and even his heavy beard did not hide the smile that lit his face.

I clamped my hand on his. Such sentiment took me unawares, but I found it in my heart to say, "If your Marta comforts you, Gregor, I am glad."

My spirits quite restored, I chose to educate my brother. "What are our added days of travel to see what few white men have seen, Gregor,—the largest of these inland seas!"

"I profess myself as eager as you, klein broeder, to discover what lays beyond Sault Ste. Marie."

"Only one, perhaps two white men are said to have witnessed the wonders of this great sea with their own eyes; yet, Gregor, as you must know, its immense size and location have been well recorded." He, not picking up the bait to tell me he was familiar with Les Voyages de la Nouvelle France Occidentale dicte Canada, I restrained from reminding him of the leather-bound volume of Champlain's, published in Paris in 1632, residing in our father's library.

By mid afternoon, we reached the end of our portage and reached the large bay at the eastern-most end of Albanel's Le Gran Lac, the same known to the Ojibwa as Kitchigami, and what Gregor says French traders are wont to call Lac Supériéur. Here, our two escorts left us to return to the Sault. The bay being fairly calm with just enough breeze, we were not long in putting up our little sail and, making a traverse of the bay. We made camp before nightfall on a point of land to the north, and could have caught enough of the large whitefish to feast on the year through, so plentiful they were.

Then followed days of skirting the lake's northerly rim westward, keeping as close as we dared to a low lying, exposed shoreline of few trees and ponderous granite shelves ranged like the backs of sleeping elephants. Or, again we gazed upon high cliffs rising straight up from the water. We skimmed across small bays, and rounded larger ones, many flumed with contrary currents. Wild white rapids spilled out of innumerable rivers and, each being for me, nameless; I dutifully assigned them one on my poor rag of a map with names such as Caribou or Fox, Cascade or Tempest to signal notable features along our route.

Though most various was the shoreline of this sea, sheer cliffs dropped down with a regularity that afforded little or no chance for securing a stopping place. Only little better for resting, were those remnants of an ancient cataclysm, those massive boulders thrust up at wildest angles. And, over all, we had only to raise our eyes to find the pall of dark forest that ran to heights and depths we—but two specks on this forbidding landscape—had no means nor desire to penetrate. Surely! there could be no need to construct fortresses in this God-forsaken country when every moat of river, lake, or stream held so forbidding an access to the land!

How pleasant, then, one day to come upon beaches of cobblestone planted there by a kindlier Deity for our respite. Smooth stones as round as the eggs of the ostrich spilled along goodly stretches of the coast, stones in pale tints of pink, green, gray or blue. And farther back, up above the banks, climbed stately white birch forests, rank upon rank of trees that were budding into green leaf. It was in one of these large inlets, we spent our fourth night after leaving the Sault. Full grateful we were to have such a shelter! At such moments, I found myself praising and thanking the God I seldom sought—unless, as during a night when rising winds shrieked on so, we feared for our safety, a prayer slid from my lips in crawling from under our canoe so as to move it, and our blankets, well up from the reach of advancing water. —Just so our fifth night passed.

I woke to quiet and the mournful cry of a loon taking up the call of its lifelong mate. Countless numbers of geese honked across a white-gold horizon and, my eyes adjusting to the intense light of the new day I saw, not far off shore, a flotilla of canoes speeding by. I wanted to rush to the water's edge and shout out a friendly halloo, but obeying a wiser instinct I roused Gregor. His judgment mirrored my own.

We moved cautiously. As always in setting up camp, we were as careful as the savages, themselves, to hide our presence from any who might attempt to steal our cargo and ornament nearby trees with our scalps. But here, now, was a fine day and, after the time we'd lost, I was impatient to be off.

"A half hour more, Pieter. Let them gain some distance, and then the weather holding, we'll push on through the day and, if blessed by a moon, on into the night."

The sun was above the water when we finally took up our paddles that morning, and for the next ten hours, we scarcely put them down. In rounding a point of land, the shore lost all gentleness. As far along this coast as we could see, stark granite outcroppings jutted in and out like Herculean hands washed by waves, waves dashing up against outstretched rocky fingers then ramming back into their crevices. "We'll look for a stopping place, early. We'll not risk our being stranded on water, tonight." Gregor's words struck me as lacking in, well,—courage.

"No," I said, heatedly. "The sea itself is glass! So long as we stay without its margin there's nothing to fear." I put up my paddle and turned full around to face my brother. "And, I remind you, Gregor, tonight promises a full moon."

"I say, we'll not risk it! Even should Jupiter and all the stars rain down light as bright as the full moon, this sea, great though it is, still lacks the ocean's depth and no chart warns us of its reefs and shallows."

Among the lessons one learns in paddling a canoe day after day is that persisting on in anger is a poor waste of energy. "Then, Gregor," I said more amicably, "let us stay on until we come to a safe harbor or, if not, think again on which peril to choose, treachery we can see or treachery we only fear."

"Well spoken, klein broeder."

The moon did rise into full and glorious gold and on those silvered rivulets of waters, I felt content with our bargain made easy on a windless night. Later, but only approaching a second hour, piney tops of trees showing first, we discerned a long spit of land lying ahead.

So, before the moon had quite risen to it full orb of whiteness, we were heading into shore to spend our seventh night enroute, caution having won out once again.

A chittering of voices woke me in the morning and, scarcely moving, I stole a one-eyed glance out from beneath my blanket. Three savage urchins stared back. They were pointing long sticks towards us as their fathers might brandish spears. I greeted them, hoping Ojibwa was their tongue. Gregor spun up, looking all the more the fierce "bear man" for being half asleep. The children froze, momentarily, and before they could flee to rouse their people, Gregor reached into his pack and offered them each a hard maple candy from the sweets he'd procured at Sault Ste. Marie. The smallest of the three, and least shy, stepped up and snatched one piece, and would have taken the other two as well.

"One for each of you," he said in, what he later told me, was a dialect of the Cree language. He chatted with them for a time, causing much laughter as he showed them tricks. Gregor, having worn his pantaloons this morning, stuffed his hands inside their wide Dutch pockets, making them magic pockets for naked boys. Finally, after shooing them off, and the little beggars scurried and stayed away, he turned my way. "Let's make ready to leave."

"Hadn't you noticed while you entertained the urchins, I was making preparations to leave and am ready? We've delayed long enough."

"Ach, so we have."

"No breakfast this morning."

Gregor nodded agreement, and after stowing our belongings inside the canoe, we got back on the water. We'd gained a fair distance before, in glancing back, I sighted a number of savages of both sexes gathered at the water's edge, waving as though to draw us back. They showed no signs of hostility, but to have returned and lingered would entail loss of precious time and goods, "gift" goods we would surely have greater need for in days ahead.

As the morning wore on and we neared groups of large and small islands, we sighted numbers of canoes moving in a westerly direction. Their numbers seemed to signify that a common destination lay beyond. Waves thrust high against the rocky margins of these islands and, from the height of land and the dense vegetation of some, we had cause to wonder if, in ages past, the islands might have been joined to the mainland. We threaded a slow and cautious passage with little conversation. But high on the rock face of one of the largest of these islands was such a glowing, red-orange brightness, I raised up my paddle. "Gold! Gregor."

"A vein of copper, Piet."

"Ah, copper, yes. I should have known." Though Champlain, himself, had not been this far into the interior to see with his own eyes, he'd reported being told of a copper lode and of the savages who mined it. As described, they would take lumps of copper and, after melting it, spread the copper out, and then with stones, smooth it into sheets. When, finally, we came around the end of this 'copper' island, parties of canoes were still within sight, and we entered a wide sweeping bay.

Indeed, a gloriously wide and sweeping bay! For this was Le Gran Portage. A magnificent bay!—one that curled into the land like an immense rippling crescent. One, that as we drew closer, looked to be cradled by stones and a beach of sand with intermittent fronds of waving grasses, to the back of which spread a broad clearing. Above the clearing, ramming the very heavens, lay yet another interminable reach of dark forest.

"Years hence," Gregor said, "this bay will be more than a gathering place for tribes. This will be the Great Gathering Place for The Trade from the North and East." I knew my brother for a pious man, but not that he delved into prophecy. Although, the bay did, most surely, inspire in me grand thoughts of commerce.

A half league or so ahead of our canoe, silhouetted in the path of the sun, five canoes of savages were racing for shore. And on drawing closer, we saw true evidence of this bay being the great carrying place. We counted some twenty or more canoes hauled up further on down the bank. One in particular caught my eye. It looked heavier, and greater by three places than Ojibwa canoes.

Gregor, perceiving the direction of my glance, said, "You are noticing that large canoe with the upthrust ends? That one is destined for Montreal." At his words, I felt a slight palpitation in my chest, the more startling because a once familiar sensation had quite diminished with each stroke of the paddle since quitting Albany.

Had I not, yet, quite abandoned the heavy obligations this ivory intermediary had laid upon me?

"The gifts, Pieter, fetch up the bundle just behind you." Urgency was in Gregor's whisper but not in his calm movements as we skimmed toward shore. I studied, clearly, what he had first seen, an assemblage of lean-faced savages were moving down the bank. To greet us? As we waded in, towing the canoe to the beach, I could not tell. They were Ojibwa, but not one swarthy face among them had I seen before. Nor among them did I detect one eye to call 'friendly'.

Chapter 37.

Guests Of The Bear Clan

Obeying Gregor's caution, I caught up a bundle of gifts we'd readied to placate savages and for the gaining of their trust. For ease of transport, these were mostly small items—beads, needles, knives, and such, to which we could add a blanket and a fine kettle. I lingered alongside the canoe with the bundle on the pretense of making a forced exit, should our welcome go awry. Secretly, I vowed to resist such a move. I saw no bow and arrow among them. And, we had weapons.

Gregor, drawing himself up to his most imposing height, raised his good hand in greeting, bowed slightly, and before any could speak, demanded that we be taken to their Ogima. Uncertain silence followed. The band of twenty or more savages—all nearly naked, stared at us or past us toward the bulky contents of our canoe. One savage with sharp, piercing eyes, sprang forward. He took a wide-legged stance, crossing his arms with elbows pointed west and east to the height of his chest. He looked me up and down with curious suspicion, then locked eyes with Gregor. No one spoke. A full minute or more later, he lofted his head over his shoulder in a signal for us to follow and, making an abrupt turn on his heels, set the bones strung across his hairless chest to rattling like castanets. A thin square of animal hide flapped against his buttocks as he started up the embankment. His cohorts flanked Gregor and me on all sides as we strode up the sandy bank, our rocky sea legs steadied by uneven clumps of sedge.

Through encounters since departing Amsterdam, I came to appreciate that the unknown makes the eye see one's new surroundings with greater clarity—and to make strange associations. In one fleeting moment, my mind's eye saw sloops and yachts sailing that bay while, above, lay a pleasantly inclined clearing bordered in linden and elm trees leading up to a tall brick house with latticed windows and green shutters open to fresh breezes. Only a moment.

For, as we and our escort gained the clearing above the bank, upwards of thirty bark wigwams were arranged in a large circle, their pole tops a-tilt like crossed hands beseeching airy spirits. It wasn't long before women and children, as was usual, streamed out to gawk at us, chattering as noisily as the pair of furious gray squirrels treed by a swarm of yelping dogs.

Our escorts, paying no attention to the commotion, steered us straight on through the assembled onlookers. They stopped at the east entrance of a long, narrow structure fashioned from tightly interwoven poles and dried grasses, then led us inside an interior, shadowy as dusk.

Ah, but once my eyes focused, what wealth! Skins of various fur-bearing animals, even the silky lynx, lay in piles the length of the lodge. And, never before nor since has so fine a display of beaver met my eyes. Light, coming in from both ends of the lodge, warmed the soft pelts to a dim, lustrous sheen. I quite lost myself in admiration — nay, this was covetousness.

By great good fortune, the most important persons among the savages fastened their attention on Gregor, not me. I finally snapped out of my greedy stupor to look from furs to bodies that were filling up the lodge. Nearing the end of the arrivals, with surprise and joy I spied the face of Animiki. She was standing among the females and she alone had a familiar face. None, not even among the row of men sitting cross-legged on rush mats in front, had I seen before. Whether Little Thunder caught my pleasure upon seeing her or even knew of my presence, I did not know. I glanced from one savage face to the next in hopes of seeing White Feather, Audaîgweos or Hadakotana. — Were so few of her clan present? I looked back often to the small figure wrapped in deerskins, but our glances did not meet, and how dispirited seemed her whole demeanor.

These hurried impressions ceased as soon as the conferring began, and I turned my full attention to the negotiations at hand — or so I expected them to be. Instead, Gregor launched into a flattering, soft-spoken exhortation. He heaped thanks upon the Ojibwa, esteeming them the greatest among all the nations, then thanked them for the great honor they bestowed on himself and his younger brother, their graciousness in receiving us, — whereupon he nudged my elbow.

On cue, I took a step forward and nodded first to one, then the other, until I had acknowledged each savage wearing a full headdress.

I stepped back and Gregor began anew. Oh, but had God given my brother an orator's vocal chords! As it was, an unnatural stillness settled in the lodge as all strained to hear that wind-whistling voice extol their wisdom, their frugality in the hunt and, based on no specified claim, praise their courage and bravery. Then, his voice rising to an eerie wail, Gregor bade them join his prayer to the Great Spirit who breathes upon all men. He wound down to the end, giving me my second clue: "We bring you gifts."

I grasped the bundle braced against my right leg, and with a princely flourish swung it before the Ogima seated near the center. He was made known to Gregor, then to me, as Wábijakwe, the famed "Grey Eagle" of the Bear Clan. Loosening the pack's leather strings, I drew out a brass kettle. An actor among actors was this kettle! In the half-light, it gleamed as though cast in gold. Satisfied grunts and moans emerged from all present. I paused until it was quiet, then drew out a blue wool blanket, spread it out before Grey Eagle, and with ceremonious wizardry, placed upon it strings of wampum— greens, yellows, blues and oranges. I finished by offering a long coil of tobacco to Grey Eagle, placing it across his upturned palms. He looked pleased and asked if we wished to trade. I, still rankled by my error in supposing "trade" to be the manner of my business with Long Smoke, hesitated but a moment. It was enough. Gregor, in his loudest whisper declared:

"We bring you gifts. We already have what we came for. White men before us told of this Great Sea, yonder." Upon which, Gregor wheeled sideways, arm extended toward Le Gran Portage.

Then, that devious Dutchman of a brother, as pompous as ever the English Sir James, thrust out both his arms as though to grasp the world, astonishing all,—most of all his klein broeder.

"We do not come to trade. We have seen, now, the Great Sea. We can return to our homes in peace and contentment and—'eternal happiness'"—or, whatever passed for such drivel in their tongue. What ailed that great shaggy head, I could not even suppose.

To his credit, Grey Eagle made a shorter speech than Gregor and offered us lodging. I wished to speak to Animiki, but an inner voice warned me, this was not the time. Her presence was nearly as bewildering as the stashed furs were overwhelming! Pipes were passed and, upon leaving, as the smoke cleared and the gloom lessened, I spotted Flying Crane, but no trace of our prior friendship lit that small boy face.

With Animiki and Flying Crane on hand, however, I felt some assurance that, sooner or later, we would discover the whereabouts of Audaîgweos and White Feather. The Ojibwa party had preceded us by at least three full days, maybe more Gregor surmised, since their canoemen had experience along Lac Superior's great coastline, its currents, shoals, and headlands. Our having been spirited away so quickly upon first reaching the great bay, even had I thought to examine the symbols on canoes drawn up along the beach, I'd not have had time to distinguish them as Loon Clan canoes or any other.

In due time, we were escorted to our lodgings, a wigwam furnished in the usual manner with a layer of cedar boughs over the dirt and a covering of furs. Shortly, a female stepped inside, and served us bowls of a hot steamy broth with bits of fish and a fatty meat floating on top. The old woman stayed on to watch, and cackled when we smacked our lips and emptied our bowls to express our enjoyment. Thanks to Gregor's foresight, we were spared the loan of their women for the night. Later, he told me of his "confession" to Grey Eagle that we had the manádapine! But, I thought, neither the clap nor scruples prompted his refusal so much as his utter exhaustion.

And what of me? I had a head full of questions to discuss! Why did he refuse the offer to trade? Why didn't he ask after Audaîgweos and the Loon Clan? Why were Animiki and Flying Crane among the Bear Clan, and what did their presence signify among a clan not their own?

My mind rumbled on and on throughout the long night forming questions that yielded no answers. Most nights, I learned to accustom myself to Gregor's snoring and, choosing an intermission, would slip off into sleep. But this night had not yet eased into dawn when— so deft and slight were the movements, it was only as a small hand clapped against my mouth and the tip of a blunt instrument pressed at my side, did I muffle into full awareness.

"Flying Crane kill Big Lake Person!"

The poor child. So brave but so clumsy an assassin was he. I let him prick my skin before toppling my body over to pin his unbloodied little fist. None too gently, I clutched his cheeks hard enough to stifle a scream; after all, he'd not had his name of "manhood" so very long.

"Flying Crane, we are your friends, I whispered. "Why do you want to kill me? You will tell me, yes?" I pinched harder. He jiggled his head to mean 'No'. Gregor lay so quiet, I knew he must be wide awake. I let go Flying Crane's cheeks and, grasping his hair, pulled his head back and ordered the defiant little knave to speak.

He did so in a kind of half whining, breathless Ojibwa which, if it made sense at all, I could not follow except for the word Bow-e-ting, which he repeated several times. All at once, either his courage buckled or he had said all he intended for he fell silent. Supposing Gregor was correct, I thought, and the Ojibwa did interpret our delay in reaching Bow-e-ting as betrayal. In that event Flying Crane could prove useful.

My Ojibwa was equal to explaining our skirmish with the Ottawa, and I did so. But for emphasis, I guided his fingers over the scab that scarred my shoulder. "Flying Crane, I know that White Feather spoke with the French trader at Sault Ste. Marie," I added, "and I know Hadakotana now carries a pâshkisigan, a white man's weapon." These and other facts of our whereabouts and theirs began to take effect. No longer was he rigid from stem to stern. He began to fidget, and I took his open discomfort as a sign that he was regretting his rashness and was accepting that I spoke truly.

"You turned Gregor's gift of a knife against me, your friend. I taught you songs." Did he stifle a sob? More likely it was the lift in his voice as he started to brag about his bravery in attacking "enemy of Ojibwa people." The sob turned real enough, though, when he told us he and Animiki were to marry into the Bear Clan.

"Marry, when?"

"Animiki after snow fall and grass grow. More snows before Flying Crane marry!"

"Where are Audaîgweos and White Feather?"

"Audaîgweos go home. Leave behind many skins. Gifts to make happy new family for Animiki. Bear Clan carry skins far, far away to trade with white men." Ah, the large canoe, I thought, the one Gregor said was destined for Montreal. I prodded Flying Crane further and asked again about White Feather.

"Audaîgweos say White Feather and Bear Clan go with white man."

White man! Surely, then, my arrival was expected, after all. I sent Flying Crane off before the camp should begin to stir. He scurried away like a hearth mouse before the housewife's broom. I wanted to mull over matters with my brother. His response only satisfied me that his sleeping had, indeed, been pretense.

"Let us rest while we still can. Give new thoughts time to churn inside our heads. As for Flying Crane, Pieter, that hatchling has better ears than sense. I was right when I gave him so dull a knife."

Chapter 38.

Grey Eagle Listens

Events following Flying Crane's disclosures were as though imprinted on my mind. No matter the danger accruing to myself, I determined to know how fared Little Thunder's alliance to a Bear Clan suitor, — that the child was not captive to some savage's lust or, equally appalling, the unwilling object of a marriage foisted on her from birth. (Of course, at the time, myself being one half of such an arrangement with Katrina, the irony of this thinking quite escaped me.)

I waited for the first glimmer of day to get up and dress. Gregor could sleep or ponder by himself in our wigwam! I was all impatience. I had to act. I would not wallow in a web of perplexities when I reached Gregor's advanced age! Always in the past, I found my thinking dull when my body wasn't moving, yet quick and equal to any encounter when I leapt into the fray. So! Charged I was in slipping out of the wigwam accorded to Gregor and myself that lay just outside the Bear Clan's compound.

All was still as I approached. Those wigwams, conical and ghostlike, and set in a broad circle, seemed as one with the gray light of early morning until coming just upon them. I could not be certain that those within all slept, and trod, lightly, stealing past one, pausing, and then on to the next. To raise the furor of suspicious savages before reaching Grey Eagle's dwelling would thwart my purpose but, in reaching the Bear Clan Ogimá's tent, I dared not hesitate. I took a wide-legged stance, inhaled deeply, and with head back my voice rang out in Ojibwa clear as a clarion in the cool morning air:

"I am Chi-o-ni-ga-mig A-nish-i-na-be, so named by the Loon Clan. I would speak to Wábijakwe, Ogimá of the great Bear Clan."

Silence. Then, like wings of vultures, flaps of tents flew open all around the circle. Sleep blankets dropped off bodies lunging toward me. Backing up closer to Grey Eagle's entry, I stared down my naked attackers, screwed my eyes into slits as narrow as their own, and my elbows poised with fists anchored on my hips, I sang out a second time:

"I am Chi-o-ni-ga-mig A-nish-i-na-be, so named by the great Loon Clan. I would speak to Wábijakwe, Ogimá of the great Bear Clan."

I'd stunned them enough to be curious or, at least, uncertain about what to do with one calling himself 'Big Lake Person Who Swims Like The Wind'. Suddenly, out of nowhere, three hothead warriors with throats a-quiver and their warbling growing louder, came upon me. I felt menacing pokes and probes and three sharp-pointed wood spears poised against my chest. If a measure of weakness would encourage them to tear me apart, limb from limb, I'd not give them quarter. "Béka!" I shouted, thrusting an upright palm to the level of their eyes. I had three pairs of eyes to gauge, and they only one in the uneasy seconds that followed. "Back up!" I demanded, again. As the warrior to each side of the savage in the middle stepped back a pace, I felt reassured, and more so, as I saw that he who remained was the same fierce-eyed Ojibwa who, after swaggering some, had led Gregor and me up to the Bear Clan encampment upon our arrival.

This time, addressing him, alone, as 'strong warrior', I repeated my demand. "Your great leader, Wábijakwe, must speak. Speak to Chi-o-ni-ga-mig A-nish-i-na-be." My last challenge flung and, having nothing to loose, I held my ground like the dominant dog. — Stronger he might be, but I was a head taller. I heard movements behind me. I did my best to mask my relief at the lowering of the spear as the Ogimá emerged. I turned to face him with head lowered and bowed stiff and solemn as would be due a king from his courtier. "I would speak with you alone, oh great Wábijakwe, you alone. You of great wisdom and the strength of your clan, must give advice to this white man." I paused to let the praise sink in before adding,"I make two requests."

I waited, hoping that deferential gestures outweighed my limited oratory, while Grey Eagle looked me over as though considering. Then eying me, intently, he made a downward motion with his hand for his people to move off. He seemed to understand that, out of earshot of others, strange and unknown requests are more easily decided. And I, knowing my speech to be doggedly slow in the Ojibwa tongue, would need to speak firmly, and so I did.

"Audaîgweos, Ogimá of the Loon Clan, has entrusted me, a white man, to teach his daughter."—Stretching the truth occurs, readily, when one speaks only simple words, and niceties of expression are beyond one's powers to voice. I expected Grey Eagle to protest and, getting none, went on.

"Audaîgweos has not yet been told what I am about to tell you, Great Wábijakwe. Audaîgweos does not know this: Enemies of Ojibwa set upon my brother Gregor and me. We kill many of your enemy. Maybe this many." I spread out the fingers of both my hands, and paused to let those words sink in and, while loosening my shirt, I showed him my scar. This was a type of wound he would recognize as made from an arrow. Grey Eagle's grunt gave me confidence in stating, more emphatically, that fighting their enemy was the cause of my brother and me losing time in reaching Sault Ste. Marie. That when we arrived at Ste. Marie, Audaîgweos and the Loon Clan had already departed.

"We were three days or more behind those Ojibwa who, like the Bear Clan, move on waters most skillfully. More skillfully than we white men," I added,—or some equivalent of the sort. Grey Eagle nodded.

"Even as Audaîgweos mourned us, thinking us dead in the water, my brother and I were working our way up the coastline of the Great Sea without the Loon Clan's wisdom to guide us. And so, Wábijakwe, these strangers to your land take much time to reach Le Gran Portage. It was our good fortune to find the Ojibwa Bear Clan; it was as though your Great Spirit guided us to this place."

The Ogima seemed a willing listener as did those, who having crowded closer, were in earshot of my words. Even the three warriors seemed less hostile than they did curious.—A curious audience is a great boon to an unpracticed orator, and with confidence soaring, I continued.

"You see that I am not dead in the water, Great Wábijakwe. I stand much among the living. Will you honor the wishes of Audaîgweos? Will you honor me, a white man who is to teach only daughter of the Ogimá of Loon Clan, the ways of white men, the ways of Waiâbishkiwed?" Now I had my audience craning their necks!

"Audaîgweos desires that the man who marries his daughter, be husband not just to his daughter, but husband of the next Wise Woman of the Loon Clan. He desire Animiki to be Wise Woman

like Nagawa, wife of Audaîgweos, is wise in the ways of the Ojibwa.—
Yet more wise than Nagawa. This is so. Audaîgweos desire that his
daughter be wise in the ways of the Waiâbishkiwed. This is so—" I
repeated in making my final thrust—"that Ojibwa people become
wise in the ways of both our peoples."

Still, all was silent. I hung on nerves taut as a line under sail,
awaiting his reply. And I waited.

When Grey Eagle was moved to speak, he said, solemnly, "You
say want more, Yellow Hair."—Ah, he, too, calls me 'yellow hair'. Or,
is every man not black haired a 'yellow hair' to them? However that
was, it was clear that this shrewd old eagle before me meant to hear
me out before he would speak. And, he was right. Animiki's fate was
not the whole of it, not by half. Flying Crane's revelation that White
Feather was to travel "far, far away" with a white man, had only one
meaning for me: I must be that white man of whom Audaîgweos
spoke and, with him not here to speak for me, I was determined to
leave with the Bear Clan. The second half of the mission Sir James's
assigned me would then be fulfilled!

Just then from the corner of my eye, I saw Gregor standing apart
and to the side of the crowd. He was a momentary distraction that
I covered up by a swat to my face to disperse a swarm of gnats. He
chooses not to interfere, I thought, yet I could read neither pleasure
nor displeasure on my brother's countenance.

Again, most respectfully, I bowed from the shoulders before
Grey Eagle. "Yes, wise Ogimá of the Bear Clan, I want more. I will
go with your people to the far away country." I waited and, when
he didn't answer, continued. "A high chief of the white man sent me
to travel with the Ojibwa and with the Mohawk, White Feather. I
learned many things from the Loon Clan on their journey to their
new home. Audaîgweos left before I could bid him farewell. He was
a good teacher, and I will miss him. You, Wábijakwe, will you honor
me by taking his place as teacher?"

Nothing of his intentions did that stoic face reveal. I was
accustomed to the withholding of secrets, and not only among
savages. And more time passed as I waited. His raised eyes paled in
the advancing light as he stared upward. Some minutes later, in a
reedy voice that softened his stony face, he looked directly at me. "I
speak with my people. You will wait."

"—One thing more, Wábijakwe. Tell me, where is the daughter

of Audaîgweos? Where is White Feather? I would speak with them, now."

"YOU, white man! Rush on like buffalo! Must you know all in the time of one sun? No. I say, you will wait."

"I will wait, Ogimá of the Bear Clan." With a sign of some sort to his people, he turned and went back inside his wigwam.

And, again, he was right. Had I been given to the practice of a flagellant penitent, I should have whipped myself for over-indulgence. Certainly my impassioned—and somewhat exaggerated—speech had won him over until I'd foolishly spouted out those last demands. I walked on past the thirty or more pairs of eyes watching me as though my head were newly shorn. And where was Gregor? He'd seen me put my case before Grey Eagle; of course his old ears may not have heard all that was spoken. In fairness, I supposed my brother owed me no explanations. Nor I him! After all, when I had the most need to talk, his silence drove me to act alone without consulting him! So I reasoned around, knowing that, had he counseled against confronting Grey Eagle, I'd have done so, anyway.   What   was done was done. And as the day progressed, I busied myself making small repairs to the seams of our canoe. Visible I was on the shore of that great lake to any who wanted me, and so I put ice to my thoughts and, obeying Sir James's admonition to watch and observe, passed a pleasant enough morning with seagulls swooping overhead in a cloudless blue sky. Now and again a hooked yellow bill plunged down to fetch up a silvery herring. The steady, low drumming in the background, I suspected would beat into a frenzy before nightfall.

About midday, I put my work aside to go and see what items were being traded with a tribe that had wandered in of the morning. I expected the usual hides, dried or smoked fish. Instead, I saw a badly dented silver chalice, and a helmet such as those worn by Spaniards laying claim to the America of the South! These were not for trade, but were being paraded as trophies. One savage wore a frock coat, it's once plush, purple lining to the outside. I saw glass beads of a deep lucent blue, and asked from where they came. These savages either did not know or chose not to reveal their source. I pointed in the four directions, and asked from which way the tribe had traveled.

"From Big Water."

My informant pointed not South, not East to the Atlantic, nor North to the Bay of Hudson; he pointed due West! I surged with excitement. "How much time to reach Big Water?"

"Many, many moons."

His response typified a people lacking our science of measurements. By words and signs and gestures I asked other questions about "Big Water." From his replies I felt assured that, as rumored, there must indeed be a water route through the interior of the Continent—all the way to the Ocean of the Pacific? If true, it must not be so great a distance. I went back to my caulking with another grand thought poking about in my mind, alongside helmets, Spanish silver—and the decisions of Grey Eagle.

I was bent over, making a last examination and well content with the tight seal of the pitch, when a voice like a thunderbolt struck:

"So! The Fur Baron of Amsterdam mends his own boat!"

Disbelief! Then so incredulous was I at the sound of that surly voice, I was like struck dumb, but only for mere seconds before, with unrestrained joy, I leapt up and clasped him by his shoulders, shoulders hard as iron. "Jan, Jan, so glad I am to see you! And more than mend it, I have paddled it, steered it, pulled, pushed, and overturned it! But, you, Jan, tell me of your journey.—No, wait. First I must tell you my great news. I've found a brother. Gregor—

"I know. I just came from meeting them, and so it is I sought you out."

"You met—them?"

"Your Mohawk, too. White Feather will accompany myself and my canoemen. We are to escort the Ojibwa up into French Canada. I can provide the Ojibwa protection. The Mohawk, however, if he values his life will not go as far as Montreal with us."

So White Feather is here, and Jan is the white man Flying Crane spoke of as going with the Ojibwa? Well, we will see.—My joy at our reunion was such that I could put aside my momentary lapse into jealousy,—perhaps permanently—if all worked as I willed it. Meanwhile, I would switch the direction of our conversation to settle the rift that had caused our parting.

"Jan, you know the truth about Mistress Mary Graves. My message explaining all, reached you? Sir James was to dispatch it."

"Many times since we fought, Piet, I have thanked my love-struck stars for our falling out—for it was that odd-shaped 'triangle' that decided my quitting Albany!—That, and the urgent coaxing of smooth-talking Sir James. Piet, there is no place in the life of a coureurs de bois for one so frail as a Mary Graves. I did not know it then. I know it now. But, friend, I had no message from you, and by the look of you, you've much to tell! You always outsized me, but now you've added shoulders of an ox to your height."

"An ox for me, and a bull for you, is that it?"

How good to cajole and chide once again. We talked and laughed, roughing one another, roundly, conscious but uncaring of those who ogled a pair of Waiâbishkiwed acting as lunatics. And in just such a gladsome mood, we headed uphill to the far side of the encampment to where Jan said we would find my brother and White Feather in counsel. It seemed, after all, Gregor had cared enough to discern my whereabouts, and had sent Jan to fetch me.

It was not the time for a brother-to-brother talk. I merely acknowledged Gregor by clasping his arm in passing as I approached another.—White Feather. From his hawkish forehead to his resolute chin, those chiseled features that seemed immobile but for his eyes, always intelligent, now kindled in pleasure, and his hand extended not to touch, but to assure me I was welcome. Seeing to Little Thunder's welfare and, to my most significant need; that is, accompanying the party onward to French Canada, could await the morrow.

Chapter 39.

Bear Clan Encampment

Flying Crane and other young boys of the Bear Clan sped across the field, imitating in game fashion, a serious battle that their elders engaged in to settle disputes among warring factions. Baug-ah-ud-o-way, was a furious game played with long sticks netted at one end with leather strings to catch and carry a wooden ball.

I watched Flying Crane flee across the grass, dodging the stick of one urchin and gleefully swinging his own with the carefree abandon of his feathered namesake. His shrill trumpeting cries gave credit to the rite of bestowing a name when the child was old enough to display a physical or mental trait to warrant it.

I found noteworthy, too, the freedom young children had to roam once freed from breast and cradleboard. Now, the cradleboard, itself, was a most efficient device for toting babes while, all around them, natural sounds and movements played on to keep them entertained.

To return to the point of this digression: As I observed and understood more, I came to respect various clan customs, such as their regard for children as belonging to all the clan's members. This was much in the way that they regarded the game they caught, the berries, acorns and other gifts of nature they gathered. These behaviors gave me pause for thought. In Nederland, indeed, and other countries of Europe, as well, one did not need to commit murder to be hung or branded or otherwise tortured. Why, in some provinces, a street urchin caught stealing bread from the baker or running off with m'lady's purse, could be flogged and branded with red hot irons.

The playing field lay near the fringe of the compound where a swift flowing stream separated the Bear Clan's circle of wigwams from those of others, and among the latter, I came across Nagawa bent over her customary pots and baskets.

She was stuffing pieces of root and tobacco into little pouches sewn of animal skin. Her presence, without that of her husband, seemed proof of Flying Crane's assertion that Animiki was to marry into the Bear Clan. The tanned parchment face raised up at my approach and her eyes flickered in recognition. I made her a deferential bow, and signed for Animiki. Nagawa half turned, motioning toward a footpath that worked its way up a point of land that gave off into a long narrow spit running clear out into the bay.

The footpath led past Jan's tent. Its flap was pinned back to let in air and Jan, at rest in a reclining position, I thought him sleeping until his head poked out as I passed and he asked where I was going.

"Up the footpath."

"Then from there, look down over the rise and after a few long hops, you'll find her."

I gave him a raised thumb and refused the bait. Same old Jan, supposing he knew something where nothing was to know! He knew only that I walked the same path as another, one who happened to be a young girl he must have seen passing by his tent.

She stood ankle deep in the marsh, hacking off reeds and pressing them down inside a long, cone-shaped willow basket hanging from her waist to just above her ankles. At my greeting, she whirled around looking pleased, her demeanor having none of the sullenness she'd shown me of late.

"I am sorry Audaîgweos is gone. Gregor and I wished to thank him for his many favors. Also Hadakotana and others, too. Why did they leave so soon?"

Grasping her basket with both hands, she sprang lightly up the muddy bank onto the grass-trodden path. She looked not quite at me but, even to the side, a bright flicker shone in her eyes. "My people have long, long journey on great wide river to the north. No time to wait."

"But, we were to meet at Bow-e-ting! My brother and I were to travel with the Loon Clan and White Feather to Great Carrying Place. No one wondered at our delay or to discover if we lived or died?"

"Audaîgweos say Big Lake Person and brother must leave. Go back to where they come. When you not at Bow-e-ting, he say you may change mind, go north and east, not come so far as Kitchigami. May be also Big Water swallow brother and Big Lake Person." She said this last with no change of expression and then as if to explain, said: "Audaîgweos say make no difference. Must leave."

Did I catch a note of pleading in her voice as she spoke next: "My people have no time to wait. Must travel to new hunting grounds." Rather breathless, she turned those dark, earnest eyes full upon me. "My people, they find new hunting grounds. Spring come, they have many many furs.—Like Bear Clan have now," she added with trembling lips and a lowered glance.

"Little Thunder, Flying Crane told me you are to marry. Do you wish this? To marry into the Bear Clan?—Not the Loon Clan?" She looked startled, puzzled.

Seconds later, she asked almost in a whisper, "Your people, Big Lake Person, would marry sister or brother?"

"No, such a marriage among us is forbidden, is not allowed. But, your Loon Clan has many men, and not one of them is your brother."

She shook her head, vehemently. "All are brothers! Loon marry Crane or Bear or Turtle or other Do-daim. Loon not marry other Loon. It great wrong!"

So that was it. The clan of one totem, even though not blood relations, think of themselves as a family, so do not intermarry. Animiki, then, had no choice.—Yet, I'd not seen one male of the Bear Clan to make her a suitable husband. Of course, I couldn't tell the poor child that, unless..."Animiki," I said gently, "You are so young. Do you wish to marry into the Bear Clan? Tell me who he is."

Again, the puzzled look and downcast expression. Arranged marriages at home at least have the merit of title or wealth or social position to encourage a loveless union, but to pair a couple attached to the name of a fish, an animal or bird? And why was she evading a simple question? Why did she act like a sheep in the pasture? If this was another of her moods, why then I preferred her to snarl and bite! She must have sensed my irritation.

"I ask you. Does Big Lake Person know who he wish to marry?" Her question took me by surprise. It struck me as snappish and deserving of no reply. While she, adjusted her basket, gathered herself together with head up, chin firm, and dark eyes glittering. "I do not know how tell more, Big Lake Person." She faced me one brief moment, then trundled off up the path.

An unsatisfactory exchange and likely our last. On the morrow at daybreak, weather allowing, our homeward journey would begin! My grandstanding before Grey Eagle worked to good effect for he agreed to my request to accompany them. But Gregor shrugged aside my part in forcing the hand of Grey Eagle in these words: "This time, you were lucky, klein broeder. Yes, the Bear Clan was moved by your theatrics. More important to them, however, is that we are useful in advancing their trade with the French. Another time, your fine Dutch head would dance on those poles." He pointed to the grisly display of scalps and skulls stuck to posts at the far side of the lodge, not the first I'd seen, but gruesome nonetheless. I allowed him the upper hand in this. He was my elder brother, and dear to me. And, no one seeming the wiser, I saw no reason to confide that, while my intercession with Grey Eagle had most to do with the politics of our travel, my self-imposed, appointment-of-the-moment as "teacher" to the daughter of Audaîgweos also bore weight—as had my appeal to Grey Eagle to be my teacher. A high compliment has been known to open a closed door. Nor, was my appeal insincere for its having been made of-the-moment. So I watched, I observed, and I learned why we were of use to them. Grey Eagle and the savage nations understood full well that the British and French pitted their energies against each other and, that to them, three Nederlanders like Gregor, Jan, and me, were a mere remnant of what our country once represented. We who posed so minor a threat to The Trade were not worth the cost of a regiment to pursue; yet, to the savages, we three Europeans with guns and knowledge of our kind, offered safe conduct and leverage in The Trade. Jan's own observations confirmed what we'd been told in Albany. "The French," Jan said, "brazenly intercept furs destined for Hudson Bay posts—an operation he seemed to favor— while the British work the other end, sabotaging traders headed for Montreal."

As for the Bear Clan,—they'd gained the bulk of the Loon Clan's furs, and with these added to their own, now had a king's ransom of furs to transport. Pleasure stretched the limits of Grey Eagle's creased and weathered face as he contemplated White Feather's declaration; it was to the effect that the Bear Clan would have three well-armed Dutchmen, skilled in weaponry, to escort and protect the Bear Clan's people and cargo against all takers, be they British, French or enemy tribes.

"Ah, that White Feather is a true diplomat," I said to Gregor and

Jan, upon our leaving the conclave. On this point, we three agreed, heartily.   It was our last evening. White Feather joined Gregor, Jan, and me around our fire, flames spitting and crackling as the last rays of an orange sun sank the great wide bay into darkness, and the moments passed, pleasantly, with little being said. After a while, Gregor standing as though at the helm of a ship, murmured, "A good omen was that red-orange sky." White Feather seemed as eager as the rest of us to be underway, but said nothing as we smoked. Even Jan was silent. Bullfrogs thrumming in a nearby marsh were more adept at chatter than the four of us. At long last, I broke in on White Feather's quietude, deeming the bond between us equal to my prying. His being of the Iroquois nation, I was more curious than ever about this new affiliation of his that would move him from the Ojibwa Loon Clan to the Bear Clan. I knew the Ojibwa still held ancient grudges against Iroquois for the bloody wars waged against their ancestral tribes. Sir James, in one of his instructive chats, had this from Audaîgweos, himself, who, he told me, was named for a Great Chief of his people, and that in the words of Audaîgweos, "Ojibwa once lived where great river meets Great Salt Water of rising sun." Sir James supposed this to mean that their centuries-old migration westward, came by way of the River St. Lawrence.

"White Feather—" I began, then waited for the austere head, freshly shorn on both sides of his crown, to make its customary slow turn in my direction; he did this most often when I sought information. "Sir James arranged for our travel west with Audaîgweos and the Loon Clan. How will it be for us—for you—traveling into strange country with a strange band of Ojibwa? Are they not enemies of your people?"

"Not strange. Food same. Canoe same. Enemies same. Water—different." Was this his humor? In all these months, I'd seen him smile only seldom. Nothing so benign as a smile lit those granite features in the flickering firelight. I persisted.

"The canoe is not the same."

"Paddle same."

"How is water different?" But before White Feather could answer, Jan cut in.

"He means the route, Piet. After we reach Sault Ste. Marie we take the French River to the Matawa to the Ottawa to Lachine and on to Montreal. You and, maybe White Feather, go with us all the way. Or, maybe you, too, will turn south by way of the Saint Lawrence, then retrace your route to Albany. But, you Gregor, what will you do?"

"I go to Georgian Bay."

I knew my brother's intention, having had a full discussion of routes through the interior with him. But Jan's instruction was meant, kindly, and I took no offense from his interruption only that, now, White Feather was tightly wrapped in his blanket; he was facing east and his breathing, even. Ah, well, many hours together lay ahead for White Feather and me, and I was sure to learn much from him. I had gained a fair facility in speaking the Ojibwa tongue, much less of the Iroquois, but what I lacked, White Feather's English could supply. I, too, needed to close my mind to all but rest, and try to quiet my excitement over a return journey that would take us into new and boundless country.

Chapter 40.

On To The Sault

All too familiar were chill dawns with a thick layer of fog lifting off the water and this, our morning of departure, was no different. By mid morning our outer clothing would be damp with sweat from paddling. By early afternoon if the sun blessed us, we'd be stripped down to our linen. But at this early hour the land held an even grayness until the thin light edging up the bay would begin to warm the eastern horizon.

We stashed the last of our bundles on the long poles stored in the bottom of the canoe in which six would ride: Jan, Gregor and myself, and White Feather and Jan's two canoemen. We would lead the brigade in a fine canoe, larger than any Ojibwa canoe I'd yet seen. It had a higher bow and stern, the ends of which curved back upon themselves with a disc-like design on all sides. Jan was told, except for the bark pieced around the curved ends, that its skin was formed from a single large birch. The bow of all three Bear Clan canoes bore newly etched ocher symbols outlined in black, and all three of their canoes stood ready.

I was fitting in a roll of bark for future repairs when I glanced up and caught a glimpse of white deerskin. Animiki, half hidden behind a clump of trees on the point of land, stood aloof, just watching. Other females had come down on the beach, lightly bantering among themselves and at us in the way of females the world-wide upon being left behind. I slipped off, expecting that Jan and Gregor would later interrogate me. So be it! I hurried up the pebbled beach, the sandy bank, and crossed down to the spit of the bay, southwest of the compound.

Was not making one's farewell a custom among her people? No matter, a sudden rush of sentiment for how she'd eased my stay among her people swelled the obligation I felt to bid her goodbye, an obligation any civilized man would honor.

"Little Thunder, you rise early."

"You leave early, Big Lake Person." For all her dusky savage darkness, she had a frail look as she stood, arms hanging limp at her sides. Her straight black hair, which she'd worn unplaited since being among the Bear Clan, was outlined in dew. And dew-rimmed, too, seemed her eyes.

In her own way, I supposed her to be honoring my leave taking. I felt moved, if not fully understanding it. Now, like Audaîgweos at Sault Ste. Marie, it was I who had no more time. Some token of appreciation seemed in order and in one rash move, I slid the gold chain off my neck, forced apart the link that held the ivory, and urged my family talisman into her hands, closing her small fingers around it.

"Keep this. Your having it will safeguard our journey."

"You come back?" Her voice radiated joy. Had I gone too far, raised some girlish expectation?

"Animiki, I cannot promise. I have a long journey through your country, an ocean to cross to my country and, should it be my destiny to return again to America, there is all that ocean, land, and water to cross again!—This I can say. If I do come back, I will find Audaîgweos and the Loon Clan. I will find Grey Eagle and the Bear Clan. I will find you. And by that time, Little Thunder, you will be married and will look at Big Lake Person through lowered eyes with, perhaps, a child of your own held to your back."

"No. I not marry into Bear Clan. I hold this. I see it always around you. I will keep it. Give back to you, only to you."

From the beach came Jan's two-fingered whistle. I brushed a finger across her wet cheek in a parting gesture, and in high spirits ran down the bank, the gold chain resting lightly upon my chest. I did not look back. I did not look back until after, having pushed far out from the bay and before starting around my self-named 'Copper' Island, I looked back at Gran Portage with a feeling so similar as on that distant morning—it seemed ages ago—when my eyes had strained for one last look at the Groote Kerk upon sailing out of Amsterdam. No high stone steeple, here, marked the land. Here lay endless dark forests of nature's own giants, until water and sky, melding together, left them, too, behind.

Chapter 41.

At Georgian Bay

Those early days out of Grand Portage slipped by all too quickly. Fair weather and six pairs of arms to ply us along in a higher-walled canoe, longer by some three places, saw us gaining easy distance on the Bear Clan. They were out of our sight much of the time. Aided by the practiced eyes of his two able canoemen, Jan had procured this fine craft in Montreal. It had wooden toggles for raising and lowering the sail, and goodly stretches of open water were skimmed across without any need to paddle. After sighting a stopping place, we lowered the sail, made for land, and had a leisurely wait while the Bear Clan was catching up.

At such times of rest, talk might be expected to flow, freely, between Gregor and me. It did not. Our knowing we might never meet, again, shrouded our conversation, he seeming as constrained as myself in talking from the heart. I sensed his disappointment in my going back to Amsterdam, though not once did he express it.—I'd never thought not to go back. As to whether or not upon my return to Amsterdam, I would remain,—events must decide; but I did not burden him with my need to return to our homeland. For his part, Gregor spoke little of our father or, for that matter, of Willem or Dirck. I asked him once, "Tell me about your boyhood, Gregor." He frowned, put a hand on my shoulder and said it had been similar to my own.

"Except, Pieter, I had brothers to wrestle and box with, and a mother who fed us full of meat pasties when Father wasn't filling our heads with the riches in furs we would bring him from the New World. So, you see, it was not so different, then. Although from the look of you, I doubt you had a mother who fattened you up on meat pasties. You are taller with a finer skeleton than your three brothers."

His words warmed me through and through—not now, or ever had Gregor referred to me as "half" brother. Perhaps, his memories of Father had faded into dimness over the years or, content in his present life, Gregor chose not to delve into the past. But, there was a 'difference'. My brothers had not witnessed Father wasting away in mind and body, having no notion of whether his oldest sons lived or died. And, although he'd never intimated the loathsome thought that a son might flourish to enrich only himself in The Trade, unworthy thoughts do slip into our mortal minds. — As to my own 'flourishing', my alliances in the New World, thus far, having produced nothing in trade to show for them, would not cheer my father! Yet my choice was clear: I would return to tell him how things stood. Then, too, there was Kristina.   We laid over at the Sault Ste. Marie. White Feather and Jan's canoemen stayed below guarding our craft and vessel, and to watch for the Bear Clan to arrive. Jan, Gregor and I, meanwhile, trod on up to look in on Father Albanel. The old priest greeted us, warmly, and introduced us to the Superior of the Ste. Marie Mission, who had come to relieve Father Albanel. Albanel, himself, seemed rejuvenated; he looked forward to going off and saving souls in the pays d'en haut, as he called this vast region's Upper Country.

Jan questioned him, closely, about his former travels to the North, the route he'd taken, and what savage tribes he'd encountered. Had he seen the Bay of Hudson. Father Albanel gave short answers to those questions, but went on at length about how fervently disposed the savages were toward the teachings of himself and his fellow Jesuits.

Upon our leaving, the two robed priests raised their crosses to bless us at the door of the mission; to preserve our divine souls and those we might save of the three heathen savages accompanying us, to find the weather favorable, our vessel and cargo water-tight, to journey in safety..., I stole a glance at Gregor. He stood head bowed and expressionless, while Jan wore the beatific smile of a Giotto saint.

Our farewells completed, I said to Jan on the way back down, "Conversing in French is not sufficient? You've become a Papist?"

"Piet, in French Canada, piety is often felt—and always useful. Some of these priests carry better maps inside their heads then are found on paper! The old priest Albanel, does, I'm certain,—which, had we time to divert him from his holy purpose, we could surely determine."

From three yards off, our noses told us that, in our absence, Muin and Nadowe had covered themselves with another layer of animal grease. In time, inured by frequent, if not constant exposure to the rancid stench, I, too, would not hesitate to smear this remedy on my person to ward off ravenous flies and mosquitoes. In time. Within the hour, White Feather sighted the Bear Clan passing right on by. All was ready and our canoe shoved off, and in short order, we too, had left Ste. Marie behind.

We must have passed them during the night. A waning moon affording enough light for canoemen familiar with the route, as were Muin and Nadowe, we kept on without stopping. Nor would we encounter the Bear Clan, again, until two days short of Georgian Bay where, again, we would waite for them to catch up.

All of us settled in for the night. But between wake and sleep a desire struck me so persistently, I rapped Gregor on his shoulder to jolt him from first sleep. "Go with me, brother. Go back home with me to Amsterdam!"

His long silence gave me hope. Then he gave a long sigh and said,"Pieter, I am home, or will be very soon. I thought you understood. Father's dreams for me—for any of us—will never, no should never be realized. We are a seafaring people; yet, when not at sea, we gravitate to the comforts of family and hearth like birds to the nest. I am no different. Though not the North Sea, I travel my rivers and lakes, take my furs, and then am anxious to be home. To wife and child.

"And you," he said, seconds later in that half-hissing whistle, "You've just begun with many years yet before you. I've come to love you like a son, klein broeder. You will come back. I'm fairly certain it is so. When you come to Georgian Bay, ask anyone you see for Gondashkwei." His chortling laughter following this disclosure, relieved the sob in my throat. "It means my manner of speaking. It suggests wind pipe to my wife's relatives."

"You are resolute, then, and with much experience to back up your purpose. And you seem well content, my brother." My good humor restored, I asked him, "Does Gondashkwei have a message for Father?"

"That I am alive? Yes."

"Nothing more?"

"Yes. Tell him I thank him for sending me here, for sending you here. That I think of him with affection.—That in many ways, I am still a Nederlander."

This would be our last chance to talk in private. At such a time of heartfelt separation, one has little to say. It is better.

From Sault Ste. Marie we followed the North Channel of the Lake of the Huron, retracing only a part of the course Gregor and I had earlier followed, alone. From that point, our brigade of canoes filed in a line. We kept to the channel throughout the long days that it took us to reach the westernmost of the fingered channels, ones that flowed out the mouth of the French River. In all, we'd covered a distance of some fifty-three leagues.

It was early evening when, at dusk, we sighted a hilly-appearing landscape, a part of Georgian Bay that, when caught by a lowering sun, showed the hills to be barren, solid granite and some quartz. We'd paddled into the wind most of the day, and were quick to stow the canoes and fall into our blankets.

Morning brought us a breakfast of cold venison and bitter-tasting, blackish berries,—berries Jan's two savages had picked in great numbers and lay spread out among us. Grey Eagle, sitting off to one side, kept leaning over to scoop them into his mouth by the fist fulls.

Jan ate hurriedly, and to urge us along, stood up and looked down on the rest of us with a sardonic expression on his face. "We haven't had to break our backs paddling, yet," he announced, "but we will! When we ran the French River downstream we flew along like geese, but now, men, we return." His gaze passed over Gregor and White Feather to rest on me with a challenging look and a laugh that rippled out the side of his mouth. "Our return will be a cracking-good duel against the current, currents to rival a mad ocean's."

I ignored his poorly disguised jest to remind me of my embarrassing 'baptism' aboard ship. "What of portages?" I asked.

"Two, to mention on the French.—The Matawa is the river for portages, Piet! We'll save those romps in Hell, for then. For, now, we'll be on our way!" He had the look and manner of a pirate, Jan did, with a red scarf draped around his head as he swung himself around in his customary abruptness. "Gregor!" My brother set his pack back down and clasped Jan's outstretched hand in both his own.

"Maybe we meet next season, Gregor Van Doorn. Maybe not.

But with both of us working the waterways, we are sure to meet somewhere, sometime." Jan's hard, slim hand wrestled Gregor's great paw, upright, and the two locked elbows, manfully, bracing against each other on legs outspread.

Their sport raised all our spirits. And Jan's savages—ones I took to be of the Ottawa band—were not to be outdone. Grunting and weaving, they gave a clowning imitation of hand wrestling that only lacked for a fiddle.—Later, I would have cause to think back on how, once, we had joined together as one in most spirited, merry laughter, even White Feather. But the infernal push of time wore any extraneous exhibition down, soon enough. And all, except for myself and Gregor, followed Jan on down to the water's edge to where the impatient Bear Clan would be waiting to be off, again. Above the beach where Gregor and I stood, hands clasped in a final goodbye, I looked up to lock-in this parting moment, the place of our inevitable separation. Sand dunes and waving greenish broom grass shimmered in the early golden light. And, above the dunes, against the backdrop of barren hills, an occasional thorny bush stuck up amid the preponderance of tiny pinks, purples, and blues—midget flowers peeping through moss-covered rocky soil.

I'd dropped Gregor's hand and was turning to leave, when, suddenly, all a-chitter, a small, near-naked, bronze-skinned boy tore down over the rocks and mossy beds, and slithered through the sand.

"Papa! Papa!" In one leap he was up in Gregor's arms. The little fellow was an astonishment. His wheat-colored mop of hair leaned into Gregor's shoulder, while his half-turned face with eyes as black as any savage's, sent shy looks my way.

While father and son, so joyously, reunited, I shouted down the beach, "Jan! I won't be long!" Jan sent me a stern, nearly imperceptible nod, but enough to let me know I should be quick.

I had determined early on that, in this our newly-joined venture, I would maintain utmost civility. I'd not challenge him even when his aire of authority sorely rankled. Little more than a year ago he'd acted the part of my subordinate. But, now, he was not acting. This expedition was, truly, in his charge. And justly so. He had hired the bowman and steersman, knew the route into French Canada, supplied the canoe, and had initiated the arrangement with the Bear Clan. That being said, I, nonetheless, needed time, now. Over the heads of father and son, I was first to see her. A short, round woman, her black hair pulled tight against the scalp, strode leisurely over the rock, moss, and sand. She stood apart when drawing near us, and smiled, broadly. Gregor thrust the child up on his shoulder, greeted her, and taking one of the woman's hands, walked her toward me. From one or another, I heard a garble of French, Dutch and English, and a tongue I supposed must be Cree.

"Knute, meet your Uncle Pieter." Gregor set the boy on the ground, and upon his father's prodding, Knute inched toward me and stuck out his hand in the Dutch manner. I pressed it, warmly, though feeling somewhat awkward myself. I had but scarcely absorbed that this little scallion was my nephew, when Gregor swept Marta forward, "My wife."

How did one greet such a sister-in-law? I took her hand, covering my embarrassment with a slight bow, repeating her name. She twittered, and Gregor chuckled, his eyes twinkling. Knute was eying his father's pack. Again, time was short as with Animiki, and I wanted to leave behind a thing of some value. Off came my gold chain. I dangled it in front of Knute's dancing eyes, and as I slipped it over the child's head, Gregor murmured, "The ivory...." A mere glance into those gray eyes was enough. I had his understanding of a thing neither of us would be quite up to discussing, not his asking nor my explaining its whereabouts.

"Knute should have something to remember his Uncle Pieter," I said, breaking the silence. The child smiled up at me in shades of his father's beaming countenance. As I kissed her hand, Marta's smile grew so big her raisin-black eyes all but disappeared into her fat bronzed cheeks. I embraced my brother, then, with the more typical cheek kissing among us Dutch. Then, turning, abruptly, I left with an emptiness I'd never known before.   I   was   fully aware that our Ojibwa "friends" looked on, and that whatever appetite the Bear Clan had for sentiment or gaiety, had been spent. The feeling that they resented our faster and easier progress had grown, steadily, ever since our canoe leapt away from theirs on the Lake of Superior. — How easy, I thought, for an ambush. The Ojibwa of the Bear Clan numbered twelve in their three canoes — how easy for them to surprise the five of us as we slept. Five? or three. Jan and I could have complete trust in White Feather, but what of Nadowe and Muin? Little about hatchet-faced Nadowe drew me to him. Of

Muin I felt somewhat better. Jan told me he was an Algonquin, but not an Ottawa; he was a renegade Micmac who'd fled Acadia after murdering a French officer, one he'd mistaken for a British soldier.

My own country gave me an awareness of how often 'mistaken identity' can account for murders followed by hangings! Why, it is a certainty that, in this huge country, I could easily mistake an Ojibwa for an Ottawa or a Micmac!—had I cause to murder one. Still, I knew not the depth of Muin's allegiance to Jan, and as yet he owed none to me. At the first opportunity, I needed to talk to Jan and settle my mind. Was losing the warmth and protective presence of my elder brother giving me a heightened sense of caution? For, I was undergoing an acute need to add to Sir James's "watch and observe" a warning to "stay prepared."

Lofting myself over the edge to kneel in Gregor's place, I took up the paddle in the same second, Jan's "Pull!" echoed over the water, and we started our run up the mouth of the French.

Chapter 42.

Ascending The French

Georgian Bay lay behind us by half the morning. My lethargy of spirit and body was caused by more than the loss over quitting my brother. My paddle lifted and fell like an iron rod. The river channel we'd entered of some twenty or more leagues spilled through outcroppings of exposed granite that, to my bleary eyes, breached and fell like gray-back whales. As for my companions, Jan listed like a ship riding out the wind. Nadowe's head drooped, and I did not need to turn my head around to know that Muin's paddle was dragging. We wearied on into the afternoon, and just before the brink of a swift, curving rapid, Jan signaled to draw in.

It was the first portage on the French, one of no great length, and should have been routine and gone quickly. But in our weak, feverish condition, we moved like overloaded hod carriers. Jan's usual martial bark had no sting to it as we plodded up and down a narrow rocky footpath. We had all the enthusiasm of the beasts of burden we were, each step an unremitting drudgery.

On finally reaching our stop, and unloading, we saw that the place overlooked a churning, sickle-shaped river rapid. We paid it little attention then, as one-by-one, we sank to the ground. Some little daylight remained, and Jan passed around a flask as a curative to ease our discomfort. It was a bitter-tasting absinthe, more foul-tasting than any old Kootermann made from herbs and wormwood. Scarcely had it coursed our gullets when, like shots from a cannon, first Jan and Nadowe, then the renegade Micmac, then myself followed by White Feather,—one after the other of us staggered off, retching and vomiting.

When we'd finished quaking, Jan and I took ourselves back down on our trembling legs to the river, flushed out our mouths and splashed cold water over our heads. By the time we'd climbed back up, the last ribbons of daylight clung to river bluffs lost in lengthening shadows. Life seemed restored.

I directed Jan's attention toward Nadowe and Muin, who sat backed against our canoe, each wrapped in his blanket. I spoke in a loud, goading voice so they'd be sure to hear me. "At least they poison themselves as well as us!"

Nadowe, the more talkative one, straightened up. "Berries bad," he acknowledged.

White Feather let loose a barrage of words in no language I had ever heard. His usual calm, unshakable demeanor had cracked at last, defeated by a querulous stomach. My surprise, giving way to laughter, was short lived as he came and stood over Jan and me, his air of authority intact.

"The Bear Clan, too, ate berries. Grey Eagle ate most." The import of his words struck us clear enough.

"So, the sickness must have struck them by now, too. You know them best, White Feather," Jan said. "What trouble will this cause?"

"We wait for them. I try talk away trouble."

"Suppose we go back and look for them?" I asked. "Show our good intentions. They were dispirited enough as it was with our ease in out-reaching them by a day and more."

"We'll not give ground where none is owed!" Jan barked. "The berries were offered, freely, with no thought of poison. So? We all got sick. Simple. Our canoe is larger, swifter. And, with Gregor gone, we still have one more of us to raise a paddle. So? We make better time." Once, again, he trained that fierce-eyed look upon us. "We'll wait over, but only until sun up. The Bear Clan should be here; they will want to catch up with us carrying the largest share of cargo. White Feather?"

"You speak truth," White Feather said. After a pause, and with the calm demeanor of a diplomat, he added: "Bear Clan not believe. Think poison, so steal cargo." When White Feather paused, it wasn't to invite comment but to provoke thought; one always knew more was forthcoming.

"Bear Clan come. I give Grey Eagle my place. I take his." He moved off, then, the matter decided. He had delivered an ultimatum, and even feisty Jan held back from arguing.

I lay down, content that Jan's arguments were straightforward and White Feather's perceptions, wise. And, mine? I upbraided myself for having spoken so rashly. Then, close to sleep I took comfort and some amusement thinking that were Gregor here, he'd not countenance my error, either; but he'd be sure to soften it with words like, "But you, klein broeder, have a good heart." Late the next morning—it being after dawn, I awoke with the nebulous feeling that I'd not yet slept. I opened my eyes to see White Feather moving, stealthily, from one to the next. "Drop blanket. Bear Clan come. Make like sick."

Having aroused us, he ran in that swift, soft-footed stride his race had perfected, and stood near the path coming up from the river. We waited. At White Feather's signal, Nadowe and Muin leapt into the brush. Pretending sickness came easy to Jan and me, listening to those two retch, and bellow like impatient milk cows in distress.

Jan sat up, crossed his legs, and bending over, held his head in his hands. I stretched out on my side, ready to moan while keeping one eye half open to the proceedings.

Grey Eagle was first to appear. He came striding over the height of the footpath, unburdened by canoes and cargo his men would bring up behind him. His face had a dyspeptic droop in spite of the paddle he held aloft like a musket. A single claw of magnificent size swayed from the amulet on his broad chest as he came toward us. I watched through an eye at half mast as he looked from one to the other of us. My moans, like the boat chain moored to a dock in a storm, filled the interludes between Nadowe and Muin's retchings. The Ogima's eyes narrowed to slits, and he spat, contemptuously. He addressed himself to White Feather, and no understanding of Ojibwa was needed to catch his meaning.

"You, White Feather, you sick?"

White Feather nodded. "Berries bad. Very bad."

Grey Eagle harrumped and sneered, "We eat berries. Not get sick."

I nearly choked. One look at the haggard faces and weepy eyes of himself and his men gave the lie to his words.

"You are strong, Grey Eagle, very strong. Most Strong Ogima." White Feather, looking him straight in the eye as he spoke, made a grand, swooping-eagle gesture of his arm. And once, not being enough, he did so in all four directions! We had all watched Grey Eagle gorge himself on the berries proffered by Jan's aides. And, just last evening, White Feather had praised Jan for speaking truth. This morning, the untruths Grey Eagle declaimed with an overweening pride were being coddled, and White Feather's feigning so obsequious a manner was, certainly, to a purpose. So, too, his gift for diplomacy was apparent. But this latest performance could easily outdo the best of actors at the Amsterdam Shouwburg! His next words, he spoke for Grey Eagle's ears, alone. We only watched as the latter's countenance beamed with pleasure.

Then, Jan, of a sudden rising up like Lazarus, boomed, "SICK OR NOT! we lose too much time!" His whistle brought Nadowe and Muin out of the brush, fully purged and cured.

Our charade seeming to have satisfied one and all, we set off in good spirits, taking extra care in reloading as we made preparations to ascend the current and maneuver the first of the rapids, the Sickle Rapid. Grey Eagle, as good as his bluff, lost no time wading into the fast-moving waters careening around a knee-high rock slab, one that afforded a slippery but solid foothold for boarding our canoe. His acceptance of White Feather's offer to exchange places was displayed with alacrity. When Jan stuck out a hand to steady him, Grey Eagle doffed it aside, hoisting himself up and over with an agility surprising for one his age.

Jan ordered me to take the bow with himself as steersman. "Good practice for us both, my friend," he said. "Nadowe and Muin will take us around the greater rapids yet to come." Those two knelt center, with Grey Eagle positioned just ahead of the stern. For now, the leader of the Bear Clan appeared so well pacified that getting him out of our canoe might pose the bigger trouble.

Jan pushed us off, jumped into the stern, and drove us skillfully into the black still of the rapids. A fast, exhilarating ride! I, making quick-darting lifts and downstrokes from the bow, felt revitalized!— joined to on-the-ready paddlers, center and stern as we brought our craft up and around the rapids, unscathed.

For some hours, our party of five sped up-river in quiet, each of us into his own thoughts. Here in the New World, too, as in fields in and around Amsterdam, small white blossoms on short stems with three pointy-green leaves poked up in low places on the river banks. Here, they budded later, after the snow melt, and would be less plentiful. Our canoes would be long past when these buds ripened to a rich red. I had only to picture my homeland for saliva to coat my tongue, longing for the taste of wild strawberries with all the lowland countryside rife with their fragrance.

On running a rise in the river, we sighted White Feather and the Bear Clan trailing behind us. Often, they were kept out of our sight by twists and turns and rocky overhangs but, most often, by the need of any who fought this river to keep a sharp watch on the current, water depth, and obstacles that lay hidden from view. These waters were far from pliant, calling for a steady lift and pull, although I thought they proved less of a strain than Jan had predicted for this stretch of river. That was my ill-formed conclusion. The most dire prediction could not have forecast, nor averted, what would lay ahead.

A second portage made, all five of us stood staring down from a headland. No one spoke, but my stomach did a turn just gazing at those frothing cataracts below. One upon the next, they mounted high as whale spouts before crashing down the rocks, each sounding a deadly pathway of roiling foam. The armada of boulders and eroded cliff rock that lined both sides of the river were as though lying in wait to eject a light bark canoe into the maelstrom and on into perdition. Nadowe pointed the way to get us through.

Grateful I was to have him back as steersman and Muin take the bow! Jan and I worked the center with Gray Eagle behind us as ballast. I was not alone in missing Gregor. There'd been one less of us since Georgian Bay. But more serious, now, was one less body to stay us in this swirling white inferno that repelled all thought. No human instinct shot each defiant stroke, drawstroke, pry, cross pry, or hold. Each floodgate charged anew, catapulting us up and over, then booming down, flinging deluges of water up and over our high-curled bow and stern. We danced hellishly about—a child's toy in the river's gaping maw. And were we not so, a mere toy? Wasn't each stroke a Jeremiah cry for deliverance to the God who made Heaven and Hell? How greater, still, should the All Powerful even hear us above those shrieking, slamming waters. Fear? No time to feel, only act: a long lean to larboard to miss a jutting rock in midstream. A thrust to starboard to dodge the current.

No brains, no mortal muscles, no strength of arms could wage a battle so ill-proportioned. Surely, the God of Christians, the god of Ojibwa, Ottawa and Micmac, were united as One God metering out mercy—and our salvation.

How might it be going for White Feather and the Ojibwa still behind us? A fleeting thought for their deliverance crossed my numbed mind as we hauled up our canoe, not troubling to unload. Each joint and sinew was a raw, knotted misery, the roaring inside my head like a funnel for gushing water. With no power left to think or feel, I fell down with the others on the soft green sedge.

Chapter 43.

Toll At the French

Grey Eagle sat hunched over a small fire. Every now and then with his head thrown back, he keened a wild, haunting cry that reverberated and filled the silence with its echo. Unnerved and dumbstruck by its power, I sat on the ground leaning into a bundle of furs, and listened. Just listened.

After a time, Jan, his face unnaturally hard and expressionless, pointed to a white sun half hid behind swollen clouds. "If they made it, they would be here by now."

He was putting words to what each of us feared. Cargo lost. Twelve men lost. Among them White Feather for whom I had come to feel more than the respect his presence commanded. Until, now, when faced with his loss, I'd not yet, as it were, pieced together the whole of his 'cloth'. Nor was I equal to looking deeper into the raw reality Jan was laying before us.

"We have two choices. We leave now, while we still have five, six hours of guarded daylight to guide us up river or we wait until morning—wait against all reason that they are coming." His sword-sharp tongue had the captain's ring to it, but I who knew him so well caught the lift of that saturnine head, the quickened intake of breath, his flared nostrils. If Jan's words denied the possibility of their safe passage after the hours that had elapsed, he spoke truth. In our hearts, each of us knew that staying upright on those tumultuous waters was the random toss of a dice.

"This, only stopping place." Nadowe, too, spoke truth.

We were resting on that same fortuitous outcropping of granite laid over with sedge, the same as had shown itself of a sudden, splayed out like feet anchoring the cliff rock walling in the river on its rampaging course down to Georgian Bay.

"There is another choice, Jan—" I broke in, hesitantly, but gained sureness with each word I uttered, speaking slow and sometimes in Ojibwa to make my meaning clear to Grey Eagle. "Remember where the cliffs breached below the last cataract? They should have made it that far." I pointed toward the layers of banded, granite-like rock that climbed up behind us. "We can ascend the rocks and retrace our route back along the ridge, then walk as far as the last cataract and sight down river. Two of you, will lower me on a rope. I'll drop down for a final, and closer look."

Grey Eagle leapt up. He came over, positioning himself so close, his upturned head could have grazed my chin. "You," he said, clutching at my arm. "You do this." I nodded, yes, not knowing nor caring if he questioned or ordered.

Jan looked grim, eying me, thoughtfully. His countenance shifted into a sidewise attempt at a smile as he said, "I know you, Piet, you and your dash-ahead, quick ways, marking a path and, later, counting the cost. Yet, my friend," he said, grasping my shoulder, "you've often won us more than you've lost."

At another time and place, this from Jan would have warmed me through and through. Then, it ignited the fire of my resolve. Muin and Nadowe, catching his bent, rose to accompany me.

Grey Eagle straightening up looked, again, the proud Ogima. "I go," he said. Long hair the color of soot fanned his face, a face formed as though from red clay hardened into stone and, unlayered by his usual puffed-up manner, looked as though, when no longer in command, his rational mind saw a way to follow, and to hope.

We took the lashings holding our bundles together and knotted them to the coil of rope stowed in the bow of our canoe, making one long length. It would drop me close, enough, if not all the way to the bottom where rocks met the river. Then, we started across the ridge on terrain better-suited to it's natural inhabitants than to men who had to be mindful of each footfall. But the ridge was terra firma, and we crossed it in under an hour. Below us ran a river full of itself from winter melt and spring rains, and thundering on at high flow.

At a breach in the cliffs, a ledge protruded out like a Roman L turned on its heel. Jan looked over the side and admitted to having a poor stomach for what I proposed to do. "I will think no less of you, Piet, should you change your mind. We cannot even see the whole of the risk ahead of you."

"It's my risk to take, Jan." Jan could not know the force of my regard for the Mohawk—I hardly knowing it myself until now. And, of the eleven Ojibwa missing from Grey Eagle's party, no one needed reminding. I left behind my moccasins, trusting to my bare feet for a better grip.

Once over the top of the ledge, and under it, I found footholds, and so could lower myself down from one crevice to the next, digging in with my knife in places where the blade could penetrate a solid layer; otherwise, I clung with hands and feet to the rocks, putting as little strain on the tether around my waist as needed to descend.

Though steep, I judged the height from beneath the L-shaped ledge down to the level of the river, to be about twenty feet. About a quarter distance from the bottom, a solid protrusion presented itself. I caught the rope around it, secured it, and jumped, landing on a sprawl of sand and rocks I thought to be lodged at a good angle to survey the river. So I thought. Some other time, I might have kept to the perch from where I'd leapt, stood a while in awe of so relentlessly majestic a river. Not now. Now, I was driven by a passion to salvage whatever that river had stolen and, carelessly, left behind. From above, the boulders below had not seemed so huge. But, now, standing on a strip of sand, I was unable to see over the mass of them.

Crawling up and leaping from one rock to another, I stood up on one to look out, again. I gasped. I saw, first, the outstretched arm and fingers. He was one of Grey Eagle's band. His body was wedged between two boulders, but his head and chest at an angle, cleared the water. Did he breathe? I moved down and, and easing the body out of its rock pinchers, draped him, belly down, across the boulder, then began pummeling his back. A thin stream of water dribbled from his mouth, then fully. He gagged some, and his eyes sprung wide open.

He tried to focus as I shouted above the roar of the water. "The others? Where are the others? White Feather?" I lifted him part way, and tried to shake him back into this world. Still dazed, he looked on me as one might an archangel or 'spirit' more in accord with his belief. He comprehended enough from my urgings to help himself up and, slowly, regain his balance. He was able enough. I led him over the boulders to the base of the cliff I had descended. "Where are the others?" I demanded, again.

"Gone," he mumbled faintly in Ojibwa. For a fleeting moment, Hadakotana and our playful game of words flashed into my mind. This was no game, and time was our enemy.

"All? All gone?"

"Gone." There was no mistaking his meaning, but how certain could he be that all were lost? I fanned the fingers of both my hands in front of him, counting them off one-by-one, and one finger once more.

"All," I repeated, "All gone?" This time, he scooped up pebbles and laid them out in three sets of four. I caught his meaning. "You," I said pointing to him. He pointed to his position represented by the last set of pebbles; he was the steersman for the third canoe. White Feather, I knew, had steered their lead canoe. "Gone? White Feather, gone?" I asked.

"He gone."

I needed some verification, something tangible. So I pointed to the stern of the first canoe represented in the sand, fearing my Ojibwa might be unequal to explaining what I had to know.

He made an upward motion of hand and arm, striking his elbow against the rock. By this means, I learned that as the bow of the canoe angled up, White Feather in the stern took the full brunt of the hit as the bottom crashed into the rocks.

Ashkote, for that was how he was called, though bruised and hurting was anxious to quit the grave site. We had reason to hurry. The sky to the east was already beginning to darken, and we needed eyes to climb, especially up under the ledge below the top of the cliff. Yet, even with Ashkote confirming the worst of my fears, I could not hurry off, not yet. I needed more proof. I signed him to wait.

Once again, common sense was at war with my instincts as I fought for balance on a narrow ledge of slimy rock, the one that jutted farthest out over the river. I scanned southward, seeing not a trace even of wreckage. Nothing. Of course, reason would have told me to expect nothing to float up against the current. I could linger no longer, and turned to go back. Weighing each step to judge my footfalls, I went forward with arms extended to keep my balance. How was it that in looking straight ahead, my eye caught a glimmer of white to the side? It lay trapped in a depression where water pooled in among the rocks. My heart pounded as I squatted belly down on the slimy ledge, and in a long reach, caught it up.

In my hand lay a feather. —Could I be sure it was his? Not the token left behind by an eagle preying on the river?

I could be sure. In the notch at the bone end, strands of black hair wound around in a tight coil. His body, swept into the undertow, left behind its frailest member. I grieved, cursing that mad river and the God who made it, choking down my silent curses lest they echo up to Jan and the others, and instill hope where none remained.

We ascended the cliff, myself first, being in better condition and better able to lead us up than Ashkote. As we came over the top, Grey Eagle gave a whoop, exuding joy at being reunited with—he may have thought—the first one of his men. "Only one," I said, shattering any growing hope.

At sunset, we held a brief ceremony on the ridge. Grey Eagle spun tobacco over the side of the cliff to placate the spirits of the dead swallowed up by the river. He and Nadowe chanted, joined by the Micmac who bestowed his own plea. Jan and I planted a cross to mark the site. All this while, I kept the feather hidden, knowing the savages might try to claim it. Burying all belongings with the deceased was one of their practices, and I had no mind to raise a quarrel by openly violating their credo. Anyway, White Feather was neither Ojibwa, Ottawa, nor Micmac. He was Iroquois.

Later, Ashkote recounted and Grey Eagle haltingly translated the telling of how Ashkote, who'd been some distance behind, watched as one twisted body after another careened on past, powerless to aid, so imperiled were he and his own men. The racked bodies of those in the middle canoe floated by first, well below the cataract. He saw the lead canoe strike and break apart just above the cataract, and the demise of his own canoe was similarly fated. It happened between a wall of boulders, where instead of gaining passageway, his canoe swerved, plunged backward, and driven into the rocks was split asunder, leaving all four canoemen adrift in the foaming rapids. Ashkote, alone, was close enough to lunge at the boulders.

A birch canoe, like the swipe of a cat's paw, might bounce off a rock and cause itself little harm. But this was like throwing oneself into the waiting teeth of a tiger. Yet, the same rocks that wreaked destruction on ten, became the salvation of one. Just one, Ashkote had been cradled by them. The river took its toll disproportionate to our number. Eleven in all.

In days to come I would look secretively upon that bone-white feather, even as I had once looked on my family talisman, but differently. Now the cost I brooded over was the cost by which survivors inherited such possessions. When the time came to part with my grandfather's and father's—and my own ghostly memento, the parting came easily. Perhaps this was because I had come to value it for what it was and was not. It's value was as a gift. Longings, promises, demands attached to an object over the generations held futile representations lacking substance. But one white eagle feather would lodge with me, forever. and so would the spirit of a lost 'brother'.

In the aftermath of disaster, my destiny took a new turn. I determined after the loss of White Feather, to stay on and go all the way to Montreal with Jan and his paddlers. Why retrace the ancient route White Feather and I had followed west from Albany, when a more well-traveled route would take me into country I'd not yet seen?

Grey Eagle and Ashkote left us at the Lake of the Nipissing, having met up with another band of their far flung people and gaining, thereby, the promise of returning to The Great Carrying Place, come next season. In exchange for gifts I still carried, and supplies Jan decided we could do without, we gained a share of furs—ones we'd transported with Grey Eagle in our canoe, and a welcome addition they were to Jan's own bundles.

The wide shallow waters of the Nipissing held to a steady chop as we—our number reduced now to four—paddled across, threading our way from island to island lest the wind pick up and force us to make a run for land. After ascending the wild French and escaping its treacherous plunder, the expansive water of this none-to-gentle lake seemed an unlikely grave. We rested at a meadowy end to the north, and the next morning entered a river of small streams, ponds, and portages, the one called the Mattawa.

I forced my mind to think of the future. I'd not forget them should I live a thousand years, but it was time to cease lamenting the departure of Gregor, natural half-brother by blood, and of White Feather, brother by esteem and affection. Jan, too, felt a need for discourse, and we talked on companionably with our paddles responding in rhythm. We talked of Sir James and our separate apprenticeships in the wilderness. Of fortunes to be made through all we had seen and learned of this land. And of its various peoples, some of whom did not fit the image of 'savage' we Europeans accorded them, and we counted ourselves fortunate for having met exceptions to the commonly held belief by which whole races were deemed "savage."

And so as long days passed. When the work of the river freed our hands, Jan and I bonded together in renewed friendship, confident that with the worst behind us, only the best could lay ahead.

Chapter 44.

The Rivers Mattawa and Ottawa

No two rivers are the same and he who thinks otherwise has never coursed the waterways of this America of the North. Yet, a river when it follows one upon the next, day-in day-out, can hold no new delight, no new torture. Only a dreary sameness sticks. Terror, monotony, and back-breaking toil. A chain of rivers, lakes, rocks, and forests will do for a cell as nicely as a prison. As for a gaoler? Consider the canoe: How many thousands of times over is paddle put to slow or rushing waters, blade turned against a current, pole pushed through shallows, cargo lashed to the backs of its toilers, toilers who then—irony of ironies—must carry their means of transport on their heads! How efficient a thing I once thought the canoe when, as a fledgling, I first skimmed along the Mohawk in the company of Sir James and Sir William and White Feather.

Whether my final judgment of this journey into the Interior would be a curse or a blessing upon Sir James who masterminded it, I left to the future somewhere on the River Mattawa, whose passage delivered all Jan had foretold.

A bewildering, formidable curse of portages, numbering upwards of thirteen were on its course. Among so many, the count ceased to matter, only the end. We saw large numbers of rude crosses stuck near rapids to mark the demise of less fortunate travelers, fur traders for the most part, and not, uncommonly, a cross named a priest or trapper. I strove hard to avoid cultivating the sense of defeat that was edging-up on me, day-by-day. Accordingly, night after night, I lectured myself: Weariness, you can scarcely hide. But, defeat even if felt, you must not display. Harden your head and shoulders! as Jan and others learned to do.

Well along on the Mattawa, Jan asked this question. "A rapid below a falls, I recollect, should be the last downstream rapid we shoot?" His question was for Nadowe, and Nadowe confirmed it. This was a timely exchange. It relieved my gloomy foreboding that ours was a virgin voyage up these rivers. Indeed, it was a virgin travail in that no two could be alike. Yet Jan's recollection and Nadowe's assurance worked to offset my gloom. I clung to the thought that others had survived our ordeal to tell of it. No one could expect promises!

On the whole, I supposed the countryside to be pleasant enough but, that it lay aside a river made each appearance increasingly unremarkable. Now, compare this to a merchant ship! A ship can take its captain and crew under sail for three or more years. Lay over in fabulous cities off coastal Arabia or Canton, feast on curried delicacies rich in fresh meats and ripe fruits; take their ease in coral islands of the Moluccas, and harbor in Cape Town, claimed by our Dutch East Indies now, a half century, ago. And, so leaving the Spice Islands, A well-laden Merchant ship voyages on home.—Ah, well, how the mind does rove and roam among verdant pastures a world away, canceling out unknown dangers and disasters.

From the Mattawa, we entered the River Ottawa at latitude 46°. Often, I had taken readings and, so many being repetitious, they seemed pointless at the time, and I'd not bother to record them. But this reading followed a singular burst of cheerfulness when Jan announced: "God willing, LaChine lays but little more than a week ahead, and with the water lower now than it was in May!" My energy renewed by his remark, I set to calculating distances in my head while questions had to wait, since he held the stern and I, the bow.

A light rain continued to fall, the kind I'd come to dread. A downpour out of nowhere will often stop as quickly as begun, refreshing the body and lifting the spirit as sun steams through the clouds, warming one around like a blanket. But steady, unrelenting drizzle, such as kept us company day and night on the Ottawa, soaks one's outer and inner clothing to a skin-tight shroud. Dampness so chills and penetrates the body that one paddles, frantically, just to work up heat! That we covered greater distances more, swiftly, was reckoned a fortunate consequence.

Pangs of longing for my native lowlands struck me forcibly, once, when scanning the countryside along the river, and I fancied a stretch of gentle hills merging into dikes bordering a canal. Or, when in place of a meadow dotted with trees, I envisioned fertile fields and tall windmills. Was this illusionary daydreaming occurring too often of late? I worried whether my mind was turning feeble. At length, I spoke of it to Jan to see if he suffered in such a way. When he stopped laughing, he said, "I have many imaginings, Piet, most every night!"

This malady, if such it was, disappeared of its own as we began running a stretch of non-ending rapids of some four leagues as one rapid succeeded another. Muin, habitually stood in the bow in high waves, calling out, "HAW!" for the two in the middle to speed up or BEKA! to brake. Before rapids, Nadowe sometimes steered us into an eddy and, while we waited, tested the river depth. Too shallow a rapid forced on us yet another portage.

All along this stretch we kept to the north-most side of the Ottawa. Apart from portaging, our only stops to repair canoes or sleep came in waiting out a derelict cross wind. Soon after the third set of rapids a yellow sky turned inky dark, and the wind gusting up a warning, we made for the first landing place to show itself along this rock-strewn river.

The routine of our chores was long since established. We all worked to unload and, since the rain had ceased we opened all the packs to the air. Jan and I overturned and braced the canoe to roof us in, then tied down canvas to make walls for a shelter. This done, we stripped and strung our clothing on willow branches to dry out by the pit that Nadowe dug to contain a low fire. Muin, meanwhile, if not gathering more sticks and, if time allowed, foraged or hunted for small game. One or both of them made our supper.

"These duties fall upon them," Jan said, motioning toward the opening of our shelter, "because my instincts told me to add 'cook' to my bargain when hiring them."

"Grateful I am for your instincts! I suppose, like myself, you've brought down a partridge or woodcock in our lowland marshes?"

"Only twice," he said. "I was better at leaving bits of forage inside the trapdoor of my mother's hut for scavenging rabbits. If they took the bait, we'd have meat."

I was well aware that hunting forest game in Holland, such as deer, had passed out of the provinces, ages ago, while great flocks of birds migrated in and out, and were legal to hunt. As for either of us cooking, I trusted our skill only with fish.

We sat hunched over like two black bears (Their skins did, indeed, wrap us) and we fell into conversation. Jan stretched out his legs, and with a looking glass in one hand and a knife in the other, began trimming his beard.

"Montreal is how many days from Albany?" I was learning much of the geography of the Interior, but of Montreal I knew only that it lay north of Albany, and desired to know more.

His mouth, pulled to one side as he scraped away at the other side of his face. When it slid back into normal position, he took up my question. "On foot through a wilderness full of streams, mountains, and scarce trails—if one doesn't fall afoul of savages—sleeps only two hours a night for as many as twenty-thirty days. Then travels by water, with few portages and none of them too arduous—that takes another eight, maybe ten days. Why do you ask?"

"Why? Because you left Montreal in late April, and spent upwards of seven months, somewhere, from the time you left me in Albany." Back to his beard, and maybe by intent, he took his time to answer so simple a question.

"I left Albany in a bit of a huff," he said at length. "Our little squabble, and Mistress Mary Graves for that matter, soon fell out my mind. Especially when stalking foot trails, alone, while keeping a sharp eye out for English militia who might take me for a Frenchman—I with this skin and hair. Nor was I eager to run into a bloodthirsty Iroquois—or Susquehanna, Delaware, Potawatomie— God only knows who'd have cracked my skull on Monday if I lived through Sunday."

I pondered the merits of this, suspecting it held more swagger than substance, a side of Jan more pronounced than I remembered. But I too had changed in the time we'd been apart.

"It was only the second day out," he continued, "when a lone Mohawk came rampaging out of the woods, running towards me with his hatchet in mid air." Jan angled his knife up as far as our lean-to permitted. "I narrowly missed losing my cover." He tapped the blade to his head, set it down, and tied his hair back at the nape of his neck. Most often, both of us left our hair hanging loose to swish away flies, our hands, since Georgian Bay, being steadily occupied with a paddle or the straps of our packs.

"I did not suppose Sir James would send you off alone."

"No, he thought not to. The two savages he assigned me as escorts were Iroquois. He said they were to accompany me until I neared Lake Champlain. When, we came too close to New France for their comfort, Sir James said I could expect them to turn tail. And so they did! Those two—I called them Nip and Tuck—had a fondness for sneaking off, well before leaving me for good. All of a sudden, they'd break out of the trees and steal up behind me, noiseless as only savages can, and break out howling and screeching. Seeing me flinch seemed a game to them, after they'd watched how I jumped when that first savage—the Mohawk—came after my skull, and I was all charged for a fight to the kill. But one of my guides. Nip, I think dispatched him with a threat,—the Mohawk was kin to them, they gave me to understand.

"But, I say to you, Piet, any I met could be my enemy or presume me theirs. I tell you Nip and Tuck set me on edge."

"Good training. Keep you prepared."

"Hmmph, before ever I set foot in the Valley of Champlain, I ordered them to leave. To go back to Sir James on the pretext, that to earn the rest of their payment, they must deliver my message into Sir James's hands before two sunrises.

"Did I tell you Sir James gave me two letters of safe conduct? One was signed by Lieutenant Governor Leisler...You know, Sir James,— he said it might do me some good should I be stopped by English militia because Jacob Leisler was their leader. But on no account was I to show it to an English officer! Leisler was a merchant, Sir James explained, not an aristocratic soldier tied to the English Crown."

"And the other?" Jan had my full attention,—and his own as he left off shaving with a quarter of his chin still bearded.

"Ah, the second paper he gave me bore the signature of Comté de Frontenac. 'Now that,' Sir James assured me, 'would take me safely into New France—padded as needed with livres.' Of course, he also warned that French soldiers when roused up on the quick were no different than any others—They'd lay me out, first, and check later to see what papers I might carry."

"The message you gave your guides—was it only a ruse to rid yourself of them, or did you truly entrust them with a message for Sir James?"

"Oh, a message of sorts. I told Sir James to expect nothing from me if I found better treatment from the French than we'd received from the English and the Dutch. Also, Piet, I said that I'd left my quarrel with you behind me. That I would do all in my power to meet you at Gran Portage, and to bring you back with me to Montreal."

Was this more bravado or was he serious? I stared in disbelief. It had grown steadily dimmer inside our makeshift shelter. Little more than reflective things like the blade of his knife caught the thinning rays of daylight, and not enough to see if his pupils bore a telltale flicker. I needed air. I held back on my burning question long enough to raise the flap of our lean-to, then check the progress of our supper. "The fire is making good coals; it's about time Muin uses them, but what I want to know is this, Jan: Am I to understand that my going to Montreal was prearranged?"

"Not with Grey Eagle, Piet!—You positioned yourself among us with the Ojibwa before I ever learned you'd arrived. But insofar as possible, our meeting at the western end of Lake Superior and the return was Sir James's intention, all along. You do not recollect that he spoke of this?—It was the day we lunched at the lodging of Widow Spence."

"I recollect his exact words,—that you and I would, God willing, reunite at Gran Portage, but never did he say that I would return by way of Montreal! You know well, it is the loss of White Feather that prevents me from returning by way of the Saint Lawrence—his destination lay somewhere near its headwaters, with his people. We spoke of this at Gran Portage, White Feather and me."

"True. But, I knew far better than you, all that lay before us before we would reach the departure point on the Ottawa for going up the St. Lawrence. If we made it that far, I had every hope of dissuading you, and to take you, at least, on to Montreal.—Sir James bade me do so, Piet. His words were, 'If taking Van Doorn to Montreal proves the more practical route, do it.' At the time, I did not question him, all seemed so unknown. Who would think we would actually meet some 500 leagues distant when for both of us, drowning or death by torture or—any one of a hundred other hazards—seemed the more likely.—Piet, does not our meeting at all strike you as a miracle?"

"Not so much as you think it, Jan. In the beginning maybe. But since then I've learned that if one doesn't perish on the way, God knows, this land with rivers for roads, and no Amsterdam or Rotterdam or Paris—or any city worth dallying in—why, meeting up seems as likely as not!" This lighter turn to our conversation quite restored us. Comparing the more 'practical' details of our two routes could wait. I was eager to know how he fared with the French, and he just as eager to tell me.

"At the Fort of Ste. Therése, I showed my papers to a squadron of French soldiers, and in their gallant company, had an escort on to

Montreal. I like the French, Piet. I'm going to endeavor to trade out of New France—I've made friends. Although I won't deny it's still a risky gamble, and more than ample reason to forget a fragile woman such as Mary Graves."

"She would have you, Jan, unless her affections have turned. Her very words were, 'You may tell Jan Carpentier that I do not object to his calling upon my father when he returns this way, again.'"

"Ah, those precise, careful, cautious words do bring back her fair image, they do." His chest heaved with a long sigh. I, misinterpreting its nature, was about to offer words of encouragement, when he leaned forward and leered, mischievously. "I've not been without women these long months." My face must have slipped into its old way of showing my thoughts for he smiled, broadly. "Only two women, my faithful Dutchman. One French and one not, or mostly not."

"And which one awaits your return?"

"Both."

I was used to Jan's way of baiting me,—as if one woman was not enough. On this occasion I outdid him, arching an eyebrow and playing man of the world as though his trysts were of no account. If my nonchalance disappointed him, my next questions did not.

"In Montreal, Jan, how is it you could establish yourself so quickly to gain a foothold in the trade? How did you manage to command your own crew into the Interior? I've heard that all traders must be licensed by the Crown, and death to any foreigners caught smuggling."

His swaggering tone returned as he talked on. "As you know, my French is not so good as yours, although I am half Flemish. I should say my 'courtly' French is not so good. I do very well in taverns, brothels, and with the French habitants of Canada, ones who are not so solicitous that we intone like King Louis. So I talked! Talked with boys who ran errands for the trading houses. Talked with peddlers, clerks, trappers of any breed, color, politics, or religion. I made friends with a priest newly arrived from a Jesuit house outside Paris—I sought shelter at his little stone church—and..."

"Let me guess! He taught you to speak proper French."

"Oui! Tu comprends bien. He did in exchange for my help—You'll never guess what that help was, Piet!"

"Oh, I suppose you prepared his sermons."

"Close! I paddled him from côte to côte as he made the rounds of his parishioners. And I carried his instruments."

"Instruments?"

"His little altar, chalice and things for saying the Mass."

"You do pass for a Papist!"

"Don't turn up your nose, Piet. I can chant the Te Deum like a choir boy. All the habitants are Papists and profess loyalty to King Louis as to God."

"This priest—" I'd all but forgotten. "I met a Jesuit in crossing the first of the Great Lakes, a Jean Baptiste, who knew..."

"Yes, I too met a Jean Baptiste! He was leaving Montreal to go deep into Huron country to the South by way of the Saint Lawrence." He made another gasp of wonderment in spite of my having just pointed out that it was not so strange for travelers to meet when routes into the Interior are few and time of travel so short.

"I learned more than to sing in Latin, Piet. I learned about the local trade. You're right about licensing! Nobody gets one if the Crown doesn't issue it, and that's about twenty-five for all of New France. So, learning how the local trade worked—and mostly didn't— I made a little offering to Father Francis's church and requested an introduction to a fur merchant's daughter.

"Probably, you do not know that parents who don't wed their daughters by a certain age are fined in New France, because King Louis is set on increasing the colony's population." I did not know, of course, nor did Jan expect me to know.

"I earned Marchand Papa's trust!—No, Piet—I made no promises to his lovely daughter. I only flourished my paper—and with only slight deception, said it was the Comté Frontenac's own wish that I be entrusted with a cargo of trade goods, the cargo to be redeemed in furs before the end of next season. And as a measure of good faith, I took Sir James's advice and padded his palm with livres. It was not too difficult. As among us, there is no great rush of Frenchmen desirous of leaving home to take up residence in a wilderness, unless they are convicts, impoverished peasants or, like yourself, bent on making a fortune, no matter the risk."

Jan knew that more than making a fortune brought me here to the New World, but my admiration for his cunning and success being fervent, I did not mention my brothers, but continued on, amiably. "Jan, had I a flagon, we'd toast properly. As is, let's be content with a cask." Muin, at that moment, stuck his head in the flap to call us out.

The enterprising Nadowe had caught up a loon as the bird slept, wings folded, atop its watery bed. Impaled over low coals and roasted crusty on the outside and sweetly tender inside, the bird yielded scant portions for two, much less four. We filled our stomachs with flat pancakes made from flour and baked over a round stone. Jan and I thanked our bird snatcher and our cook for the feast by presenting each with a dram. Jan poured from a small flask kept for just such a purpose. Savages are inclined to drink liquor like one catches water from an overhead spring. Heads back, they let it flow into their mouths, taking great gulps to keep up with the stream. But on this occasion, there would be no stream.

Nadowe thrust out his wood cup for more. Jan upended the flask and let the final dregs drop inside. Nadowe grunted his displeasure, but grew content as he and Muin, drawing out otter-skin pouches, filled their stone pipes with tobacco. They lit up with embers from the fire. The smoke soon gave off the aroma of a trade tobacco. The rain having abated some, Jan and I sat on by the fire in silence, and waited for them to finish smoking, and then move ourselves inside the shelter. We heard the snores of first one, then the other. Then, we set-to at the choice wine we'd saved for ourselves.

Jan wasted no time in launching into an earlier theme of our conversation. "What about you, Piet? Have you had no woman? The one you left in Amsterdam must be pale and drawn by now."

Compared to Jan, I had nothing to tell. But his words held such expectancy as the embers of our little fire burned down, and warmed by good food, too much wine, and in the presence of a trusted companion, I fell into telling an amorous tale of a lover. A lover she was not, but with no suitable women braving the hinterlands—I could scarcely invent such and be believed! In short, I found myself without naming names, embellishing upon the charms of Animiki. How bewitching she looked in white deerskins! How she'd befriended me, even saving me from the wrath of the odious Long Smoke, whom I likened to a witch of Modoch, gluttonous for my life's blood. Jan hung on each word and never had I guessed at my talent for storytelling! I blabbered on without ever disclosing Little Thunder's tender years, nor the brotherly affection in which I regarded her. It was apparent that what Gregor had so wrongly suggested about

Animiki's own affections—being the discrete brother he was—had not been passed along. Jan could think what he would. Knowing him as I did, he would think all the better of me. On the morrow, I was sure to think less.

Chapter 45.

Montreal

Jan pointed to cinders in the campfire that morning, saying, "Blacken your hair, Piet. It's not uncommon to see light hair in Montreal, but the darker yours hangs, the less people will take notice of you.—Let it mask your grin!"

Indeed, the expression he took on of a stern, tutorial professor was so at odds with his absence of schooling, I could not hide my smile. While, at the same time, I chided myself, knowing how little my bookish education at served me in this New World. And, as noted on several occasions early on in this record, I did not lack for understanding of sooting up one's face, and had done so when my white face might draw unwanted attention. Still, I made no rejoinder. Like Gregor, Jan had a need to instruct. Nor was he quite finished.

"Listen, Piet. The French will relish Dutch meat as much as they do the tasty British. Besides, that haughty nose of yours might be mistaken for an Englishman's."

"This nose serves me well enough, Jan. But, does yours sniff so well? You profess a strong liking for the French, yet you paint them with the nature of cannibals."

"Not so, not as regards the race of them." He turned, thoughtful. "Though, I have heard of the flesh of an enemy afloat in a stew pot."

"Well, such things are known to happen. The ancient Gauls ate human flesh thinking to cure diseases. You've not heard of this foul practice, elsewhere, Jan?"

"Yes, but I'd not known one who had done so, until in talking with Jean Baptiste. He told me, himself, of such a time when he was off visiting among the tribes. He felt uncertain when invited to feast with them, if he was to be their guest or their hostage; that he felt quite faint upon seeing human fingers eaten as we would eat cake. Maybe, it was to impress his savage hosts—I don't know this—the priest said only that he felt 'most strongly obliged' to partake."

Once he started, Jan could go on with lurid tales, one after another. I did as he bid, blackened my hair, and listened with half an ear. On this day I had no real cares. I felt buoyant as a fresh sea with a bright sun roaming an azure horizon. If all went well, this day should see us close to our destination. The winds having calmed, and ourselves refreshed by sleep, our clothing board-stiff, but dry,— we had determined to make all possible speed to reach Montreal. Getting to any destination would spur me on.

My own reactions in outrunning currents and rapids was no less than my companions, and had by now approached second nature. After these long months of reading waters—flat, shallow or fast,— placid surroundings slipped by me as in a dream. What was one more mass of rock, cliff, forest, stretch of river, lake, or stream. Not that I was unwary, but my sensibilities lacked engagement. I felt distanced from the river running under us or ahead of us; it was as though all the round world and everything in it moved on by in a fluid state. This period of detachment stayed with me for some time, and stayed until we were nearing a portage by rapids of the Long Sault. I roused myself enough to remark upon what I perceived to look like charred remains of pikes sticking up from the bank; that these might once have walled in a palisade.

"So they did...more or less." Jan spoke with a rare tone of awe in his voice. "It did serve as a palisade once, only its hurried construction was fence more than fortress. You'll find that all of New France honors a fiery young Frenchman by name of Adam Dollard. It was about 1660, when Dollard led seventeen men of New France and a mere handful of friendly Indians against a band of Iroquois, surprising them before they could attack. Dollard and his men took cover on that self-same spot you're looking at.—And, you see what's left of it." His voice trailed off as we began besting swift running currents.

Once back in the calm, I asked him to tell more of what he knew of this Dollard.

"Why, had sheer bravery been enough, Piet, Dollard's men would have won straight out! They held the growing ranks of the Iroquois off for five days, first with muskets, then swords—hatchets, then hands. But in the end, Dollard and his men were either slain or burned to death. A Huron who escaped—or deserted—lived to tell about it.

He claimed to have fought on the side of the French, and that the Frenchmen had held off some seven hundred of the enemy."

"Do you believe those odds, Jan, sixteen against seven hundred—even one hundred?"

He shrugged, noncommittally. "It's what they say—the habitants. They say, too, that Dollard's stand held back the Iroquois from warring against Montreal and Quebec. No doubt the savages lost heart. Wouldn't you?—if so many of your warriors were killed by a few armed men in a flimsy barricade? That battle was some forty years ago. Of course, the Iroquois still come. Only, now, they tend toward coming in small numbers, and kill and raid in the dead of night."

"Citizens of Montreal, I suppose, keep their guns loaded and doors locked at all times, just as in Albany."

"They do. And so, also, they bathe in the river, till their fields, and visit taverns by twos and fours."

We reached Lac des Deux Montagnes, the next day, and made a crossing of this lake, one that formed a wide path in the river, and was of some seven leagues long. We left a village and, what looked like a mission, behind us, choosing not to stop for rest; and, going on made another thirty leagues or more on mostly fast water. Then, as though daylight had charged into night with no dusk forthcoming, the most wrenching sounds, thunderous and pounding, assailed our ears. On the instant we swerved landward, before Muin could even "HAW". What a formidable sight just ahead! And, why had no forewarning come from Jan? I knelt as though glued to the planking to stare, open-mouthed, at the most deadly falls I'd yet beheld!

Jan, eying me, and laughing like a raucous crow, alerted me to a joke of a kind of which I was ignorant. Nadowe in the bow looked on, expressionless. No grunt came from Muin in the stern. Either the pair were as puzzled as myself or better mannered than our captain.

"Spit at those rapids, Piet! Those are the boiling rapids of LaChine.—But, my friend, we will reach Montreal by way of land."

How quickly does growing anger turn to exaltation at such glorious news. I fairly breathed "LaChine, at last!"

What satisfying assurance is solid ground underfoot. Nadowe and Muin stayed behind, while Jan and I walked not so short a distance;

nor did it seem overly long; for our purpose was to engage a cart and horse that would haul us and our bundles into town. Nor, did we discuss or quibble over the high cost of procuring the service of cart and horse.

Yes, the ground beneath our feet was solid enough. Also, it was visibly scarred. I was aware that scarcely two years had passed since the massacre of LaChine's populace by some fifteen hundred warring Iroquois. Where once had stood dwellings, I saw signs of desecration sticking out from the rubble all around us.

"Tell me, Jan, what are a town's defenses in New Canada?"

"Each little côte fends for itself in an attack," Jan said with a grim face. By 'côte' was meant a settlement of six to ten houses or so, built close together along the river. "But, he added, jovially, one of the huts is certain to be a dram shop."

We bargained for a kind of plough horse and a cart strong enough to carry our load of furs. And so, as we were joggled along back to the spot where Nadowe and Muin awaited our return, Jan enlightened me more about this New France.

"Thievery, Piet, puts everyone on guard. And why not, I ask you. Let me tell you.—Stealing is reasonable—if not respectable. Supplies from abroad are so scarce. And promised shipments face such long delays. Few are delayed or never received because of shipwrecks or piracy. No, the Crown is outright negligent. Can't or won't see an inch beyond their lofty noses.—Do they think their colony can turn furs into tools and trees into iron, squeeze flour from soil? The habitants have little industry or even the makings for it. No, Piet, we'll not risk leaving our canoe and our belongings to be raided by some prowling citizen."

After transferring our bundles from the canoe into the cart, Jan ordered Nadowe and Muin to stay put, make camp, and wait for our return, upon which, they would be paid as promised.

"It's a mere precaution," Jan had said. But I, knowing him so well, surmised that thievery was a lesser fear than how we might be received in Montreal. Leaving our trustworthy Nadowe and Muin with the canoe would assure us of having a way out, should one be needed.

All looked peaceful enough as we bounced along in the cart passing a field in harvest, the glint of a farmer's scythe catching the last shreds of golden twilight. In the distance a great hill stood darker than the sky, and as we drew nearer, saw just below it, dots of lamplight flickering in little houses. I reveled to be once again in civilization! In spite of Jan's stern warnings, I was ready to overlook the 'French' in these French citizens of New France. And, I'd even ignore the threat of hostile savages. I must say, having heard much talk and many stories about the evils perpetrated by savages in the New World—and I don't for a moment doubt them—I do confess to having witnessed very little savagery with my own eyes, except for that butchering band of Hurons.

We lolled on toward town at the slow pace of the old dray horse who, aware of his purpose, would not be hurried. With no habitation save hut, wigwam or overturned canoe these many months, I was fired with impatience to reach the town, and pleased to see, looming ahead, the outline of a great stone building, one that turned out to be a mill. As we clopped on by, I saw it was fortified with holes to deploy cannon. A row of wood houses stood between the mill and the Hôtel Dieu, and next stood a building with huge stone towers.

"It belongs to the Sulpitians," Jan said. I pleaded ignorance. "An order of religious,—missionaries like the Jesuits, although the Jesuits, themselves, may not think so."

The cart slowed just past the Hôtel Dieu. Across the front, light glowed at the edges of its shuttered windows. "Well done, Jan!" I said. "Rein in so we can install ourselves in a fine feather bed!" He shook his head. Alas, his destination proved to be at the rear of an adjacent building, a warehouse that bore the sign: LeBer, Marchand.

For some moments, I heard only the rustle of leaves, the lapping of waves from the nearby quay, and the clinking of the brass knocker. The town was asleep. No doubt sleeping, too, had been the gruff-looking man seconds before the small wood panel rattled to one side, and arrayed in candlelight his nightcapped-head leaned out the window. Squinting, and in a rasping flurry of French, he demanded: "State your names and your business with me, that you come knocking at such an hour! And if you be Constabulary, I have my weapon loaded, so be off."

"I am Jan Carpentier, Monsieur LeBer, and just returned. With me is a friend who wintered in the far country among the savages."

"Ah, Carpentier. You have merchandise?"

"I do. And more than is owed to repay you my debt."

"Good. Come back in the morning."

"Monsieur! It is true we are done-in from our long journey and in need of lodging, but there is more than that; I will not risk the lot being confiscated by officials or stolen while we sleep. Receipt me for delivery of eight bales and a cart. We can deal with the particulars of transfer in the morning." Jan's unpolished French was well suited to bargaining. Monsieur LeBer relented, and doing as he ordered, we took ourselves around to the warehouse dock to wait.

Some time it was before we heard a latch lifting, saw one side of the double doors swing back, and one length of heavy iron grillwork clang open. I, having already hitched the horse to a post, helped Jan push the cart up into LeBer's warehouse.

And what of a feather bed? This long, long day begun in the wilds off the Lake of Two Mountains was not yet, nor soon, to be concluded.

Chapter 46.

The Merchant of Montreal

"Eh, thirty bales castor sec, I pay 20 francs, 10 sols each. My best offer."

"No! No, castor sec, castor gras!" Jan retorted. "Castor gras from the Interior's Great Lake."

Jan and Merchant LeBer bickered back and forth over the quality of beaver spread out on the warehouse floor. Jan insisted that his furs were castor gras, the most valued of the beaver furs for their winter thickness and silky hairs. A seasoned merchant like LeBer, even were he born sightless, had only to feel them to know their worth. But he was a shrewd dealer of cards. It was apparent to me he was testing the mettle of a man years younger than himself and, therefore, one he would presume to be ignorant unless proven otherwise. Seeing Jan would not budge, the merchant acquiesced, not by word, but by an approving grin and a sharp slap to Jan's shoulder. The bargaining continued.

"Silver fox, two francs."

"Two? No, Monsieur LeBer, four is the going price." Jan persisted, and next demanded four francs, ten sous as his due for winter otter. LeBer also cut the going price of otter by half, and so on it went.

The merchant in a pious throwing up of his hands, reminded us in a wheedling voice that he had to pay for the permit, that the price of his trade goods had doubled, and he must recoup his losses for his good heart in having extended Jan credit. What followed, he spoke in so rapid a French and peasant-profanity, I could only guess at it, myself. Thankfully, Jan missed himself being named the equivalent of a 'no-nothing, beggarly bastard'.

As the bargaining continued, I fell into listening with a curious detachment as to the particulars, but not through disinterest, no indeed!—Our forty bundles were a small transaction, surely; yet I reveled in the thought of all that they represented. A whole continent held like opportunities! One ought to be reconciled to months of grueling toil and unrelenting hardship to esteem oneself a fur trader. Why, I had built strong friendships with the Loon and Bear clans, had means of procuring trade goods through Sir—My reflections halted. Negotiations in the warehouse were getting out of hand.

Whatever might be said of LeBer, Jan had become ever less circumspect as the haggling heated up. "In Albany, these fine, winter skins would bring triple your offer! You know it!"

"Aha, I do," acknowledged LeBer. But, have you means, so easy to transport skins to your English friends? You call yourselves free traders. Such a trade exist only when you have friends—a friend like me who take high risk to help you. Here, my young friend, the authorities enjoy to call your furs contrebande. They will enjoy to have you whipped and strung up for trading without the license." LeBer paused, lending silence to the effect of his words, turning a bleary one-eyed look on Jan. "The authorities, they pay good bounty for the scalp of an enemy.

"Before me, in my own warehouse is no friend? Is two enemy?" His eyes, shifted from Jan to me then rolled heavenward and, between the full flaps of his moustache radiated the confidently smug smile of the wily trader practitioner.

LeBer as he spoke, even to the red cloth draping his head, gave off the bold bluster of the pirate he was, and not for a moment did I doubt he would see that one or another of his threats was carried out, should we cross him. Broad shouldered and muscular with legs flared out in the blousy-blue pants of the French peasant, he stood foursquare in the warehouse aisle, mounds of pelts occupying two thirds of the packed dirt floor. Animal hides of beaver, otter, fox, lynx, wolf, even to some of moose and deer.

He stood against the inside wall, arms folded against his chest. But my attention roved from the man to the open cupboards on either side of him. They held a stash of items which, if LeBer's total inventory, indicated a sadly reduced supply of trade goods. I looked from him to Jan. The latter's hard leanness made a taut shell for the temper I knew was set to explode.

"You speak of License? You, Monsieur LeBer, drew up the note yourself for the trade goods we carried! And you well know, I paid in advance for a part of them, a thing not too usual among free traders! My canoemen were present; they will bear me out."

"Oui!" he whistled. "Sauvages? You would pose their word against mine,—the word of Henri Marcel LeBer, Marchand de la Nouvelle France, licensed to trade in furs by His Royal Sovereign, His Majesty, King Louis XIV of France, and...." He prattled on in a sustained mockery as though oblivious to Jan's heaving chest and dark-eyed scowl that, any second, threatened to lose us, everything, even life itself!

I brushed past Jan with feigned ease, bowed, and in a tongue more proper than he himself spoke, addressed le Marchand de Montreal.

"Up there, above your head, Monsieur LeBer, please be so kind." My role being that of the patient bystander, I had spoken little until now, so assuming a carefree nonchalance, I pointed to a shelf high up on the wall and to its folded stack of coats. "I have a liking for a capote, a fine capote. Serge, are they not? I wish to see the blue one, up close." LeBer obliged. As he was getting himself around the counter, reaching for the hooked pole stored aside the wall whereupon the shelves were bolted, and in the time he took to snag the blue capote, lying between the grays in the pile, I whispered a muffled, firm command in Jan's ear.

"Go easy, take less. He holds all the cards—and, he is well supplied with skins." Jan, arms locked across his chest, gave me a withering glance, but he looked around into the darkened corners, saw the warehouse's abundance of furs, and he knew I spoke truth. Could his swarthy complexion blanch, it would have paled into white.

LeBer returned, doffing the garment. I caught it up in three fingers and swung it over my shoulders with aplomb, just as though it had the fashionable cut worn by a courtier of Versailles when, in truth, except for the French button to the right shoulder, Dutch fishermen wore much the same.

Meanwhile, Jan having made an all-out effort to collect himself, took hold of the hem of the capote and made much of examining its coarse fabric. "It becomes you," he said, evenly. I took his taunt in good grace. In short order he turned on his heel and faced the merchant, squarely.

"Monsieur LeBer, one so honored by his King as yourself would not stoop to cheat. My apologies for misjudging your intentions." I expected the worst! Jan sounded as fatuous and scornful as the other had when mocking him, and Jan hadn't finished. "Monsieur, I believe you will sweeten our payment by being as generous to us as your King is to you. Include two capotes, one for my friend and one for myself.—I'll have a gray," he added, swinging on his heel. To his credit, LeBer threw back his head, laughed heartily, and acquiesced a second time. Jan, thereby saving face, concluded his business, and the two of us strode out into the night, newly cloaked.

"A bath and a good meal, Jan, are as close as the front entrance of the Hôtel Dieu!"

But, no, Jan informed me that, first, the cart and horse had to be restored, and Nadowe and Muin, eager to return to their own villages afar, must be recompensed without delay.

"Ah, of course, you are right. It is only fair." I acknowledged his decision, graciously, without conviction.

It was by now well past midnight, and with clouds obscuring the moon, we let the horse find us our way back to the quay, along the same path we'd taken earlier. We clomped on past the row of sleeping houses and were near the mill. I remembered the fields just beyond as they had looked in the golden twilight being freshly harvested. "Let's stop, here, Jan. We'll not find a better place to rest this night. Besides, your canoemen are dead to the world. We have the cart and our coats and, if need be, the horse to keep us warm."

A hand was tugging at my sleeve—I awoke all at once, and in the gray light of dawn, saw leaning over the edge of the cart, close—too close—that stealthy face with small ferret eyes. "Sarkey!" My gasp caught Jan in his sleep, even as Sarkey had caught me. On the instant, Jan leapt up, toppled Sarkey to the ground, and throttled him like a madman.

"St-op! Hol-d of-f!" Sarkey cried in a whining snivel.

A good pummeling is his just deserts, I thought, to sneak up on us so. Jan's frame of mind matching my own, he let loose of Sarkey somewhat later than recognition had set in. "Lucky you are, I mistook you for a habitant! Had I thought you a savage, I would have twisted that turkey neck of yours 'til it bled." Jan's apology, as half-hearted as I could wish it, strained the facts. Had Sarkey been a savage, it is certain Jan and I would both be dead, stripped of our clothing, scalps, and all else.

Once he quit sputtering and caught his breath, Sarkey, with a look of injured reluctance, slid his fingers inside his shirt and withdrew from a concealed pocket, a tightly-sealed missive. He eased it toward me like a recalcitrant child. The missive was cunningly creased and folded to forewarn the intended recipient, should another have tampered with it, first. Only one person could be its sender, and the handwriting confirmed it.

"Greetings to Pieter Van Doorn IV and to Jan Carpentier, singly or jointly. It being my expectation that the two of you will be well met in Montreal, I address you both.

In late October or by first November, I sail for Europe. Before departing, I desire to formalize our working relations if, having adjudged your dispositions correctly, you have indeed gained useful knowledge of the Interior these past months, and still continue in your enthusiasm for The Trade. My having other business more personal, you will please remain in Montreal to await my arrival which, if all goes well, should occur within a fortnight. Avoid the Hôtel Dieu, and request lodgings at The Cove Inn nearest the Quay.

Make no mention of your intentions to Sarkey, nor to any other. Sarkey has his instructions. Destroy this missive after reading, and keep its contents to yourselves alone. In the pleasure of seeing you both, again, I remain as I am, and unsigned."

Who but Sir James furnished such scant detail while promising so much! Sarkey's clipped tongue revealed, upon our pumping him for information, that he'd been posted to Montreal some weeks earlier to spot our arrivals, and, if what he told us could be understood and believed, he had tracked our movements within hours of our arrival. The draymaster was paid to inform him of persons hiring a cart and horse, a circumstance to be expected of fur traders making it all the way to LaChine.

After answering our questions, he finished by saying, "An', I nought be hang 'n roun' Mont'ral waitin' for y's more longer, being 's it' s' gett'n on in th' seezin. A've 'portant bizness a m' own." Jan made a rush at him, as though to throttle him again, and Sarkey, knowing no different, fled into what was left of the early morning hours when respectable persons sleep.

Jan was incensed. Having passed himself off among French officers, clergy and citizenry of Montreal,—and in particular, I surmised with one mademoiselle at the Hôtel Dieu,—Jan was having none of Sir James's ordering us about. "And to think," he stormed on, "I've been tailed by that vile ape of a Sarkey!"

We'd no more discharged our duties of returning the horse and bestowing generous gifts on two well-satisfied canoemen, when Jan began ranting, again. "Sir James be dammed! I've served him better than well! If he wants more, he can himself be the emissary and not set a sneaking Sarkey after me!"

"What rot!" I said with equal vehemence. "Sir James has the inclinations but not the endurance. Who is better skilled to steal his way from place to place than Sarkey? Could a bulky Englishman like Sir James? We know and Sarkey knows this. It's Sarkey who slipped through the English and French lines and found us. I say, if paid well, your "vile ape" delivers well."

"Like a dog he delivers! and only for his master Sir James. Don't try your luck with him, Pieter Van Doorn. He'll not serve you."

"It's not my intent to hire Sarkey. But I will accord to any who deserves it, his just due."

And to myself, also, was due some simple pleasure after long months of deprivation. I kept in eager step—No, I kept ahead of Jan on our way back to town and let him work out his surly mood, alone.

With my heightened expectations of the Hôtel Dieu, Sir James' advice to avoid it, could be easily ignored. I would begin with an order of cheese,—an entire platter along with bread made from wheat, and with butter. I couldn't expect from the French of Canada, to procure our fine Gouda cheese or Leyden butter, but the French reputation for Le cuisinier français ought to produce a dish somewhat like our hutsepot. Ah, weren't those special days when Ma-ma, herself, chopped up quantities of mutton and beef, green vegetables, and prunes, added a sprinkling of lemon and a strong apple vinegar. And after all boiled for three-four hours in a mixture of fat and ginger, ah, what aromas! We feasted on hutsepot the week-long.

Time had constrained Jan and I from eating most of one day and well into the next. I craved solid food! The people of New France— rather the habitants as Jan insisted they be called—must eat more than game. Perhaps squashes grew here or the potato. Not that we Dutch prized the potato. "Hah!"

"If it's a good laugh, Piet, let's hear it."

"Nothing much, Jan, I was just remembering Ma-ma coming home in a fluster over gossip she'd heard at the market. "Mevrouw

Toren!—She is said to have poisoned her husband by feeding him potatoes!" Pa-pa reminded her that it was a favored crop in Ireland, now, some 100 years. But, as you know, the potato still is not popular among us Dutch lovers of turnips and haricots and cabbages."

"Food's not so far, now." Jan's lethargy bespoke the void in his gut.

"It is not.—Look there." Limp, withered berries stuck to shriveled vines along the wayside. Jan's wan smile was as weak as my attempt at humor. Months must pass before either of us would be tempted, even had plump, red, juicy strawberries remained on the vine. My thoughts ran on, disjointed and to no purpose. All the while, my stomach rumbled, hungering for what lay ahead.—A fulsome meal at the Hôtel Dieu!

Chapter 47.

The Hôtel Dieu

Along the way, we passed nine or ten low-built, small log houses mortared with mud and sitting on squat posts, each close up to its neighbor with only stove wood piled between. Not enough fuel, I thought, to outlast a long harsh winter. Hay, too, was stored close by for the habitants' cows. I called Jan's attention to one house. A pump sat nearby, smaller, but fashioned much like the Dutch pump which came into use after a large warehouse for storing rope burnt to the ground.

"So? You stare like it's the first you've seen."

"Why, so it's for dousing water on the house in case of fire!"

Jan shrugged that I should think it such a wonder, but I was forcing myself to study all I saw. "Filling the mind eases an unfilled stomach!" I said. I spared him my observation that wood houses, here, were roofed with thatch much like those of Dutch farmers. Although in our cities, one saw houses with tiled roofs.

Finally! In passing the palisade we could look beyond to the stone exterior of the Hôtel Dieu. Coming out of wild, open country, the structure seemed most imposing, surrounded by its low wall and open gate. As though announcing our arrival, a toscin rang out from the belfry, setting the pigs to running about and hens to squawking. At the side of the Hôtel Dieu, an old man was picking through a garden already shriven of its summer produce. From the rear of the building came the sound of children's voices, a sweet, prayer-like song.

We rattled the clapper, and receiving no answer, let ourselves inside. No one was in sight—not the hotelier or attendant or maid. Nor was there any sign or sound of them. What's more, I was sniffing a heavy odor of what seemed like camphor and castoria.

On wide-legged planking rested well-scrubbed table tops, sanded to a high polish. Rows of these long tables stood in formation inside of a room of spacious size. The back wall was appointed with a large portrait of an ornately-robed Louis XIV in front of his gold palace of Versailles in its three-directional radiants. (No Dutch painter would produce so waggish a work.) On turning about, I faced a niche displaying a gaudy statue of a sainted figure. Off to the side, and cordoned off only by a grate, sat a kneeling bench before a lit candle and a large wood cross.

"What manner of inn is this, Jan? And is no one here to greet travelers?"

Jan gave me his sidewise smile, saying only, "Wait and see."

We had not long to wait. A drab, gray-garmented, plumpish woman descended the wood stairs wearing the headdress, not of a demoiselle or madame, but from out of a nunnery! She looked to be in her forties, but sprang towards us with the eagerness of a young woman. She held out her hand for Jan to kiss and, with extravagant praise for l'Enfant Jésus, Our Blessed Savior, Our Most Holy Mother of God, All the Holy Angels and Saints—and all this was in gratitude for Jan's deliverance from the ravishes of Iroquois and the Wilderness.

With a puffed-up look of pleasure, the toe of his new sabot tapping the floor, Jan interrupted her litany with one of his own. He praised the beneficence of her prayers, hers most particular. Then, hastily, he introduced me as his bon compagnon, and rushed to make his point before she could utter another word.

"Mother Magdaléne, I would like, also, to see Terése LeBer. Do me the kindness of granting a visit."

"Non possible!" Mother Magdaléne exclaimed, her eyes flickering to the ceiling, if not to Heaven, as she prattled on in a flurry of gestures and apologies, the crux of which seemed to be that, of the lady in question, an eligible gentilhomme having asked for her hand and she not yet promised, she was married before God and all Montreal just three short weeks past.

Jan appeared nonplused. He thanked her, profusely, and we escaped before she could put into action her heart's desire that we visit, in place of Terése LeBer, the chambers of the lonely sick installed on the second storey.

"A poor joke, Jan," I said, when once again I breathed fresh air.

"What, that you mistook the Hôtel Dieu for our lodging? You who sputter on in French as though born to it!"

"Here, it seems 'hôtel' suffers a new meaning. But, why were you incensed that Sir James should urge us to avoid the place? And, you giving me to understand—"

"Ah, I was angry. His interference makes me so. His orders are couched as requests, but we both know he means his way or no way. However, Piet, Sir James's warning does have purpose. Every manner of infection and disease descends upon the Hôtel Dieu. Who but the good nuns are here to care for the sick and ailing? Without them, who is here to instruct the growing number of children the settlement produces?—The King, as I told you, pays to increase his colony, but his coffers give far too little to support the urchins that live past infancy.

"But, of more import to our avoiding the Hôtel Dieu, Piet, is that strangers are suspect. Should any at the Hôtel Dieu learn of our stay in Albany—even though that was of a year ago—we would be highly suspect. Word would fly from the Hôtel Dieu to the Sulpitians—to the Intendant—"

Now, I interrupted. "You spent seven months in Montreal. Surely in that time you must have spoken of Albany!"

"Learn a rule with women and nuns, my friend. Speak little of yourself and say much about them."

"Your rule wouldn't hold with the French officers who gave you escort into New France! They had to know you weren't French. You had only to open your mouth—

"Ah, but I was already in French-claimed territory. I approached them; I was not their captive. Besides, I could drink and play cards with the best of them, and also bribe as needed. Anyway, they were to garrison in Quebec, not Montreal."

I had one more question as we continued on toward the quay. Already, the route was familiar, nothing in the town being at too great a distance from the Palisade. "Why did you not ask the Merchant LeBer after his daughter?"

"She was not my business with the father."

How many new parts one discovers in a friend when found in new circumstances. That Jan was shrewd, yes. But I'd not suspected he could so deftly divide business from taking his pleasure.

Now appeared both a church and a tavern and, gratefully, we stopped before the latter. It could have been staged the way, as one, all heads looked up from their cards and cups to stare. I'd been the subject of inspection on ship and among the tribes, but here I sensed more than curiosity lurked behind the looks leveled upon us as we came through the entrance to the Bon Temps. Clearly, some unknown approval was needed. Feigning ease, I looked down, across, and about us. On the inner wall, a long counter served all manner of operations. The counter was mid-point for the setting down of trays of drink and food from the kitchen, and from them emanated steamy smells, both rich and rank enough to make one swoon. Behind, at the mid-point, the innkeeper in leather apron and small pointed hat was setting down a tray. He nodded our way, giving a broad wink.

His wink was for Jan and I comprehended why, on looking beyond the innkeeper on down the rail. The counter served also as a backrest for three les femmes. Gaudily overdressed, they were, and moved out, conspicuous as peacocks in a barnyard. In fact, they flew up to ascend upon Jan. He clasped two around their satiny waists, and leaned forward to kiss a third, catching her on the cheek as she turned her lips away. That one was by far the prettiest of the three and more properly attired; that is, while less fulsomely exposed in her yellow, pleated bodice, she was the more fetching. I was in the act of slipping on past to arrange our night's lodging. and inquire about a table, when Jan released a waist to grasp my elbow.

"Mon ami, not so fast! Mon charmants wish to meet you," His deplorable French showed another side of him I'd not known before. (His encounter with Mistress Mary Graves could, scarcely, be called flirtatious, so shy and tongue-tied had been his demeanor but one year past.) He introduced me as Petri with flamboyant gesturing, and paying audacious compliments to each of us in turn.

For my part, I acknowledged them with "I'm honored," and bowed once, twice and, the third time bowing with more deference to one Jeanéne, my eyes lingering somewhat on her person in yellow satin so in contrast to skins, hides, and blankets. The similarity of their sizes—this Jeanéne's with Animiki's, struck me as though the little savage, were she to wear yellow satin with her dark hair spun in curls...The image would not form itself. I could no more envision Little Thunder with curls and in yellow satin, than I could Jeanéne in braids and deerskins.

By the time we were served, an hour or so later, even the thin soup with bits of chicken and herbs, served with a heavy and expensive dark bread, tasted most delicious, and should at two sous per bowl.

And one bowl was far short of being sufficient. The ladies trailed off, one by one, seeing the two of us engrossed in our meal more than their recitations about privations déplorable in Montreal.

In the days that followed, I saw little enough of Jan. By noon, some days he might rise up, dress, and then we'd lunch together. By the end of the first week, I had a churlish need to indulge my curiosity and, in so many words, asked with whom he spent his nights.

"I think, Piet, you really wish to know if there is one with whom I do not sleep. And, yes, there is one. Jeanéne turns her back on me. She goes the way of Terése! Marriage is the law you know, God Save the King."

Chapter 48.

Under Fire

Into the second week, this Montreal—this Nouvelle France I had so anticipated had lost its luster. Yes, even in the dim light of early evening, the spire of the church inside the bastion of Fort Ville-Marie rose up imposingly. Yes, houses of royal officials serving at the King's pleasure, like the Governor General's house of stone, stood out against the spare wood huts of habitants. And, yes, one could look down upon well-tended farms rimmed with forest, and beyond to the wide waters surrounding this widesome island. All this from the summit of Montreal's highest landmark,—a hill to some, perhaps, but a mountain to me.

Still, I could not bring myself to share Jan's enthusiasms for things French, nor for that matter, the 'French' of the habitants, themselves. This may be supposed, in part, due to the necessity of keeping our conversation so controlled as to be contrived. I steadfastly upheld Jan's stated principle of speaking little about ourselves, certainly nothing to link us to Albany or to the English, and if I slipped in a mention of the Dutch, it was in a manner as offhand as I would speak of the Portuguese or Russians!

In the frivolous company we kept, evasion was made simple since nothing consequential was expected of 'drawing room' conversation.

"Petri, if you please, you are you say from Picardy?

"Ah, mademoiselle, you are perceptive. Some ancestor was born there—just where, I cannot say. As for me, home is where I am at the moment."

"Jacques, it is certainement you are from Gascony."

"Ah, mademoiselle, if you wish it, it is so."

"Your hair, Petri, is blondeur, is it not? The sun, it make it so, oui?"

"Light or dark, some help is to be supposed from my father and mother, Mademoiselle Lorraine."

"But, of course!"

And so it went, the main thought in their cabbage heads touching on laces and buttons, and when a ship would arrive with new dresses—even if they be long discarded Paris fashions. My bookish French measured against the patois most of them spoke, sounded stiff, setting them off into gales of laughter which, at first, in their agreeable company with glass in hand, I was a full participant.

Though, as these occasions continued on, hearing laughter spilling out of their mouths for whatever silliness Jan or I might utter—be it witty or droll or mean nothing at all—boredom sat on me like a burr underfoot. Effort, then, was not in exchanging pleasantries, but in hiding the ennui I felt that might lapse into a telltale yawn.

All too soon, I would have pause to reconsider my harshness in prejudging the mettle of these pretty creatures and the town's habitants in general. Surely, frivolity and indulgence must be forgiven a populace so wearily beset by deprivation and savagery.

In the midst of one of our parlor conversations, a toscin rang out a strident, unmistakable warning. "FIRE!" screeched Monîque.

As one, we leapt up and crowded to the door. Clouds of smoke billowed above the Strand and orange flames riveted skyward. The mistress of the house rushed in and, opening a small closet, fetched an armload of leather buckets. At that same moment, a voice shrieked, IROQUOIS!" Only an instant did the horrific portend of that single word stick in our throats. "FUIR! FUIR!" clamored Lizette and, as one, each female grasped a bucket, picked up her skirt and fled to the Palisade.

Jan, yelling, "Arms are at the Palisade!" ran off, no doubt in expectation of me following right behind him. Instead, I beat up the stairs to our room, fetched both our pistols, and scrambled back down.

At the Palisade I found men well accustomed to defending a colony under siege. Jan, equipped like the others, held musket in hand. All were engaged and ready at the barricades—with no enemy yet in sight. And, as we watched the thickening flames, steadily spiraling upward over the Strand, I told Jan I might be needed more by the fire brigade.

In passing the far end of the Strand, I saw the roof of a house starting to crackle like a pile of dry tinder, while its neighbor looked to be beyond saving. I remembered the house with the Dutch pump further down and, hurrying on, lost no time in wrestling the latches to remove the pump. I'd about succeeded, when of a sudden, the lady of the house swooped out her door shaking her fists. Broad and red of face, she screeched, "THIEF! you dare steal my pump? Leave it! Leave..." Her scream died in a gasp; she looked half-crazed. And with cause!

Their throats a-quiver like ten thousand shrieking ravens, seven or eight war-painted savages, tomahawks raised, came leaping over the woodpile wedged between her house and shed. "God helpen!" My oath met with a pistol in each hand. I fired. One dropped, then a second. Stunned, by the unexpected attack, the five or more savages left dove back over the woodpile. The houses, torched or not, would make no bulwark against their return. The old woman could never make it to the Palisade. I thrust her behind me. To shield her as best I could, I ordered her to stay put and keep watch on the road, while I kept a constant watch on the perimeters of her house. For, unless the savages should retreat or circle around from the road, I expected them to divide and come at us from both sides of her house or its neighbors, and so close in on us.

In less than minutes, one hulking savage leapt over the woodpile and, zigzaging to keep out of pistol range, dashed toward us launching a tomahawk. He was swift; so was I. The blade edge only sideswiped my right arm, but deep enough, I dropped a pistol. The old woman, God bless her, retrieved the tomahawk, and was stooping for my pistol when two more came howling toward us. I caught the first square in the chest, then needed to reload. She was ready. Wielding the tomahawk like an ice axe, she took the second one down. I, meanwhile, still held one loaded pistol and dared the two savages who seemed to be coming back, to come at me. Why they came not at us and, instead, chose to carry off their dead did not figure. I waited, listening. After a time, I judged the battle over and told the woman I'd take her to the Palisade.

The poor dear stood all a-tremble as we turned to leave,—I thought in safety—until a flaming log struck me full in the back, bowling me to the ground. In the instant, I rolled over and up, just in time to fire at close range. He was badly wounded, blood oozing from his mid section. To be certain he was gone for good, we waited while he staggered off toward the river and out of sight. I sent up thanks heavenward for my having had the foresight to have fetched our pistols, and told the woman I would go to the Strand.

"Take my pump," she offered as she finished binding my bleeding arm with the cloth of her apron. She didn't know taking it with or without her permission was my full intent. "Be certain you return it," she added before I left her at the Palisade.

I kept a sharp eye out for any lingering savages in going back for the pump, then dragging it along the path leading to the end of the Strand where the bucket brigade still battled. The flames were receding, somewhat, but a second pump would shorten their work. I handed it over, making it clear to them that I was going to maneuver my way down river. "Cautiously," I added. "I will scout the area for any Iroquois still lurking about or for and of their reinforcements.

"You do that? No need," said a pock-faced habitant who introduced himself as Germaine. "We've had a poor harvest. The savages know there's little to steal. Also, they know If they burn too many houses, there will be less to steal. They come in small parties to frighten us. Usually, they come at night. We sleep not so good for fear they kill us and take our women and children."

"Will they be back, later, then, Monsieur Germaine?"

"They come back, yes, but no more today. The old lady, Veronîque. You saved her. To loan you her pump, she must to you be very grateful. She take better care of her pump than her husband!" He chortled, good naturedly, elbowing a short, stocky man whom I took for Master of the Pump. The pains Jan and I took in New France to avoid undue attention to ourselves, seemed for nought, and I tarried only long enough to tell the pump's "master" that his wife seemed well able to take care of herself, and the pump was being left in his capable hands to restore.

My swelling arm agreed that I was not needed, and having no liking for resuming life at the Bon Temps, just then, I pursued my longing to see what ships might lay at anchor on the River Saint Lawrence, east of the rapids of LaChine. A clean, clear walk to quit the smoke-filled sky was what I most desired!

The air freshened as the river widened into a deep bay, then narrowed again to where even a small ship would founder if it met low tide. And low tide had worked fate against the English fleet just one year past. A favorite boast heard round Montreal was how its clergy—officers, habitants, coureurs de bois—everyone young or old—swarmed to the aid of the Comté de Frontenac when Quebec was under siege by the English. When the battle was over, Sir William Phips and his royal fleet—what was left of it—had to limp all the way back to the Port of Boston Town.

But here now at this place all sounds were peaceful. I listened to the creaking of pinnace and caravel, barque and bateau, all lying at anchor to the soft lapping of waves meeting the shoreline. Screeching heron gulls circled overhead in an azure sky fading into purple. Peacefulness could lull a man, and I dared not venture too close to the shore where I might be seen. And, I stayed a discrete distance, too, taking sheltering among the trees on my walk back to the Bon Temps, walking with the stealth I'd learned in another place, had learned from another Iroquois.

Chapter 49.

The Embarking

I was awakened from first sleep by Jan opening the door to look in and make sure I'd returned. He stayed only long enough to inform me that the "heroic exploits of Pieter Van Doorn" were circling the town. With no further explanation, he slipped back out to 'pay respects' as he'd called it, to his 'liaison'.

Thereafter, I slept lightly, and not for long for, next I knew, I'd bolted upright. It was not rain I heard pelting the shutters but something like small stones. My mind flew to Iroquois seeking revenge. Cooler thinking quickly prevailed. It was not by tossing out early warnings would these savages terrify their intended victims, but by blood-curdling shrieks in the midst of attacking. My better sense reviving, I slid out of bed and crawled to the base of the wall beneath the shutters, that were still being lobbed by pebbles. More expectant, now, than fearful, I unlatched the shutters and, indeed, saw his figure outlined below.

"'Tis Sarkey, Sir," he whispered. "Hie 'erself down." He pointed to a hefty woodbox he'd 'borrowed'.

Some ingenuity, he had; but the power to fly, I had not. "Up-end it, Sarkey. Stand it tight to the wall!"

I threw on my clothes, tore strips off the bed covering to twist into a rope, and secured it to the bedpost. Grasping the ledge of the window, I lowered myself down on my 'borrowed' rope to within inches of the woodbox. Stealth was the only sure exit this time of night. Always, the outer doors of the Bon Temps were securely locked well before midnight, and even earlier on moonless nights.

The sum of what Sarkey was ordered to make known, and I struggled to catch, was this: Jan and I were to gather up our things. "Neow, neow," he repeated in a voice more cat-like than human. We were to board a vessel that would take us up the Saint Lawrence and around Quebec to the Strait. There, a British ship, with Sir James aboard, waited to sail. Not tomorrow or the next day, but "T'night, neow!"

At last! The finer points of what the future held were obscure, but to think I'd be once again under sail made my heart swell. Within some four to six weeks, if God blessed the ship's helmsman (as He had my pistol hand this very day) my present journey would end. And another could begin.

I grappled back up to our room the way I'd come down. That came easily. But now I must choose among four rooms in the Bon Temps. Jan would be ensconced behind one, but which one? Monique's came first.

I knocked softly and, ear-to-door, could hear the deep breathing that sleep brings. Hers? His? Wooden bars took the place of locks on rooms at the Bon Temps; they were to aid a quick exit in case of attack. A little jiggling and coaxing thrust the bar aside. The door creaked as I opened it, as did the floor. I heard a stirring and a woman's gasp. Then, sitting straight up, and her scream being imminent, I launched myself next to her person and clamped a hand over her mouth.

"My deepest apologies, mademoiselle,—I thought to find Jan, a—a Jacques." I stammered in my loudest whisper into her soft little ear.

"Petri! Ah, mon ami, I am so afrighted. Please to sit awhile with me. Do!"

"MONIQUE?

I sat just long enough for the weight of my questioning voice to sink in before asking another.

"How is it I awaken here at your bedside? It must be my old sickness is upon me. Please, please, mademoiselle, I beg of you, accept my apologies that, again I have wandered in my sleep! Ah, to have frightened you, I am most sorry." Then, having apologized profusely—and provided myself with a cover should one be necessary—my retreat back into the hall came just shy of rudeness.

At Lorraine's door, minutes wasted away. Jan's answer to my knocking was with a moan and words uttered most endearingly to his companion. "Later, mon cherie, later," and so he fell back to snoring.

I knocked again, whispered Jacques and, then throwing caution aside, knocked and yelled, "Jan!"

He grumbled, and said, surly, "Whatever it is can wait for morning."

"No! It cannot. Come now, right now, you must!" Sufficiently aroused, he stumbled out, having the forethought to bring his nightshirt with him, and he followed me to our room.

My possessions were far fewer upon leaving than when I'd first come to the New World. I stowed them in my valise while I listened to Jan, who, wide awake now upon hearing my news, remonstrated that he was determined to stay in New France, and why I, too, should remain. "The best lies ahead of us, Piet. After dallying away the coming winter in Montreal, a gentle spring and a rush for the rivers will be upon us. We are not only experienced coureurs de bois to command a decent price, but have led a brigade!—Well, I have.— A small one," he added, more humbly, when my raised eyebrow betrayed my thinking that both he and I owed our very lives in large part to his Micmac and Ottawa guides.

"We could go and see Quebec. Ah, it is a fine place and grows as a city. A high chateau raises up on a.... "

"Enough, Jan." Not my words, but my raised hand silenced him.

Time was short. I would not be dissuaded, nor would he; and so we embraced, each with his private world of misgivings, yet mingled with some relief that in parting, we were each fixed in our decision.

Sarkey, and another hand and arm more capable than his, rowed me out to a square-rigged fishing barque, anchored a stone's throw from the bank. The barque was the same as those that coursed this river for a catch of perch, eel or pike, and we left with the tide. We passed a few small settlements, Trois-Rivières, north and east of Montreal, seeming the most prosperous along the banks to either side of the River Saint Lawrence.

By sunset of the following day, we came to the broad widening of this river that led to the Strait. We rounded steep, gold-gilded cliffs and came upon a grand promontory of lofty exposure, it being the very site upon which Samuel de Champlain had built his château. The residence, now, of Comté de Frontenac, Governor of Quebec, showed no signs of opulence, at least not from this distance. But, I pondered the thought that should Louis XIV ever sail into these waters and look up to see the fleur-de-lis breasting from the ramparts, surely then, the Sun King would erect above this marvel of an entry to the New World, this Quebec, a Palace Royale to grace so magnificent a harbor.

By nightfall, a brisk wind swept us into the Gulf. We were within breathing sight of the Great Atlantic and so sought a mooring. A signal lantern being raised and at once answered by a flickering glow above the dark sea, the barque pulled alongside the ship. What a joy to again be climbing Jacob's ladder! To stand on the deck and again inhale the salt air of the great Atlantic! But, now, De Engelenburg was flying the colors of The Bird Of New England.

"Show me to Sir James's cabin," I told the boatswain's mate. For what reason, I did not know, he gave a raucous-sounding laugh, and in a confiding tone of pronouncement, said, "The old sparker's 'nought'n—is sheets, an's nought t'be row-de-dowed."

The hour was late, and content that all would be made known on the morrow, I exchanged his offer of quarters, below, for a blanket. I stretched out on the deck, and lay in high spirits to be lulled asleep by gently heaving swells below and a star-lit roof overhead.

Chapter 50.

The New Day

"Wake up, Van Doorn! A new day dawns—a most propitious, bounteous new day."

I shook awake, and looked up from the frock-coated-portly belly bearing down on me to the jowled and beaming face of Sir James.

"Sir!" I rolled from my blanket to my feet, and would have embraced him in the Dutch fashion, had he not so vigorously gripped both my hands in both of his. Our heads turned when, jauntily stepping down the deck in her wide bouncy skirts and bodice,—a dark crimson in the glow of a brilliant morning sun, came the Widow Spence.

Arms extended, she came at me, rosy-cheeked and all smiles from ear-to-ear. "Bend down, Dutch boy!" she ordered, laughingly. And I accommodated by lifting her high enough our lips could meet, then planted the triple kiss on each cheek. Such greetings! such a reunion! I expect never again to have should I live one hundred years!

I understood in short order, however, that their effusive welcome was not entirely to honor my safe arrival nor my success in furthering the mission Sir James had laid upon me those many months ago. I was about to be honored as a witness, a witness to the marriage ceremony that would, that very day, take place before all the ship's company.

The decks, I saw, were gleaming, and the hands were already beginning to gather around the rails of the lower deck. Shirts scrubbed white in the light of dawn had, by now, dried in the breeze, and their long hair slicked back and held at the neck, was festooned with ribbon. Three of the crew, whom I judged to be Melakans from the Dutch East Indies, must have polished their shaved skulls no less than the shine on the planking.

Captain Von Streppe strode out onto the quarter deck shortly before the noon bell to join us for the occasion and, in greeting me, said, "I see the savages left you all your limbs to decorate, even to your plumaged head. Welcome aboard my ship, Van Doorn."

Ah—I failed to mention, that well before these festivities ensued, Sir James had again come on deck and, this time, to offer me his quarters. "You'll be freshened up," he said. I expressed gratitude, knowing how unkempt I looked. But, I should have known better. For, once inside, I was nabbed to be bathed, barbered, and tailored; that is to say, I was worked over from head to foot.

And, so it was that some hours later, I emerged onto the quarterdeck, only too aware that I glittered like a colorful bird of paradise from my silken hose—gartered to match a much-embroidered frock coat—to a stylish cavalier's hat, broad-brimmed and feathered. I did not inquire to whose unfortunate end I owed this beneficent wardrobe, only knew that the garments were made for one shorter and stockier than myself, and frayed cuffs and elbows showed them to be well worn.

This once luxurious attire in over-done French, was in stark contrast to Sir James when he strolled up the deck in a modest brown frock coat, yellow shirt waist, and stiff linen collar. He gave me an approving nod, and we waited with the Captain. Captain Von Streppe had trimmed his beard for the occasion. His Dutch navy jacket must have been from a former lifetime, though replete with brass-buttons and shiny medals.

Soon, a seaman piped a pleasantly brief, flute-like tune, and Amelia sauntered toward us in a lush burgundy, but plain satin gown sheathed in a white lace shawl. Two fingers of one gloved hand pinched the edge of her broad-brimmed hat; its plumes of ostrich feathers swaying lightly in a southerly wind. Sir James met her halfway, locked her free arm inside his own, and then the two took their places, facing the Captain.

Captain Von Streppe's head moved a slow right to left as his eyes took in all those assembled, then opening the ship's Bible, he began in the sonorous voice of a pulpit preacher to pronounce the words that would bind Sir Richard Blackman James and Amelia Crawford Boulé Spence in Holy Matrimony. The 'I take thee' vows were spoken, and no dissenters to the union presenting themselves aboard ship, the love feast began.

Toasting the bride and groom began with cognac that, with their broad smiles and finery, lent a warm sparkle to the newly-paired James's advanced years. Rum was to be dispensed to jolly all the ship's company and, one by one, the deckhands were let on the quarterdeck to pay respects and be issued a round.

The festivities then moved into the Captain's quarter for more raising of the cups. Later, as the air began to chill and Sir James grew more unsteady on his feet, the Surgeon, First Mate and myself, escorted Sir James and his bride to their cabin.

Untoward noon of the next day, Amelia came on deck, appearing rested and cheerful. "Sir James, the poor man," she announced, "lies abed. He pays the price of last night's excessive drinking and eating. He tries to forget that his body lags behind his active mind and spirit, and so must suffer. Ah, well.

"So, Pieter, tell me of yourself." Before I could reply, her quick eyes perceived the ugly gash down my lower arm. "How did that happen, my poor lamb?"

I had forgotten my rolled-up shirtsleeve, and hastened to apologize. "My excuse, Madame, is that I removed the cloth wrappings to let the fresh sea air work its cure." Her womanly solicitude, unnecessary as it was, touched me. Yet, she was not a silly woman for all her charming ways.

"You had many encounters with the natives?"

"I did, and for the most part, they were friendly. But it will take me some time to think and sort through so many experiences in the New World, crowded into so short a time. I do know that I value them, exceedingly."

As we chatted on I kept the talk to impressions of the habitants of New France, the recent ordeal they'd undergone and their on-going deprivations, supposing that these would be of most interest to Amelia who, herself, was born in France, but would be of least interest to Sir James. I did acquaint her with the fortuitous circumstances of meeting my brother Gregor. A look of pure delight lit up her face and eyes, warming me through and through, and the afternoon wore on as pleasant as the calm sea, itself. Surmising my eagerness to talk with Sir James, she assured me before returning to their cabin, that "the dear man" was certain to be at my service on the morrow; she would see to it.

Our early November crossing met with fair seas, and when not in their cabin, Sir James made himself available to me. He spoke freely and unguardedly. Amelia often sat with us, attentive, but not venturing into our conversation. Sir James was aware of Jan's French leanings, and when told of his decision, said only that he expected as much. He was eager to know all I could tell him—how fared Audaîgweos, how far north the tribe had wintered, their most needed, or desired, items in trade goods, and business matters of the sort. His interest took a visible rise upon my telling him that the Loon Clan planned to ascend into the Athabasca country and, indeed, must already be well on their way.

"Audaîgweos goes to Athabasca? You are certain of this?"

"As certain as were the Ojibwa, themselves, when last we spoke."

I did not choose to share with him that my learning of the clan's departure was made known to me by the daughter of Audaîgweos, not by the Ogima, himself. Sir James looked thoughtful but did not, at the moment, enlighten me on the cause, leaving me to my own speculations.

He expressed genuine pleasure at my reunion with Gregor, and profound sadness upon learning of White Feather's demise, but after a reverent pause, he ushered us back into the main flow of his dialogue: "Our Company at the Bay undergoes constant harassment. These costly incursions by the French cannot be tolerated. As you have learned on the waterways of lower Canada, their coureurs de bois have routes well marked into the Interior and, as you also know, claim loyalty from Ottawa, Algonquin, and certain of the Christianized Iroquois. But Upper Canada, Pieter, is vastly different as are the tribes we engage. Our Company, moreover, has the merchant ships and the means to navigate from the Atlantic Ocean clear into the bay of Hudson. And, should we need it, we have our Navy to aid us should outright war break out over disputed territory with the French. So much is expected.

"Now, Pieter, you may ask, what is the mechanism to drive this Trade, this 'machine' one might say." His eyes held the old gleam. "The Company has in place a solid group of London investors, whose profits aren't lavished on a Sun King, mind you, but hold tightly to one aim—to prosper The Trade. You, my young friend, can be a part of it." He looked at me, expectantly. I said nothing, and waited.

"I've sent word to Marlborough, in expectation of your consent, for an appointment to serve The Company at York Factory or wherever he should deem you to be most needed. So, you can appreciate my interest, Pieter, when you informed me that the Ojibwa were heading to the far North into the Athabasca country." He paused, again, but as was customary with him, not for long. "What say you?"

I took my time. I would not permit him to rush my answer. Nor did he press me. Sir James's manner toward me had undergone a deep change. No longer, it seemed, was I the greening youth in need of raising up. Though I was far from regarding us as such, he treated me as he might an equal. I walked over and leaned into the rail to stare out to sea and to consider this new circumstance. A pod of dolphins leapt so joyfully, one might take the sighting as a fair omen. When I turned about to face him, he was sitting in the parlour chair brought along for his comfort, and rocking in time with the heave of the deck.

"Sir James, your offer gratifies me. It gratifies me for the confidence it expresses in my ability to serve you.—Nor does it quite surprise me, since something of the kind you once intimated. But I am mindful at this time of a more paramount need. Most immediate is the necessity of my return to Amsterdam. I have either to settle my affairs there or, perhaps, to begin them. I've made both promises, and no promises."

"That is good enough, Van Doorn. Nothing happens between now and late April. Our ships next sail for the Bay of Hudson by mid or late June. Send me word or, better yet, come to London by mid March. That will give you time to meet with our Directors, and to examine our operations from the inside." He reached a hand into his jacket pocket as though to pull out a cigar, and as quickly, withdrew it. Recalling his agreement with Amelia to quit the habit,—At least, when she was in range of discovery,—I gave him a knowing wink.

One cheek slid into a half smile as he continued on: "The real work, of course, lies at the Forts. Our Bay men are the soul and heart of The Trade! Our Forts are in harsh locations, sea miles and a world away from all the misconceptions and weighty trifles that beleaguer our fine Lords and Governors in London. On the other hand, our Londoners have pressures put upon them that, when translated into orders to our men in the field, appear as stupid, insidious, unwarranted—and, admittedly, Pieter, more than some are just that."

Sir James did not raise the subject of my deployment, again, nor did I, until close upon their departure when he said, grandly, "I will await your decision, patiently, Van Doorn." His paunchy cheeks collapsed into a mirthful grin, one eye winked, and he all but roared, "You'll not be subjected ever again, my friend, to a "banishment" such as occurred at the Handelaar Tavern!"

I laughed along with him, making a quick rejoinder much to his and Amelia's enjoyment. "You're right, of course, Sir James! I will not be so hornswoggled ever again, for I've learned how not to be from the Grand Master of Hornswogglers!" Our parting came soon thereafter.

Sir James and Amelia disembarked at Harwich. I was continuing on to Holland and, sailing before the wind, we made our crossing of the North Sea, then laid up at Hoorn for repairs. We waited out four long days inside the harbor at Hoorn. Slow, slow days. Yet, being quite alone and idle, except for an occasional chat with Captain Von Streppe on the plight of exports, imports, and such, gave me hour upon hour of time to reflect and scribble in my journal. Persons and places and New World experiences ran around in my mind along with the possibilities that lay ahead of me. Well into the fifth day, with the ship declared ready, at long last, we were once again underway.

The Bird of New England sailed into Amsterdam harbour in the early light of morning. My joy in beholding my native soil, again, was not without trepidation. Twenty-two months past, I knew all that my father expected of me. And, now, having seen and learned much he could not know, could not understand, I had no expectations of him, nor even that he would listen or, if so, hear me out.

Chapter 51.

Return To Amsterdam

Old Kootermann looked even more stooped than I remembered. He was fitting bales of straw against the house to buffer the strong sea winds that invade the lowlands, bereft as they are of shielding hills and forests.

"Mijn brave Kootermann." I called to him from the gate so as not to alarm him. His bent body turned, his head raising to let his eyes follow the sound from the gate, then brought himself up on his legs, each move in its own time. The callused fingers of one hand tugged at the visor of his cap in a kind of salute. It was as though I was watching old age unfolding in those moments of silence. It struck me that time no longer went forward for Kootermann. He'd been a part of my life for as long as I could remember and, now, it seemed he dwelt in some day-long present.

"God be with you, Pieter." He spoke, softly, and with the calmness of one who'd seen me but yesterday. I wrapped my arms around those hardened bones, and stepping back, pressed into his hand a small flask of French brandy. His furrowed brow creased with wrinkles, and the lopsided grin of an upraised lip showed more missing teeth than I recalled. "Dank u, Pieter. The master lies in his bed, Pieter."

"Ah, Kootermann, is it so." Not wishing to startle Ma-ma with my presence unannounced, I waited just inside the door while he went to fetch her.

The room sat in the wintry moistness of many cloudy days of veiled sunlight. All had stayed the same. The house was as I remembered it to the last detail of drapery and furnishings. In place of comforting the familiar appeared strange. But only I had changed.

I shook off this unwelcome melancholy, in studying as I had so many times in the past, my father's wall map of North America. Only, now, so engrossed I became in those upper regions, ones I could correct and enlarge! extend the knowledge of cartographers— I heard, then, her light footsteps descending the steep, narrow staircase leading down from the upper room.

"Pieter! It is you, my darling. Ah, my Piet, my Piet, my son!" She flew into my open arms and clutched me fast. Then, standing back to look me over from head to foot and back again, she dried her tears and spilled them anew. As we gazed upon one another, I noted the dark auburn hair streaked with some gray and, in spite of her warm smile, her face seemed more weary than I remembered it. A sadness shadowed the light in her eyes. Not altogether new. Her sadness lay under the surface, concealed inside through long years of practice.

Switching into gaiety, her small fists beat upon my chest, then tapped my chin with a finger tip. "Your letter, Pieter, stayed us all these months, but said so little! Now you must tell me all. Come sit." She led me to the cushioned window seat and we sat close together, she holding both my hands. "First—before you start, you'll want to know about your father."

"Yes, please, Ma-ma. He was always on his feet so early, and Kootermann says he lies in bed."

"Always he is abed, now, Pieter. His suffering intensifies, and grows worse with each day. The doctors do nothing—know nothing. I think they bleed him because it is all they know to do."

"Does he complain of a..."

"That's the worst of it! He has always grumbled, if not about the plight of our Navy then about our merchants, and if not about commerce than the power of the French—the English, or the manners of the clergy.—I seldom attended, closely, knowing all his peeves by heart. But now, Pieter, he is so silent. His lips scarcely move to form a word unless it is to ask for water or the need to shed water. I fear for him."

"And he never leaves his bed?"

"He has neither the strength nor the will to walk. But, my darling, we'll go see him when he stirs. Just now, we'll have Kootermann stay close by him, while we go have tea and our talk. I want to know everything,—everything, Piet." Yet, she kept up a chatter of this and that, leaving most thoughts unfinished, before she led me to the kitchen.

She set a covered wood box from the pantry on the table and, as she set out her best Delft cups to mark the occasion, I took the steaming kettle from the grate and poured our tea. How grandly nourished I felt, demolishing a half loaf of bread with one slice after the other off the solid round of Edam cheese. I ate as she exclaimed over the high cost stall-holders wanted for a mince meat pie, white cabbages and a portion of haricots. "And, Pietor, just guess the cost of a few codfish!"   "Why, I don't think I can guess, Ma-ma." I let her tell me as I fell into a kind of stupor as though all my journeying, all that I had witnessed in the New World was slipping away as decidedly as were the tea leaves sinking to the bottom of my cup.

"So begin, begin! I am eager to know!"

I roused myself. "Ah, Ma-ma, you would find the New World a much, much different place from what you know, here. It is so vast a country, and so differently peopled, one cannot know how vast..."

"Oh, I want to know all. All!—But before Father wakes, Pieter, you must know that Kristina has asked after you. She, too, complained of your short letter that told her nothing. Why was that, Pieter? Do you not care for her?"

An honest, direct question. But how was I to answer? I sipped my tea. "She is well, I hope."

"Oh, yes, well, but how long she will be well, you should know cannot last forever. You and she are no longer children and must face up to the making of your future."

"I am still shy of twenty, Ma-ma. That is not so old."

"Not for you, perhaps, you men—out and about the world and doing as you please, but for Kristina, it may be half her lifetime!"

Ma-ma may not recognize it, I thought, but she was speaking of herself, only she names Kristina. I reached for the kettle warming by the fire, and in turning back too quickly, struck my arm hard against the table.

"Your arm, it is injured?" she asked, seeing me flinch.

"It is almost healed, Ma-ma. So much so, I sometimes forget and put too much weight on it."

"Ah, I'm relieved to know it, with all the moving about you've done in and about the New World, getting there and back, again."

I smiled. In one sentence, she'd summed up close unto two years of my life, and it would seem, she might never learn even one full day of it, if she continued to interrupt my telling of it.

"You must tell me all!" she said while getting up and, after she'd lit a candle on the mantelpiece, sat down again. "But do think on Kristina, Pieter. She—Ah, your father calls. I can feel it." Her chair clattered on the well-scrubbed tiles as she rose up to leave.

"Stay, Ma-ma, Kootermann will fetch you if you are needed. We've just begun..."

"No, oh, no, I must go to him. And you, Pieter, finish your tea, then come to the door and knock gently, but give me a bit of time with him, alone first,—to prepare him for your coming."

I listened to the tapping of her feet disappear up the stairs, and the slow thud of Kooterman's footsteps coming down. In passing through the kitchen, he patted my shoulder with a "Goedjongen, Pieter." I rose up and saw him out the door with a smile. To him, I was still his 'good boy'.

He had not changed much nor, in my absence, had Ma-ma. Her quick little ways of flitting about were as though if quick enough, she'd not trip over her thoughts or fail to perform some self-imposed mission. I stirred the fire, took more bread from the cupboard. Refreshed my tea. I sat.

Thoughts, too long avoided, turned on Kristina, and I found myself wrestling with the idea that a bridegroom should rejoice to see his bride—if such I was to be to her. I concluded that, surely, this—this feeling of malaise was only that I was too anxious after so long a separation!—She was beautiful. Though their exactness did not come to me, I knew her to have delicate features, a soft blush to her cheeks, and hair the color of the flesh of lemons. And, she herself had their tartness, this Kristina I remembered, along with a disposition as might stoke or ruin the ambition of a man.

I knocked gently. Ma-ma, opening the door, beckoned me to his bedside, then left the room. I listened to his faint, labored breathing. It was my first time to ever see my father in repose. His skin looked so pale, so translucent that, were he given to asceticism, here lay a saint. The low stool of my childhood now sat in a corner for Ma-ma's comfort. I drew it up to the bed, and pressed my hand over his. The eyelids raised, and I shrank back. Like etchings of Dante's shriveled damned! so sunk in hollows were the black pits of his eyes.

I waited and, when his lids closed, got up to stand over by the window. I looked out on the sorry little orchard. Stringy, unkempt shoots reached down to the ground. Here and there a shriveled apple still clung to a bare branch. I thought back on the field's many seasons of neglect and how, odd that Father, never once, assigned me to work it. I would have done so, eagerly. No, my daylight work laid inside his books. Ah, well, so the benevolent Van Doorn's left their orchard for birds and mice, rabbits and other creatures.

I went back to the bedside and, again, covered his hand with mine. "Father—Do you not know me?" The head, whitish hair thinned to his pale bony skull, turned slowly, oh so slowly, and the eyes quivering, roved up.

"I...know...you...." The once stern voice that used to fill me with dread had lapsed into the merest whisper. "Tell me...." I felt a pressure from his fingers. It was the pressure of impatience from one still aware, but too weak to express even his simplest thought. Mother's fears were justified. My father was at death's door.

I would not dissemble with a dying man. I bent close and spoke so he should not miss a word. "I have news of Gregor to make you happy, Father. Gregor lives! He lives well, trapping and trading his skins with the natives. He lives amid giant forests and great lakes, rivers and streams.—Gregor, and I too, can walk on snowshoes, most useful wooden devices the natives make in order to cross over snow fields, and very cleverly made they are, too. Snows in that country can be very heavy." Suddenly, aware that I'd been racing on as though my energy would give him energy, I paused, then began, again, and more at ease.

"Father? Your son Gregor has married. You have a grandson! His name is Knute.—The little fellow does not go by a Cree name— rather, I do not really know that he does not, Father.

"And, I have learned from my own experience that not all savages are so—that is, so 'savage' in the way they are mostly regarded." I pressed his hand. "I had a close friend, Pa-pa, an Iroquois we called White Feather, though that was not his real name. He drowned when his canoe—Ah, but, Father...." I stopped talking, sensing that his distress had worsened. Maybe, listening so long was too difficult for him. Or, I thought better, it was because of what I had chosen to tell him.

Only a short time I stayed silent, thinking that, if not now, very soon, the chance to clear my slate would be lost forever. So, again, I enclosed his cold, limp hand in mine, cleared my throat and, once again began to speak.

"Gregor sends you a message. It is this: I am to tell you, Father, that Gregor thanks you for sending him to the New World, and for sending me, his half brother, there, also. Gregor thinks of you with affection. He said to tell you that in many ways, your second-oldest son Gregor is still a Nederlander." I waited, hoping he would make some response.

Minutes passed so slowly. Was there a faint trace of a smile? Were his lips trembling as though he would speak, before they closed? I could not be certain of what I might be seeing. I was certain there was more I must reveal.

"Father, listen! I could not do all in America that you sent me to do, Father. Some few fortunes in furs are still made by the established Dutch handlaers in the colonies. But, fortunes are not so easily amassed in this America, as were once made by-by the Van Doorns, and by the Van Rensselaers with their grand holdings. But, Father, descendants of the Great Patroon still control their Van Rensselaer holdings. Their wide and lengthy fields stretch far along the River Hudson...a River of great length and size. The beaver that were once harvested in close territory and supplied Fort Orange, are all but gone and have been gone for the better half of this century..."I am tiring you, Pa-pa—"

His head moved, slightly. "No? Then, Father, do me a great favor. Tell me, tell me if you can...that you forgive me, that you understand.—I did not come back with riches for our family. Yet, Father, I have learned much. I have made friends with native people who do know, and took me to the new land of the beaver. I have much to tell you when you are stronger, Pa-pa.

For now, it would please me greatly to know that my conduct in the New World—that it pleases you.—Father?"

His head lobbed to the side, and I thought him asleep when with a great effort he exerted himself enough to lift a trembling hand, and he tried to speak. From his throat came sounds not unlike, when from a distance, wheels of a loaded cart rattle over stones. I listened. Oh, how I listened to catch each word.

"I...forgive all...and...ask none in return."

I did not know, then, that these would be his final words as he sank back on the pillows. He wasted away for six more days, and died in the night on the last day of December. Ma-ma and I prepared the body ourselves, and he was put to rest in our family plot in the graveyard behind the high-stepped stone church near Kanaalstraat. I gave the hired pallbearers coins, and the small gathering of mourners departed, slowly. I had told Ma-ma, I would follow, shortly.

A peculiar thought had taken hold of me that did not lighten my already somber mood. Two other graves lie aside Pa-pa's, those belonging to his mother, and his first wife, Matilde. The first Pieter Willem Van Doorn, had doubtless set aside this generous space of ground, fully expecting that as time went on it would be occupied by himself, and his growing number of descendants; but Grandfather was lost at sea. Would all four of his grandsons be lost to the New World? How fragile are plans we humans make. Ah, Piet, I told myself, seconds later, Hang it up! Live life! I swung around, walked swiftly, and caught up with Ma-ma.

As was customary after a burial, friends of my mother came to sit with her in our parlor, partaking of spiced wine, white bread, and sweet cakes. Now and then, an elderly man stopped by to console Ma-ma or talk with me. I expressed my thanks to each, caught my breath, and then went to stand apart by the window, allowing grief to be my excuse for remaining uncommunicative. The room itself was mostly quiet with only the low murmur of voices and tinkling of cup or glass. Then, from the window, I saw her.

She was walking in the opposite way that her parents were moving. She walked down past the dark-limbed beech trees stripped of their leaves, then stood as though lost in thought. I wondered if she might be reassessing her coming here, and was feeling uncertain of her place. She'd not been at the gravesite. At the clap of the knocker on the front door, I hurried out the side door, thereby missing the certain arrival of Meneer Planck and his wife.

Summoning my courage, I found myself running to her in gladness. "Kristina!—Kristina, so happy I am to see you!" I clutched both her hands, eagerly, and would have embraced her. But so solemn she stood in her deep blue full skirts and white whimple, only a few wisps of hair straying across that smooth alabaster forehead. Her full blue eyes looked past me, keeping her thoughts hidden. I waited for her to look up at me, to speak.

"Your grip has hardened, Pieter. It is not now I would talk with you. I come only to bring words of sympathy to you and your mother upon the death of Meneer Van Doorn. How is it with your mother?"

"In time she will come around to seeing many things that she has been denied these many years."

"In this, she is then not so different from other women."

"Ah, no, I suppose not," I said, trapped into her earnestness and feeling thwarted by my having expressed in all honesty, my mother's condition. It was left to me to break the dead pause that fell between us.

"Is it now you wish to speak with her?"

She made no reply, only nodded, so I took her arm and we started toward the house, the way I had come. Had she nothing to say? Did she not wonder that I'd not called on her? Her father would, of course, know of my return if not on the very day, then the day after. Those who go to sea and, like myself, return, are always marked more, I suspect, for what news we can provide about the far-away World, than for the pleasure of our company. She looked straight ahead as we walked. When turning halfway toward me, I thought she might speak. She did not but, truly, she was beautiful.

"Come, inside, Kristina, I said, putting a gentle hand to her back. "Your company will give Ma-ma and myself much pleasure."

Chapter 52.

The New Year

The New Year came, and in the weeks that followed I sought Kristina out. Of an early evening, we'd walk along the marshes that hadn't yet been drained to make more land. Many warehouses and passageways for shops were being built. On one occasion, our stroll took us through the High City Gate, up the half-moon bridge and down that crossed over the canal. We stood to watch the water coach, a long boat pulled by a horse. The cabin above the deck was filled with some forty or more merry passengers who, having visited the saloon below, bellowed out drinking songs, which would the farther they traveled, surely lapse into sad, slow songs.

"The water coach goes to Harlem, would you like that, sometime, Kristina?"

"Perhaps."

"I'd like to see the Palace, again. It's close by."

"The sun will set, soon. My father will worry."

"Then, we will hurry."

More than a Palace was this architectural wonder of Amsterdam with dome and bell tower in the French style. Not just government did it house, but commerce, a court of law, an arsenal, and a prison. 'It still stands proud," I said to Katrina. "It's tall windows and seven small doors that cross the facade haven't caved in."

"You sound surprised."

"No, Kristina, I'm not surprised, just glad. After all, constructing an edifice of such grand proportions arouses one's betting instincts!" I didn't bother to repeat what she must already know; if the stout pilings on which it rested, failed to bare the weight, all would sink down into the watery subsoil that menaces much of Holland.

The next afternoon, Kristina came, saying she was to take tea with Ma-ma. I invited myself. The two spoke back and forth, easily, whether over lace making or the current gossip. I held back from laughing outloud when Kristina announced she'd seen the new canal boat to Haarlem as though I'd not been present.

Ah, well, if talking was to be strained between Kristina and me, there might be some benefit to be had. I, myself, was not interested when she enthused about her father's new venture into sleigh-making; I just listened. Her person had changed little. In any man's eyes she was desirable, and at times I longed to caress her, indeed to test her further, but held back. Often, her grace of movement helped relieve the stiffness of her demeanor; yet always I discovered my mind comparing her unfairly, comparing her sharpness with the lilt of another's voice and manner.

One evening stands out. Ma-ma, Kristina and her mother, and myself had finished eating. We waited for Meneer Planck to swallow his last portion of roast pork, finish his beer, and belch. Raising his head, he looked at me, pointedly, and said: "Now that you have the New World out of your blood, Pieter Van Doorn, you will be useful to me in my new business. Then, fondling Kristina's chin, he added, someday, mijn lieveling, it will be your business."

His words drew me quickly to my full height and, on that occasion, I refused the offer of an after-dinner cordial, while pinning Ma-ma with a look she dared not ignore. I made the shortest of farewells in deference to Ma-ma's weakness, should she fail to bed down before the bell rings the tenth hour,—a weakness Ma-ma knew not she had. I did not like Meneer Planck, nor that Kristina suffered her father's coddling with so broad a smile, when for me her smiles were so scant.

My mother's companionship, too, began to lay on me heavily. I sensed she knew this, but had not the gift of breaking through her pattern of established chatter. Married to my father, her opinions would scarcely be valued. More than once I tried talking with her about the New World and of Gregor. She'd not known my stepbrother, and I tried, earnestly, for her sake to look as though she was following the thread of my conversation. I'd stop, abruptly, sometimes in mid-sentence to raise a response, and when none was forthcoming, knew her mind had wandered off into her own concerns.

One day, to her reoccurring complaint of headache, I sought her understanding in a far different way. "Ma-ma? You have nothing to do."

"Nothing to do? Nothing to do, you say? I have this large house—

you to cook for and, now—your father's grave to tend. Kootermann as you know is a dear part of this household, but is of little use as a servant. Everything! I have to tend to and care for."

"No. No, Ma-ma. You have but yourself to care for. Kootermann has had long years of self-sufficiency. And, in spite of his ailments, it is he who cares most for this house. It keeps him alive. But, one day, and soon perhaps, he'll no longer be here to feed and milk the cow, nor look to the house. As for the field, it is a wild expanse of trees that are left unworked. No, Ma-ma, you have too little to occupy your body. And your mind, also, I added, gently."

My words shocked her into a profound silence, a silence I indulged her with for quite some time. I had no wish to hurt her; I wanted only to rouse her from the mental, metal armor that acted upon her mind like a deep sleep. Tame conversation would not answer! She began to tremble. A tear slid down her cheek.

"—Ma-ma? Are you listening? One day soon—in about three weeks—I will leave Amsterdam." Her soft brown eyes fluttered up at me, now fully rimmed with tears. Her fear and dismay were apparent.

"I have made a firm decision, Ma-ma. I will return to America." She raised up such a piteous face that I laid my fingers across her lips. "Hush. Hush my dear mother, and listen. Please, listen to what I have to say.

"I wish you to go with me as far as London. Sir James Blackman and his wife—you will like Amelia,—she and Sir James will help you to resettle in a fine house. A far finer house than you have here, Ma-ma. With scores of shops, nearby to choose from and places to see. And, after a time, should you wish it, and when I myself am settled, you can come to America. To visit. Or to live." She took a deep breath, and sat motionless. Speechless.

"It is time, Ma-ma, you leave this dreary house! It is drafty, old, in need of repairs,—and, this place is full of memories you'd best be without." I put my hand on hers, and feeling only a slight pressure of withdrawal, tightened my grip, forcing her attention.

"You are still young and pretty enough, Ma-ma, to catch yourself a husband! Someone to love and care for you.—To care for you in the way—in the way my father never did."—There. At last I'd said it.

Her breath came in gasps as she stumbled up from the couch.

Instinctively, I started forward, then sat back down. She would not faint. She only needed time to reflect.

She needed time to face her future, honestly. I would see to Kooterman's welfare. She needed time to think of herself. Make her farewells, dust off her valise, and to pack!

Epilogue

When first I began setting down at length the account of my introduction to this America, I was removed from those events by ten years, and well into my twenty-ninth. I did then, and continued in successive years, to stay as faithful to the true events as scant notes in my journal and imperfect memory, allow.

Of the many promises made or imposed upon me on first departing from Amsterdam, many were not kept. I failed to find any word of my brother Dirck, and only heard unhappy rumors of Willem. I failed to redeem the wealth of my ancestral family. I broke my parent's betrothal promise to marry Kristina, daughter of Meneer Planck. I failed in other ways. I still do.

In some matters, I succeeded. And so I take up my pen again, these many years later, to remember persons and to relate how some pivotal events played out:

My second farewell to Amsterdam became permanent. Ma-ma needed but little more persuasion and, once the idea nested in her head, she flew into preparations. She accompanied me to London, and there took up residence. She was most graciously introduced into the society of not just the 'Sir James's' but, as Ma-ma insisted, of the Sir Richard Blackman James's. Less than two years, thereafter, I received word that Ma-ma was being happily provided for by one Lord Bayard, and was until her untimely death in the fourteenth year of this new century.

In America, I have become known as Peter Dorn. I honor my Dutch heritage in other ways, while this shortening of my name is but a small accommodation to traders who grapple with Dutch sounds, and spell even more poorly.

After much yearning and scant soul searching, I sought out the Athabasca country and, to my great joy, succeeded in making Animiki my beloved wife. She sings often. Little Thunder had kept hidden my ancestral ivory, she said, "for Big Lake Person to come back."

Audaîgweos gave us his blessing because, he told me, "Once, I see your nábikawágan in dream. Same I see now around neck of my daughter." (So long as I am still alive, I need not count as a failure that the one other family talisman is still unfound; there is yet time.)

My wife has given me two healthy sons with the expectation of a third child soon to be born. During the long cold months, we all look forward to summer visits with Gregor and Marta, and my sons' cousin. Gregor is now so old and stooped, he grows feeble. I fear for him. Knute, a fine sturdy man, does the winter trapping.

My affection for Jan Carpentier remains strong. But he, enmeshed with the French of Canada, and I in alliance—if not always in agreement—with The Company on the Bay, our paths, Jan and mine, I fear have diverged, irrevocably. At least during these times of unrest.

Of Sir James? As my sworn enemy, he became my trusted friend. As an arch manipulator and disposer of men, he taught me as much as I know about freedom. He, too, is dead, now, by some twenty years and still I miss him. He was a man well ahead of our times. I know this to be true because, for myself, I strive only to know this life, better. This present, better.

Had I the choice to bring back from the dead, just one man, who would I choose? Some might say, "Your father, of course." Or, "Sir James who enabled your "rise" with The Company." No. My heart chooses the Iroquois savage. My Mohawk friend.

His white feather mounted on red silk hangs framed above my desk, from whence I look out on a harsh landscape—some would say forbidding, bleak. No tall, majestic forests, here,—and few balmy breezes cross this north-lying land on The Bay. But to each place God has sown its own beauty.

Animals of many kinds—foxes, hares, and musk oxen, caribou and reindeer, the great whales and polar bears, seals and walruses. And, each spring, tern and geese return in great numbers, and the tundra wakes up bright with jeweled flowers and soft green mosses.

As to my "rise," which some persist in calling my association with The Company on the Bay, this is a false perception. In late spring of 1694, I had refused the appointment to go to York Factory, preferring to live my life like my brother,—a free trader. I remain so today. Yet, most welcome is the friendly, comfortable association I maintain with the Bay men. This is a harsh land where every man must be your friend. And is, unless that trust is broken.

My eldest son and I keep busy the year long, securing the richest of pelts and preparing them. Animiki dries our fish and, although the season is short, she grows most magnificent vegetables and preserves them. As a family, once a year we travel to the Bay Forts to exchange for commodities our family needs.

We live, for the most part, peaceably, in a stout warm house, one built of stone, mostly, and log beams bartered off a ship. And, yes, a carved lintel, once above another's doorway, now greets our family, and beckons the occasional stranger to our fireside.

From this house on this broad bay—of this inland sea—we observe all the surrounding wildness, and we watch. We watch ships sail to and from any of this wide world's oceans. Some few men sail for adventure. Many more sail for The Trade. I will do both one day, very soon.

129264